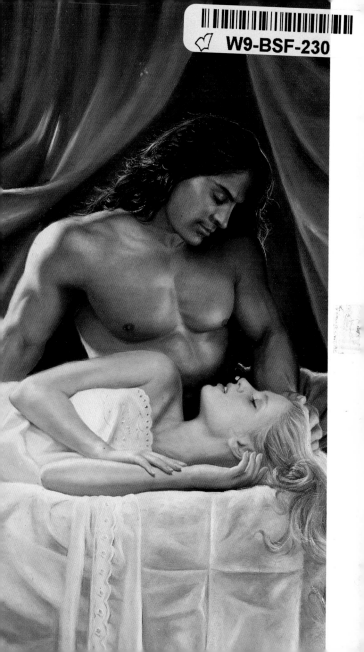

I WANT TO TOUCH YOU

Her hands slipped beneath his shirt, peeled away the linen bandage that kept his skin from her exploration, followed the line of muscle over his shoulders. He closed his eyes, drinking in the sensation.

"I want to touch you."

"Touch me," he breathed, desire robbing him of sensate thought, mindlessly mouthing the words she gave him.

She clutched a handful of shirt and he shrugged out of it, jerking his arms free of the sleeve and pitching it away.

"*Houri*," he murmured, taking her hand and pressing a kiss into her warm, soft palm. He flicked his tongue across her delicate wrist. She was so small, so perfect. "Pleasure's dark-eyed maiden, sandalwood and ambergris. Always love."

She touched his lips, teased them open, and ran her fingertip lightly across the seam. Her own lips parted and her breathing deepened. "Your mouth. I want—"

He groaned, sucking her fingertip into his mouth. Her eyes fluttered shut and she gasped. He knew full well what she wanted with his mouth. Her words were clarion, even in memory. . . .

CONNIE BROCKWAY

As You Desire

A DELL BOOK

Published by
Dell Publishing
a division of
Bantam Doubleday Dell Publishing Group, Inc.
1540 Broadway
New York, New York 10036

Copyright © 1997 by Connie Brockway

ISBN: 0-440-22199-4

Printed in the United States of America

Published simultaneously in Canada

February 1997

10 9 8 7 6 5 4 3 2 1

RAD

For Doc Danger, who holds my heart in every one of his many guises

I would like to thank Dr. Richard Cummings, program director of the Learning Disabilities Association, for making available his expertise and kindly sharing with me his research on the medical history of dyslexia. The Egyptian poetry in this book is derived from the wonderful translations of John L. Foster. Thank you, sir. I would also like to thank my editor, Marjorie Braman, for her fantastic enthusiasm and most especially for "now wanting to go to Egypt," and my agent, Damaris Rowland, for her unflagging belief and encouragement. But most especially, I need to thank Michelle Miller and Doris Egan of the Black Hankie Brigade, for finding the tender spots, and Kathy Carmichael and Terry Kanago, for always wanting more.

CHAPTER ONE

*A*bove the vast Egyptian desert the midnight sky reflected its own eternal emptiness. This was the High Desert. Its uncharted surface offered convenient oblivion for those who sought to hide in it.

Squatting sullenly at the base of a sand dune, the slave traders' encampment was peopled by such fugitives. It was a small compound: a string of camels, a half-dozen tents set around a fire, a score of lidless crates piled within reach of the campfire's illumination.

Inspecting the contents of these crates were several dozen men. Some were obviously merchants who, having come into the desert from towns miles away, were here to acquire the black market goods being offered. The merchants were Arabs, relative newcomers to Egypt—fourteen centuries being relative in this ancient land. The others—heavily veiled even now, at night—were Tuareks, of Coptic origin, the true descendants of the ancient Egyptians. They were the sellers. And, sitting just beyond the reach of the firelight, was the rarest and most precious *offering among merchandise rife with the unique and invaluable: a young, blond Englishwoman.*

A slave.

The pale and proud girl faced her captors, making no effort to hide her disdainful glare. When first snatched from the Cairo market four days before, fear had paralyzed her usually agile intelligence, terror had crippled her spirit with the certainty that soon she would become the plaything of some cruel desert sheik.

But now four days had passed and no desert prince had come for her. Indeed, no one came near her at all, and the sweet, tender flower of womanhood found that terror, numbed by the potent drink her captors forced upon her, had given way to . . . to . . .

Boredom?

Desdemona Carlisle slouched tipsily against a pile of Persian rugs, gravely considering the word. It seemed too cavalier for her situation, but she couldn't claim she felt exactly terrorized anymore. She stuck a finger under the wretched *chadar*, the face veil her captors insisted she wear at all times, and scratched.

Impatient? Yes!

The young lady, courageous and valiant, was impatient to confront her fate.

But first, thought Desdemona, the young lady would have another swig of the unique, and not altogether unpalatable, milky beverage that the sullen-looking boy, Rabi, spent most of his free time encouraging her to imbibe.

Indeed, other than sitting about being bored—impatient, penning entries in an imaginary diary, and sipping this stuff—there wasn't much to do. The fake papyrus scroll Rabi had given her as a means of keeping her occupied was fascinating, yes, but a bit too . . . absorbing . . . to be studied properly here and now. It was more suitable reading for a private setting.

She was sure she could have found other interesting things in the crates heaped around camp. She had glimpsed glints of shining metal, colored stone, shapes and figurines. But every time she ventured near the crates, her guards barked at her; every time she tried to run away, they fetched her back—with increasing ill grace—and every time she tried to hold a civil conversation, they stared at her in mute contempt.

The most obvious explanation for their aloofness, she concluded, was that her purity was being safeguarded to ensure she would command a greater price on the auction block. She shivered and groped around in the sand for her tin cup.

She found it and looked up. Rabi was staring at her. As soon as he noted the direction of her gaze, he turned and slunk away like a cadaverous Anubis puppy. Wise lad, she thought darkly.

It had been Rabi who'd kidnapped her. One minute she'd been examining a nice, authentic-looking canopic jar and the next she was being gagged with some hideous cloth, her head stuffed in an equally vile sack, and she'd been flung over a bony shoulder. A moment later he'd thrown her atop what—judging from the smell and lumps—could only be a camel.

She'd spent an entire day jolting about in front of him, sweating beneath the heavy sack covering her. Once they'd arrived, he had plopped her on her feet for her unveiling and, his young voice flush with the pride of conquest, hailed the camp. Then, with a spectacular flourish, he'd snapped the sack—and her headdress—off.

Confused, frightened, and seasick from the rocking camel ride, she had squinted into the sudden blinding light, peering at the silent, shadowy faces crowding around her. Someone said something that sounded suspiciously like the Arabic equivalent of "Uh-oh." In a flurry of motion, the men had snatched their *burkos* in front of their faces. She'd not seen an unveiled man since.

Soon after, they'd taken Rabi aside and given him the thrashing of his young life. She assumed it was because he had attempted to assert his masculine rights of ownership over her. Her mouth twined at the thought. A fifteen-year-old boy-child was not her idea of— What ever was she thinking about?

She lifted her tin cup to her lips and sipped nothing. Drat. It was empty.

"Hey, Rabi!" she called. "I say, I could do with a spot more of that what-have-you!" As if by magic, the sound of her voice cut off all conversation in the camp. Every man, especially the town merchants, turned and stared at her. Within five minutes the Arabs had fled, leaving her alone with her veiled captors. They glared at her, looking decidedly unhappy.

"Well? I'm sorry but *they* certainly weren't going

to buy me. They couldn't even afford your fake faience. Not a sheik in the lot, I'd wager," she said with alcohol-imbued logic. Indeed, the departed men had looked more like middle-age—and none too prosperous—businessmen than proper white slavers. She glanced about, trying to determine where they'd gone and if she could go with. Maybe she had this white slave thing all wrong. Maybe she . . .

It was then that she saw him.

Wind and darkness coalesced in the distance. A rider so much a part of his steed that he seemed more centaur than man crested the moon-silvered edge of a dune. His cape billowed in the wind like great black wings. Closer he sped, myth embodied, galloping across the midnight-shrouded sands, racing toward her.

Her destiny.

She stood up, swaying. Rabi dropped the goat bladder he'd been filling her cup from and caught her elbow, steadying her.

"Who is he?" she breathed, her gaze riveted on the figure now almost to the camp.

"He came for you," Rabi said.

Her head snapped around in surprise. She'd thought "drink, you drink" the extent of Rabi's English vocabulary. He looked positively jubilant.

"You mean . . . he's taking me . . . tonight?"

"Yes, yes," Rabi said, pulling her forward. "Tonight you go with him. Everyone will be happy." He dragged her toward the campfire and she stumbled to her knees.

"Hup, hup, you hup," one of the veiled men grumbled, coming and standing over her.

She tilted her chin haughtily. "Why should I?"

He made a grab for her and she scooted to her feet. She would not give him the satisfaction of swinging her over his shoulder like a sack of grain and dumping her back in that hot, smelly tent—the way most of her previous acts of defiance had been met.

She was an Englishwoman; she had her pride. With a brave toss of her hair, she swept into the bright circle of light.

"Here is *Sitt*," the man ahead of her mumbled, flicking his hand in her direction and snatching up Rabi's goat bladder as if he needed it. He took a deep swig.

She looked around and found the one unfamiliar figure in the camp. Her heart started racing. Her breath caught in her throat. Without doubt, without reason, unequivocally and absolutely, she knew this man would *own* her.

He hovered on the periphery of the darkness, licked by shadows, studying her. When he came forward, it was with the soft-sure footfall of the panther. He approached at an oblique angle, his head cocked as he considered her. Somehow she contrived to remain erect beneath that keen and heartless perusal.

He flung back the inky cape suspended from a jeweled clasp on his shoulder and set his gloved fist on his hip. Only his eyes were visible; his expression was obscured by an indigo *burkos* tucked beneath the edge of his *khafiya*.

Another Tuarek tribesman, Desdemona thought breathlessly. The most savage of the lawless desert nomads.

Above his veil his eyes narrowed and glittered in the uncertain firelight. Dangerous, sleek, and arrogant, he stalked toward her. She swallowed hard and, her self-possession breaking with his predatory approach, scuttled back from his advance.

He laughed, a cruel, barbaric sound. It stopped her retreat. Generations of British pride steeled her backbone, and she met his gaze defiantly, even courageously. His hand shot out with the deadly speed of a striking cobra and he grabbed her wrist, dragging her to him. She fought fiercely, knowing the slavers would do nothing to intercede, fear replacing her former defiance.

He held her easily, her strength a negligible thing, and called over her head to the muttering slavers in hoarse, guttural Arabic. Why, oh why, she asked herself, could she never learn to *speak* the dratted language, only *read* it?

One of the men, a dirty individual in a lopsided turban, flapped his hand toward the tent where she slept. With another low laugh, the stranger snatched her forward and hauled her into its dim interior.

The sudden severity of her situation exploded in upon her, erasing some of the torpor from her drink-befuddled mind. This was no romantic prince of the desert, this was a hard savage, a man who would use her body as casually as an Englishman would soil a napkin and just as casually discard her when he was done.

She screamed. His big hand clamped over her mouth and he spun her about, dragging her against the unyielding wall of his chest. He hissed something in her ear but she couldn't make out the words, her stifled screams reverberated too loudly in her skull. She struggled, kicking and flailing.

"Would you bloody well stop it?" he thundered in her ear.

She froze, her surprise at hearing not only an English accent but *that* English accent so great she couldn't have moved. He unclamped his hand from her mouth and wheeled her about. In their struggle his *burkos* had fallen, uncovering his face.

She stared at him, disbelief turning to amazement turning to fury. "Harry Braxton, if *you* bought me, I'll kill you."

CHAPTER TWO

"*I*s that any way to behave?" Harry Braxton ducked her windmilling blow and caught her wrist above her head. Clucking his tongue, he whirled her in an impromptu pirouette and looped his arm around her waist, pulling her against him. "Particularly as I have just saved your scrawny hide from some horrifying fate?" His warm breath tickled her ear. "What, by the way, horrible fate had you dreamed up with that vivid imagination of yours?"

"Whatever it was, it couldn't possibly be more horrifying than to be owned by you," Desdemona declared, abandoning her struggle.

She was simply no match for Harry. She could feel the hard muscular planes of his chest, his heart pumping intimately beneath her shoulder blade. She looked at his arm belting her waist, noted the golden down covering the ridged sinew of his forearm and supple wrist. Damn it, he was all masculine strength, arrogantly unconscious of his own superior power. The thought caused her to go still. Without Harry, she wouldn't be getting out of here. He may laugh at her, but he'd come for her, too. Masculine strength had its good points.

She relaxed and it seemed to her that his arm tightened, pulling her into an embrace that did not merely restrain, but that translated something urgent and potent . . .

Oh, no! She wasn't going to make that mistake again. While she had no intention of giving up the habit of scripting romantic scenarios, she wasn't going to be casting Harry in any of her daydreams' leading roles. She had done so once and too painfully learned the difference between dream and reality.

"Why didn't you tell me it was you?" she asked gruffly, pulling free of his embrace. Though in retrospect, she should have realized. No one, not a desert prince or American red Indian or even captain of the Oxford polo team, which—if memory served her right—Harry had been, rode a horse as well as Harry Braxton.

"I didn't want to spoil all the fun you were having playing defiant captive. Besides," he went on, "these men and I have occasional business transactions."

"So?"

"I have my reputation to consider. Egypt is a male-dominated society. I was merely being dominantly male. I wouldn't want these chaps losing their respect for me."

"No one respects you, Harry."

As this blatantly untrue insult didn't have any noticeable effect on him, Desdemona got down on hands and knees and started feeling under the edge of the thick carpet lining the tent.

"What are you doing?" he asked.

"Gettin' my things," she responded, and then, hearing the slight, unfortunate slur in her speech, she said very carefully, "You are, I assume, going to take me back to Cairo? I see no need to prolong my stay, charming as my hosts have undoubtedly been."

"Things?" Harry echoed. "What 'things'? Abdul said Rabi took you from a market. You don't have any 'things.' "

"I do now."

Harry's pale eyes lit with a familiar, avaricious gleam. *This* was the Harry she knew. "What kind of things?"

"Only an ol—" She caught herself in time. Just the thought of Harry discovering what kind of material she'd been reading was enough to send the blood boiling to her cheeks. If he ever suspected what she had, she'd never live it down. "Never mind."

"You are a remarkable woman, Dizzy. Here you are, half sotted on the fermented goat's milk Rabi claims was the only way to keep you quiet, having convinced yourself that you're nothing but a pitiful slave heading for auction, and still you manage to buy—" His eyes widened as her guilt betrayed itself on her cursed face. "You didn't *steal* these things, did you, Miss Carlisle? *That* would be wrong. One is tempted to say *unethical*, not to mention *immoral*. A

virtuous young model of English womanhood like
you—"

"I did not!" she protested. "That boy Rabi gave
them to me. They're mine."

"You actually talked your captors into giving you
presents?" He was staring at her in open admiration. "Marry me."

"Stop that," Desdemona snapped, finding her
bundle and extracting it from beneath the carpet.
Hurriedly she shoved it under the waistband of her
skirt and drew her loose native blouse over it.

Marry, indeed. Harry never missed an opportunity
to remind her of her one-time infatuation. If he'd
ever actually suited his actions to his words— She
stopped, chastising herself for that dangerous line of
thought. "And stop calling me Dizzy. No one calls
me Dizzy. I am in no way, shape, or form *dizzy.*"

Liar. The inside of the tent felt preternaturally still
and warm, and she felt all loose-jointed and breathless.

"It's the irony that makes the nickname so piquant. Besides which, I think I've earned the right to
call you pretty much anything I like. According to
the laws of many cultures, of which the Tuarek are
one, you belong to me."

She stared up at him with unblinking eyes. So
odd. Even though light-headed, she could see him
quite clearly: the way the moonlight cast interesting
shadows beneath his cheekbones and in the hollow
of his throat, the laugh lines about his eyes, even the
fine, clear texture of his skin. Yet drunk she must
undoubtedly be, because despite his insouciant

tone, she saw something sharp and yearning in his expression that simply could not be there. More than desire, and yet that was a part of it. Desire and . . . She shook her head, trying to clear her thoughts. She'd drunk too much.

Yes, she thought drawing her legs up and wrapping her arms around her knees, she was half done on fermented goat's milk. It was the only thing that could account for that inexplicable something she swore was betrayed on Harry's lean countenance.

She closed her eyes and pressed her fingertips into her temples and massaged them. When she opened them Harry's face reflected nothing more than his usual ironic self-assuredness. Just, she nodded sadly, as she'd thought.

"What is this *present?*" Harry asked.

"A royal sarcophagus," she said, though her tone was not as cavalier as she wished. "And what do you mean I belong to you?" She struggled to her knees.

"Don't you?" he asked softly. "I have rescued you. And you haven't even thanked me."

She froze, caught on the horns of a moral dilemma. He was right—drat him. He had rescued her, possibly even saved her life, and she supposed she did owe him something for that.

She glanced at him. He was giving her an abused lapdog expression that she didn't buy for an instant. There was nothing in the least bit domesticated about Harry Braxton. He was a complete jackal and, like the jackal, a born opportunist. Still, God knew how long he'd been searching for her, struggling over blistering sand dunes, broiling beneath the interminable desert sun, sleeping out alone in this barren, blasted landscape. She felt herself softening.

Utterly unwise. Unfortunately unavoidable.

"I imagine you had to pay a lot for me," she said despondently.

"Oh, yes."

Just what would it cost to purchase her from these slavers? Probably a small fortune. She didn't suppose harem blondes were that easy to find.

"I'll find some way to repay you, Harry. Perhaps I *can* find time to translate those papyri you filched off that American archeologist. At least then you'll know what to charge your . . . *clients* for them."

She staggered upright and confronted his telling silence. She should never have gotten involved in this conversation. In her present highly vulnerable and emotional condition, he would doubtless take appalling advantage of her.

"Harry," she said plaintively. "You know we don't have any money. Grandfather is a horrible accountant. I have always suspected—" She leaned close, glancing one way and another to ensure that any forthcoming indiscretion wasn't going to be overheard, and nearly pitched forward on her face.

Harry caught her forearm and tilted her back upright. His hand passed gently by her face, pushing the fallen locks out of her eyes. She shivered at the warm, sparkling tendrils of sensation his touch left behind. His lips parted slightly and she could see the clean white gleam of his teeth within his mouth. Had Harry been unveiled when he rode up, she thought inconsequentially, she would have known it was he at a hundred yards. She'd know the shape of Harry's lips anywhere.

His breath sluiced delicately over her forehead and cheeks as if he were consciously attempting to gauge his exhalation. He loomed closer and her own breath jumped, catching in her throat, her body startling her with its involuntary response to his. He backed away immediately, but though he moved only a matter of inches, it seemed he'd removed himself much farther.

"You were saying?" he prompted, a line between his brows, a harried note in his voice.

She blinked, disoriented. Something about Grandfather . . . Ah, yes. "I have always suspected that one of the primary reasons Grandfather took this post was to get away from his creditors."

Not that Harry wouldn't have known that. Everyone in Cairo knew that Sir Robert Carlisle, head of Antiquity Acquisitions for the British Museum of History, though an excellent archeologist and middling bureaucrat, was a complete failure as an economist.

"He has never understood the concept of profit and loss."

"But you do," Harry said.

"Yup. If I can just raise enough money, Grandfather will be able to accept the post the museum offered him in London."

"And that's important," Harry said. "Your grandfather's triumphant return to England."

Desdemona bobbed her head affirmatively. "He's

been wasting his genius here for twenty years, Harry. Once we're back in England, he'll finally achieve the recognition he deserves. Can you imagine, Harry, how much it hurts him to watch would-be archeologists arrive here, scrape around for a season or two, then return to England and immediate international recognition?"

"I think I can."

"But he won't go if he thinks it'll mean I'll have to live in reduced circumstances. If we could just get these past debts settled, I'm sure he could make a proper living what with the stipend from the museum and lecture—"

"Yes," Harry interrupted. "But what about your desires?"

"Me?" She blinked. "I'll love it there. Of course. We'll have a little thatched-roofed cottage with hollyhocks and a privet hedge and—"

"—a leaking roof and an old biddy next door who'll be clucking her tongue every time you appear in your harem trousers."

"Oh," Desdemona said quietly, "I'll give up all those once I'm home."

Harry shook his head. "Do you really want to go back to England?"

"What do you suggest as an alternative?" She tried to keep the hopelessness out of her voice by giving a dismissive snort. "Do you think I'd like to spend the rest of my life here, an object of curiosity? I've had enough of that, thank you very much." She hurried on. "I want a normal life. I want to meet people who have no interest in dead cultures, dead people, or dead languages. I want to be introduced to gentlemen with at least some expectation that they might be more interested in *me* than in whether I can translate a grimy piece of papyrus they always 'just happen to have' in their pockets. That's certainly not going to happen here."

"Well, before you start tatting lace curtains, you have that translation to do for me," Harry said, apparently unswayed by her tale of woe. "Since that's the price you put on my efforts."

She heard the reproach and responded immediately. "It'll take weeks to do those translations, Harry," she said, England forgotten. "Isn't that recompense enough?"

He nodded dubiously. "Oh, of course. What's four days of brutal sun and heat to me? Not to mention the, er, the expense this little rescue has entailed. That's the problem with us poor mortals, Diz. A damsel's smile"—his face grew somber and he reached out and traced her jaw with his knuckle—"ravishing though it might be, doesn't put soup on the table. Plebeian concerns, but there you are."

With the touch of his hand she went still, which among all the odd, garbled, and jumbled episodes of the last four days was oddest of all because Harry touched her often—familiar, fraternal touches—and yet *this* touch seemed staggeringly different from a brotherly caress, imbued with tantalizing awareness, shivering reverence, discovery, or . . . acknowledgment.

She wanted to arch into his touch and so she did the opposite, certain this reflexive desire was counterfeited by her mood, the drink, and the scandalous shape of his mouth. Angry with herself for being such a simple-witted, suggestible chit, she snapped at him. "Why can't you just do something admirable, Harry, without always trying to"—she cast about for the right phrase and found it in an Americanism she'd lately heard—"figure the angles? Why can't you, for once, just be noble?"

"Because then you'd expect I *was* noble." His words came out low, harsh. Harsher than he'd intended, perhaps, because he suddenly dropped his gaze and shook his head slightly. "Wouldn't want you forming any wrong impressions about me." He glanced up and his mouth twisted in self-mockery. "So, what's it to be, Diz? No joy for the hero despite the out-of-pocket expenses incurred on your behalf?"

Whatever her ransom had cost him, Harry could afford it. He was well on his way to being one of the more successful jackals in Egypt.

She sighed, vaguely relieved and oddly chagrined that the intensity of the past moments had vanished. "I'll see if Hammad might be willing to sell that Nineteenth-Dynasty collar to you," she offered. "It really was decent of you to come after me and all, Harry. In spite of your taking advantage of me."

"Think nothing of it," he said.

"I wish I could," she muttered under her breath, aware of how grudging her gratitude sounded. "I hate being beholden to you."

Harry had that effect on her. With everyone else she could be composed, mature, gracious. Harry brought out her worst qualities: sarcasm, impulsiveness, competitiveness. He constantly shot holes in her attempt at self-Anglicization.

Well, Harry old boy, she thought, brushing her fingers against the packet held beneath her waistband, if one were incited against one's finer nature into being competitive, one might as well win. There was bound to be a market for the type of merchandise currently jabbing her in the midsection. Those markets would be hard for her to find, but still . . .

"Brax-stone!" The Egyptian with the lopsided turban flung back the tent flap. Impatiently he motioned them outside. Harry ducked under the flap and Desdemona followed him. The Egyptian waved his arm toward her, making angry sounding invectives as he did so. Harry responded heatedly.

Something was wrong. Maybe the slaver had decided not to part with her. Maybe he'd found a wealthier buyer.

"What is it?" She grabbed Harry's arm. "What's he saying?"

"Nothing. Nothing at all. You just go wait over by my horse," Harry said. The old trader sputtered. "Go on."

She had just started to sidle past them when the Egyptian suddenly reached inside his robes. She started in horror, certain he would pull out a razor-edged dagger. Instead, he pulled out a bulging satin purse. He flung it at Harry's head. One-handed, Harry snagged the missile from the air. Gold coins spilled from its mouth.

"You take!" the Egyptian shouted. "You take *Sitt*! Take this for your trouble! But *take her back!*"

Every hair on the back of Desdemona's neck stood at attention. She should have known. Of all the people on this earth, *she* should have realized: Exit Harry the Hero. Enter Harry the Hound. *Passion and something inexplicable.* God, she was a fool! She stomped forward, hands clenched at her sides.

"Desdemona," Harry said, backing away from her. "We don't have time for this. Abdul is very angry we're still here. He wants us—you—gone. Now."

"Ha!" Nonetheless she stopped, glancing over at Abdul. The Egyptian looked apoplectic.

"Honest, Diz," Harry said. "He says he has some buyers who have been waiting to trade for two days. They won't wait any longer and they won't come near the camp while you're here."

"Really?" she asked dryly. "Why? And *you*"—she speared the slaver with a glare—"can just button it, Abdul. I'm not leaving with Harry until I have some answers." Abdul must have understood; his grousing subsided into a low, incessant mutter. "Explain, Harry."

"You're a genteel English lady, Di—Desdemona. Our dear Sir Baring—You know, Over-Bearing?—may not be the titular head of Egypt, but he rules the country. Do you think Abdul here would risk an international incident in order to make a few pounds?"

A few pounds? So much for her princely ransom.

She was glad it was dark so Harry couldn't see the red color flooding her cheeks.

"Think again," Harry went on. "If word got out that you were kidnapped, not only would every right-thinking"—the word dripped sarcasm—"English gentleman in the country be after Abdul's head, so would every one of his native cohorts. Kidnapping young Englishwomen is bad for business. So he sent for me. This money is merely a gratuity of sorts."

"So why," she asked coldly, "did Abdul kidnap me in the first place?"

"He didn't. Rabi did. By mistake. And he is, by the way, very angry at you for your deception."

"*My* deception?"

Harry nodded sententiously. Abdul kept muttering. "Rabi says you fooled him into thinking you were a poor unattended slave. He thought of himself as rather a knight errant, saving you from the clutches of a negligent owner. And after he'd picked you up, his suspicions that you were badly mistreated were confirmed. Skinny, bony, weak—"

"Oh, for heaven's sake!"

"Rabi's words, not mine. He feels very poorly used. He had, he claims, only the highest principles in mind."

"Rabi must be related to you."

"Why would you say that?" Harry cocked his head.

"No reason." She glanced again at Abdul. With his swollen cheeks and purplish hue, he looked as if any moment his skin would split. "Are we going to stand here talking all night?"

Harry let out a *whoosh* of relieved air. "Of course not." Without a glance at Abdul, he led the way to where his Arabian mare waited. He swung up lightly onto her back. Desdemona had to admit it; Harry was graceful. He nudged the horse forward and held out his hand. She took it.

Without further ceremony, Harry pulled her up, lifting her sideways across his lap.

He looped one arm around her waist, settling her closer. "Are you sure you wouldn't be more comfortable if I took whatever it is you stuck under your waistband?" he murmured against the nape of her neck, his lips velvety-soft and warm.

She shivered from the feel of his mouth on her skin and shook her head. "I am absolutely certain, Harry." Her voice sounded too high. "Thank you for your concern."

She must be more exhausted than she had realized because now, with the cool night breeze ruffling her hair and Harry's hard thighs bracketing her own to keep her from falling, she was feeling very drowsy, very . . . content. The world that had for the past few days seemed surreal and unfocused and—yes, she could admit it now—frightening, was beginning to feel safe and familiar once again.

She closed her eyes and let her head roll against Harry's shoulder. Harry might be lean, but his shoulders were broad. Comfortable. Far more comfortable than the dusty, sweaty tent in which she'd spent the past three nights.

"Diz?"

"Hm?"

"What did Rabi give you?"

"Love letters," she murmured.

He laughed and kicked the mare into a canter.

Sir Robert Carlisle looked up from the book he was reading as Desdemona straggled through the front door. He peered over the edge of the glasses perched on his nose. "Oh. Hello, Desdemona."

Hello? She'd been kidnapped, spent four days and three nights in a sweaty tent, and nearly been sold into slavery. She was tired and filthy and her head felt like it was being used as an anvil by a blacksmith demon, and all her doting grandfather could say was "hello"?

"Grandfather, do you realize—"

"Hello, sir."

Her grandfather looked up and squinted. His expression sharpened. "Oh, it's you, Braxton. What are you doing here?"

"I met Dizzy on the way in." Her grandfather closed his eyes. He disliked Harry's nickname for her almost as much as she. "I thought I'd take the opportunity to pay my respects."

Her grandfather snorted. So did she.

"Grandfather, I have been—"

"Dizzy has been telling me what a lovely time she had visiting the Comptons."

"She has, has she?" her grandfather said. "Well, next time you go visiting, Desdemona, please tell me

of your plans in person rather than leaving a note
with the housekeeper."

Note? With Magi? A surreptitious glance at
Harry's innocent expression told her who'd au-
thored her "note." She gave an unhappy inner sigh.
As much as she hated to, she was going to have to
lie to her grandfather. Either that or spend the next
year in her room. *Damn.* Now she owed Harry another debt.

"I realize things are done differently among you
young people nowadays," her grandfather was saying. "I have tried to adjust. But still, it is important
to keep up appearances. And since we have
broached the subject of appearances, why are you
togged out in that getup?" His gaze traveled over
her bedraggled native garb and even more bedraggled self.

She groped around for an acceptable lie. If her
grandfather ever discovered her unchaperoned and
absolutely forbidden trips to the Cairo *suqs,* she'd be
locked in her room for a year.

"Dress party," Harry said.

"Oh?" her grandfather asked.

She narrowed her eyes on Harry. He smiled graciously. She could almost see him checking off another mark in his mental "Debts Desdemona owes
Harry" list.

"Dress party, Desdemona?"

Desdemona nodded glumly.

"Well, I also suggest that the next time you feel
you must dress like a native, you find some clean

garb in which to do so. Gad, Desdemona, what can you have been thinking of? You smell like a camel."

"Goat's milk. Fermented," Harry supplied helpfully.

The warmth in her cheeks turned into an inferno.

"I'm going to bed," she announced.

"Jolly good plan. Let yourself out, Braxton." Her grandfather wandered off toward the back of the house, once more engrossed in his book.

Without waiting for Harry to leave, Desdemona climbed the stairs. A bath, a light meal, a bed, and then—she patted the thick packet at her waist—and then she would reread the shocking, titillating, downright indecent poems of "Nefertiti."

CHAPTER THREE

If ever, my dear, I am gone,
  where will you offer your heated stalk?
If I cannot hold you close deep within my body,
  with whom will you know love's satisfaction?
Would your fingers follow the line of another's thighs,
  learn the curve of her breasts, and the rest?
It is all here, now love, for you
  quickly uncovered.

Desdemona flipped over in her bed. The words kept her from sleep, teasing a deep warmth from her body. All evening she'd pored over the papyrus. Not an authentic papyrus, of course. Akhenaton and Nefertiti's tombs had never been found.

She could have offered the scroll's creator a few pointers on counterfeiting age on papyrus, she thought. This was too clean, the vegetable dye too fresh looking, the whole too well preserved. The author's imaginative abilities, on the other hand, were another matter altogether.

Not only were the verses erotic, sensual, and graphic, but they touched the heart as well as aroused the, er, spirit.

At ten o'clock Desdemona had been interested, by midnight she was riveted, and by one A.M. she'd developed such heart palpitations only a brisk sponge bath in cold water had relieved her. She'd been lying in bed for the last hour, unable to get the verses out of her mind. They were nothing like the romantic books she kept hidden in her grandfather's library and far more graphic than anything her own imagination had thus far come up with.

When she'd been twelve, she and her parents had stayed with a professor of antiquity in Hamburg. He had a daughter Desdemona's age, Maria. In her, Desdemona had found her first real girlfriend. Each day the two girls would excuse themselves to go study. In reality, they would lie on Maria's great featherbed, staring out the window and trading daydreams. They made up stories that had nothing to do with philosophies or academics or politics, but instead recounted deeds noble and worthy by men, honest and brave, who loved their beautiful ladies far better than they loved wealth or fame or power.

It was a harmless pleasure she nurtured during the seemingly endless rounds of symposiums and conferences her parents—and she—attended. She would take the dry, sterile little episodes of her life and build elaborate, wonderful stories around them.

As she grew older she kept up the practice, secure

in the knowledge that being a romantic did not mean being a fool. What harm did it do to weave a little magic around mundane events? She knew the hero of her imagination didn't exist. But if a few flowery words could help assuage the nameless longings . . .

She moved restlessly beneath the sheets. Romantic she might be, fanciful she was not. *Longings, indeed.* If she kept up this nonsense, she'd convince herself Harry was simply misunderstood rather than a self-confessed, unrepentant, charming rogue. She forced her thoughts back to the matter of the papyrus.

This wasn't the sort of things one picked up on the sidewalk outside Shepheard's Hotel. This was geared to a highly specific type of collector. A male collector.

Men, Desdemona had learned, were fascinating, often self-delusional creatures. The same man who would not consider looking at, let alone owning, such steamy salaciousness when printed between the covers of a modern book jacket would pay ten times over for that same verse when written by an ancient hand on a decaying piece of pounded vegetable pulp. And that man would not thank anyone to point out that new ink on old weeds does not an antiquity make.

A buyer was out there. She only needed to find him. Discreetly. She couldn't very well stand about on the street corners hawking Egyptian pornographic verse. Such activity was bound to ruin one's chances in society. Or, at least, the society she'd join once they returned to London.

The thought brought a frisson of discontent that she quelled. Hopelessly longing after something one could never have was pointless. Having learned the benefits of ruthless practicality, she'd long since decided that if her future lay in England, then England she would love.

She couldn't stay in Egypt without her grandfather, and her grandfather wanted—and deserved—to return to London. He was nearly sixty. He ought to have the opportunity to enjoy some well-deserved acclaim.

She sighed and rolled her cheek into a pillow clad in Egyptian cotton so finely woven that it felt like brushed satin. She'd miss Egyptian cotton.

She felt Harry's mouth, a thing fashioned for ecstasy and sin, roam with wicked delicacy along her throat, trace the wing bone jut of her clavicle, and follow the incipient swell of her breast to the very . . .

Desdemona woke in slow, delicious increments as a light, warming breeze soughed over her through the netting that surrounded her bed in the Egyptian style. Wonderful sensation, though a curious one since she distinctly recalled Magi closing the shutters last night. A slight noise, exactly like the cushioned fall of a foot, caught her attention. Without turning her head, she opened her eyes.

Through the gauzy tenting she saw a man moving about with economical—and devious—grace. Harry

Braxton was expertly and stealthily rifling through her drawers.

There would, Desdemona thought, have been a time when Harry would have found something in her drawers. Not now. Five years had taught her everything she needed to know about Harry, and no amount of fermented goat's milk could erase that cautionary knowledge.

Her very first lesson had been never, ever, leave anything of value in an easily accessible location. Like a drawer. Well, she amended as he scowled and straightened, his hands on his hips as he looked around her room in exasperation, maybe not the *first* lesson. The first lesson had been that looks were deceiving.

When she'd arrived in Egypt five years ago, she had promptly fallen madly, passionately, desperately in love with Harry. She'd just come to live in a strange land with a grandfather she'd never met. She'd been as credulous as only academic parents could make an only child. In short, staggeringly credulous. Harry Braxton, young, charming, and athletic, had seemed like the quintessential storybook hero.

Now, with five years of hindsight to guide her, she realized that anyone—indeed, any *thing*, including a crocodile lurking in the Nile—was better suited to the role of romantic hero than Harry. He wasn't even that good-looking, she thought, watching him through half-closed eyes.

Once she'd likened him to a Greek or Roman god. She nearly snorted. About the only thing epic on

Harry's countenance was his nose; a nice, bold specimen. The rest of his face was pure north European, not Mediterranean. He had high, broad cheekbones; a clean, canted jaw line that clipped out in a ninety-degree angle from his throat; thick, nut-brown hair; and pale blue eyes banked by dense bronze lashes. A god would have had soulful obsidian orbs. There were times when Desdemona doubted Harry even had a soul.

Nope, she thought with satisfaction as Harry disappeared into her closet and returned a few moments later, she was over her childish infatuation. She could not help it if her dreams occasionally forgot the lessons daily life had taught her. It had to be enough that during her waking hours she was wise enough to know the difference between fiction and reality.

Indeed, she congratulated herself, she was so well over it that she could even admit the points of Harry's physical appearance that did not suffer in comparison to a Greek god's.

Like his mouth. Harry had a nice mouth. No, honesty compelled her to admit, Harry had a *beautiful* mouth. It was wide and mobile with firm lips, the upper bowing into a sensually pronounced philtrum above the full, sculpted band of the lower. Harry's lips looked sensitive. Harry's lips, thought Desdemona, looked like they could read Braille.

His smile was disarming, too. Seductive. Why, last night—while granted she'd not been herself—hadn't even the most casual of his smiles seduced her, appealed to her, made her read into it a warmth that simply didn't exist? Too bad he not only knew this but used it to shameless advantage. If she had a pound for every woman who'd fallen victim to Harry's grin, she'd be living on custard and foie gras instead of hiring out her services as a translator, correspondent, and whatever else she could to augment the household's overextended funds.

And finally, she had to admit Harry had a nice form—if one were partial to a rather attenuated version of the classic physique. Which, drat it all, she was. He was lithe and supple and strong. Rather like a feral cat, she thought as he suddenly dipped and felt along the bottom of her desk.

She allowed herself a small, victorious smile. *Nothing there, Harry, old chap.*

He stood up, looking annoyed, and after pulling a chair noiselessly over to the wall, leapt lightly atop it. He peered into the wall sconce.

"How stupid do you think I am?" Desdemona asked curiously. "Anything hidden there would be set on fire the minute the jets were raised."

Harry whirled. The chair started tipping over. An ordinary man would have tumbled and fallen flat on his face. But then, an ordinary man hadn't spent so much of his life sneaking about. Harry simply jumped out of the range of the toppling chair like a house cat avoiding the crash of the furniture it upturned. And just as nonchalantly as that cat, he gazed at her.

"Dizzy, m'dear, you're awake," he said with unfeigned pleasure.

"What are you doing here, Harry?"

"I've come to see how you are?" The assurance came out as a question. "I stopped by this morning and Magi said you were still snoring away. Next time you visit a trading camp, avoid the fermented goat's milk. That stuff will lay a strong man out for a week."

Uncomfortable, she looked away. At least being tipsy accounted for all that nonsense she'd been thinking about "desert princes and harems" before she had realized just which prince had come for her.

The Prince of Jackals.

Mythic creature formed of wind and darkness, indeed. Tipsy? She'd been *drunk.* The thought was comforting.

"Well, as you can see I'm fine. Now would you care to explain why you are looting through my things?"

"Looting? What a vulgar choice of words," Harry said. "I was merely waiting for you to wake up and looking about for something to do."

"Theft is an interesting pastime."

"You used to be such a sweet creature. So trusting." He *tched* gently. "Whatever happened to you?"

"You."

"Dizzy, you wound me. You really do. Actually," he hurried on, doubtless reading her willingness to do battle in her eyes, "I have come about that papyrus you promised to translate."

"I only promised that when I thought you had risked life and limb to save me from the clutches of heinous villains, not simply answered a call from your reprobate pals to come and take me off their hands—for a hefty fee, I might add," she finished darkly.

"Abdul went through a lot of trouble to see you were safely—and discreetly—returned."

"Abdul is a smelly desert rat and runs with the same." Her eyes narrowed suspiciously. "How *did* you get involved, Harry?"

"Don't look at me like that. I did not arrange to have you kidnapped."

"Oh?" she said. "You were pretty quick with a suggestion of how I could repay your heroism."

"You should be relieved I don't demand the obvious and customarily accepted mode in which a damsel repays her debt to the man who has saved her life." He moved around to the side of her bed and placed one palm flat beside her hip, drawing the sheet tight over her lower body, leaning over her. His face was suddenly lost in shadows, his expression inscrutable. For a long moment he studied her.

"Little temple cat," he finally murmured. His voice filtered like smoke through her thoughts: dangerous, warm, obscuring smoke. "I said you belong to me." He leaned closer. She could hear the slow intake of his breath.

Confusion raced with arousal along her nerves. Last night she'd thought he'd seemed different and now, today, again, their familiar relationship was off balance, skewed. "Or do I belong to you?" he mused in that hypnotic whisper, longing and irony intertwined in his gaze. *Longing.*

She closed her eyes. Her skin shivered with electric awareness, her blood saturating the nerves with restless stimulation. She forced her breathing to a regular pace. Her reactions were simply the last vestiges of fatigue and inebriation.

She counted to ten. Her muscles tightened involuntarily with the notion that all she had to do was move forward a few inches to feel the lips that had tormented her in her dream touch her in reality.

But this wasn't a dream and she had none of the excuses for her unruly thoughts that she'd had last night. She may not yet be in control of her body's reaction to Harry, but she could certainly control her thoughts.

"Would I take the reward, were it offered?" A layer of desperation lay beneath his casual tone. Nonsense. She forced herself to smile and opened her eyes. He was toying with her.

"You know there is absolutely no chance of collecting *that* reward."

"Do I?" he mused. A shadow of . . . self-mockery? No. More probably fatigue crossed his face. He straightened abruptly, his face carefully blank. "Well, I didn't have you snatched. Do you think I'd resort to such measure just so you would translate some scribblings?"

"Yes."

"I wouldn't. I didn't. You're not the only translator in Cairo. The place is rank with translators."

"But I *am* the best."

"Such self-conceit." He shook his head sadly. "It

isn't at all desirable in such a pretty, delicate, and fragile-looking young woman."

Hearing the twist he gave words that she'd applied to herself only a day ago, Desdemona's face grew hot. He grinned. Evil, mind-reading wretch.

She stabbed him with what she hoped was a superior glare. "I *am* the best and you know it. The *wunderkind* of Egyptology. Why, my father had me—"

"—'translating glyphs when I was six years old,' " Harry finished in a bored voice. "Yes, yes. I've heard it all before. I hate to think what your life would have been had your parents finished what they started."

"What is that supposed to mean?" She rose up on her arms and her light blanket slipped to her lap. Harry's light eyes skittered over her, jerking away.

"For God's sake, Dizzy, have you no modesty?" He lifted the ragged lace strap from her shoulder. His fingers shivered as they brushed her shoulder. Or was that her own response? Her belly muscles tightened. "More important," he said tersely, "have you no decent bedclothes?"

He was not so unsusceptible as he would like to be, she thought triumphantly. Drat him anyway, teasing responses from her body and then chastising her for her immodesty! Well, she wasn't the only one prey to human failings, susceptible to certain unaccountable but undeniable attractions. And if rumor was to be believed, Harry was more "susceptible" than most.

"May I remind you that you are in my bedchamber uninvited? If my lack of modesty or my choice of nightrails offends you so much, go." She sat up straighter, aware of the swing of her unbound breasts beneath the thin, worn cotton nightrail, the flush blooming across her chest and flowing up her throat at her unaccustomed boldness.

"If you'd stay decently wrapped under your blankets instead of traipsing about in that flimsy—" He broke off. His eyes fixed somewhere over her left shoulder. "May I remind you that I am not your ancient eunuch, your cursed brother, or your feeble uncle? I'm a man, Dizzy," he said, his breathing rapid and angry. "Just a man. But sometimes that's enough."

Her pulse quickened in response to his low, urgent tone. All of Cairo viewed this man as someone to be reckoned with, and all of Cairo's women saw him as desirable. Including, damnation take it, herself.

But the ability to awake a man's baser interests wasn't the same as awakening his heart, Magi had adjured her on many occasion. And that is what she wanted, a man who loved as well as desired her. That man wasn't Harry. He'd made that clear long ago. Regardless of how he teased her.

"Then don't come in here unless you're invited," she snapped angrily, abandoning her plan to punish Harry with longings similar to those she felt. What purpose could it possibly serve? "And stop mocking me about my former . . . delusions. Someday, Harry Braxton, the tables will be turned. Someday you'll be the one humiliated by an ill-conceived and absolutely unwarranted fascination."

"So you promise . . . repeatedly."

She wriggled down against the pillows, tucking the blanket up under her chin. "Someday you'll be on your knees—yes, *on your knees*—because of some woman, Harry—"

"Sounds painful."

"—and when you are, I'll be there to see it."

"I don't doubt it," he said, suddenly serious. And then he grinned, switching from grave-eyed male to reckless, charming rogue and in the process confusing her. "You're a fascinating woman, Diz."

She snorted.

"I mean it. Just look at you," Harry said with something that might, if one were of a fanciful disposition, been approval. "Self-confident, competent, vivacious. Egypt has made a woman of you. Why ever would you want to go back to that mold manufacturing plant called England? Egypt reeks of romance and a good half of Her Majesty's officers are madly in love with you—"

"For heaven's sake, Harry, do you honestly believe that this palaver will twine me about your little finger?" she asked. "You just want me to stay here because I'm the cheapest of the translators you hire."

"I want you to stay." His gaze locked with hers. For a second, shadows moved in his bright eyes. "At any rate, Dizzy, my dear, until you've done my translations." He chucked her lightly under her chin, but one finger lingered to touch her cheek. "Now, now. Don't look like that. You have only yourself to blame. If you didn't insist on indulging your thespian impulses by dressing up and lurking about the bazaars looking like some poor fool's angel or a *houri*—" He rose and thrust his hands deep in his pockets, sauntering away from the bed.

"I wasn't lurking. I was attempting to blend in."

"Exactly," he muttered in a distracted tone. "You know you are much safer dressed as an English citizen than an Arab woman. You have no idea how poor Abdul was sweating when he discovered who, or rather *what*, his youngest son had brought home from market." He stopped near her battered desk and hitched his hip up against it.

"Why didn't you come get me straight off?"

"I didn't know where you were. I just about went mad—" For an instant his expression tightened into something resembling pain. No. Frustration. Harry would have hated being thwarted.

"Abdul was so distraught by the situation he neglected to impart that rather pertinent bit of information in his note." Incredibly, his gaze fell away from hers, as if *he* were uncomfortable. "So I scouted around until I found you."

"It took you long enough."

"I started north of the city. He went south. Poor Abdul."

"Oh, for heaven's sake, Harry. They're *slavers*."

"Abdul is not a slaver," Harry said. "It's enterprising young Rabi who wishes to expand the family business into a new, lucrative sideline."

"I'm surprised you haven't thought of it."

"Oh," he said, "I've thought of it."

Desdemona's mouth twisted in disgust. "Have you no decency?"

"Certainly," Harry said. "I just choose to ignore it. As you did when you took advantage of poor Rabi and accepted . . . ?" He trailed off invitingly.

"Aha!" Desdemona crowed. "Now we get down to it. That's the real reason you've sneaked in here."

"Why *is* Braxton here?" her grandfather asked from the doorway.

It said much about her grandfather's confidence in her that he did nothing more than raise his eyebrow at Harry's appearance in her bedchamber. And, too, Harry insisted on acting under the completely unfounded assumption that he was somehow looked upon as a member of the family.

"Why are you here, Braxton?" her grandfather repeated.

"I came to see how Dizzy was and to ask you both to dinner at Shepheard's this Friday evening."

"Why?" Sir Robert asked suspiciously.

"My cousin is here, healing from a broken heart. Or so my mother writes. I promised her I'd introduce him to the assorted *Inglizi* littering the place."

"Cousin?" Desdemona asked.

"Lord Blake Ravenscroft."

Desdemona's interest awoke. She knew Harry had a family in England. An extensive, loving one. After each Christmas he sported new shirts for weeks on end. She hadn't realized there was a lord among them.

"Really?" she asked.

Harry gave her a sardonic smile. "Oh, you'll love

him, Desdemona. He's so damn English I expect he carries a piece of Buckingham Palace around as a talisman. And romantic! Broad, dark . . . bulky. I assume he spends a good deal of time pouting—though you'll doubtless call it 'brooding.' At least he did as a child. The most boring, humorless companion I've ever been forced to spend a summer with. I can't think that a dozen years will have changed him much."

Harry didn't like his cousin; she was half in love already.

CHAPTER FOUR

Sir Robert glanced out into the hallway and then back at the alabaster cylinder in his hands. He was having a hard time dating the dratted thing and as of yet there was still no sign of Harry. What in God's name did Desdemona and Harry spend so much time discussing? He blew his cheeks out in self-mockery. Hieroglyphics and chronologies, of course. The tie that binds.

He looked around his environs and sighed. The makeshift library cum office cum sitting room was ugly, granted. But even though cluttered and crammed with artifacts and relics, at least its contents had the virtue of authenticity. The rest of the small, cramped domicile did not.

Narrow, drafty, and in need of repair, the house was outfitted with second-rate furnishings and reproductions, an odd and eclectic conglomeration of English furniture Desdemona had scrounged from English military couples returning to Great Britain and the odd bits and pieces she'd dragged home from the marketplaces, the *suqs*.

It was not a proper home for a young English-woman, though it was more than adequate for his own needs. In fact, he could think of no place he'd rather be than here, among his beloved treasures, a stone's throw away from a land that had fascinated him since he'd first read of it over fifty years ago.

He didn't want to leave Egypt.

But if there was one thing he loved more than Egypt, it was his granddaughter. He'd spent the first decade and a half of her life nearly unaware of her existence except for the infrequent mention of her as a child prodigy in some scholastic journal that found its way to his desk or the sporadic letter from his son, a son he knew only slightly more than the granddaughter.

After her parents had died and she'd arrived here, he'd learned more of his son. That knowledge had horrified him. Sir Robert had spent the last five years scrambling for a way to rectify the grave injustices his son and his wife had done to their only daughter.

Desdemona, the protégée, the fascinating linguistic oddity, had never had a childhood. She'd been hauled all over Europe, from city to city, from conference to convention. She'd spent her youth on podiums and in libraries and on stages, amazing brittle scholarly old men with her uncanny ability to translate ancient written languages.

When she'd first arrived here, Sir Robert had asked her what she wanted. He'd never forgotten her response: shy, hesitant, and heartbreakingly brief. She wanted, she'd said, to be a normal English girl.

He'd do anything to see she fulfilled that gentle aspiration, and it certainly wasn't going to be achieved in Cairo in the company of ex-patriots, obsessed archeologists and dilettantes, politicians and despots. Sir Robert knew his duty and his heart, but he also knew Desdemona. The only possible way she would return to England was if she thought he wanted to go, too. Desdemona was so damn willing to sacrifice herself to others' needs. She'd never leave him here.

But now—a beatific smile touched Sir Robert's lips—perhaps there was a way they could both achieve their desires. A footfall in the hallway alerted him and he rose from the desk. As unlikely as it was, Harry Braxton might be the answer to all their problems.

"Braxton!" Sir Robert called as Harry passed by.

Harry reappeared, framed by the door, hands thrust into his pockets, his expression a trifle suspicious. "Sir?"

"Come in, m'boy. Come in and have a seat." Sir Robert set the alabaster piece aside and smiled.

Looking behind him as if to assure himself there was no other "boy" in the hall, Harry entered. Sir Robert indicated a chair near an empty sarcophagus and Harry lowered himself cautiously into it.

"Well." Sir Robert steepled his fingers in front of his lips and nodded invitingly.

"Well."

The silence hung between them.

"Well, then. Anything interesting happening with you, Braxton, m'lad?"

"No." Harry smiled pleasantly and Sir Robert gave an inward curse. Leave it to Harry to do nothing to help an awkward silence. Casting about for some subtle, ingenious way to introduce the subject he wanted to broach, Sir Robert rifled through the disarray of papers on his desk. He found an article on Aton and monotheism and handed it to Harry. "What do you think of this drivel?"

Harry barely glanced at the pages before handing them back. "Fascinating. Did you have anything in particular you wanted, sir?"

"Oh, no. No. Just haven't had the opportunity to have a chat with you lately. Man-to-man sort of thing, you understand."

Harry's expression grew uncharacteristically grave. "If this is about my being in Dizzy's room, sir, nothing—"

"Of course nothing happened!" Sir Robert sputtered. "What do you take me for, boy? You and Desdemona!" He snorted. "Most unlikely thing I can imagine. Oh, granted, at one time I know she had rather a *tendre* for you. Thank God, she grew out of it. 'Spect you were relieved, too."

"Oh, yes."

"No. That ain't what I wanted to talk to you about. I was, er, wondering about this cousin of yours."

Harry relaxed. He stretched his legs and crossed

his ankles, folding his hands across his chest. He raised his brows expectantly. "Yes?"

"A lord, you say."

Harry nodded.

"Thought your father was a dean or a don or some such thing."

"He is."

Sir Robert toyed with a pen, studying the nib as he asked, "But gentry, too?"

"No, sir. I am related to my cousin through my mother's side of the family."

"He's broken-hearted, you say?" This gambit brought no response, and Sir Robert ground his teeth in frustration. "Would he have . . . been at fault in the matter? Not, you understand, that I'm prying. I just wouldn't want to expose Desdemona to company unbefitting a young, sheltered girl."

Harry burst out laughing and Sir Robert stared at him, his ire rising at the thought that Harry would laugh at Desdemona.

"You are really a blackguard, Harry," he said tightly. "Have you no sense of what is proper? No nicer impulses?"

"Apparently not." Harry grinned unrepentantly.

The anger that invariably came whenever Sir Robert thought about how Harry Braxton had wasted his considerable talents and intellect burned hotly to life. "You could have been a premier Egyptologist, Harry," he said tightly. "You could have achieved something profound. Something lasting. With your abilities and your knowledge, you could have made a name for yourself. But instead, you've chosen to squander your talents on"—he cast about for a suitably derogatory term and found one—"grave-robbing."

"It's a living."

Sir Robert rose to his feet, leaning over his desk and slamming his palm down on its surface. "Don't be impertinent!"

A hard light flashed for an instant in Harry's pale eyes and then abruptly died away, leaving his expression once more unrepentantly insouciant. "Forgive me."

"If you would just apply yourself. Just buckle down and start writing—"

"Too much work. But you didn't ask me here to give me this lecture again, did you, sir?" he asked pleasantly.

With a deep sigh, Sir Robert sank back into his chair. "No. You're right. I didn't. Too bad, really. I like you, Harry. If things were different—"

"You mean if I were different," Harry said flatly.

"Just so. If you were different, I'd even have encouraged Desdemona's infatuation for you. I can't help but think you would have learned affection for her. She's a fine woman."

"Undoubtedly."

"Deserves a fine, upstanding man. A man of importance, a man of property, a man of higher learning."

"Yes. I know."

There was a tension about Harry's posture at odds with his casual tone, and it occurred to Sir Robert that Harry wanted out of this interview. Well, by

God, even if he wasn't husband material, he and Desdemona were friends—great friends—and solicitude was the responsibility of friendship.

"I don't think you do. Desdemona deserves the best man in the world. She deserves to have her desires realized. God knows, her parents never heeded her wants." Normally, he wouldn't have disclosed such private information, but Harry had pricked him on the raw with his laughter.

Harry's lids obscured the direction of his gaze. He appeared to be studying his hands. Color rose on his lean cheeks. Good, Sir Robert thought, good. He should feel some shame for his carelessness.

"Sir?" Harry murmured softly.

Sir Robert hesitated. He'd never confided any of the more painful aspects of Desdemona's childhood to anyone before. Certainly he'd never said anything to Harry. But then, he'd never wanted to enlist Harry's aid regarding Desdemona before.

"She wasn't like other children."

"I would assume not."

"She could read before she was two years old. My son was afraid her prodigious talent would be wasted."

"I can imagine his concern," Harry replied, watching him carefully.

"Concern?" Sir Robert echoed. *"Fear*. Desdemona scared her parents. Rather than accept responsibility, they hired tutors, scholars, the most prestigious they could afford, and they gave her to them. Old men more interested in dead languages than live children. And when they'd packed her head with all these languages, they carted her about Europe so she could impress the world."

"Yes?" Harry's voice was so low Sir Robert had to strain to hear it.

"They forced her to work for hours, these zealous instructors, intent that not one measure of her vast intelligence be wasted or distracted. But every time she learned a new language, there was another to be learned. Every success was met with another challenge. There were no friends. A mind like hers could not be tainted with exposure to normal children."

"Did she tell you this?" Harry looked stricken.

"In fits and starts. Little pieces she dropped casually over the years. That's the most piquant part of it, Harry. She doesn't even know how truly bizarre her upbringing was. She has nothing with which to compare it. Only her books, those romantic adventure stories she thinks I don't know about. She doesn't even realize how odd her life here is. But she guesses and she longs for something—"

"—something English and wholesome and romantic."

"Yes." Sir Robert leaned over the desk. His face grew warm. "There are few opportunities for Desdemona to meet acceptable gentlemen here. Is your cousin . . . an acceptable sort of man?"

Harry was silent for so long Sir Robert feared he was not going to answer, but then he cleared his throat and said, "Yes. Inasmuch as I know of Blake Ravenscroft, which is not so much after all, he is an unexceptional and very standard example of the breed."

"The breed?" Sir Robert's brows dipped in confusion.

"Worthy, dogmatic, dull."

"Dull as in unintelligent?"

"No. Dull as in predictable. Blake can always be counted on to do the proper, the honorable thing. Always."

Sir Robert grinned. "Sounds a fine young man."

"Does he?" Harry cocked his head mockingly and Sir Robert shook his. Harry would never understand the appeal of integrity, principles, and probity. While Harry was loyal to a degree and trustworthy to another, he was utterly a rogue.

Still, Sir Robert had found out what he'd wanted to discover, and it was gratifying knowledge. He sat down, his gaze falling on alabaster cylinder on his desk. "What do you think of this, Harry?"

Harry rose and came stiffly across the room. Probably rigid from posing in that insouciant position for so long, Sir Robert thought.

He took the cylinder from Sir Robert and turned it over, his gaze traveling over the smooth surface a minute before he placed it on the desk. "Old Kingdom. Cartouche is blurred. Possibly a seal."

Sir Robert scowled. "Why would you say it's Old Kingdom? I see no evidence—" He bent his head and studied the faint carvings in the stone.

Harry turned, his movement mechanical and graceless. "That's Osiris' cartouche. Osiris was worshipped from 2200 to 2100 B.C. I think it might be a funerary seal."

"By heavens, Harry, I do believe you're right!" Sir

Robert looked up excitedly only to find himself alone. Damn waste of a wonderful mind, he thought soberly before returning his attention to the seal in his hand.

Carter looked up, absendly only to read stories

within Carter hopes, for now a period stand in hopes to

where ------ have way, but and start on the man used to

the agents.

CHAPTER FIVE

Everyone who was anyone eventually dined at Shepheard's Hotel. Occupying the site of what had once been the palace of the Muhammad Bey, the hotel had just undergone a sumptuous refurbishment and drew even greater crowds of cosmopolitan tourists than it did before. The wealthiest, the most elite, and the most cosmopolitan company Cairo had to offer dined here, and these days, that was cosmopolitan indeed. Old money and new, titles and scholars, dilettantes and adventurers crowded the spectacular, ornate terrace.

Harry, of course, had managed to secure a table not only on the terrace but at the rail, overlooking the lovely vista of parks and palaces.

Marta Douglass, the only woman in his party, looked over her fellow diners: Colonel Simon Chesterton, a fixture in Her Majesty's Egyptian army for over twenty years; Cal Schmidt, her own distinctly American escort; and Lord Blake Ravenscroft,

Harry's darkly handsome cousin. Pleased with the ratio of men to woman, Marta wondered whom the other two chairs awaited.

"I'd like to propose a toast." Lord Ravenscroft raised his glass. The others followed suit. "To Lenore DuChamp."

Marta Douglass waited for some further revelation regarding the woman they'd just toasted. None was forthcoming. Lord Ravenscroft was being purposefully enigmatic, for which Marta was distinctly relieved. Listening to men drone on about other women was tiresome.

As soon as they'd been introduced she'd recognized Blake Ravenscroft; an aristocrat, confident of his superior looks, his superior social situation, his superior breeding. Something of a rake, too, she decided.

Pity, so few rakes truly *liked* women. They clung to their cynicism like a talisman. Now, scoundrels were a different matter, she thought fondly. Her deceased husband had been a scoundrel. Too bad he had not lived. If one were a romantic, which she most certainly was not, one might even say tragic.

She had been widowed when Colonel Hick's campaign of '81 had resulted in her lieutenant husband's death. Rather than return to the restrictive embrace of her husband's disapproving family, she'd stayed in Cairo. It had proven an entertaining—sometimes even lucrative—decision.

But now it was time to think of the future. Soon she would be thirty-two. She had no substantial wealth, and her looks, while still impressive, were beginning to show subtle signs of age.

Thankfully her sunburned American escort didn't appear to notice the half-dozen years she seniored him. Beneath the cover of the linen tablecloth, his hand seemed to be taking on a life independent of his brain. Dear boy. She took a sip of wine just as Georges Paget, the deputy director of the Cairo Museum, appeared beside their table.

"Madame Douglass." The plump, middle-aged Frenchman inclined his head.

"Monsieur."

"Paget, join us," Harry invited, waving a waiter forward and requesting another place be set. Immediately the waiter scurried to comply.

"If I do not interrupt," Paget said, having tallied the accumulated wealth represented at the table and gauged it worth his attention. French national interests not withstanding, Paget's real interest was making a lucrative living "distributing" high-end relics. He'd apparently decided there might be a buyer present.

"Not at all," Harry said, as the setting was completed and a waiter brought Paget another chair.

Throughout the introductions, Simon sat back in his seat, his enormous beard settling over his uniform like a dingy laprug. He stroked the graying mat, regarding them thoughtfully. Though first and foremost—so he claimed—an officer in Her Majesty's army, Simon was also one of the world's most renowned collectors of Egyptian artifacts.

How fortuitous that he'd been assigned duty in

Cairo, Marta thought wryly, glancing at the thick gold band adorning his little finger. She masked her tweak of chagrin. A life-long bachelor, Simon could well afford to play the role of collector. It seemed monstrous that the only women Simon spent his money on were embalmed ones.

"How's business, Georges?" Harry asked, drawing Marta's attention. Not that she'd forgotten him. Not for a moment. His collar was rumpled and his jacket was creased. It didn't detract from his appeal in the least.

"Business is thriving, Harry," Georges said. "Only last week I was brought a piece I would stake my reputation came from Akhenaton's tomb."

"Come now, Georges, Akhenaton?" Harry asked.

"Who is Akhenaton?" Cal asked.

"*Who is Akhenaton?*" Simon echoed in such extravagantly shocked tones that Marta wanted to laugh. "My dear lad, you really must spend some of that Yankee cash on books. Especially if you intend to take up archeology."

"Akhenaton was a pharaoh," Harry explained, his face alight with the avidity it often wore when he spoke of ancient Egypt. "A pharaoh who took it into his head to promote his own god above all the others. Rather adamantly forced the issue. Renamed himself after his god, built a city dedicated to him, compelled his people to worship him."

"And this is the fellow whose tomb Mr. Paget thinks has been found?" Cal asked.

"Oh, I very much doubt that," Simon said with a superior smile.

"Why not?"

"As you can imagine," Simon said, "Akhenaton wasn't very popular fellow with the priestly sects dedicated to the usurped deities. Put them all out of jobs, you see. After his death, the priests had a field day obliterating every instance of Akhenaton's name, every physical reminder of him, his family, and his god. They abandoned his city and certainly desecrated his tomb. No royal artifacts have ever been found."

"Before this." Georges smiled like Mr. Carroll's Cheshire cat. "I know where I will search. But it is hard work, a far distance from any towns. I need to hire an aggressive foreman to oversee the job."

"What about that French fellow, Maurice Chateau?" Simon asked.

"Maurice Franklin *Shappeis* is no more French than you," Georges said, obviously insulted. "Besides, he is no longer in my, er, the museum's employ." He turned to Harry. "I would watch very carefully the shadows, my friend. Maurice Shappeis harbors you no goodwill."

"What did you do to this man, Harry?" Lord Ravenscroft asked, speaking for the first time since he'd made his toast.

"Nothing much."

Georges snorted. "Harry demonstrates that Maurice's method of enlisting young workers is not healthy for Maurice."

Ah, Marta thought. She remembered now. Rumor had it that Harry had fought Maurice after the foreman's work practices had resulted in the death of some poor Arab boy. Maurice had fared badly in that fight. Very badly.

"I see," Lord Ravenscroft said.

"I doubt that, Blake," Harry said mildly. "In Egypt, being a site foreman is one of the more lucrative positions open to an uneducated man. Unless one knows where a cache of antiquities is holed up." His glance at Georges invited confidences. Georges merely waggled his brows at Harry.

"Oh, but I do see," Lord Ravenscroft said. "The opportunities open to an . . . uneducated man are limited in every part of the world." Something subtle passed between the Harry and Blake, and Marta realized that they did not like each other.

Beneath the table, a hand caressed Marta's knee. Calmly she reached under the cloth and swatted it away. Undeterred, Cal Schmidt winked at her and Marta nearly laughed.

Cal was so impossibly American. A self-confessed neophyte in the game of antiquities collecting, and with apparently no knowledge whatsoever to guide him, Cal had arrived in Cairo a month ago. They'd been introduced shortly thereafter. He was blond, lanky, and rich. Marta could have become fond of him if only—

She looked up, chancing to meet Harry's gaze. He smiled absently, his gold-flecked blue eyes glinted with humor, and her heart triphammered in her throat. Lord, what a man! There was so much magnetism about him; not only charm, but wit and depth and a generosity that was all the more fascinating because there was nothing in the least naive about it.

Half a decade ago they'd had a brief, delicious affair. When they'd parted it had been without recriminations. She had assured him that her interest, like his, had been satisfied.

She'd lied.

She'd never really gotten over Harry Braxton. She looked away, unwilling to have him read too much in her expression. A wise woman did not wear her heart on her sleeve.

"Dining room's awful crowded tonight," Cal offered into the ensuing lull. "Why's that?"

"Another of Mr. Cook's famous Nile Expeditions—fares all-inclusive—must have disembarked," Simon explained with a sneer. "I swear each year that chap hauls more and more inquisitive old biddies up the Nile. The country is littered with Englishwomen. One can hardly see the pyramids anymore for the bustles swarming them."

"Surely not all of these people are with Mr. Cook?" Cal asked.

"No," Harry said. "Only the well-dressed ones. The poorly dressed chaps are archeologists. Assorted nationalities represented."

"Yes," Georges said, "and I see one nationality represented that I am sure is looking to declare war—of a personal nature."

Marta looked over her shoulder. Red-haired Gunter Konrad—a would-be archeological expert— sat behind them, thick arms crossed over his barrel chest. His brow jutted above his nose and his jaw bulged at the corners as he stared at the back of Harry's sleek, brown head.

"I think Herr Konrad is upset with you, Harry. You should not have cheat—" Simon glanced at Lord Ravenscroft. "You should not have *maneuvered* him into selling that Middle Kingdom collar of his so cheaply."

"A man should know the value of what he holds." Harry took another sip of water. "Besides, I've made arrangements to make amends."

"I say," Lord Ravenscroft suddenly breathed. "Now, there is a treasure worth coveting. Have you ever seen such a piece of tiny, golden perfection?"

"Gold? Where?" Simon asked, hastily peering about the room.

Georges licked his fingertips, following Lord Ravenscroft's stare. "Pretty, is she not? That's Desdemona Carlisle."

Marta followed the direction of everyone's gaze to where Miss Carlisle's progress through the room was marked by a wave of men scurrying to their feet as she passed.

She should have known whom those empty chairs were for. Any party Harry arranged was bound to include Desdemona Carlisle.

"She's lovely," Lord Ravenscroft said.

"Oh," Simon said, finally catching sight of the chit. "Desdemona." He sank back in his chair, deflated. "Nice girl. Odd. A walking encyclopedia. Knows more about glyphs than any ten men in this room and a dozen or so languages. Grandfather's an ass."

"A dozen languages?" Lord Ravenscroft asked. "Surely you're mistaken."

"I am not, sir," Simon said indignantly. "She was an internationally acclaimed prodigy as a child. Written up in all sorts of newspapers and circulars, exhibited at the National Geographic Society conference in '80."

"You mean her skills were exhibited," Harry corrected softly.

"Course," Simon said. "Caused quite a sensation among the Egyptologists. I attended one of her performances myself."

"How extraordinary." Lord Ravenscroft's gaze had not left the petite woman. "However did she end up here?"

"Orphaned," Simon replied shortly. "No family left in England so they shipped her off here to live with her grandfather. Poor little girl. Jolly lucky bugger—'scuse me, Mrs. Douglass—but old Bobby Carlisle would probably be living in a hut if not for Desdemona. She quite takes care of her grandfather."

Marta made herself study the approaching younger woman. Lord Ravenscroft was right; Desdemona was exquisite.

Her hair, twisted in a loose—and unfashionable—knot low on the nape of her neck, gleamed like antique gold. Its color was echoed by her delicate, though unladylike, tan and further augmented by the topaz sheen of her outdated evening gown.

She came quickly through the throng, oblivious to the rapt attention her passing caused. Though she moved with fluid grace, there was too much impatience and expectation in her pace, as if she were racing forward to meet her most fervent desires. Marta felt old watching her, so delicate, lovely, and quicksilver, her face alight with pleasure. Trailing behind her, her grandfather spied the gleefully smiling countenance of his nemesis, Simon, and scowled.

A few feet away, Desdemona slowed as the men at the table rose. And now, this close, one could see the unexpected and startling duskiness of Desdemona's nearly black eyes beneath straight dark brows. It was no wonder that if—as rumor had it—she did wander masked among the natives, she did so successfully. Veiled, with a long *chadar* covering her dark blond hair, her eyes alone would lead one to assume she was some exotic Ottoman hybrid.

Reluctantly Marta glanced at Harry. He'd gone quite still. Intensity, so at odds with his usual offhand charm, had crept into his expression. There was a barely perceptible tightening of his shoulders and jaw and a slight forward attitude to his posture . . . as if he were drawn to Desdemona by some magnetic force he resisted.

But for all his covert anticipation, Harry's greeting was insouciant. He grinned, the last to rise, shedding the lambent, dangerous aspect of his character, like a lion playing at being a house cat.

Damn, damn, damn. Marta wanted to shake him. What could he want with this little, sloe-eyed hoyden? She was unfashionable, bizarre, far too vocal in her opinions, opinionated and restless. She was not nearly woman enough for Harry.

And yet, for all the familiarity Desdemona allowed Harry, as intimate with her as he undoubtedly was, there was a distance—subtle, unfathomable, unspannable—that Harry himself kept between them. Even though, Marta noted miserably, his gaze leapt hotly to bridge that gap and consume the gilt-colored chit. If a man ever looked at her like that, she would follow him to the ends of the earth.

She disliked sitting there, an unwilling, secret observer of such devastating passion. Harry should be looking at *her* like that. Time was running out. She would have to do something and do it soon.

Someday Harry would tire of this odd, cautious courtship and run Desdemona to ground. Only a fool would refuse such a man. And though Marta fervently wished Desdemona was such a fool, she didn't believe it to be so.

CHAPTER SIX

*W*hat did Harry mean by watching her like that? Caught for that instant, Desdemona could not help but respond although she recognized that he was purposefully exerting his considerable charms. Although for what reason, she could not imagine. He was far too sure of his masculine desirability. He probably listened outside of doors after he left to see how many times his name was mentioned.

She would not give him the satisfaction of seeing that he affected her with his crooked smile and his welcoming gaze, his skin shaved as smooth as amber, his deep tan emphasized by the cool white of his shirt. She gave her head a fractional shake and stood tiptoe, peeking over his broad shoulder, hoping for a glimpse of his cousin. But her view of Lord Ravenscroft was obstructed, and other than scurry around Harry with the obvious intention of winning a view of the English viscount, she could only await an introduction.

Georges Paget bowed gallantly over her hand and Cal Schmidt greeted her with a broad smile. "A pleasure to meet you again, Miss Carlisle."

"Miss Desdemona," Simon said, bowing slightly, "how delightful to see you," and then, after an overlong pause, he jerked his chin in her grandfather's direction, "and him."

"I see you are introducing your relative to Cairo's more disreputable element, Harry," Sir Robert said, staring stonily at Simon. "A simple lapse of taste? Or did this brigand foist his company on you?"

"Why, you sanctimonious—"

"Pathetic old war horse—"

"Now, Grandfather," Desdemona cut in hastily. "How have you been, Colonel Chesterton?"

"Fine. Excellent. Been acquiring antiquities at a rate that makes my head spin."

Sir Robert's face colored to an unpleasant mauve shade. Simon and he were embroiled in an ongoing battle to see who could acquire the most relics.

"I didn't get a chance to thank you properly on that *translation* you did for me last week, m'dear," Simon went on. His little blue eyes gleamed malevolently. Desdemona could have tipped the old brute over. Her grandfather had expressly forbidden her to act as a translator; the occupation was "unbefitting a Carlisle woman." Little matter that the household was in part supported by those services.

Sir Robert scowled. "Desdemona, you promised you wouldn't—"

"I'm afraid I'm to blame," Harry broke in. "I asked Desdemona to look at some pottery I was in possession of before, er, Simon came into possession of it."

"What pottery?" Sir Robert demanded, successfully decoyed. He was vigilantly jealous of anyone else's acquisitions. "And why doesn't Harry do his own translations?"

"That would be interesting," Blake muttered, winning a tense look of dislike from Harry.

"New Kingdom." Simon grinned like a fat gargoyle. "Glass inlays."

"That's very rare, isn't it?" Cal Schmidt asked.

"Yes," Marta Douglass purred, and with her breathy, deep assent Desdemona's self-confidence teetered. Marta, as elegant as an ibis with her long, pale body and deliberate, graceful movements, always made Desdemona feel short and incidental and . . . inexperienced, as if the older woman were in possession of a mystery she knew Desdemona would never own.

"You are a collector, too, Mrs. Douglass?" Cal asked admiringly.

"Heavens, no. But if one hangs about with hounds, one eventually learns to bark," Marta said, winning laughter from the gentlemen.

Sir Robert, however, was not to be sidetracked. "Good Lord, Braxton," he sputtered. "How can you let this . . . this person steal treasures from your own country whom I, and the museum, represent?"

"*My* country?" Harry asked mildly, feigning surprise. "I was under the assumption we were in Egypt, sir."

Desdemona stifled her laughter behind her hand. He was impossible.

"You know very well what I mean, Braxton."

"Well, sir, if *my* country were willing to pay as handsomely for purloined treasures as Simon here . . ."

"My point," Sir Robert broke in, "is that as historians we must take the long view. The Egyptians can't afford to look after their national treasures. They can't even manage their own government—"

"If we gave them the opportunity, instead of allowing those Turkish—" Desdemona began until she saw one of Marta's pencil-thin brows jump. She felt the rebuke Marta sent out as sharply as if the older woman had slapped her hand.

"It is our obligation," her grandfather went on, "as the cultural guardians of the world to safeguard Egypt's treasures for her until the Egyptians can do for themselves."

"I see," Georges said, chomping fiercely on his Turkish delight. "Once England decides Egypt is capable of self-government, you'll simply pack up all their relics and ship them back from London's museums." He sneered. "I don't think so. The British Museum is nothing more than the world's most successful looter. And you are no less a graverobber than . . . than . . . poor Braxton there."

Poor Braxton? Desdemona thought in exasperation. Poor Braxton was smiling like a crocodile.

"I think Georges has a point," Harry said. "Even the prince is not above the odd spot of . . . grave robbery. At last count he personally owned fifteen mummies and was giving them away like party favors to various friends."

"How would you know?" her grandfather asked.

"I sold him his last one."

Georges burst out laughing, and Cal and Marta sniggered. And this time, in spite of her best efforts, Desdemona could not contain her laughter. Harry's gaze locked with hers and something intimate and piercing and dangerous moved between them, frightening her with its intensity.

How and why had their relationship suddenly become unclear and unsettling? She was certain she was somehow to blame for Harry's toying with her. She shouldn't let him see how he affected her. What a fool she was!

Her grandfather's face had turned an alarming shade of red as he searched for a response to this outrageous—and undoubtedly true—remark. He sputtered, recalling her to her senses.

"It *is* a point of shame, though," she said almost by rote. "All these governments, crawling all over Egypt, like ants on a felled animal, rending it apart. At least Harry doesn't pretend higher purposes for his acquisitive activities."

"And what would so young a lady know about national interests?" a deep voice asked.

Everyone turned, including Harry. The movement finally brought his cousin into Desdemona's view. Her eyes widened. Lord Ravenscroft was spectacular.

The perfect antidote to Harry.

* * *

The wonderful authoress Ouida herself couldn't have penned a darker and more intense-looking man. Even Desdemona's favorite fictional hero by that prolific romantic writer, the manly and suffering Bertie Cecil, would have been hardpressed to match Blake Ravenscroft's spectacular good looks.

Just above middle height, his perfectly tailored dinner jacket stretched tautly across broad shoulders. His snowy-white shirt provided a contrast for the ebony curls tumbling across his pale, noble forehead. And he was watching her with the . . . with the .

. . . with the rapt and alert intensity of a falcon. His black eyes gleamed from beneath black, winged brows. His lips were stern and straight beneath his aquiline nose. His features chiseled and noble.

"Comes from all those languages she can read," her grandfather was saying. "Everybody made so much of her as a child she's developed the notion that her opinions, no matter what they are, deserve expression," he muttered with the air of one confessing a relative's secret voyeurism.

"Oh, she does, does she?" Lord Ravenscroft's utterance was warm with amusement.

"Ahem." She cleared her throat, giving Harry a hard look of reproach.

"Oh, yes," Harry said. "Sir Robert Carlisle, my cousin, Lord Blake Ravenscroft. Dizzy, that's Lord Blake Ravenscroft. Blake, Miss Desdemona Carlisle."

Of all the ungracious—

Blake—such an exciting, manly name—cut in

front of Harry and claimed her hand. He raised it to his lips, his eyes never leaving her face. "I am delighted to make your acquaintance, Miss Carlisle." He brushed a kiss across her knuckles before slowly relinquishing his hold and turning to her grandfather.

"Won't you be seated, Sir Robert?" Blake gestured toward an empty place across the table. "Miss Carlisle?" He yanked out the chair next to his.

"Thank you," Desdemona murmured, settling gracefully.

The old debate over the disposition of recovered artifacts, having been brought out and attended to with monotonous adherence to custom, was summarily dismissed, and for the rest of the dinner the conversation stayed—more or less—on neutral ground.

Because she was trying so valiantly not to stare at Lord Ravenscroft, Desdemona spent the dinner uncharacteristically quiet. She found it a nearly impossible task. Blake Ravenscroft could have been fashioned directly from one of her daydreams. Big, dark, intimidating, and brooding.

"Who," Blake finally said in his deep, aristocratic accents, "would have imagined I would travel thousands of miles only to find an exquisite little English rose blooming in the desert?"

Bertie Cecil couldn't have said it better himself! In fact, he may have said it just the same in Chapter Fourteen of the romantic epic *Under Two Flags*. She smiled at Blake.

"Nice plantings, aren't they?" Cal Schmidt asked,

peering over the balcony to the famed Ezbekiya gardens spread below them.

"I was speaking of a flower blooming nearer at hand," Blake said.

"Oh. Yes. Of course," Cal said, dividing his beaming appreciation between Marta and herself. "Though I can't say I can appreciate roses myself. Give me a cactus blossom any day of the week. Though I'll confess they're a mite harder to pluck than a little old rose." Desdemona started to chuckle but, catching the severe expression on Lord Ravenscroft's face, she turned it into a choke.

"Fish bone," she said, pointing at her throat, fighting down the tiniest flutter of disappointment. Well, she'd never made a sense of humor a prerequisite for her romantic heroes. She glanced up and saw Harry. He wore a huge, delighted grin, and she had a hard time suppressing her own answering one. Harry's smiles were infectious, particularly when they were inappropriate.

"Ah." Harry nodded knowingly. "Spiteful things, fish bones. Fearful the way they'll stick in the old craw. I say, gulping down a great wad of bread can sometimes wash down the particularly tiresome spine. Just pop one of these down whole and you'll be right as rain." He wiggled the bread tray under her nose.

"No. Thank you. I'm fine."

"Have some wine then, Miss Carlisle. Shepheard's reputation is well warranted," Blake said, his dark eyes on her. "Its wine cellar is superlative." He edged his chair nearer hers. Around them the others continued talking about the latest site being excavated. Blake swirled his glass of ruby-colored burgundy and held it invitingly. She smiled shyly and sniffed. Lovely bouquet. At least, she assumed it was a lovely bouquet. She preferred lemonade herself.

"They use the dungeons as the wine cellar," she said.

"Dungeons?" Blake asked. "What dungeons?"

"The Mameluke Bey's," Harry answered. Desdemona hadn't realized he'd been attending. "The previous tenant," he elaborated. "Shepheard's is built on one of the old Mameluke palaces."

"Interesting, the things you manage to *hear*, Harry." A piquant expression softened the harsh line of Blake's mouth. But rather than winning a matching warmth from Harry, it seemed to sting him. Harry's brilliant eyes shimmered, a sharp unreadable chill spreading over his usually open, animated face. Deliberately, he turned from Blake.

"I am sure you will find your stay in Egypt fascinating, Lord Ravenscroft," she said, trying to ease the tension that had sprung up between the two men.

"I already do," he answered. "I'm intrigued."

Harry rolled his eyes. Just because he didn't find her womanly charms worth remarking on did not mean other men did not.

"I didn't realize you had any interest in Egypt, Blake," Harry said.

"Indeed. Considering your successes here, I'm becoming quite interested. I was hoping to persuade

you to take me on a tour of some of the nearer mon-
uments," Lord Ravenscroft said. He turned back to
her. "I am eager to explore the pyramids. Imagine
the thousands of years they have stood witness to
civilization. Men's lives fade and their names are
lost in the passage of time, yet that which they build
endures. If only I . . ." He broke off suddenly.

There was no mistaking the sudden unhappiness
that descended on him. His black brows dipped, his
lips closed into a thin, tight line.

What troubled this brooding, handsome man?
Heartbreak, Harry had said. Well, she knew about
that. Impulsively Desdemona touched the back of
his hand. Whatever it was, it might be assuaged by a
sympathetic ear.

He leaned closer to her. "If only—"

"Sorry, old man," Harry broke in, his voice as
bright and cold as a desert moon. Desdemona jerked
away from Lord Ravenscroft, the moment of intimacy shattered. "Can't do it in the next few days.
Have to make arrangements to go to Luxor to see a
man about a cow."

"Cow?" Her grandfather and Simon chimed in
with equal interest.

"Yes," Harry said.

"Well, then," Lord Ravenscroft said sardonically,
"I shall have to go alone."

"What cow?" her grandfather asked.

"Just a cow. A . . . very . . . old . . . cow."
Harry settled back. He might as well have thrown a
firecracker on the table. Conversation exploded
around them.

"What's this about a cow?" Cal Schmidt asked in bewilderment.

"He's talking about an Apis bull!" Simon said to her grandfather.

"An Apis bull?" Georges said. "You know where there is an Apis bull? The Cairo Museum had one but we, ah, misplaced it. We could use another."

With a sigh, Desdemona sat back in her chair. She'd been privy to this sort of fanatical conversation for years. It could be half an hour before conversation returned to another subject.

"These Apis bulls are rare?" Cal asked.

"Very rare," Marta said in her laconic fashion.

"What do they look like?" the American asked.

"Like a bull," Marta said blandly.

"I like bulls. Raise championship pure-blooded Brahmans myself," Cal said. The rest of table ignored him, shouting demands that Harry share information with them. "But I sure haven't any bull with a pedigree the length of the one you all are discussing," he said thoughtfully.

"Excuse me, Miss Carlisle." Lord Ravenscroft touched her arm. She looked at him with surprised pleasure. He, at least, had no interest in a bull, Apis or otherwise. "I am hoping to find myself a dependable, English-speaking guide while I'm here," he said beneath the din. "Could you recommend one, Miss Carlisle?"

Desdemona looked at her grandfather.

"Harry," he was saying, "you must give your own country first opportunity—"

"I say, Harry, if you *have* come into possession—"

"You realize, *mon ami*, that you must report any—"

"Can you help me, Miss Carlisle?" Lord Ravenscroft asked. His gaze swept over her, making her vitally aware of the rhythm of her heart.

"I certainly can, Lord Ravenscroft," she said. "I would be delighted to show you the sites myself."

"I shouldn't compromise your valuable time, Miss Carlisle, but I cannot refuse your charming company. You honor me."

"When did you wish to go?" she asked. "You really must see the Giza pyramids when the first light hits them."

"Sunrise?" She nearly jumped at her grandfather's barked query. She hadn't realized he'd been paying the slightest bit of attention. "What's this about sunrise?" he asked.

"I've offered to guide Lord Ravenscroft to some of the local sites, Grandfather," she said. Around them the conversation ebbed.

"Capital idea. Capital," her grandfather said. His chest swelled out so prominently that the other diners were in danger of being pelted by buttons exploding from his waistcoat. She could read his matchmaking intentions like a book, and she felt herself warming with embarrassment.

Sir Robert smiled. Marta smiled. Lord Ravenscroft smiled.

"Yes, capital," Harry said softly, the smooth expression he characteristically wore a shade smoother, his gaze as brilliant and dismissive as a god's.

"You know what?" Cal said suddenly, drawing everyone's attention. "I want one of these Apis bulls. It tickles my fancy, the thought of me, a rancher, owning a three-thousand-year-old bull."

"Does it?" Marta asked.

"Yup. And once I set my mind on having something, well"—he shook his head smiling boyishly—"I just have to have it, is all. I tell you all what. Anyone who brings me a good-size, mantel-size—Texas mantel-size, that is—authentic Apis bull, I'll pay him ten thousand dollars cold American cash."

Every table within a twenty-foot radius went abruptly silent.

"Did you say *ten . . . thousand . . . dollars?*"

Desdemona's eyes glazed over. Harry was grinning like a fool; even Blake looked nonplussed.

"I did, ma'am."

Ten thousand dollars would pay off every debt her grandfather had and even some he hadn't. It would pay for repairs to the house, purchase first-class passage to England, a new suit for Grandfather and perhaps even a dress or two for her.

"For an Apis bull?" her grandfather asked in astonishment. "An Apis bull is rare but it isn't that—ouch!" He shot her a wounded look and reached under the table to rub his shin. Enlightenment dawned in his eyes. "Sorry, banged my leg. Where was I? Oh, yes. Ten thousand dollars. Well, you might be able to get someone to part with it for that."

She might be able to find that bull, Desdemona

thought, *and* act as the handsome viscount's tour guide.

She wasn't the only one who decided ten thousand dollars was worth a little effort.

Georges bolted upright from the table and upended his chair. He backpedaled, stammering good nights before turning and trotting away. Her grandfather rose more sedately, his expression sharp with greed. "Ah, Braxton . . . be a good lad and see Desdemona home. I have a . . . a headache. Don't want to spoil her fun. Good night."

Simon, smiling and beaming, lumbered to his feet. "Ah, look at that time. Late for an old piker like myself. I . . ." He frowned at her grandfather's quickly receding back. "I . . . Night!" He spun and hurried off, leaving Cal Schmidt blinking at the half-empty table.

"Was it something I said?"

CHAPTER SEVEN

"*W*hy are you looking at me like that?" Harry asked. He twirled Desdemona on the dance floor, spinning her so quickly the breath caught in her throat. She laughed with delight, filled with pleasure first that she and Harry had found their way back to this familiar ground, and second that in Blake Ravenscroft she'd finally found a man who could supplant Harry in her imagination.

"Well?" he prompted, smiling down at her quizzically.

"I was wondering why you didn't race off to hunt up an Apis bull with the rest of the pack after Mr. Schmidt made his offer," she lied.

"Simple. Your grandfather asked me to see you first entertained and then safely home. I take my responsibilities seriously," he said glibly, looking over the crowd.

She took the opportunity to examine his profile: the deeply sensual bow of his upper lip, the short, thick fringe of bronze lashes, the strong, cleanly shaved throat. He glanced down, well aware she'd been studying him, his expression gently—nearly tenderly—amused.

She cleared her throat. "I know why."

"Why what?" He cocked his head.

"Why you aren't scuttling about the streets of Cairo looking for Mr. Schmidt's Apis bull."

"Yes?"

"It's because you already as good as have one in your pocket. Probably sent a message to your teen-age apprentice, Rabi, somewhere between the fruit and cheese course at dinner. I swear I saw him lurking about the outside of the hotel earlier tonight."

He grinned. "Just another lovesick male under your spell, Dizzy."

She made an unladylike sound. "I don't believe that for a minute."

"I know you don't, it's part of your charm." He directed her attention to the line of young officers gazing morosely in her direction. "There's your devoted following now."

She laughed and shook her head. "Unfortunately that's all they do . . . follow. None of those lads ever comes to call, hardly ever ask me to dance, and the only person who takes me out, besides Grandfather, is you."

"Not that you're complaining."

"Of course not!" she exclaimed seriously. "If one of them did take me out, it would probably be for a walk in the gardens. No one would think to take me to the places you do. The really interesting places."

"The forbidden places," he suggested gently.

"Now, Harry, you know if I were expressly forbidden to go somewhere I wouldn't go."

"You know, Diz"—he leaned close so his lips were just an inch from her ear—"you're something of a blackguard yourself."

"Pshaw." She fought and lost her battle to remain unaffected by his warm approval and covered her confusion with a sniff. "Diversionary tactics won't work, Harry. As I was saying, the reason you aren't running around, bumping into Simon and Grandpa and Georges in dark alleys, is either because Rabi will find you an Apis bull or you'll just purchase that one you were talking about earlier. That one from . . ." She trailed off invitingly.

"You are the least subtle woman I know. And, no, that Apis bull won't do for Cal's purposes. Far too small."

"But you know where to get the right-size one, don't you?" she prompted.

He shrugged and she felt his shoulder muscles bunch beneath her palm: silk-smooth economy. "You give me more credit than I deserve, Dizzy. Apis bulls aren't that easy to come by. Especially a 'Texas mantel-size' one. I wonder what else old Cal has on his Texas mantel—one of the Elgin Marbles?"

She couldn't help but laugh again. As if to reward her mirth, he spun her madly once more along the dance floor's perimeter. Her breath staggered thrillingly in her throat and she gazed up at him, feeling merry and wicked and strangely exhilarated. "Aha!" she teased when she'd caught her breath.

"Won't you be surprised if my grandfather does come up with one and cuts you out of a lucrative deal? That would put your nose out of joint, Harry Braxton."

"You're right. It would. Not, you'll note, that I'm particularly worried." He twirled her once more and she clutched his shoulders, enjoying the sensation of being caught in a vortex, spinning as lightly as goose down in his arms. Harry wasn't a polished dancer, but he moved with an athletic grace. "Fortunately, while your grandfather is a marvelous scholar, he doesn't know a damn thing about dealing."

"Such arrogance, Harry. Did it ever occur to you that *I* just might search for one myself and I *do* know something about dealing?" It was mostly bravura, but the idea that had taken hold earlier had become more and more appealing. What did she have to lose?

"I grant you, you've a wicked way with fruit vendors." He grinned condescendingly. "But an antiquities trader is not a street peddler."

"You know, I've half a mind to prove you wrong."

"Please do."

"Oh!" She pushed at his shoulder. "You can be the most provoking, patronizing . . ."

"You think I'm patronizing?" he asked, suddenly serious. "You, my dear, haven't a notion of what patronization means. But if you end up back in England, you'll learn soon enough."

"What do you mean?"

"Your life here is singular, Dizzy. Exceptional. People respect your judgment, they ask your opinions. In England, no one is going to give a little blond chit more than an ogling."

Those hated words. *Singular. Peculiar. Exceptional.* She answered them rather than his meaning. "No."

"You've never lived in English society, Diz. It isn't free and cosmopolitan and delightful. It's narrowminded and restrictive and punishes those who do not conform to its concept of normalcy."

"I'll take that chance."

"Why?" He stopped her suddenly in the middle of the dance floor, his hands gripping her upper arms, his expression demanding.

She squirmed. Immediately he let go of her arms, recapturing her hand and leading her off the floor. Around them, dancers swirled apart and drifted back together as they passed, like water birds settling in the wake of a swiftly sailing *dahabiya*.

"Why?" he asked again, his voice quieter.

She paused, uncertain how to voice the subtle longings the word "home" and "England" and . . . and "normal" aroused.

"Miss Carlisle?"

She turned. Gunter Konrad towered over her, preening his bristling red mustache with the back of his forefinger.

"Mr. Konrad," she acknowledged the huge Austrian. She smiled, fixing Harry with a bright glare, willing him to do something to get her away from Gunter. A year ago, not an hour after their first introduction, Gunter had publicly declared himself her slave.

Dizzy might have pitied Gunter except that his "devotion," tame and courtly in the extreme, was so patently a device to push himself to the fore with the rest of the archeological community. She resented him using his "infatuation" as an excuse to get close to her grandfather and Simon and Georges.

"You are wonderful beautiful tonight, little tiny girl," Gunter bellowed. "You do not know the joy you have given me. I was ecstatic, *transported* when Braxton told me."

"Harry told you *what*?" she asked.

"About the polka festival at the Austrian Club tomorrow afternoon. That you and your most eminent grandpapa will be my most honored guests there. It will be most gay. Schnapps and music— perhaps your grandfather will bring a friend? The director of the Cairo Museum? I have invited him, but he does not answer—"

"*What* polka festival?"

"Ah!" Gunter waggled one sausage-shape finger playfully. "You are shy that you have told Braxton how much you wanted to go to the polka festival with me. This coyness pleases me very much."

"Harry told you that I wanted to go to a polka festival with you?" Her stomach felt hollow.

"Yes. He said you would all enjoy very much. You, your grandfather . . . Braxton." Gunter smoothed the scowl that appeared the instant he'd said Harry's name. "I see my ploy works."

"Ploy?" she repeated numbly.

"Yes. I, too, can play 'hard to get.' "

Her gaze swung on Harry with the deadly accuracy of a dervish's blade. Oh! She quivered, furious she could feel such acute disappointment that Harry would use her. Of course he would use her. He was Harry.

"Ah, Gunter old son, I'd go a bit lighter on the—"

"You be quiet, Braxton. It is only because you bring me such good tidings that I do not squash you like a bug for the double-dealing, conniving blackguard you are. If you interfere with me again, I *will* squash you. You got off easy this time, Braxton. Next time, I will not be so munificent."

"You promised Gunter I'd go to a polka festival with him so he wouldn't exact whatever punishment you undoubtedly deserve at his hands?" she asked in a small, stilted voice.

Harry's face tightened in sudden recognition of her hurt. His dark brows lowered. "Diz, I—"

"What is wrong?" Gunter asked.

She took a deep breath and pitched her head way back so she could look up into Gunter's face. "Mr. Konrad," she said clearly, "I am sorry to have inform you of this, but I did not tell Mr. Braxton that I wished to attend a polka festival with you."

Gunter's eyes widened and then shifted frantically about the crowd surrounding them. He attempted a gruff, dismissive laugh. It sounded as if he were croaking. "No matter. Gunter sees the way you look at him, little girl. I note how you always just 'happen' to be where Gunter is," he said loudly.

With each word, Desdemona's sense of injury

grew. Gunter had padded after her for a year, and now he was declaring to all within earshot that *she'd* been hounding *him*.

"We still go to the polka. And your grandfather. And the director your grandfather will want to invite, too." He winked.

"No, Mr. Konrad. I will not. I have prior commitments."

"You do? Well, at least your grandfather and the director—"

"Oh!" She was tired of being used. As a translator, as a door prize, as a rung on someone's ladder. "Mr. Konrad. My grandfather will not be able to go either. I do not have the vaguest notion what the director's social calendar looks like. If you're interested, I suggest you ask him yourself. And furthermore, I must inform you that I have no romantic or professional interest in you. Nor have I ever. If you wish to continue under this delusion, please do so from a distance."

She tried to keep her voice as low as possible, but others heard. A few shocked gasps arose from those nearest, and Desdemona felt a surge of guilt. Gunter's mouth dropped open, slammed shut, and dropped open again.

"Miss Carlisle, perhaps you should reconsider—" Gunter said, his face turning an alarming shade of purple.

Harry stepped between Gunter and her. Harry was not so big as Gunter, but he was big enough. His breadth, always so supple, now seemed formidable . . . even protective. Which was ridiculous.

Gunter Konrad would sooner eat ground glass than be caught intimidating a lady, let alone actively threatening her. In that area at least, Mrs. Konrad had done a good job with her behemoth son.

"You heard her," Harry said pleasantly. Gunter's hands twitched at his sides as he glared with unmistakable hatred at Harry's bland face. Harry stood his ground, his nonchalant grace a direct contrast to Gunter's rigid fury.

For a long, silent moment—well, not that silent; she could hear Gunter mouth-breathing like a congested dragon—they stood toe to toe. And then the silent confrontation was over. Stiffly Gunter stepped back. Harry smiled. "Sorry old chap, I must have been thinking of some other Desdemona."

"I hold you responsible for this, Braxton!" Gunter ground out. "That's twice you have embarrassed me. This time, you'll pay."

"Send me a bill," Harry suggested, taking her elbow. Unhurriedly, he threaded their way back toward their table where the others waited. She kept her face averted from him the entire time, fighting the sharp ache that had replaced the earlier pleasure of dancing with him.

When they were nearly to their table, Desdemona saw Lord Ravenscroft looking about the room. As soon as he saw her, an appreciative smile lit his face. She allowed herself to feel warmed by his interest. He may not be Bertie Cecil, but he was undoubtedly as close as she would ever come to finding him in the flesh. Certainly closer than Harry.

She lifted her chin and turned to Braxton. "How

dare you tell Gunter I wanted to go somewhere with him, Harry?"

"Oh, for heaven's sake, Diz. It was an invitation to a polka, not a brothel. Your grandfather was planning to go. I was going to go. It was for luncheon. Nothing could be more innocuous. I simply told Gunter what he wanted to hear . . . at a very opportune moment. Just before he was going to hit me. It saved me a sore jaw.

"And as soon as I realized that you really did not want to go with him, I intervened, didn't I? I'd never let anyone, anything, ever—" He broke off. "If you can only approve of actions ruled by rote rather than reason, you'll never approve of me. I am what I am, Diz."

She barely heard his words, being too incensed with his actions. "You shouldn't have promised anything in the first place!"

"How was I to know you'd take such strident exception to spending a few hours stomping around with that great oaf in order to save me from a few potential bruises? He wants to hurt me."

"Someone always wants to hurt you, Harry," Desdemona muttered. Blake rose and Harry drew out her dining chair.

"True," Harry said under his breath, bending near as he pushed her chair back in, "but only one has thus far succeeded."

CHAPTER EIGHT

Blake Ravenscroft opened the door to his suite, ushering his cousin in ahead of him. The evening had proven what Blake had suspected; Harry had embraced this alien society utterly. It didn't matter. Blake was here for one reason: to convince Harry to sign the papers that could save Darkmoor Manor from ruin.

"Have a seat, Harry. There's a matter I'd like to discuss with you."

"Of course," Harry said, sauntering into the room. Blake studied his manner. Harry's self-confidence, at one time no more than an assumed veneer, was now real. Yet, by Harry's own admission, he was little more than a grave robber.

The appellation repelled Blake. Harry had finally found a new way to put a blight on the family name. From his birth to the scandal that had resulted in his expulsion from Oxford, he'd been an embarrassment to the family. And now grave-robbing.

Blake forced his knotted fists to relax. Only the piquant and individualistic charm of Miss Carlisle had saved the evening from being utterly onerous.

"She's a remarkably lovely young woman," he mused. "Imagine anyone knowing twelve languages."

Harry did not pretend to misunderstand. "Stay away from Desdemona, Blake. You're simply not up to her. She'd destroy you."

"Destroy me?" Blake asked in genuine amusement. "Well, there's a turn. Miss Carlisle is little more than a girl. Men are generally accounted the *destroyer*, not the *destroyee*."

"Not this time."

"That sounds possessive, Harry," Blake said, shock awakening with recognition. Harry wanted Desdemona Carlisle. "Is there something between you and Miss Carlisle?" The idea of his flawed cousin and the bright, gifted young woman offended every sensibility. Blake did not bother to keep his distaste from his tone.

"No." Blake detected a degree of torment in the way Harry made the denial. But more than that, sincerity. At least Harry realized that she was not for his likes.

There had always been something nearly noble in Harry's willingness to endure pain. Blake reluctantly replayed that cursed scene from their shared youth, the scene that had hounded him for years: Harry facing his enemies with just such a look of resigned yet eager expectation. As if there were joy in being able to confront at least these enemies—

even knowing they, through sheer numbers, must win.

A wave of pity welled up in Blake and with it the attendant guilty disgust he'd always had for the man who stood before him, his head cocked as if he could read Blake's mind. Harry was remembering that episode, too. Everything about the mocking regard with which he was watching him declared it so.

If Blake wanted Harry's cooperation, he could begin by gaining his respect, and that purpose would be best served by making a clean breast of the past. "I shouldn't have run."

"Run?" Harry echoed, looking baffled.

"From the lads at Eton."

"What?" Harry's eyes narrowed.

Good God, Blake thought in stupefaction. Harry had *forgotten*. Forgotten the incident that had haunted Blake for nearly two decades.

How could any *normal* person have forgotten that harsh episode behind the headmaster's house?

"That first day at Eton," he said tersely, "when the lads first found about your . . . problem, that you had no right to be there, that you couldn't possibly compete with them—"

"—scholastically," Harry interjected in a seemingly bland voice.

"Scholastically," Blake allowed impatiently. "Remember how they tormented you? How one day they cornered you?"

"Oh. That. Yes," Harry said. His brilliant eyes

held no more than mild interest, and yet Blake was suddenly certain that Harry had *not* forgotten.

"I should have stayed and helped you fight them. I didn't. I ran. It was cowardly of me."

Harry shrugged and sprawled down in a chair near the windows. "So? You didn't want to get the bloody hell beaten out of you. Can't say I wouldn't have done the same."

"No," Blake said. "You wouldn't have run. You know it and I know it. And I wouldn't have run away either except . . ." He lifted his chin. Bravely. "A part of me wanted you to be thrashed."

Harry gave only a light sigh in response.

Blake drew himself up, facing him squarely. "I thought you deserved it," he said defiantly, "for bringing the taint of abnormality to our family name. That's really why I ran away."

For a few seconds, Harry gazed at him, his face unreadable. And then he dropped his head against the back of the chair, staring up at the ceiling. "Oh, bloody hell," he finally muttered in a tired voice, "you were a boy, Blake. You were ten years old."

"And you were eight. I'm your cousin. I should have stood by you. No matter what my private inclination, I should have been better than that. It had to be said."

"Did it?" Harry lifted his head. "Don't ever consider converting to Catholicism, Blake. You'd wear out the knees of untold trousers seeking absolution."

Blake jerked, stung by the coldness of Harry's tone more than his words.

"I certainly hope your little admission has comforted you," Harry continued calmly. "Can't say it's done a whole hell of a lot for me. Sorry to inform you, old man, but I am no priest. And I don't really give a damn for your confession."

The blood leached from Blake's face. He'd thought to give Harry a chance to feel superior—morally superior, if nothing else—and had assumed Harry would leap at the opportunity. It had been a hard confession to make, but no harder than the self-knowledge of his own mean-spiritedness that had plagued him through the years.

And now Harry had flung his apology back in his teeth.

Anger rode down what shame still burned in Blake's cheeks. "Always were so damnably flip. Isn't anything important to you?"

"Nothing," Harry shot back, surging forward, his hands gripping the armrests. For an instant, a lightning strike of ferocity lit his eyes, but then he settled back in his chair . . . and yawned.

Outside a pack of dogs set up a fierce and noisome howling. Blake paced behind Harry's chair toward the open window, his mind racing.

What bitter irony that this cavalier . . . *defective*, without principles or loyalties, with no thought of anything beyond his own survival, was to inherit Blake's home, Darkmoor Manor. How could he persuade Harry—Harry, who did not *care*—to sign the mortgage papers that Darkmoor Manor's future depended on? And persuade him he must. The bank had been absolutely clear on this: They would give a loan only to the designated heir.

And Harry didn't even know he was that heir. Yet.

Blake slammed the window shut, muffling out the sound of the grim, nightly serenade.

"Why doesn't someone just shoot the poor beasts, put them out of their misery?" he muttered.

"They've tried," Harry said. "There are always others there to fill the void."

"If that's supposed to be some sort of—"

"Take it easy, Blake, old man. It isn't supposed to be anything. You've always acted as if you were personally accountable for every twist of fate. Made you a monotonously morose childhood companion."

"Not all of us could spend our youth risking life and limb for a few moments of excitement."

"Well"—Harry smiled, but nothing of humor reached his cold, bright eyes—"what else did I have to do?"

"I'm sorry, Harry."

"Don't be." He leaned back, tipping the chair on its back legs and balancing there, the picture of relaxed insouciance. "Don't ever be sorry on my account. I'm doing fine. As you can see."

"Yes. I can."

It was true. Harry had made a fortune in Egypt. The means were suspect, but the results could not be denied. As Darkmoor Manor's owner, Harry would be able to make the repairs and restorations that Blake, through all his efforts, had not. On the other hand, Harry may well let the place rot and tumble into the sea. Out of spite or revenge.

Blake clamped his jaw against the pain of such an image. Whether their grandfather ever reinstated Blake as his heir or not, right now Darkmoor Manor was in danger of falling into ruin. And only Harry could prevent it.

"How's your family?" Harry asked. He sounded tired.

Blake occupied himself with opening a bottle of wine, carefully gauging his response. "My mother," he said shortly, "lives in London, complaining about her lack of means. My sisters are with her, doing their best to emulate her sterling example."

"What? In London? I'm amazed your grandfather let them go. You must have hired on new servants to act as his whipping boys."

"He's your grandfather, too."

Harry grinned. "Not to hear Grandmother tell it. She always swore my mother was the product of a passionate, fleeting encounter."

"She only said that to infuriate Grandfather."

"Succeeded, didn't she?" Harry actually chuckled. "Old sot never could bring himself to publicly renounce my mother for a bastard. Couldn't have society laughing at him, could he?"

"It must have been hard on your mother. I'm sorry."

"Sorry again, Blake? You're in danger of being redundant. And once more, for no reason. Grandmother's announcement regarding my mother's sire was, I suspect, a stroke of maternal genius. It got them both kicked out of Darkmoor Manor."

Blake frowned. "She moved straight off to Cambridge, didn't she?"

"Where else would a bluestocking like Grandmother have gone with a young daughter?" Harry asked. "All the scholars and dons indulged and cosseted them. Including my father. No, don't waste your pity there, Blake. We're a nauseatingly happy little clan. If you pity anyone, pity your father and yourself. You had to grow up in that great rubble heap under the rule of an old man as miserable and cold as the rocks of his lair."

Blake wheeled around angrily. "Darkmoor Manor is not a lair. It's the family manse. It has been the property of the Ravenscrofts for three hundred years."

"About two hundred and ninety years too long, I'd guess."

"Do you hate it so much?"

"Hate?" Harry asked, clearly surprised. "One doesn't hate a pile of rocks, Blake. I save my stronger sentiments for the living."

"It's my home." Blake's voice rang out sharply. "Haven't you ever wanted a real home, Harry? Not just a warehouse filled with merchandise, like that place you live in here. I mean a place among your own kind, a place you can bequeath your heirs?"

Harry was silent a moment. "Being leg-shackled to a house isn't important to me."

"Apparently not. But even you must understand the importance a home has to others."

"Even *I*?" He seemed to consider the question. Then he shrugged. "No. Not really. Is there some reason I should?" A slight air of puzzlement crept into his expression.

I should tell him now, thought Blake. I should tell him that Grandfather has cut me out of the will, that he has been named heir to Darkmoor Manor, and that as such only he can sign the mortgage papers that will save my birthright. Aye, he thought frantically, and then I should tell him that as soon as he's signed those papers, I will do everything in my power to change Grandfather's mind and regain my inheritance, leaving him once more a man without a country or a home.

He stared at Harry's clever, sun-bronzed face, caught the animal shrewdness in his brilliant eyes and he could not do it. He needed time. He knew nothing about Harry beyond the fact of his defectiveness, the bizarre hole in what appeared to be normal intelligence.

Harry had always been an enigma. As a child, he'd an inexplicable ability to find humor when he, above all others, had had no reason to laugh. It was a quality that had ultimately overshadowed his handicap, gaining him a few loyal friends at Eton. And then there'd been Harry's fierce determination to achieve goals he could never conceivably reach. Blake had found it offensive and pathetic; others had applauded it.

But if Harry had been a mystery to Blake as a boy, the last decade had made him even more so. He didn't know what the last ten years in this primitive land had rendered Harry capable of. Blake needed a few more days to try to gauge what Harry would do. A few more days before he told Harry that everything he valued in the world lay within Harry's power to save . . . or destroy.

"No," he finally said, handing Harry his glass of wine. "There is no reason at all."

CHAPTER NINE

The mantel clock struck six A.M. as Desdemona looked up from the account book. In order to balance the household finances, the numbers in the right column of the ledger needed to outweigh the figures in the left. It was a close contest, but this month the income column lost. How was she ever to find enough money to repay her grandfather's outstanding debts in London when she couldn't even come up with the fourteen pounds necessary to make this month's ends meet?

Something would have to be done. But then, there was always *something* that could be done. And she was the one who invariably did it. She bent over a sheet of paper and began writing.

Most darling one,
Each day that passes without seeing your face or hearing your voice, I count as wasted. You are glorious to me, the shining lodestar by which I am guided.

*Without you I flounder, adrift and without direction,
carried on chance currents of fate and the whims of
others.*

*Are there others? My eyes cannot see them, my ears
cannot hear them. I see only the vision of your ethereal
form, only hear the sweet music of your voice whispering "I love you."*

Not half bad. Now it only remained to add a loving closing, and Lieutenant Huffy could come fetch
this latest letter to his jealous wife in England. Desdemona added another five shillings to the income
side of the ledger and then steeled herself in prepa-
ration for writing the next missive.

She took a deep breath and marched over to the
bookshelves lined with leather-clad volume after
leather-clad volume of scholarly treatises and tomes,
histories and scientific data compiled in English,
French, Arabic, and Latin.

She stood on tiptoe and toppled Pliny on his side,
reaching behind it and groping around until her
hand closed on a small paperbound book. Quickly
she withdrew it, glancing down at the title to make
sure she'd gotten the right book. *My Sins Be Scarlet*
was by far and away the most lurid of the books sent
to her monthly by the New York–based publishing
company.

Certainly—she checked the imprint on the face
page—Hamm and Ham would not be shy about
publishing some Egyptian love poems, even if they
were modern Egyptian or more likely some modern
European. She noted the address of the publisher

and carefully stowed the book back in her hidden cache of romantic novels.

She returned to the desk and spent the next ten minutes penning a polite and professional query to Mr. Hamm. Then she sat back and rang for someone to come and take the letter. While she waited, the thought occurred to her that the publisher might like to see a sample of the poems. She reached down beneath her grandfather's desk and slipped her hand behind the drawer. A small, dropped shelf was tucked alongside the sliding mechanism. Carefully she withdrew the brown paper-wrapped parcel containing "Nefertiti's" poetry.

She unrolled the scroll and started reading:

A fountain plays in the center of my garden, love.
You need only bend your lips to quench both our
thirsts.
Why do you hesitate? Dip your—

"*Sitt* requires?" Desdemona dropped the scroll and snapped upright, cheeks burning. Magi had entered the library. Quickly Desdemona retrieved the scroll and rolled it back up.

"What did you say, Magi?"

"You rang the bell a few minutes ago. May I so humbly inquire what it is the *Sitt* requires?" the housekeeper asked in an ultra-soft voice, her almond-shaped eyes lowered deferentially.

Desdemona grimaced. Magi was still mad at her for being kidnapped. Well, that had been four days ago, it hadn't been her fault, and it was high time Magi got over it.

"Yes. *Sitt* requires this letter to be brought down to the docks and mailed to New York forthwith." With any luck, Mr. Hamm would have the letter by early next week. And then there was the possibility—remote but real—that the Albanian dealer, Joseph Hassam, might know where she could get her hands on an Apis bull. She picked up the note she'd written him earlier. "And if you would take this to Mr. Hassam's establishment."

"Of course, *Sitt.*" Magi bowed and clapped her hands. Immediately the houseboy, Duraid, appeared. His ungainly young form reminded Desdemona of yet another potential problem.

"Duraid, did you notice a young man, a few years older than yourself, hanging around outside?"

"Yes, *Sitt.* Tuarek. Dirty people," the boy answered promptly, and with a certain relish. "Do you want I should have the scum arrested?"

"No, Duraid."

"I could have a few of my friends beat him—"

"No, Duraid." Desdemona sighed. Duraid was a horrible snob. How they'd managed to raise such an elitist in their midst was beyond her. Still, something would have to be done about Rabi. He couldn't, as Harry had suggested, have a crush on her. On the other hand, if he thought to kidnap her and sell her again, he had another think coming.

Magi delivered a few curt Arabic words to Duraid and the boy took the letter and sped off, leaving the housekeeper standing in the doorway, hands clasped in front of her waist, eyes to the floor. "Your bidding is done."

"Good," Desdemona said.

"Whatever *Sitt* desires, she must have. I live to serve. She is wisdom, I am but a poor stupid old woman who subsists on her benevolence."

Magi, ten years her senior and gorgeous, was trying to provoke an argument. Well, two could play at this game. "Allah will be pleased with your humility," Desdemona said.

"Allah?" Magi speared her with a dark look. *Bull's eye.*

"Yes, apparently you have finally learned to control your restless woman's tongue and achieved a proper humility in your dotage."

Magi's nostrils widened. "Yes. Mayhaps my transformation is an example for every headstrong, sharp-tongued woman."

Point for Magi.

"Now," Magi said, "does Revered *Sitt* require anything else? Would Revered *Sitt* like to *borrow* my yashmak . . . again?"

"That's terribly thoughtful of you, Magi. Actually, your veil may come in useful when I—"

"No!" The obsequious manner fell away, as did the soft, broken accent. It was replaced by a perfectly crisp English one. "How many times must I warn you, Desdemona, it is not proper for a lady of your standing to dress up and go into the bazaar? It is only a wonder you have not been kidnapped before. Praise be Master Harry was available to save you."

Desdemona shoved the scroll back under the

desk, irked by Magi's relentless and completely unwarranted hero worship of Harry. In all other things, Magi was so discerning. Where Harry was concerned, she was blind. "Humph. Harry was nothing more than a courier for his thieving pals."

Magi swept across the floor on bare feet, her early years as a pasha's concubine evident in her graceful movements. "Master Harry was most distraught. He will always come for you," she said.

"Yes, I expect he shall," Desdemona said, "as long as there's something in it for him." She picked up the silver letter opener and began slitting open the correspondence stacked on the corner of the desk.

"Harry will come for you at whatever risk to himself. Whatever cost. Why are you so unkind to him?"

"I'm not. You romanticize him." She inserted the tip of the blade into the end and sliced it open with more enthusiasm than she'd intended.

"I do not."

"You do."

"I do not." The older woman's face softened. "Oh, Desdemona. In so many ways you are such an astute woman. But in the matters of the heart you are so . . . monumentally stupid! It is you who are the romantic."

"There is nothing wrong with being a romantic," Desdemona said. "But thank you for making me reconsider my words. Your insistence on vesting Harry with heroic qualities isn't romantic, it's self-delusional. Harry Braxton is the least romantic man I know."

"That is not what the other ladies in Cairo think," Magi said slyly. Desdemona snatched another envelope from the stack and ripped the end off the damned thing.

"There is a huge difference between romance and . . . appetite," she said tightly.

"Desdemona"—Magi cocked her head in sudden inspiration—"is it perhaps that you do not feel yourself woman enough to satisfy a man of Harry's experience?"

"No."

"Because, if it is, I can teach you some means of securing and keeping a man's interest," she offered.

"No." Desdemona blushed, which was ridiculous. Long ago, she'd asked and received from Magi certain explicit information regarding the nature of physical relationships between men and women. She'd received that detailed information unblinkingly. Why that knowledge when spoken in conjunction with Harry should now make her blush was a mystery.

"Just as well." Magi shrugged. "I do not think Harry requires experience of you."

"I don't give a damn what Harry requires!"

"Language!" Magi scolded. She folded her hands at her waist. "Why cannot you see? What happened that you have built this wall between Harry and yourself?"

"Wall?" Desdemona said. "There's no wall between Harry and me. We understand each other perfectly. We're friends. Kind of."

"Friends." Magi said the word as if it were sour.

"Bah. This is a nothing word. You use it to protect yourself."

"From what?" Desdemona asked, honestly startled.

"This is what I would like to know. I have never pursued the subject, certain that in your own time you would come to see that which is clear. But next week you will be twenty-one years and I have seen a troop of young officers parade through here without ever touching your heart. What do you protect yourself from, Desdemona?" Magi's voice was soft with concern. "Why do you insist on playing the part of this sleeping person from one of your English fairy tales? Why do you not try to attract Harry?"

"No challenge." Desdemona took a deep breath, striving for a light tone. "The entire female population of Cairo has already accomplished it."

"I do not know." Magi cocked her head, frowning as she studied Desdemona. "I do not think this is simply jealousy. You are not by nature a covetous woman, Desdemona. Is it something else. Perhaps . . . did Harry at one time become too ardent? Too demonstrative?"

Desdemona cut off the sob—whether of laughter or pain she would never have been able to say.

But Magi was quick to read her and stared in astonished dismay. "Oh, my dear. If when he was younger, bolder, more unruly, he overwhelmed you with his—"

"Good God, no!" She cut Magi off in a voice low with embarrassment and hurt. "Quite the opposite."

"Desdemona?"

"Harry doesn't want *me*, Magi."

"Impossible."

"Oh, quite possible. In truth, a fact." She laughed, a splintered sound. "I am loath to admit it, even to you dear friend, but he was offered *me* on a silver platter! I, you see, did the offering."

"Oh, my."

"Yes. So now you understand, there's no need to—"

"There is every need. You must have misunderstood. I see how he looks at you. I see how he cares for you."

"Magi, there is no possible way I can have misunderstood. I went to his house, dressed in"—her face burned with fire—"in a most provocative manner. I . . . I kissed him. He told me to go home."

She told Magi the story then: how she sneaked into his home and found him in his library. He had jerked away from her kiss and scooped her up against his chest. His arms had been wrapped so tightly, so fiercely about her, she had thought he was taking her to his room. But he hadn't, and she knew now that the tightness of his clasp had been from panic. He'd practically run to the door of his house and set her down on the front steps. He hadn't even called a carriage for her. He'd told her to go back to England to find her Galahad and slammed the door shut.

He'd avoided her for a week, then two. And after she'd cried all her tears and forfeited all her illusions regarding Harry and love and happily-ever-afters, then, anxious and uncomfortable, *then* he'd arrived.

It had been the one and only time she'd ever seen imperturbable, affable Harry truly nonplussed, when he'd gravely suggested they discuss what had occurred.

She'd stopped him cold. She simply could not have borne his pity or compassion or weak, watered affection. She'd fixed him with a bright smile—a brilliant smile—and told him not to be so damned full of himself. She'd said she didn't want to discuss the matter. Ever. It had been a stupid little fancy she'd taken into her head. It wouldn't be repeated. She was quite over it.

And she was. Dammit, she was.

"So you see, I tried," she finished, somehow finding a light tone.

Magi was frowning. "When did this happen? You sneaked out of this house dressed like a *bintilkha'ta?*" she asked, using the Arab word for prostitute. "I did not see you. How did you accomplish this?"

Desdemona shook her head. Leave it to Magi to focus on that aspect of the mortifying debacle. Magi prided herself on knowing every single movement of those under her care.

"It was three years ago. A lifetime."

"Aha," Magi returned, mollified. Her eyes grew large. "Then perhaps Harry has changed—"

"No." Desdemona shook her head. "Harry has not changed. Leave it alone, Magi. We're comfortable as we are. Harry teases me about my one-time infatuation and that's fine. I . . . I would never admit this to anyone, especially not him, but I value his friendship, Magi. It is important."

"Still, something does not fit. And now there is this man, this cousin of Harry's."

"Lord Ravenscroft."

"I do not like how you say his name. You sound like an awe-filled child whispering the name of a favored bedtime story."

Desdemona scowled. "Oh, for heaven's sake, Magi. First you pester me about Harry, now you don't like his cousin. You haven't even met Lord Ravenscroft. He's a fine man. A handsome man. A viscount."

"I do not need to meet him," Magi said, crossing her arms over her chest.

"What's that supposed to mean?"

"He will be a wide man with too much hair and a cross expression on his face."

"Cross?"

"Unhappy, crabby. You will say he broods," Magi said.

"I'm sure I don't know what you mean." Desdemona sniffed.

"Yes, you do. Now Harry . . . he is—"

"Stop it, Magi."

"I will not. You must—"

A light rap on the door interrupted Magi. A young Arab house girl poked her head in. "Master Harry is here," she said, grinning broadly.

"Show him in," Magi said before Desdemona could say a word. With a triumphant smile, she glided to the door.

CHAPTER TEN

"*A*ny chance of some coffee appearing?" Harry asked. Magi murmured assurances that coffee, dark and sweet, would be immediately forthcoming and hurried off to see that it was so. As soon as she left, Harry turned to Desdemona. "Where is it, Diz?" he asked.

"It?"

"Rabi came to see me last night. He insists that you took something important from the camp. He says now you will not see him and give it back."

"Took?" Desdemona exclaimed indignantly. "He *gave* it to me."

"He says that this . . . thing"—he raised his brows invitingly. She ignored him—"is of a personal and highly sentimental nature."

"Ha!"

Harry grinned. "That's what Rabi says."

"So that's why he's hanging around. Well, you can tell Rabi that I consider this . . . *thing* compensation for being kidnapped, and that hell, or whatever its Islamic equivalent is, will freeze over before he'll see it again."

The boy had probably pilfered the papyrus from his disreputable sire's personal library of erotica, Desdemona thought. She banished her urge to return them. Sometimes the best lessons were those hard-learned.

Harry held out his hands in capitulation. "Hey, don't kill the messenger. I told Rabi I'd try." He crossed to the window, looked out, and made a slicing sign across his throat.

The morning light, still translucent and fragile, bathed Harry's features in gold, ennobling his aggressive-size nose and curling lovingly around his lips. The first clear rays of sun glanced off his irises, making them seem to gleam from within like colored votive glass.

Desdemona wondered if he knew the effect and had positioned himself accordingly. But, as much as she'd like to think otherwise, she doubted it. Vanity—at least regarding his appearance—had never been one of Harry's flaws. Not that he didn't have plenty of others to compensate.

He turned back and approached the desk. "Rabi wants that thing very badly. What is it?"

When she didn't reply, he leaned over the desk, bracing his arms on either end. "I can wait here as long as it takes for you to answer," he said. "What did Rabi give you?"

If Harry knew about her possession of blatantly erotic poetry, he'd never let her forget it. She blushed profusely at the thought of his endless teasing. "A scarab."

Harry captured her chin and lifted her face to his, studying her for a long moment, a tenderness in his expression that matched his gentle touch.

"You're lying . . . to *me*," he said, softly quizzical, almost aggrieved sounding. His hands, like the rest of him, were an odd combination of elegance and toil. Though his nails were clean and trim, his fingertips were callused and the backs of his hands were covered by telltale glyphs: white scars from toiling through tomb rubble; an overlarge knuckle on the finger he'd broken during an excavation; a pair of white dots, reminders of a cobra's unhappy waking.

"Dizzy, look at me," he coaxed.

How could she help herself, regardless of how stupid or useless? She shook her head. Magi had awakened old thoughts, old mistakes. They were better left sleeping. Better yet, dead.

"What?" she asked. "You wouldn't want to know all my secrets, would you, Harry? I'd lose my feminine mystique."

"Never."

"And are you willing to tell all yours in trade?"

"Would you really want to know them?" he finally asked, the seriousness of his tone catching her by surprise.

She sensed a slight withdrawal on his part, but discounted it, being too aware of the copper shards in his pale eyes, the laugh lines radiating from their corners, the thin red line beneath—

She frowned. "You've hurt yourself."

Without thinking, she touched the freshly shaved skin on his throat where a narrow gash angled across the vulnerable-looking flesh. He was warm. His skin was fine-grained and smooth. He swallowed. His pupils had dilated, his lips opened.

She dropped her hand. He dropped his.

"It's nothing. A razor cut."

"It could become infected. I'd better have Magi bring—"

"Don't." He straightened. "I have to leave in a few days, and I want you to be careful."

"You're off after the Apis bull? You've found one to sell to Mr. Schmidt?" she asked, her hopes toppling. If Harry already had arranged to procure a bull, how could she, with her few contacts in Cairo, hope to compete?

"I'm off," he said shortly, "and while I doubt Rabi would do anything stupid, he's a young male and 'stupid' is rather synonymous with that breed. If you won't return his . . . gift . . . at least promise me you won't go adventuring."

"Of course not," she said with a twinge of guilt. How she was planning to spend the afternoon wasn't adventurous, it was simply business.

"Regardless of what you might think, I'd . . . nothing must happen to you. You are . . . You are too . . ." He trailed off.

She could hear him breathing. The room had grown preternaturally quiet. The fragrance of night-blooming jasmine drenched the air, and the faraway cry of a hound throbbed through the still morning.

She stood up, disoriented. Had their friendship shifted into something else, become something . . .

No. She dipped her head, closing her eyes tightly. It was all in her imagination. She had thought this once before and she'd been abysmally wrong. She arranged a smile and looked up. He was standing motionless, a frown scoring his brow with a deep line.

"Well, if you're planning to kick about the desert with your Egyptian cronies, you certainly aren't dressed the part," she said.

He glanced down at his white linen suit and back at her, puzzled. "Oh. Yes. I'll wear appropriate garments."

"I suggest that Desert Prince ensemble. Classic. Very impressive. Most chic."

"Whatever are you talking about, Dizzy?" he asked, clearly bewildered.

How could she answer? She didn't know herself. All she knew was that the room seemed too small, that she could smell the sharp, antiseptic tang of his soap mingled with the cool, dry scent of book leather, still feel the exact degree of warmth her fingertip had stolen from his throat, the pressure of his thumb tipping her chin.

"I'm talking about your trip," she said. "What else?"

His frown deepened. "I wish I could take you with me."

"Oh, really?" she asked lightly. "You'll be needing some verification on some translations?"

"No. I don't like you being left alone."

She was suddenly angry; at her racing pulse, the phantom of her infatuation, his paternal concern. "I won't be. I have Grandfather and I'll be spending quite a bit of time with your cousin."

"Oh?"

"Yes. We're lunching together today and we'll be going to Giza later. So you see, I'll be well looked after. Not that I think it necessary, but should any need arise, Lord Ravenscroft looks to be more than a formidable protector."

"Yes," Harry muttered. "I'm sure he is everything a hulking young aristocrat should be."

"He's not hulking! He's very—" She was saved from getting into an argument by Magi's arrival. The housekeeper slipped into the room, her face wreathed in benevolent smiles, and set the silver coffee service down. She fussed a moment with the toast rack and the jam pot, sent Desdemona a stern look of encouragement, and glided out.

Harry seated himself and poured out two cups of coffee. He settled back, raised his cup to his lips, and took a sip. "Quite taken with His Lordship, are you?" he asked in a bored fashion.

"Taken?"

"Smitten. Besotted."

"I'm sure I haven't any idea what you mean. I don't *know* Lord Ravenscroft. Please refrain from ascribing your own base nature to me. Just because you are incapable of being in the same room with an attractive woman without falling all over her does not mean I share the same proclivity."

Harry burst out laughing. "Falling all over?"

"Yes!"

"Oh, Dizzy. Someday I'll have to properly demonstrate *'falling all over.'* "

"Don't bother."

"Although old Blake and you were doing a passable job of it last night."

"Lord Ravenscroft was a complete gentleman and I, I hope, deported myself as a lady."

"There was more fluttering going on at that table than from the handkerchiefs on the deck of one of Mr. Cook's steam liners."

"I wasn't fluttering."

"And Blake." Harry shook his head in disgust. "Such affectations."

"*You* are calling someone affected?" she asked, raising her brows. "You, who employ two secretaries, one for your Arab dealings and one for your English? You, who are too high and mighty to write your own correspondence?"

Harry grinned. "That's different. At least I don't commit the sin of triteness. Calling you a 'rose.' An 'English rose' at that. You must forgive him the hackneyed compliment. Old Blake's not much for originality, I'm afraid."

"I thought him charming."

Harry made an unconvinced sound.

"I *did*. I suppose you could do better?"

"Well, were I to make the effort to extol a woman's beauty, I could certainly do better than to drag out some tired old cliché about a rose."

"You are the most monumentally egocentric man

I know," Desdemona said, trying to keep the trace of admiration out of her voice.

"You are unconvinced?" Harry asked, taking a sip of coffee and crossing his legs. "Allow me to demonstrate . . . and please bear in mind that I improvise."

He spread jam over a piece of toast, studying her quizzically as he did so. She felt like a specimen, standing there under his scrutiny. She took the chair next to his and started buttering her own toast with supreme indifference. She was not a specimen.

"Let me see. Nothing floral. In fact, I think we'll dispense with the vegetative allusions all together. Animal?" he asked rhetorically. "Perhaps a gazelle? No," he dismissed the idea, chomping into his toast. "Too meek. Too inconsequential. This is difficult, Diz. To blandish a woman about her physical appearance is so limiting."

"Yes," she said dryly, burying a pinprick of hurt. He couldn't think of anything to compliment her on.

"All right, then," he finally said. "I'd begin with the way you stand."

"Stand?" He'd caught her off guard. She blinked.

"Slender. Upright. Face lifted for the sun god's caress," he murmured slowly, musingly, as if to himself. He cocked his head, his eyes traveling lingeringly over her body, and she recognized the potent attraction other women must feel when Harry looked at them this way. As if she were the central point upon which all of his world turned. As if he lo—

"Why, look," he asked in a hushed voice, something surprised and painful and pleased in his tone, "even Ra himself cannot resist you. Only see how he lathes your cheeks and brow with his heated tongue"—he reached out, brushing his fingers over her tanned cheek—"marking you with his golden kiss?"

His words were too graphic, too carnal, and she was too aware of his fingers skating along her cheekbone and over her jaw line. He'd never spoken to her this way before. Her heartbeat quickened, thrumming in her throat and in her wrists. She shivered. He smiled. His hand retreated.

"How can a mere mortal man stand a chance if even the gods are so enamored?" he whispered. "And how can one single image describe you? You are a *country*, a country of unexplored sensation and whim, veiled in dawn, shining, shedding light. See how the long fluid line of your throat flows to your breasts?" If he heard the intake of her breath, he ignored it. "Or how their blue-shadowed curves ripen above the smooth plain of your belly?"

She should stop him, he went too far, but his voice mesmerized her, like sweet, honeyed wine, warm and languorous.

"Your mouth." He paused, and her lips felt suddenly sensitized, tingling as his gaze fixed on them. "Your mouth is a sweet well sealed against me, keeping me thirsting for the clarity of your kiss. Your flesh is like the desert sand, warmth and shifting strength beneath its golden color. Your palms open, fingers flexed, are minarets, delicate and elegant. And your body . . . it is the Nile itself—the camber of your back slipping so easily by the narrows of your waist and jettied hips to the lush delta below."

He stopped. She heard the intake of his breath. "You are my country, Desdemona." Yearning, harsh and poignant, and she felt herself swaying toward him. "My Egypt. My hot, harrowing desert and my cool, verdant Nile, infinitely lovely and unfathomable and sustaining."

She gasped.

His gaze fell, shielded by his lashes. An odd, half-mocking smile played about his lips. "You'll never hear old Blake say something like that."

She swallowed, unable to speak, her senses abraded by his stimulating words, her pulse hammering in . . . anticipation? Trepidation?

"Remember my words next time he calls you a bloody English rose."

CHAPTER ELEVEN

Damn, damn, damn Harry Braxton, Desdemona thought. Ever since he'd left that morning, Harry's words had played through her mind like the underlying ostinato in an intricate melody; deep, recurrent, and inescapable.

. . . The camber of your back slipping so easily by the narrows of your waist and jettied hips to the . . .

She fanned herself with her fingertips. Her lips tingled.

"Miss Carlisle?" Blake Ravenscroft's voice recalled her to the present with a nearly physical jolt.

"Hot," she declared. "Unseasonably hot. Usually winters here are much more temperate."

"You were woolgathering, m'dear," Blake said indulgently.

He tucked her gloved hand more firmly in the crook of his arm, leading her down one of the Ezbekiya gardens' more traveled gravel paths. She glanced behind her and looked away again, chagrined. Above the rail on Shepheard's balcony, her grandfather beamed down at them.

He was so openly exulted by Lord Ravenscroft's invitation to lunch. As was she, she reminded herself. Then why did she keep hearing Harry's low, yearning voice?

You are my Egypt . . .

"I had asked how you came to Egypt, Miss Carlisle," Blake said.

"My parents died in a train derailment when I was fifteen. As my grandfather is my only living relative, I came here to be with him," she answered.

"I'm sorry." He stopped at a wrought-iron bench, sheltered beneath the dusty boughs of an ancient acacia tree, and bade her have a seat. Carefully he positioned himself so that she was shielded from the traffic. He was a broad man. He made a good shield.

"You must miss England, Miss Carlisle. It must have been devastating to lose both parents and one's home." He caught her hand and squeezed it sympathetically. "How alone you must have felt. It is a testimony to your courage that you have managed not only to exist in this forbidding land but flourish."

"It wasn't all that bad," she said, embarrassed.

"No?" Lord Ravenscroft asked, his brow climbing.

"Certainly I missed my parents but I had Grandfather."

"True," he said kindly. "Still, for a gently bred and sheltered young girl to be uprooted like that . . ." He trailed off, inviting confidences.

Rooted? Since when had she ever felt rooted in any place, any time? she wondered. "Gently bred, sheltered, but extremely well traveled," she answered. "I feel quite at home among my grandfather's colleagues. Obsessive Egyptologists are a universal lot if nothing else. My own parents were among their numbers. Not that I follow after them," she added hastily.

"But surely," Blake said, "Egypt itself must have seemed alien."

"Enigmatic," she corrected with a fond look about her. "Rich and evocative."

"Rich? Except for the riverbanks it's all dry and barren."

"Oh, no! You have to understand—" She broke off suddenly, realizing how her defense of her adopted country would sound. She adored England. She *would* adore England. Her grandfather—and she, of course—might soon be living there. "What I miss most about England is its emerald green color, the wee crofter's hut, the shaggy moorland ponies."

"Ah!" Blake nodded understandingly. "You were raised in Scotland then."

"Oh, no. No. I was raised in London. Mostly."

He blinked in perplexity. "Forgive me. When you mentioned craggy moors and a crofter's hut I assumed—"

"Well, I've never actually been in Scotland but I've read about it. A lot. The craggy moors and Heathcliff and—"

"Heathcliff?"

"J-just a name," she stammered flustered. "Anyway, I distinctly recall Hyde Park and it was most wonderfully green."

He smiled. He had straight even, white teeth. One of Harry's front teeth was slightly crooked. "What do you find to like about *this* place?"

"Egypt? Everything," she answered, sweeping her hand in a casual, encompassing motion. "The fairy-tale minarets, the sun-scraped desert, the damp, chalky smell of the Nile. I love the colors: bleached high country, roan-striped *wadis*, green-gold floodplains. I even love her sounds, from the hiss of the desert sand to dervishes' finger cymbals to the street vendors' music."

"Music," Lord Ravenscroft repeated sardonically. He laid his arm across the back of the bench and his fingers brushed the nape of her neck. "Well, the din I heard when I wandered through the bazaar yesterday could hardly be called music."

"Oh, but it is. Listen." She tilted her head. Around them the ululating call of the date vendors and water sellers mingled with the clomp of donkey hooves hitting the cobbled earth, the creak of braking carriage wheels, and the chirruping voices of countless street urchins.

"Perhaps if one understood the, er, lyrics," Lord Ravenscroft said doubtfully.

"Oh," she said, "I don't understand the words but I still appreciate the orchestration."

"I thought that you were something of a linguistic genius," he said in surprise.

She laughed. "Well, I am. In a way. I can read twelve languages. I simply can't *speak* them."

"I don't understand."

"Not everyone is like Harry," she explained patiently. "Translating the written word is a far cry from understanding the spoken one. There's the matter of accents and speech patterns and the frustrating rapidity with which people speak. It's a skill I've never mastered. A natural gift for Harry."

"A trick," Lord Ravenscroft said flatly. "Thankfully he has one he can put to profitable use."

It was her turn to pause. "I wouldn't call Harry's talent a trick. He speaks at least six dialects like a native. Indeed"—her lips twisted ruefully—"he's been adopted by one tribe as an honorary member— the Tuarek ruffians. He takes particular pride in it."

There was polite indifference in Blake's expression, but beneath that something like exasperation. "Well, I'm glad he's found something here. I'm afraid poor old Harry has never had anything of his own. I imagine it was hard for him as a child, wanting things he couldn't have and I did. It rather colored our relationship."

"I've never thought of Harry as being . . . envious." *Mercenary to a degree. Ambitious, certainly. But not envious.*

"Perhaps you are not as well acquainted with my cousin as you believe," he said coolly.

. . . *the clean, sweet well of your mouth freshening but sealed against me.* She knew Harry. Didn't she?

She straightened. She was wasting entirely too much time thinking about—and talking about— Harry. She would far better spend her time discovering more about the enigmatic gentleman by her side. She studied him.

The shuttered expression had returned to the English lord's classic countenance. His square jaw jutted in dramatic profile. His brow beneath his glossy black hair was pale as a pearl, his expression as fierce as an eagle. He was magnificent, even his shirt was clean. Few in this country managed a shirt that blindingly white.

"Tell me about your home in England, Lord Ravenscroft."

"My home." He lifted his square, cleft chin. "Darkmoor Manor is the most magnificent place on earth," he began passionately. "It is a great gray-stoned house, crowning the bleak, wind-lashed headlands of Cornwall. It is a harsh land, harried by winter gales and steeped in fog. It is a land that challenges a man."

It sounded more like a sentence than a challenge, but she forbore comment. He gazed at her, obviously awaiting a response.

"I bet it's hard to heat."

He stared at her for a second and then gave a sharp bark of laughter. It was the first time, she realized, that she'd heard him laugh. The sound was rusty, she thought, unused. Someone should teach this man to laugh often and openly.

Like Harry.

"It is that," he said, his amusement evaporating abruptly into reverence. "Chill majesty, raw, stern. Some would say Darkmoor Manor is a forbidding place, and they would be correct. But it is my heritage, my birthright. I only hope I am someday able to act as its conservator."

"Why wouldn't you?" she asked in confusion. Hadn't he just said it was his birthright?

"I will." He spoke as if making a vow. "If there is any justice at all, Darkmoor Manor will be mine. And I will be able to restore it to its former glory."

Never having owned a manor—or a house for that matter; every place she'd ever lived had been rented—and never having owned anything of value that was not destined for a museum, she could not quite understand his vehemence. She shifted uncomfortably. "Well, even if you can't restore it, you still have your health and you—"

"Darkmoor Manor is the one thing in this world I love."

"How sad." The words were out before she could stop them.

"You think so?" he asked bitterly. "Well, I have not found human attachments particularly successful. My own—" He stopped. "Suffice to say my mother has spent a lifetime amassing transitory pleasures. There have been times I've suspected that all women were like that. But you, you are different."

Different. How she loathed that word. And it was untrue. She was a normal girl. She wanted pretty fribbles and lawn tennis games and a smitten swain . . . all the things she'd read about and never experienced.

"But I do not want to bore you," Blake continued. "Let me just say I find it more satisfying to invest my passion in something lasting. Like Darkmoor Manor. I think you'd like it. Anyone who can grow to love this land would have no trouble learning to love my home."

She smiled weakly. Well, of course she could. It is what she'd always wanted, to return to England, and didn't it sound wildly romantic, all cold and remote? She glanced across the street at the vibrantly clad throng milling among heaps of gaudy silks, fragrant, ripe fruit, and shimmering brass goods, a chaos of color and texture dazzling beneath the brilliant Egyptian sun.

She gazed wistfully at the riotously sensual scene, recognizing the flaw blotting her planned return to English. She loved sunlight and warmth and wearing gossamer light clothes and sipping iced lemonade and wandering barefoot over hot terra-cotta tiles in a tea-scented garden. But surely England had some warm places, with cloudless skies?

"I would love to show you Darkmoor Manor," Blake said. "Read each impression as it is reflected on your guileless little face."

Luckily, she wasn't nearly as guileless as he imagined. She proved so now. "That sounds wonderful," she enthused. Unwilling to commit herself to further equivocations, she searched for a new topic of conversation. "Are you enjoying your stay with Harry, Lord Ravenscroft?"

"I'm not staying with Harry. He insists his quarters were inadequate for housing guests. I'm staying here, at Shepheard's."

"Harry's right," Desdemona replied. "He lives in

a dilapidated old Mameluke palace. It is little more than a warren of boxes and statuary and books."

"Books?" Lord Ravenscroft frowned. "Now why would Harry have books?"

"Why wouldn't he?" Desdemona asked.

"Well, it's not as if he's going to be using them for research, is it?" he answered with odd, bitter compassion.

"What are you talking about?"

His face reflected his surprise. "You don't know."

"Know what?"

His frown disappeared. He reached over and clasped her hand, looking at her gravely. "I thought you and Harry were friends."

"We are," she answered, thoroughly confused. "What do you mean, Lord Ravenscroft?"

"I'm sorry, my dear. It isn't my place to tell you. But next time you've the opportunity, ask Harry why he was expelled from Oxford."

CHAPTER TWELVE

Cairo's narrow streets twined and coiled along ancient footpaths. They wended their way beneath the shadows of the myriad balconies that clung to the sides of the buildings like cliff swallows' nests and crept through cramped passageways. They disappeared into blind alleys, occasionally reappearing and widening enough to allow a view of the fairy-tale skyline, the light-pierced stonework of striped turban-topped minarets and parapets filigreed against the dazzling afternoon sky.

Desdemona strode through the crowded streets with feigned confidence. If Duraid realized she was lost—and really it was not so much lost as uncertain as to where she was—he would nag her to distraction by insisting they return home. Duraid, though twelve, had the soul of a mother hen with one chick.

Well, Desdemona thought, she wasn't going to go home, at least not until she'd met with Joseph Hassam. A note from the well-known Copt *antika* dealer had been waiting for her when she'd returned from lunch. He had something "interesting" available for her consideration. *If* she could come at two o'clock.

It was one forty-five.

Perhaps Joseph had an Apis bull the likes of which her own message had asked him about. It was admittedly a slim chance. Such coincidences rarely occurred in the world of *antika* dealing. However, the only way to be sure was to find Joseph's shop.

"*Sitt* doesn't know where we are, does she?" Duraid asked dolefully from a few paces behind her.

"Yes, *Sitt* knows where we are," Desdemona replied without turning. "*Sitt* simply wishes to absorb the local color. Isn't it splendid?"

Duraid grunted. Being a lady, she ignored him. To prove her point, she stopped, drinking in the flood of sensation like a connoisseur sips a rare and potent brandy. The scents of cardamom-spiked coffee mingled with the sweeter ones of cinnamon and cloves, oranges and lemons. Beneath these wafted the heavier aromas of dust-laden donkeys, warm human bodies, and the flat mineral scent of sun-heated stone. And over this rich concoction, like the final ingredient in a cauldron of aromatic sensation, lay the densely green, fecund fragrance of the Nile.

It was a pity Lord Ravenscroft hadn't yet learned to appreciate Cairo's sensory pleasures, she thought. Doubtless he would. Anyone with a poetic soul was bound to become enamored of Cairo. Even Harry, the most pragmatic of men, savored Egypt's rich complexity.

The thought of Harry slowed her steps. She wasn't too surprised by Blake's hinted disclosure. Knowing Harry, he'd probably been expelled for selling test answers.

"*Sitt*, can we go home now?" Duraid asked.

Her eyes snapped open. "Nope. We're almost there." She struck off purposefully toward the river, breathing an inaudible sigh of relief when she saw the small plaque advertising Joseph Hassam's establishment.

"See?" She pointed at the low, dark doorway. "What did I tell you? Lost, indeed. We've arrived."

"Yes. I see. *Sitt* has the luck of the *afreet*."

"I resent being compared to little devils, Duraid."

"There *is* no comparison," Duraid said. She gave him a sharply suspicious glance. He gazed back innocently.

"You stay outside," she said. "I am here to negotiate."

"You should not go in there alone. It is not proper."

Duraid was such a stickler. "Yes, yes. Well . . ." If given the opening, he would keep her here arguing for hours; he'd done it before. "Well . . . sorry."

Before he could reply she'd ducked beneath the low lintel and was squinting as her vision adjusted to the cool, dim interior. Inside, the shop was long and narrow. A low, round table stood at the far end, fat pillows lining its circumference. Brass goblets, an ornate hookah, and a pitcher stood on its top, along with several irregularly shaped flat stones. *Ostraca*.

It wasn't the hoped for Apis bull, but then, she'd never really expected that windfall. And *ostraca* always sold well to tourists who were inevitably charmed by the diminutive pictures etched onto shale or plaster, the ancient equivalent of doodling.

"Hallo?" Desdemona called, threading her way past a cluttered Louis XIV desk. Her gaze fell on the papers scattered over the desk. Harry's name leapt out at her. Craning her neck, she scanned the top sheet. Her scowl deepened as her eyes narrowed.

It was a bill of sale—the sum of which made her catch her breath—written out to a Mr. Hatfield for "an authenticated Middle Dynasty papyrus with attendant, extensive English translation." It named Harry Braxton as the original owner—a fact that made getting it through customs easier.

"Extensive translation" was a tepid term for the weighty tome that had accompanied that papyrus. She knew. She'd done it. And she had been promised 10 percent of the selling price.

She hadn't gotten it. She hadn't made 5 percent of the stupendous figure staring her in the face.

Harry owed her money.

"Ah, hallo!" A small, middle-age man in a European-cut jacket and white turban emerged from behind an embroidered curtain. "Miss Carlisle. I am so pleased you have come."

She smiled tightly, gesturing toward the bill of sale on the table. "How good of you to invite me here, *Sid* Hassam. I could not help but notice that you have sold a papyrus to a Mr. Hatfield. He seems to have left his bill of sale here."

"Ah, yes. Mr. Hatfield." Joseph said the name with such tender fondness, Desdemona could only suppose that Mr. Hatfield had not bothered to haggle over his purchase's asking price. "He has left Cairo. I would send him this bill, but"—Joseph shrugged—"I do not know where he has gone."

"Perhaps I can be of service." She smiled winsomely. "I'll just pop this in at the British consulate on my way back home, shall I?"

"Oh, that would be most generous of you, *Sitt* Carlisle. Thank you."

Without further ado, Desdemona snatched the bill up and stuffed it into her pocket. Proof! She couldn't wait to wave this under Harry's nose and demand her back wages.

Joseph motioned her toward the table. "You will find I offer only the very best, most rare of items."

"We'll see," Desdemona said, trying to remember Harry's attitude on the few times she'd actually seen him conduct business. "Even if you don't have anything I fancy, I have had a lovely walk on a lovely day. I am enriched by the experience. Nothing could disappoint me after such a nice walk. Nothing. Not even faked relics, which, of course, I am sure you would not bother showing me."

She smiled. There was an appreciative glint in Joseph's raisin-dark eyes. "A woman who knows to enjoy the journey as well as the goal. How delightful. Won't you please be seated?"

Gracefully she sank onto one of the pillows, carefully arranging her skirts over her feet and folding her hands in her lap. When negotiating, Harry always gave the impression he was simply idling away a few free hours and that the results were of no consequence to him.

"Lemonade?" Joseph offered her a goblet.

She received it with a murmured thanks, taking a sip and carefully avoiding looking at the *ostraca* placed so temptingly beneath her nose.

"I have a question—" she began.

"Are you all right, *Sitt?*" Duraid's young voice suddenly bellowed from through the doorway.

Desdemona smiled again. "My bodyguard," she explained.

"Ah." Joseph nodded.

"*Sitt?*" Duraid's voice came more stridently.

"He's very loyal."

"I see," Joseph answered.

"*Sitt?*"

"Yes!" she shouted back, winning a startled glance from her host. "I'm fine! Buy some figs. Take a nap. Be quiet!"

"Yes, *Sitt*. As you wish, *Sitt*. But first I would like to see you, *Sitt*," Duraid said stubbornly.

"Oh, for heaven's sake," Desdemona said, raising her arm and waving it over her head. "Here. See?"

"No."

"Duraid—"

"Should I come in, *Sitt?*" Duraid asked. "I should come in."

"No." Muttering invectives, Desdemona scrambled to her feet and flapped her arms up and down. "See? I'm fine. Fine!"

The small head silhouetted against the bright outside street nodded. "I see. You are well. I am most pleased."

"Now, *go away*."

"Yes, *Sitt*."

Suddenly realizing how this must look to her host, Desdemona glanced down. "He wouldn't have quit squawking until he'd seen me with his own eyes," she explained.

"You are much loved by your servants." Joseph murmured.

She blew a gusty sigh. "It's a curse."

Joseph's eyes widened. Few people understood the tribulations that came with loyalty.

"Duraid will behave now. About my question . . ."

"Absolutely authentic, *Sitt*."

"That's not what I was going to ask."

"Ah, forgive me. And that was . . . ?"

"Why did you decide to offer the *ostraca* to me? Who told you I would be interested?"

"Why, Master Harry," Joseph answered in surprise.

She should have known. Still, she could not suppress the prick of disappointment. "He wants me to translate the glyphs on them before he buys them?"

"Oh, no. No. He simply told me that if I should ever have some pieces he would—" Joseph left off abruptly, swallowing hard.

"—not bother with," she finished for him. "He told you I might be interested in his *leavings*?"

Joseph shook his head in quick, hurt denial. "No, Miss Carlisle. It is not this way at all. I handle only the finest pieces of the ancients' art. Master Harry does not handle smaller consignments, that is all. He said you might be interested."

She sank back, trying to sort out her emotions. As tightly as the reeds clung to the banks of the Nile, Harry was twined in every aspect of her life.

"I see. And you, *Sid* Hassam. Why did you choose to take his advice?"

The Copt lifted his hands. "A whim. I was preparing for a transaction with a very wealthy foreigner. In clearing house, I chanced upon these forgotten treasures. I then recalled Harry telling me of your interest in such things."

Foreigner? Desdemona wondered. Could it be the American, Cal Schenkle, and could the merchandise have been an Apis bull?

"And then, too, there is the matter of the turkey factory."

Startled, she looked up. Joseph was smiling at her.

"Your activities on behalf of the street children of Cairo are not unknown, Miss Carlisle. They are appreciated."

"I haven't done much. Just bought a few turkeys—"

"—and purchased the property on which they are raised. And trained the children in the manufacture of the scarabs and suggested the most likely areas in which they might sell them."

She felt herself blush. Hard-nosed dealers did not blush. She had certainly never seen Harry blush. "It's not charity. I take a percentage of the net."

"But of course you do! Only a saint or a fool

would do otherwise. Saints, blessed as they are, are such uncomfortable business associates. Fools are dangerous business associates. But you—lovely and practical. A rare combination," Joseph said approvingly. "You are different."

Different. All her warm cozy feelings vanished. This was not her idea of a proper negotiation. At this rate Joseph would be giving her the *ostraca.* She didn't need another person to be indebted to, especially since Harry had apparently already filled that category to capacity.

"Hm," she said, glancing down. Her breath caught.

There were three *ostraca.* Each, though thousands of years old, was vibrant with color and emotion and humor. One was a leopard seated at a table, offering a lotus blossom to a tiny, crabby-looking monkey. On the other, a mouse dozed beneath a palm frond. But the third . . . the third was exquisite.

It showed the half-completed sketch of a woman, a royal personage from the sheer pleating of her girdle and the scepter by her side. Her palm was raised. Seeds filtered through her gracefully opening fingers, scattering in an unseen breeze.

"Lovely, aren't they?" Joseph said blandly.

"They're wonderful," she breathed. She clamped her mouth shut. Too late; he'd heard. His smile was benign and remorseful.

"Yes," he said. "I have always thought to keep them myself."

Liar.

"I would not sell them at all, having just decided such when you arrived. But now, being only a weak-willed male, I find myself entranced by your beauty and enticed into foolishness by your charm. For you, and you alone, I am willing to part with them for the ridiculously small sum of twenty pounds."

She allowed herself one last glance at the lovely woman sewing seeds. "Twenty pounds?" She lifted her brows, echoing the remorse in his tone with a milder version of her own. "Oh, well. Perhaps I can have another glass of lemonade before I go?"

"But, Miss Carlisle—" he protested. She grinned. He grinned back. The negotiations had begun.

Duraid came abruptly awake as a fly landed on his lip. Swatting irritably, he uncurled himself from his post near the door and rose. He stretched, looking around. He'd been asleep longer than he'd intended. Quickly he ducked his head through the open door.

Sitt Carlisle was sprawled against a pile of pillows. She was babbling cheerfully. Duraid sighed with relief. Magi would flay him alive if anything happened to *Sitt*.

He looked over his shoulder, noting the purple-stained shadows creeping across the dusty street. He did not want to be in the bazaar after dark. He did not want *Sitt* to be in the bazaar after dark.

Perhaps he should advise *Sitt* of the hour. Once more he stuck his head through the door.

"—I do not know how I have let you rob me of

such a treasure," the Copt was saying. He sounded gleeful.

"I don't know why I paid so much for them."

"It must be charity on my part."

"It must be pity on mine."

Both started giggling. Duraid frowned.

"My children will starve if I continue to allow my good sense to be overruled by my silly sentimental nature."

"Your children probably go to school in Paris," *Sitt* answered in a tone that made the desert sands seem moist.

"You can starve in Paris as well as Cairo."

Both broke into gales of laughter. *Sitt* fell over on her side. She made no effort to right herself.

"Do you have any Turkish delight around here?" Duraid heard her muffled voice ask.

"No," the Copt said.

"Anything . . . crunchy?"

"Crunchy? I do not think so."

"Rats."

Something was not right. *Sitt* was still leaning on her side.

"But"—the Copt's voice brightened with inspiration—"we can always partake of another bowl from the hookah. To seal our bargain."

Another . . . *bowl?* In horror, Duraid rose to his feet.

"Again?" *Sitt* asked thoughtfully.

"As is custom."

"Oh! Well, I wouldn't want to flaunt custom."

Once more they burst into laughter.

Allah alone knew what effects hashish would have on the *Sitt*. In the best of times, she was unpredictable. If she took it into her head to be difficult— Before the thought was complete, Duraid was running. He had to find Master Braxton.

CHAPTER THIRTEEN

"*I*'ve missed you." There, Marta thought, she'd said it. She hadn't felt this uncertain for decades. She looked up to find Harry regarding her with bright, unreadable eyes. He reached across the small table and touched her hand in a fleeting, comforting caress.

"You are too kind, Marta."

He didn't pretend not to understand the invitation her admission offered. It was only one of the qualities she found so appealing in him.

"Am I?" she asked lightly, unwilling to push him, afraid that if she forced him to make some sort of decision, he'd make the wrong one. "I've never been accused of that before."

"Kind *and* lovely," he said. "Would you care for a glass of sherry?"

"That would be nice," she answered. He rose and went to the sideboard where he unhurriedly poured out a glass.

She wondered if he was taking the opportunity to fashion a reply, and her pulse accelerated with a foreign sensation of self-doubt. She shouldn't have come. She shouldn't have arrived on his doorstep, unannounced and uninvited. Not so soon after he'd spent an evening watching Desdemona Carlisle with such painful intensity.

She *had* missed Harry. He was a zealous, ardent lover, concentrating more on the pleasure he gave than that which he received. But even more than the physical relationship—delectable though that had been—she'd missed the intimacy after they'd made love.

She had the distinct impression that Harry had spent years on the outside looking in, had wanted things denied him. And that those years of exclusion had been improbably translated not into bitterness but into a fervent appreciation of those who allowed him entree. He'd always seemed surprised by her interest in him and had expressed his gratitude in the most physical way possible. It had been heady.

"Your drink."

He was standing over her, holding out the sherry. She could see where he'd knicked himself shaving. She took the glass and set it on the table beside her, impulsively reaching out and capturing his hand, tugging it.

"Please, Harry. Sit beside me."

He obliged, pressing her hand between both of his big, warm palms.

"We're quite a pair, aren't we?" she asked. When he didn't reply, she went on. "How long have we been in Egypt, Harry? I've been here a decade. You arrived shortly after Ned died. What does that make it? Eight years?"

"Hardly seems possible."

"Think of all the experiences we've racked up between the two of us. All the winks we've given to custom and convention. We're a reprobate lot, we are." She tried a laugh.

He smiled. "Indeed."

It wasn't working. She could see it in the steadiness of his gaze, the unwavering concern in his expression. Whatever he thought, he did not pair them in his mind. He had never even considered it.

There was still another course open for convincing him.

She leaned against him, just enough so that her breast pressed his upper arm. She felt his biceps tense. If she could engage his body, afterward she might engage his heart.

"Harry," she whispered, pulling her hand free and laying it against his chest. His heart beat steadily beneath her palm. "Harry. We were good together."

"Yes." He sounded sad. "We were."

She did not like the slight emphasis he placed on the past tense. She dipped her head, touching his throat with her lips.

"We could be again." She watched him carefully, waiting for a sign of awakening sexual awareness in the dilation of his pupils.

"I haven't any doubt," he said. "If only—"

"Master Harry!"

Harry's head snapped up at the sound of the breathless voice. Marta frowned but made no move to disengage herself from his side. A thin Arab boy stood panting in the doorway.

"What is it, Duraid?" Harry asked, concerned when he should have been irritated.

"It is *Sitt.*"

"What?" He surged to his feet, Marta forgotten.

"*Sitt* is in the bazaar."

"Yes?"

"I think she . . . She may need you. She is—"

"Tell me as you take me to her," Harry broke in.

And then he was out the door, following the boy, not a word to her as he left, his entire concentration focused on Desdemona Carlisle. His entire bloody world.

Marta picked up the abandoned glass of sherry, lifting it and studying the way the amber fluid prismed in the late-afternoon light. Harry Braxton to the rescue. Why the hell couldn't the brat have gone for Lord Ravenscroft?

Abruptly she hurled the glass against the wall.

The foolish woman had wandered off, alone and untended. Joseph wrung his hands, apologizing profusely when Harry questioned him further.

"But she said she had smoked the hookah before, Harry!" He practically wept.

"Filled with tobacco, you ass. *Tobacco!*"

"It was tobacco! The bowl had been used for hashish a few days ago. I did not realize that she would be so susceptible to the residue. How was I to know, Harry? At first, she seemed quite at home with the effects. No fear. None."

"She doesn't *know* to be afraid. At least not about things like this. And most especially not—" He cut the words off. Even though he realized that Joseph was not to blame, it did not keep him from wanting to throttle the miserable-looking dealer. "Which way did she go?"

"I do not know." Joseph flung up his hands in despair. "I thought her bodyguard was with her. I did not attend."

Bodyguard. Harry swung around. Duraid flinched.

"You know how she is, Master Harry," the boy said. "I knew I would be unable to make her do anything she did not want to do. And I thought that if she took it into her mind to do something danger-ous . . . well, you know how she is!"

"Yes, I know how she is." He shook off images of all the potential danger she might stumble into in her present condition. Usually Desdemona's com-mon sense overruled her impulsiveness. But under the influence of hashish, her inhibitions may well have been stripped from her. The thought made his blood run cold.

"Duraid, you go toward the river. I'll go east in case she's taken it into her head to wander alone into that section of the city. She *couldn't* be so reck-less," he said to himself.

"She may," Joseph said miserably. "She was feel-ing very triumphant. Very secure. And if she was worried about the boy—"

"Dammit to hell!"

Harry strode out of the shop and into the warrens creeping through the crowded buildings. If he was Dizzy— He swore. Trying to think that way was an exercise in futility. It was his luck, his curse, to love such an independent, unpredictable, and valiant little romantic. But love her he did. With all of what he called his heart and every piece of his soul, he loved Desdemona Carlisle. And she was missing, damn her.

He stalked through the emptying streets, asking questions, finding no answers. No one was willing to admit they'd seen an unattended young Englishwoman, and with each passing minute his fear grew. Though Cairo was safer than many large cities and Dizzy's nationality guarded her from most dangers, there were always a few men desperate enough, debased enough, or stupid enough not to resist the lure of easy prey.

He quickened his pace, trying to drown his building panic. Perhaps Duraid had found her. Perhaps even now she was lying in her bed at home, fighting the sapping lethargy that came with hashish. Perhaps she had a headache. He hoped to *God* it was a horrible headache.

At the entrance to a cramped alley he spotted a boy playing some solitary game in the dust. He stopped. The child looked to have been there for hours.

"A lady," he said in terse Arabic, "an *Anglizi* lady, very small, pretty, yellow hair. Have you seen her?"

Without pausing, the boy nodded.

"Where?" His heart pounded. He held out a pias-
tre.

"Yes, yes!" The boy nodded vigorously, his eyes
fixed on the coin. "A golden-haired woman. Crying."

"Jesus—where?"

The boy jerked his thumb toward the alley entrance. "A quarter hour ago."

Harry flipped him the coin and turned.

"She was followed, *Sid*."

Followed? Harry broke into a trot, following the
upward incline of the dirt path. A sense of hushed
anticipation pervaded the abandoned lane. His boot
heels hit dully against the ancient packed earth. A
door closed behind him. A whispered voice, another
corner . . .

Six men stood in the deepening shadows, like a
pack of jackals on the periphery of a campfire. They
waited with animal patience as they eyed the small
figure crumpled against the wall where the lane
abruptly ended.

Dizzy.

He strode through their numbers, heedless of
their snarling recoil, and bent, snatching Dizzy up in
his arms, fear and rage thrumming in his temples.

"Dizzy, are you all right?" he demanded urgently.
He waited until he felt her nod before turning.

The men had closed in behind him. He did not
look at them. He did not dare look at them. Muscles
cramped, bunching in his jaw. He lifted Dizzy
higher. Her arms twined around his neck in child-
like bid for comfort, and she burrowed her face

against his throat. He could feel the salty moisture of her tears on his bare skin.

He walked into their midst. He felt his upper lip curl as he stared straight ahead, afraid that if he saw one threatening movement directed at Dizzy he would explode with violence, further endangering her. He could feel them closing in around him, the press of their malevolence, the violence implicit in their silence, and he struggled to restrain his impulse to turn and confront them.

How dare they? The thought threatened his reason, swamping cool intellect with hot rage. *How dare they think of hurting her?*

And then, as quickly as danger had presented itself, it was gone. Some unseen signal passed among the men and they shrank from his advance: silent, surly, and watchful.

He carried her through the alley, past the boy and down the road, down a dozen roads and a dozen more lanes and knew that he could have carried her thus forever. Only when they were in sight of her house did he look for a deserted side street. As much as she would have laughed at the suggestion, he did not want her encountering her grandfather in her present condition.

He stopped, hoping to give her time to compose herself, but he could not yet bring himself to set her down. Not yet. He needed to feel her: the graceful strength of her; her lush, light weight; the texture of her wilted dress; the warmth of her skin beneath it. He needed to inhale the scent of her damp brow, her hair, the faint tobacco flavor of her breath. Everything about her was precious and essential to him and he had so few chances to hold her though, like a thief, he always looked for an excuse, stole any opportunity, to touch her. He couldn't relinquish her, not yet.

"Dizzy. Are you all right?" His voice sounded hoarse and foreign to his ear.

She lifted her head, her dark eyes luminous in the odd twilight. "What took you so long?" she wailed. "I was afraid!"

He started to grin.

"Don't smile. I *was* afraid. I was lost."

"You shouldn't have left the shop."

"I know," she admitted. She'd always been honest, even with herself. It was as unique as it was tantalizing. "But Duraid was gone and I was worried about him and I thought . . . I thought—Oh, Harry!"

"Shh," he murmured, rubbing his lips against the silky cleanliness of her hair until a faint odor of hashish rose from the spilled strands. He scowled, abruptly recalled to her condition. "What the hell do you think you were doing, smoking hashish?"

"Hashish?" she asked, her fine, dark eyes clouding. She was, he realized for the first time, still under the influence of the drug. "I didn't smoke any hashish."

"What do you think you and Joseph were smoking?"

"Tobacco? He *said* it was tobacco."

"Bullshit."

"Okay. I admit that after a while I thought it was

interesting tobacco, but I've never—okay, once. Okay, half a dozen times—smoked tobacco, so how was I to know?"

"Common sense?" he asked sardonically.

She wiggled in his clasp, as if to remove herself from his embrace. Fat chance. He wasn't ready to let her go yet. But then, he never would be.

"You don't have to be so unchivalrous about it," she said in a grumpy, offended voice, settling back in his arms after what appeared to be no more than an obligatory attempt to dislodge herself.

"I *am* unchivalrous." His voice was flat. There it was again, the wall separating them, Dizzy's insistence on fairy-tale princes. No, not *some* fairy-tale prince. An *English* fairy-tale prince and an *English* happily-ever-after, a role he could never fill in a setting he would never return to. "And unscrupulous and ungentlemanly and untrustworthy."

"You don't have to remind me." She twisted in his arm and gazed accusingly up at him, obviously having been reminded of some grievance she had. "You owe me money."

"I do?"

"Yes. You should pay me."

He bounced her in his arms and leered down at her, once more falling into the familiar pattern they'd found for their relationship. "Usually when a woman demands payment it is for either a service or pleasure. Sometimes both. Now, I don't specifically recall receiving either from you, but if you'd care to remedy—"

"Ha!" she crowed, ignoring his suggestive tone.

She must be farther gone than he'd thought. "You have *so* received service from me."

"Have I? Odd that I would have forgotten."

It didn't seem to occur to her that she was conversing with a man who held her as tightly as if his life depended on it, and for this he was grateful. He needed only to keep her distracted in order to steal a few minutes of physical pleasure. Something he was not, nor ever hoped to be, above.

"Yes," she said. "You owe me money for all the translations, transcriptions, and authentications I've done for you over the years."

"I've already paid you."

"Yes, but you paid me too little."

"How do you conclude?" he asked, amused. "I paid you what you asked."

"You took advantage of me. I didn't know to ask for more."

He was quickly losing interest in the conversation, being distracted by the way she kept fiddling with his shirt collar. Her fingers, brushing idly against his skin, teased him as tantalizingly as butterfly wings.

"You'll have to enlighten me. I'm feeling particularly dense." And he was suddenly tired of playing the affable, immoral scoundrel she thought him. He wanted so much more.

Her mouth flattened with disbelief. She was as slender and supple as a temple cat and he wanted to stroke her. He couldn't. He could only hold his breath each time her breast pushed against his chest, each time her words washed her breath over his lips.

She squirmed until she'd managed to push her

hand into her skirt pocket—a hand that came dangerously near a certain part of his anatomy that was fast becoming oversensitized. He breathed an inaudible sigh of relief when she found whatever it was she'd been looking for and withdrew her hand.

Jesus. She had no idea what she did to him. She never had.

"There!" she crowed in woozy triumph, shoving a crumpled piece of paper against his chest.

"There, what?"

She smoothed the paper out and held it under his nose. "Read that, you blackguard."

Mutely he stared at the paper. He would have gladly offered a limb to be able to follow her directive. But he couldn't.

He couldn't read.

CHAPTER FOURTEEN

"So?" He balled the cursed sheet up and threw it aside. "How much do you figure I owe you?" Surely she felt the hammer beat of his heart beneath her ear.

"You said you'd pay me 10 percent of whatever you made. That Middle Dynasty papyrus sold for one hundred and six pounds."

"I see." He relaxed. At least now he knew how to go on. "Dizzy, Joseph may have gulled some fool into parting with one hundred and six pounds, but he only paid *me* forty and I distinctly recall handing you a five-pound note."

His words deflated her righteous ire. She wrinkled her nose and glanced sheepishly up at him. "Oh." A long pause. "I'm sorry. I shouldn't have accused you." She turned her head into his shoulder.

"You're forgiven." He rubbed his chin lightly over the top of her bowed head. Her hair felt as slippery and clean as the finest silk. And his secret was a secret still.

Word blindness.

He remembered the first time he'd heard the term. The doctor who'd said it. Not that the word or the doctor had made any difference. Whatever its name, his inability to read had permeated every part of his life, fashioned not only how others saw him but how he saw himself. It had created him.

Until he'd arrived in Egypt.

Here he'd found a place where his expertise and ambitions hadn't relied on written words, words that one day made sense and the next were transformed into an incomprehensible mass. Here he'd fashioned how others saw him.

It hadn't always been blamelessly done. He'd taken advantage of his native ingenuity, of the raw resources available to him, because a man who cannot read has nothing else. He'd manipulated his competitors into confrontation and then taken advantage of their distraction. He'd used guile and, when necessary, fists to get what he wanted. And it had worked.

He'd wrested a portion of respect from the scholarly community here, a feat he'd once thought impossible. He'd finally found an avenue for all the knowledge and ideas that burgeoned in his mind, mocking him with his inability to express them on the written page. The impossible had ever been his carrot and he, fate's mule.

He'd learned early and in the harshest manner possible that some things were exempt for him. That no matter how strong his desire, how much he was willing to sacrifice to achieve his goal, there were some things he could not do, some things he could not have. He'd tried overcoming his deficit through sheer willpower. He'd promised himself that no matter what it took, he would somehow learn to read.

Well, he'd sweated, railed, petitioned heaven, and bargained with hell, and he still couldn't read English. He never would be able to. But he learned an immutable lesson from that: Pain is the only reward for clinging to impossible dreams.

So he'd taken that lesson and transferred it to every area of his life. Including Dizzy. He'd given her up without ever telling her his secret.

What good would it have done? Dizzy was destined for England. And he *would not* go back to England. He *could not* become the Ravenscrofts' halfwit relative again, the object of his parents' well-meaning concern and his own self-scorn. And that's all that awaited him as the son of scholars, the student with some of the highest oral exam marks in Oxford's history . . . the man who could not read.

No, he couldn't go back to England. But Dizzy would. It was her dream, and it wasn't an impossible one. Doubtless some strapping young lad in country tweeds would sweep her off her feet. Or someone like Blake. His lips curled back and his hold on her tightened, and he cursed himself for a liar and a fool.

No matter how he'd warned himself and threatened himself and tried to convince himself, he hadn't given Dizzy up.

His heart hoped in spite of being brutally cognizant of the dangers of self-delusion. His love refused to die no matter what reason and experience argued, in spite of her determination to go "home."

Damn her, home wasn't an island or a cottage. It wasn't a place. Home was *her*. And she was leaving. God, how could he let her go? How could he ask her to stay? What, he wondered in anguish, would she do if he told her, if she learned of his . . . inadequacy? As always, his imagination offered myriad scenes, all of them untenable.

If she wrestled his dysfunction into some melancholy, romantic bit of— If she felt pity— If she nobly offered herself as compensation for his—

God. He closed his eyes. How would he survive *that?*

"I had lunch with your cousin today," she was saying. She had reached up and was smoothing the roll of his shirt collar between her fingertips.

"What?" he asked, seizing on the distraction presented by her words.

"Lord Ravenscroft and I had lunch together. With Grandfather. We had a very interesting conversation."

She was still lost in her fascination with his collar.

"Blake can be a font of information." He took a deep breath. He had to know what Blake had told her. "Dizzy, did he—"

"I really do think you've been awful."

He wondered if she could feel his arms trembling. "Oh?"

"He came here thinking you were barely making ends meet. Why did you let your family believe you're just managing to scrape together the bare essentials of existence? Why don't you share your wealth with your family?"

"My family? Papa and Mama Braxton and all the little Braxtons are doing very nicely, I can assure you."

"I meant the Ravenscrofts. How could you, Harry?" She sounded acutely disappointed in him. "How could you let the Ravenscrofts struggle along while you enjoy yourself?"

"Struggle? My, my, Blake has been busy," he murmured. He bounced her higher in his arms. "Listen, Dizzy. Though I realize your present condition makes it doubtful you'll remember this, do try to attend."

She blinked up at him.

"Blake's family owns a great moldering pile of bricks—"

"Darkmoor Manor," she chimed in like a student with the right answer to a question.

"Yes, Darkmoor Manor. It is a great rotting hulk of a house that squats among the most godforsaken rocks in England. For whatever reasons—and I strongly suspect mental instability—each successive line of Ravenscrofts cleaves to it as if they'd been bequeathed the Holy Grail itself."

She nodded with drunken sageness.

"Blake and his father and his—our grandfather

poured every bit of money they had into hare-brained schemes. Schemes designed to generate enough money for Darkmoor's restoration. They weren't very successful. In fact, the Ravenscrofts barely find enough money to keep pace with Darkmoor's deterioration."

"Okay. Darkmoor Manor is a white elephant. What's your point?" she asked.

He grinned. How could anyone with such syrupy fantasies about England be so astute and pragmatic in all other instances? "My point," he answered, "is why should I pay a succession of repair bills that would never end?"

"That's awfully cheap of you, Harry."

"No, it's not. Admit you'd do the same thing in my position. Why should I lay out money so Darkmoor can have a new yew maze?"

She scowled fiercely at that though her unfocused gaze still wandered unhappily over his shirt. She plucked at a button. "Well, perhaps."

There was that honesty again, that unassailable clear-headedness and practicality that she tried so hard to deny and that was so much more appealing and so much rarer than mawkish sentimentality.

"Still, you shouldn't allow Lord Ravenscroft to think so poorly of you. It's obvious to everyone that there are hard feelings between you. And I suspect it has to do with more than money."

"I really don't give a damn what Blake thinks of me."

She was going to try to convince him otherwise. Desdemona-Make-It-Right. It was there in the set of her jaw, the earnest compression of her lips. And all the time, she continued her unthinking exploration of him.

Slowly he had become aware of her hands on his body. It was so unexpected, so startling that he hadn't even registered it until now, but fondling him she was. Little touches and pets, feathering like sunlight over his skin. Most astonishingly, he would have wagered his entire fortune she didn't even realize she was doing it.

She frowned at his throat, moving her thumb gently to and fro over the nick he'd given himself shaving, as if by doing so she could erase it.

"Lord Ravenscroft thinks you're a scoundrel," she said in a distracted voice, her gaze still on his throat as the button slipped from its hole, exposing more of his skin to her regard—and breath-stealing caresses.

"Hm." It was all he could manage.

She winnowed the hair from his temples, brushing it away from his face. "Of course, you *are*. But not in the way he thinks."

"Hm."

"You might try for a reconciliation."

She had, he realized, lost all concept of the personal boundaries between them. It was as if she no longer recognized where her body left off and his began. She was touching him as familiarly as she would her own person, casually—shatteringly casually.

His breath quickened and he opened his mouth, stealing a breath between his lips before giving himself fully over to the sensation of her voluntary touch. Her fingers flowed up the back of his head, fingering the short nape hairs intimately. He went absolutely still, unwilling to do anything to remind her they were separate beings, that his body was not hers to touch and use and handle in any way she desired. Even though he knew the effects of the hashish were responsible for her hazy abstraction, he would not break that contact.

Her emotions were labile, her thoughts disjointed. He knew better than to seek honesty in her clouded gaze, but at least in this state her body revealed a certain clarity, certain undeniable reactions to him.

"You need a haircut," she mused lazily.

"Yes."

"Lord Ravenscroft's hair is terribly long, isn't it?" She sighed, her full lower lip just a shade exaggerated, the beginning of a pout. "He has lovely hair."

"Gorgeous."

"Very dark. Like a—" She searched for a word.

"Let me guess. A raven's wing?" he supplied helpfully. She didn't look very grateful but apparently couldn't think of a better comparison.

"Yes. Yours is—I've never been able to say exactly what shade." She was serious, her inability to define the color of his hair actually troubled her. "Cured tobacco, maybe, or burnt almonds? Or the color of a desert shadow. More bronze than gold, but nothing so hard or metallic. Like warm sand at twilight. But soft." Her expression reflected her dissatisfaction. "You know that color?"

"I know."

She nodded and gave another gusty little sigh. "He's broader than you are."

Damn that troglodyte Blake, he thought. Her fingers slipped across his chest as if measuring its span inch by lingering inch. He felt marked with liquid fire. All thoughts of Blake fled.

"Is he?" He could barely hear himself.

"Much broader. But not as tall." She paused, frowned. Her palm covered his breast, pressing, testing his firmness. "I wonder if he's as hard as you are."

He felt his loins tighten instantly and hoped desperately that she wouldn't notice exactly how hard he had become.

"There's no give to you. None at all." She sounded plaintive.

"I'm sorry."

"I am, too," she whispered. "Why must you be hard? Too hard."

He wouldn't even begin to guess at her meaning. She was an enigma to him, had always been.

Three years ago she'd come to his house, bent on seduction. He'd been first stunned, then stimulated, and finally angered when he'd realized that she had come to offer herself to some hero she'd dreamed up, a hero that would sweep her up on his silver charger and race her straight back to England. With Sir Robert riding pillion.

He hadn't handled the situation well. His gut instinct had been to take advantage of her infatuation and her youth and make love to her. Well, he'd been young, too. He gave himself credit for not acting on the impulse, driving though it had been.

Too bad he hadn't been able to think of any wonderful, tactful way to get her quickly out of his house, maidenhead intact. Instead, he'd done the only thing he could think of in his highly stimulated and tense state; he'd laughed.

He'd not realized then that his laughter had, if nothing else, banished his chief rival: himself. It would have been an understatement to say he'd fallen from his pedestal. He'd plummeted. Which had been fine with him. He wanted Dizzy to see him as he was in truth, or as much of the truth as he was willing to allow.

Until now.

Until Blake.

Until Blake he hadn't realized that she thought him irredeemable, in fact worse than he was. It was almost laughable that in seeking to disabuse her of one fantasy, he'd merely replaced it with another.

He couldn't find a smile for the painful absurdity of it. Not now, here, when she was suddenly so meltingly attainable. Her mouth was close, her eyes drowsy and unguarded. And it was getting harder by the minute to remember his resolve not to take advantage—

"Lord Ravenscroft has a nice mouth."

—especially when he wanted to seal her lips with his, keeping them from forming Blake's cursed name again. Ever.

"But not as nice as yours. You have the most wonderful mouth, Harry," she said, and sighed. "Your lips look like they could tell the difference between grains of sand." She touched her index finger to the center of his mouth, and his eyes drifted closed with that intoxicating sensation.

Who was more drugged? He couldn't tell anymore. His body was tense and liquid, a hard veneer filled with molten energy.

Her fingertip tickled his upper lip. "I think it's the way your upper lip dips down in the center here," she said thoughtfully. "Or maybe"—she traced the underside of his lower lip—"maybe how firm and yet extravagant your lower lip is."

She tugged his lip open and gently stroked the slick inner lining. He shuddered. She inhaled on a breathy little hiss and caressed him again. Her pupils had merged with the fluid darkness of her irises.

"Sometimes," she confided in a faraway voice, "when I look at your mouth, the very tips of my breasts tingle, inside, where they can't be itched. It almost hurts. And I think about your mouth and I wonder if your lips could—"

"Jesus! Stop it, Dizzy." She was a hair's breadth away from finding out the answer. His arms were tightening involuntarily and the faint, delicious, but unmistakable scent of feminine arousal inundated his senses. He wanted to find its source.

Her hand dropped away. Her brow furrowed. "*You* talked about my breasts," she said in an accusing tone. "Why can't *I*?"

"I didn't—" He stopped. He had. But he hadn't played with her body while he was doing so, hadn't fingered her lips, though in his mind he had been roving every satiny inch of her flesh with hand and mouth and tongue.

"Aha! You did. If you can talk that way, so can I."

She was drugged, unaccountable for her actions. He had to keep reminding himself of that.

With a conscious effort he slipped his arm from under her knees, easing her to her feet. She looped her arms around his neck and he could feel her breasts, dragging softly down his chest. Her eyes were . . . shining? Cloudy? Damn, he couldn't tell.

"Have you ever wondered what it would be like if we made love?" Her tone was detached, quizzical. Her body was not. He could feel her nipples, hard and delicate, like pearls, through his shirt.

He couldn't answer, could barely breathe.

"Well?" She cocked her head. "Why don't you answer?"

"You want a yes-no answer or is this an essay test?"

She ignored his words, staring into his eyes. "You look at every woman like you're looking at me, don't you?" she asked mournfully. "You can't help yourself."

"Jesus." He really could not take any more. He was beyond frustrated working well into recklessness. He couldn't seem to untangle his gaze from her lambent one, and when she smiled at him— trusting, uncomprehending—he made one last bid to keep her impromptu and utterly unconscious seduction under control, to shake her from this sweet, befuddled incomprehension.

"Dizzy, if you'd like to find out how far you can tease me, I suggest we go inside. *Now*. I'll be more than happy to show you." His voice was strained, harsher sounding than he'd intended.

It acted like cold water on her drowsy mind. Her musing, unfocused gaze sharpened, her soft lips snapped together. "*Tease* you?" she echoed.

"Yes. *Tease*, as in arouse without giving satisfaction."

She laid her hands flat against his chest and pushed. "*Me* tease *you*?" she asked. "You're the one who filled my head with all that nonsense about being a desert and a river and being your 'country'! What do you call other women . . . your continent? Your hemisphere?"

He laughed. He couldn't help it. She hadn't been as serenely unaffected by his words as she'd pretended. She was everything he'd wanted and dreamed of in a lover: wit and competence, shrewdness and generosity . . . and a nice right jab.

She thumped her fist into his chest. "You are the most monumentally low-minded, disreputable, unromantic—" she said. "Why can't you be more—"

His humor vanished. "More what?"

"More . . . more . . ." She stumbled around his name. Harry didn't.

"Like Blake?" he finished in soft, glacial tones. His arms tightened. Damn it, he'd not give her up to Blake. Nor to anyone.

"Exactly like Lord Ravenscroft," she said, falling gleefully on his suggestion. "He would never be less than a perfect gentleman. *He* would never say such crude things to a lady."

God, he hated the way she said Blake's name. Like she was proclaiming a new king's ascension to the throne.

"No," he said tautly. "He'd tell you he was in danger of being 'carried away' by your beauty—your roselike beauty—before striding manfully off to some brothel to do with a courtesan what he wanted to do with you. Well, I'm not going away, Dizzy."

He knew frustration was responsible for his anger, frustration, and jealousy. They burned clearly, hotly, rending into ashes his resolve never to want that which he couldn't have. It left one essential truth: He loved Dizzy.

His beloved set her jaw and swung her fist at him, nearly falling over with her impetus. There was no possible way she was going to navigate the way to her house under her own power.

He plucked her off the ground and slung her over his shoulder, dropping her upside down.

"Put me down!" she demanded. "I *hate* being carried like this!"

"Too damn bad."

She pounded her fists against his back. He ignored her, striding down the empty street that led to her home and stalking angrily up to her front door. Without a word, he set her on her feet and reached past her, pounding on the door.

She sagged against the wall, her knees starting to buckle. He caught her under her arms and she sank against him, her unblinking gaze still locked with his.

"What do you want from me, Harry?" she whispered, her chin angled upward, her eyes so damn innocent.

"Dizzy—" He didn't get any further. His mouth covered hers in a hard, succulent kiss. Her lips opened on a purr, and he took advantage, unable to help himself, unable to stop, delving his tongue into her mouth. She was yielding, supple, making little whimpers of pleasure deep in her throat. It was the sweetest sound he'd ever heard.

He moved closer, catching her face between his hands and using his thumbs to tilt her face up so he could—

—hear a carriage clatter noisily down the street. He stopped, lifting his head, breathing hard, senses slowly returning. Damn it, he was making love to Dizzy in the streets, in full view of all Cairo, as if he were some randy soldier and she was a doxy.

And she was drugged.

He leaned her back against the wall.

Her eyes were dark, her lips ripe. He wanted to taste her again. "Please," she whispered, "don't stop."

"Allah, God, and heaven." He raked his hair with shaking fingers.

"Please."

He swayed forward. The sound of bolt on the inside of the door being driven back stopped him. "I can't."

She shook her head. "No. You won't. *Again*."

CHAPTER FIFTEEN

"*Is* the *Sitt* awake?"

At the sound of Magi's dulcet tones, Desdemona rolled over and buried her face in her pillow. She didn't want to talk to Magi. She felt awful: foggy-headed, feeble, and embarrassed.

"I can see that revered *Sitt* is indeed awake."

"No, she's not."

"Yes." Magi sounded positively perky. "She is. I can tell from the moaning she makes. Very different from the moaning she made when she was asleep. But this is stretching the definition of 'sleep.' I would be better served by saying 'unconscious.'"

Desdemona turned her head. The rest of her body refused to follow. "I really don't feel very well, Magi."

"Oh? Really?" Magi cooed. "I am devastated to hear as much. I am sure your discomfort far exceeds that felt by certain people upon hearing from Duraid that you sneaked into the *suq* and were smoking hashish."

Desdemona groaned.

"Or upon hearing that you were kidnapped by white slavers."

Desdemona closed her eyes.

"Or that you had been drunk on fermented goat's milk." She waited.

"I've had a rough week."

"How could you, Desdemona?" Magi demanded, sweetness abandoned.

This time Desdemona managed to roll over. Magi stood over her, her hands planted on her hips, dark eyes flashing. Even though lying on her back put Desdemona at a distinct disadvantage, she couldn't find the energy to rise.

"I didn't even *know* it was hashish."

"Humph. You are not a fool, Desdemona. You must have suspected you were not imbibing in a simple puff of *sheesha*."

Sheesha. Tobacco. Harry had said the same thing . . . hadn't he? But Joseph had assured her that—

At the thought of Joseph, she bolted upright. With the sudden movement, pain hammered through her temples. She grabbed both sides of her head, squinting in pain. "Ow! Where are the *ostraca*?"

Magi pushed her back down, clucking impatiently. "They are fine. Harry brought them over and gave them to Sir Robert. Your grandfather is most pleased, Desdemona."

Damn! She couldn't ask her grandfather to give them back. She bid good-bye to her projected five-pound profit. *Thank you, Harry,* she thought. At times it almost seemed he was making a concerted effort to sabotage her plans to return to England. She shook her head.

The entire preceding day was an inextricable tangle of images and voices and sensations—all of them profoundly uncomfortable. The most disquieting one had Harry attached to it. She remembered a kiss. Or was that a three-year-old memory? Could hashish conjure up the past—textures, fragrances, flavors—so clearly?

She *had* to have been reliving that one long-ago kiss. The memory of disappointment was the same, the feeling of frustration and abandonment. It had ended the same way it had then—with him setting her aside. Hadn't it? Lord, she was so confused!

"I cannot stand by when you endanger yourself," Magi was saying.

"I'm sorry. It won't happen again."

"It had best not. Hashish is for fools," Magi exclaimed passionately. "In the *seraglio* there were many women who smoked hashish and opium. They smoked it to flee the boredom of their lives, to wander in dreams where they were forbidden to go in reality. Pitiful creatures making fantasy their only truth."

"Don't worry, Magi." She meant it. If she never saw another hookah, it would be too soon. She could not remember ever having felt so dull and sluggish . . . and stupid. And if what she half remembered did indeed happen, she'd certainly embodied that last attribute.

"You must promise me—"

"For heaven's sake, Magi, I promise. You and Harry. The two of you should open a school of naggery. No wonder Harry is so good at what he does . . . he bullies his clients in acquiescence."

"I am glad Master Harry has lectured you." Magi sniffed. "I do not mean to harass you. I only want you safe, Desdemona."

Magi's mouth turned unhappily and Desdemona, suddenly aware of her ingratitude, caught her hand, squeezing it. Magi's concern for her was real, her affection unfeigned. Magi was as much a mother as Desdemona had known. "I know, Magi. But please don't worry. I have no intention of ever smoking hashish again."

"Good." Having gotten the answer she wanted, the worry promptly evaporated from Magi's expression. She pulled her hand free, fussing about at the foot of the bed.

"Desdemona?" her grandfather called from the other side of the bedroom door. Desdemona glanced at Magi. If her grandfather got wind of what had—

"He doesn't know," Magi whispered.

Desdemona sighed with relief. If he heard of yesterday's misadventures, not only would her grandfather be scouring the English countryside for long-lost relatives to dump her on, it would break his heart.

"Yes, Grandfather. Come in." She pushed herself to a sitting position as Sir Robert entered.

"Desdemona—" he began, and then stopped

short of the bed, peering at her in concern. "Are you feeling quite the thing, dear? You don't look well."

"Headache," she said. "You were about to tell me something?"

"Yes! My word, yes. The most wondrous thing has occurred, Desdemona. I think I've found an Apis bull. In El Minya."

"Really?" She scooted farther up, ignoring the hammer hitting the anvil of her brain case.

"And *I'm* the first in Cairo to know about it. I have to go down there as quickly as I can make arrangements. Before the horrible Chesterton finds out."

"Of course you do."

Her grandfather beamed approvingly at her, and then his expression turned glum. "You realize that this means that I won't be able to escort you to that Turkish chappie's dinner on Friday night?"

"He's the khedive's secretary, Grandfather. The *khedive,*" she repeated when he stared at her blankly. "The ruler of this country?"

"Whatever," her grandfather said. "At any rate, though I was hoping to chaperone you and young Lord Ravenscroft, I simply cannot eschew such an opportunity. How I would love to be able to set you up properly in a London town house."

"Set me up?" Desdemona raised her brows. "If we could sell Mr. Schmidt a bull, we'd use the money to repay your debts and send you and your collection on tour."

"Oh, that would be nice. But not as nice as seeing you in your own garden, surrounded by English spaniels and plump, ruddy-cheeked English babies."

"Yes." Dear man, he was always more concerned with her future than his own. "That would be nice. But not as nice as seeing you standing in front of the National Geographic Society."

Her grandfather flushed. "Yes, that would be delightful. But visions of your chubby tots make any self-aggrandizing schemes of mine seem quite insignificant—"

"Yes. Well, fat children are certainly a fond dream of mine, but when one has a lifetime of knowledge to impart—"

"Oh, stop it, you two!" Magi broke in. "Always trying to convince each other how wonderful England is. It is maddening! The issue today is that Desdemona does not have a chaperon."

"Oh, that," Desdemona said. "Don't worry, dear. I don't need a chaperon. I'll be fine."

"Well, of course you'll be fine," her grandfather said, rolling his eyes. "It's not a matter of whether or not you'll be *fine*. It's a question of appearances. There are proprieties to observe. As a viscount, Lord Ravenscroft is bound to be sensitive to the look of a thing. We won't want him to be disappointed."

"I'm sure Lord Ravenscroft is not as stiff-necked as all that."

"Perhaps not, but still, we have to ask ourselves, is it the done thing? I mean, in England, would it be proper? We don't want Lord Ravenscroft to think that just because we're in Egypt we've forgotten what is and isn't done." He wrinkled his brow.

"And there's the question of who will accompany the two of you on your trip to Giza tomorrow, too."

"I will be pleased to act the doyen," Magi volunteered. Sabotage was written all over her face.

"No. Thank you, Magi," Desdemona responded quickly.

"I'm afraid that won't do, Magi," her grandfather unexpectedly concurred. "Though I thank you. I'm expecting a shipment from England tomorrow. Someone will have to be here to see the thing isn't mismanaged." He rubbed the bridge of his nose thoughtfully. "I suppose I could ask Harry—"

"No!" Desdemona burst out.

Her grandfather blinked in surprise.

"I mean, no, *sir*." She didn't remember much of what had happened between Harry and herself yesterday, but what she did remember made the thought of Harry acting as her moral guardian not only absurd but mortifying. If she recalled correctly, she'd asked him to make love to her. No. Harry was her last choice as a chaperon. In fact, he wasn't a choice at all.

"I think it's a fine idea, sir," Magi piped in.

Desdemona speared her with a glare. "No, it's not."

"Why not?" her grandfather asked.

"I've enjoyed my liberty and been guided by my own good sense for five years, Grandfather." She ignored Magi's snort. "I cannot suddenly pretend to conventions I have never adhered to and have no intention of adhering to. Even to make our guest comfortable." The words, though initially offered as an excuse, were, she realized, nothing short of the truth.

"I suppose you're right, Desdemona. You've had far too much license." He passed his hand across the crown of his head. "I haven't done an exemplary job as your guardian."

"Nonsense. You've been wonderful."

"No," he said, shaking his head. "I haven't. I had you shipped to Egypt, exposed you to obsessives like Chesterton and criminals like Paget, allowed you too much freedom in some arenas and not enough in others. It hasn't been the best circumstances in which to raise a young woman. But once you're back in England I'm sure you'll adjust. But for now . . . ?" He sighed heavily. "I've done my best. I won't try to restrain you at this late date."

"Nope."

"You've been socializing with those Americans again, haven't you?" He sighed, not really expecting an answer. "Very well, then. You have my permission to go off unattended with Lord Ravenscroft." He glanced at her out of the corner of his eye. Devious, he was. Subtle, he was not.

"Hadn't you better be making travel arrangements?" she asked. She settled back against the pillows and closed her eyes.

"Oh, my, yes. I'll be leaving this evening if I can arrange it."

"I still think Desdemona should not go alone with this Ravenscroft. What do we know of him?" Magi protested.

Her grandfather paused. Desdemona could hear

the honest surprise in his voice as he replied, "Why, Magi, he's a viscount."

Harry paused outside of the Carlisles' front door and wiped his palms against his trouser legs. His heart beat too rapidly and his mouth felt dry. He was afraid.

He did not know how much of yesterday's adventure Dizzy would remember, or how much she would fault him for. He could not forget her forlorn and lost expression as she'd accused him of spurning her. *Again.*

A wave of self-disgust swept through him. She'd been in his arms and he'd acted like a bloody, prideful knight-errant. What a complete ass he was. She'd been willing, his flesh had been more than willing, and yet he'd held back, tethered by some notion of chivalry.

He was becoming some sort of aberration, controlled by fantasies as peculiar as Dizzy's.

He rapped sharply on the door and waited. A moment later Magi ushered him inside. Absently he noted the dingy interior, the threadbare carpet runner, the chipped plaster molding in the corner of the ceiling. All of Sir Robert's money was devoured by his consuming passion for Egyptian antiquities. There was scant left over for necessities, let alone creature comforts.

"Do they need anything?" he asked Magi. "Do they need money?"

"They always need money. But"—she lifted her shoulders—"I do not know if the household finances are harder-pressed than usual. Desdemona no longer lets me see the accounts. She does not want to worry me."

And that worried *him*.

"I've come to see her."

"She's not up yet." Magi's sniffed response gave clear indication of her feelings on the matter.

"Then I'll see Sir Robert."

"He is gone." Magi was obviously displeased with him. Normally she was one of the more loquacious women of his acquaintance.

"Fine. I'll just trot along and see how Diz is do—" Magi stepped in front of him, blocking his way to Dizzy's room.

"Listen, Magi. I didn't drag her to Hassam's store and force that water pipe in her mouth."

"You should have been more attentive."

He lifted his hands, palm upward, in frustration. "How? What would you have me do?"

"Marry her."

He shook his head. "She doesn't want me. She wants some English paragon, a bloody knight in shining armor. And dammit," he muttered, "she deserves to have those desires realized. If anyone deserves it, Diz does. Sir Robert"—he caught his breath, outrage making him breathe too harshly— "Sir Robert told me what her childhood was like."

None of the hazily detailed memoirs Dizzy had sporadically related had prepared Harry for Sir Robert's confidences. After hearing Sir Robert's story, Harry had realized that Dizzy had made up a childhood to take the place of the one she'd never had, told him of playmates he knew now were imaginary, of parties that had occurred only in her imagination.

The reality had been that Dizzy had been forced to sit ramrod straight for hours on end, reciting and memorizing . . .

A visceral image flooded Harry's mind: leather straps tying him to a straight-backed chair in an empty classroom; trickling sweat itching beneath his prickling wool jacket; a voice thundering in his ear hour after hour "Read the words, you stubborn, stupid boy! Read them!"

Impossible to believe that a child prodigy, the antithesis of what he'd been, would ever have endured such loneliness and isolation. But Dizzy had. Regret and anger raced through him. His laughing, life-loving Dizzy had . . .

"Christ."

He gazed beyond Magi's stiff shoulders outside at the brilliant, sun-dazzled courtyard. In his mind's eye he saw the child Dizzy, her feet tucked under her, secretly reading from forbidden books, books meant for entertainment, not edification, trying to snatch some knowledge of a world and life her genius had denied her. The sunlight was too bright. It hurt his eyes, made them water.

"I think you are wrong, Harry, to let her go to England. I think both you and Sir Robert are wrong." Magi touched his shoulder. "Here, in Egypt, Desdemona is a part of life, not a spectator. She is important, her talents useful, not merely an oddity. She accumulates responsibilities as other girls collect hair ribbons: the household, Duraid, the street children.

"Sir Robert doesn't see the satisfaction she derives from this, only the work." Magi shook her head. "He only knows that her upbringing was unorthodox and unpleasant and he vows to make it right. Like you. You are both wrong."

As much as he wanted it otherwise, Harry found no solace in her assurance. Magi loved Dizzy like a daughter. Of course she did not want her to leave. And he didn't either. But Sir Robert's conversation a few days ago had had its impact. And Egypt wasn't as safe as England, as the last week had all too clearly proved.

"I'm sorry, Magi," he said, slipping by her and heading down the hall. Behind him, he heard her emit a gusty sound of exasperation.

CHAPTER SIXTEEN

He took a deep breath and pushed open the door to Dizzy's bedroom.

"I don't remember anything." The lump beneath the sheets spoke before he could say a word. "Nothing. Awful, horrible, noxious stuff. Completely robbed me of my memory. Absolutely no recall of yesterday afternoon's proceedings. None at all."

He turned his laugh—of relief? of delight?—into a polite cough and waited.

After a prolonged moment, the sheet slipped down just enough to reveal a tangle of golden hair and two bloodshot, suspicious eyes. "It wouldn't be very nice to make up awful things and then try to convince me they really happened, would it?"

"Most unkind."

"Just the sort of thing you're liable to do. Well, I'm telling you forthwith, Harry, I won't believe anything you tell me. Anything at all. So save your breath."

"You sound most adamant."

"I'm not in the mood to be teased."

"I wouldn't dream of it." He crossed to the foot of her bed and gazed down at her, clasping his hands behind his back to keep from hauling her up into his arms. Somehow he conspired to look unaffected.

"You would so," she said accusingly, a bit more of her face coming out from beneath her linen burrow. She was very pale, the golden skin touched with an unhealthy ivory sheen. Served her right, the adventurous baggage.

"Not I." If she did not want last night to have occurred, then it hadn't occurred. For the time being.

He raised one brow and looked down at her with all the imperviousness at his disposal. "You know. I'm having a distinct sense of déjà vu."

Her head popped fully clear of her bedding now. Her hair fell in disarray about her straight shoulders, her sable eyes gleamed amid the pale oval of her face. Shadows lay beneath them.

She was pretty, he thought inconsequentially, even as he noted her combative glare.

"I'm sure I don't know what you mean."

Things were back on their normal footing.

"The indisposed heroine . . ." He trailed off as if an idea had just occurred to him and it was distasteful. "Indisposed." He tasted the word and shook his head. "Not a strictly accurate term, is it? You know, Diz, I've read *Wuthering Heights* myself and I am certain I do not recall Catherine ever having been *hung over*"—he stressed the label, ignoring her indignant gasp—"and that makes twice now that you've been . . . four sheets to the wind, shall we say?"

"We shall not!"

"You're not intending to make a habit of debauchery, are you, Diz? Because as much as I'd like to oblige you, my calendar simply cannot accommodate too many of these impromptu rescues. I do have a business to conduct."

She raised herself up on stiff arms. The hair fell across her dusky eyes, making her look feral and dangerous. "Self-important"—her voice was no more than a growl—"narcissistic, egocentric—"

He ignored her. "Where was I? Oh, yes. The wan, feeble heroine languishing in bed as she awaits the arrival of her champion. Do try to languish a bit more, Diz. You look all tense."

"And I suppose *you're* my champion?"

"Well"—he smoothed his hair back, smiling modestly—"that does make twice in one week I've rescued you. Doesn't that qualify me as some sort of hero?"

She gave a most unladylike snort of contempt and flopped back against her pillows. The sudden motion caused a million dust motes to take flight and dazzle briefly in the light spilling from the open doors and windows making up one wall of the tiny bedroom.

She looked disgruntled and comical and enchanting lying there amid the age-faded sheets in this shabby, dilapidated room.

He found himself by the side of the bed looking down into her upturned face before he realized he'd even moved. Her eyes were dark, mysterious, knowing, and shatteringly innocent. He swallowed.

"I let it pass before, being a gentleman and all," he heard himself murmur as her eyes grew nearer and his sense of being lost to time and place increased, "but I really must insist on the hero's portion this time."

He could hear her breathing. The memory of each velvety soft centimeter of her warm lips on his overwhelmed him with desire. He drew closer still, saw her pupils grow larger, the faintest brush of heat color her throat, surprise surface in her expression. Closer . . .

"You're right." She drew a sharp breath, pulled back from him. He straightened smoothly, wiping his face of expression. Her gaze leapt from his and she lifted her chin, turning away.

"Polish up that Anubis head, Magi," she called loudly. "Harry here wants a trophy."

He burst out laughing. "Really, you're so troublesome."

She grinned and he reached down, brushing the hair away from her eyes.

"Harry?"

Like satin, or silk . . . Why wasn't there a better term for something so healthy and exquisite, something that captured the life as well as the texture—

"Harry?"

"Hm?"

"You . . . you won't have to tell anyone about my little . . . adventure yesterday, will you?"

He let the strand of hair slip from his fingers. "Someone like Blake?"

She nodded eagerly. "I mean, I wouldn't want your cousin to take a disgust of me, and yesterday was a unique occurrence. I wouldn't want such an episode to unfairly color his impression of me."

Blake. Who had everything to offer Dizzy. An ancient name. A manor and its attendant heritage. The respect of his peers.

He dredged up a mock salute. "Dear Diz, Blake shall hear nothing of your escapade from me. God forbid that he should see you as anything less than a perfect little rose of femininity."

"Thank you." If she realized he mocked her, she gave no indication. "I have sworn off inebriants of all forms," she said solemnly. "And you can rest assured that you won't have to interrupt your business meetings on my behalf again."

"I'd be grateful."

"Though how one can call a five-second swap of goods and money in some disreputable alleyway a business meeting is beyond me," she muttered dryly.

"Business is where you find it. And the alleyway trade has been very good lately."

A shadow crossed her face. He felt himself tense. "What's wrong, Dizzy? Lieutenant Huffy no longer hiring you to write his letters to his wife, the divine Tanya?"

"No," she said distractedly, "I'm still assuring Tanya she's the point upon which Lieutenant Huffy's world turns." She smiled crookedly. "I suppose you'll be leaving for Luxor soon. Picking up that Apis bull. Making ten thousand dollars." She sounded forlorn.

"The Luxor piece is stone. Cal, so he informs me, wants metal. Hell, I think Cal wants gold, and don't we all?" he said, watching her carefully. She brightened. "Is that what you were doing at Joseph's, looking for an Apis bull?"

Her silence was answer enough.

"Is it so important?"

"Some people call eating important," she said irritably. "I'm afraid I'm one of their frivolous company."

"Ten thousand dollars is a lot of crème brulée, Diz," he said sardonically.

"Crème brulée?" She laughed in honest amusement. "Ten thousand dollars is a lot of fruit and vegetables and bread and . . . Ten thousand dollars would pay the bills, the debts, buy us a house of our own, one with a roof that doesn't leak and windows that actually shut. With ten thousand dollars I could buy the turkey farm, buy a dress, sponsor a little speaking tour for Grandfather." She closed her eyes and smiled dreamily, luxuriating in the images her imagination created.

Harry looked at her, all rumpled and content in her raggedy room, dreaming of pleasures she shouldn't ever have lacked. He reached down while her eyes were still closed and brushed her hair lightly.

"I'll see you later, Diz," he murmured, and left.

* * *

As the sun fell from its zenith, Harry searched districts of Cairo that Europeans did not see, did not even know existed. He questioned a bookseller, a pair of petty smugglers, looking for an Apis bull.

No one had any leads for him to follow. It didn't deter him. He was a patient, tenacious man. He'd had to have been. Otherwise, he'd never have gotten as far along in his protracted education as he had.

No one knew how fiercely he'd struggled to make sense of the written word. Or how, when all the struggles had proven useless, he'd found other ways of learning. He'd badgered and bribed his sisters into reading his textbooks aloud, rhymed names, studied pictures, made up pitiful jingles to aid his memory.

Then, four years ago, suddenly, unexpectedly, he'd discovered that there was one language that, in its written form, was not completely denied him.

He'd come into possession of a section of stylus that he'd offered Simon Chesterton. Like a lover, Simon had fondled the thing, insisting that Harry, too, outline the delicate raised patterns of the hieroglyphics. Simon had murmured the name on the cartouche as Harry had traced it.

Over and over again, Harry had repeated the name to himself as his fingers played over the bas-relief. When he'd stopped, he could *feel* the form shivering beneath his fingertips and he could put a name to it.

His hands had achieved what his eyes could not.

He'd hurried from Simon's house, the enormity of what he'd done stunning him, making him tremble with fear and apprehension. There were times, fleeting, unpredictable, when words made sense, when the pieces of the treacherous puzzle fell together and a sentence had meaning for him. But the next day, the meaning was gone. This might be the same thing. But the next day and the next, he'd been able to recall the feel of the cartouche and trace it in the sand, been able to put a name to the pattern, until ultimately he hadn't needed the crutch of being able to touch the cartouche in order to remember the feeling of it. And in remembering its physical shape, its visual shape became familiar. Amazing. Stunning. He'd been able to see a glyph and read it.

And so, slowly, tenaciously, he'd begun adding glyphs to his vocabulary, painstakingly pressing pictographs onto thin sheets of tin with a stylus and then fingering the raised patterns over and over again until language for him became a physical experience.

It had worked. He could read hieroglyphics. Not perfectly—not nearly as well as Desdemona—but he could actually read them.

"Harry! Psst! Harry!"

Rabi Hakim glided from the shadows near the steps of a disreputable-looking coffeehouse.

"What are you doing here, Rabi?" Harry asked.

"I am following you. I come to ask if you have brought my petition to the *Sitt*. Will she return to me the thing I lent her? Did you ask?"

"Oh, I asked, all right."

"And?" the boy asked eagerly.

"Forget it, Rabi. You have about as much chance

of recouping whatever it was you gave her as a crocodile has of crossing the desert."

The boy's dark face twisted and he spat at the dirt.
"Bah! Stubborn woman. I *gave* her nothing."

"Regardless, she has it, you don't, and I don't see
that changing in the near future. Stop harassing her,
Rabi."

Some men came up the street, apparently heading
for the *kahwi* house. Instead of entering they stopped
and eyed him, muttering among themselves. For-
eigners did not often appear in this section of the
city.

"Bah!" Rabi spat again.

"What's so important anyway, Rabi? Nearly everything your father sells is fake or common, good
tourist fodder but not worth any effort to recover."

"It is of a personal nature," Rabi said shortly,
glancing in the direction of the men lounging
against the low doorway.

Harry wasn't buying. He tried a different tack.
"Where have you been this past month? Luxor?
Gurnah?" Had the Rassuls' discovery of a royal
cache in the Valley of Kings been repeated by Rabi's
family?

"No." Rabi's mouth clamped shut.

Harry gave up. The boy was saying nothing.
"Well, Rabi, unless your father has a gold Apis bull
to trade, I wouldn't be bothering *Sitt* Carlisle again.
She'll have you arrested."

Rabi glowered at him, flipping the edge of his
khafiya across the lower portion of his face. "That
woman is most unreasonable."

Before Harry could agree, Rabi had left, his footfall dropping emphatically on the packed earth. Harry was smiling after the boy's departing figure when movement near the coffeehouse caught his eye.

He turned his head, noting that the idle spectators were dividing into two pairs. They did not look quite so idle anymore. They telegraphed their intention with furtive glances. From long experience Harry knew just what that intention was. He'd been the recipient of such intentions before.

One twosome was approaching him directly while the other pair took off behind the coffeehouse, obviously intending to box him in.

They weren't, Harry noted, very good thugs. If the presence of a skinny fifteen-year-old lad was enough to delay their assault, they shouldn't be too much trouble to deal with. True to his assumption, the two burly men stared at him in confusion as he politely excused himself, slipped by, and headed up the street.

Behind him he heard the rapid beat of footsteps as the men suddenly gave chase. Four against one might be these blokes' idea of fair odds, but it wasn't his. Harry increased his pace, outdistancing them easily. He trotted onto a main thoroughfare, cursing the midafternoon vacancy of the streets.

There were no crowds to get lost in, no open shops in which to dart. It didn't overly concern him. Although the shouts of his pursuers still resonated in the deserted streets, they were fading. He loped along, secure in the knowledge that he would soon be far ahead of his pursuers, his thoughts racing far faster than his feet. Who had hired these men? The list wasn't all *that* long. There was the Syrian who'd taken offense at being outbid. A Swiss deacon who'd—

"Harry!" Blake hailed him from the opposite side of the street.

Harry swore. Blake was the last thing he needed right now.

He sprinted across the road, grabbing Blake's upper arm and spinning him around, shoving his cousin out in front of him. "Run! Hurry!"

"For God's sakes, man!" Blake said, his face suffusing with angry color. He jerked free of Harry's hold. "What the hell are you doing?"

"We've no time for this, Blake. There are some men after me. We have to run."

"What have you done?"

He didn't answer. The sound of his pursuers grew louder. What a moment before had been ample time to escape was no longer enough. They'd be here any second. "Damn it," he muttered, scanning their surroundings.

They were in a small courtyard with two corridors running from it. One, Harry knew, narrowed into a mere slit before widening again and entering the road just above his house. The other corridor ended in a blank wall a few hundred yards up the hill.

"There." He pointed at the one that gave egress. "Follow that alley. It leads to my house."

Blake didn't move. "What about you?"

Harry shoved Blake toward the opening.

"If you need help, I'm not running away again," Blake said, his jaw setting with determination.

"Of course not," Harry said, the lie coming easily. "I'll go up the other. It'll confuse them."

Blake frowned, disapproval and contempt flashing across his features. "You'll go up the other alley?"

"Yes, yes." The four men appeared at the entrance of the courtyard. They stopped, panting and murmuring among themselves before starting forward.

"Now!" He shoved Blake into the alley. With a snarl of frustration and one last glare, Blake moved forward. Harry jumped back, out of Blake's line of sight.

There was simply no other way. With his bulk, Blake would need every spare second Harry could give him in order to force his way through the bottleneck in that alley. And he couldn't allow Blake to get into a fistfight with these men. Blake, with his exalted sense of fair play, wouldn't last a minute. There were no Marquis of Queensbury rules in Cairo.

Harry had no such constraints. At least he stood some chance of fighting free.

The first man reached him. He grinned. Unpleasantly. "We have been sent to deliver a message," he said.

CHAPTER SEVENTEEN

Desdemona smiled in dreamy satisfaction, replaying the morning's events in her mind . . . making only slight modifications to the romantic adventure and that purely for the sake of her muse.

The great pyramids pierced the earthbound cloud, ascending from the depths of that thick white sea of mist and climbing to the very seat of heaven. Two mortals voyaged in this unreal world, a broad young man and a girl on the cusp of womanhood. They approached the gilded pinnacle of this lost civilization silently, marveling at the spectacle.

The man was handsome, his bold, hawklike features framed by a wealth of tumbled curls the hue of a . . . a raven's wing. His step was panther sure on the uneven ground, his keen falcon's gaze vigilant for any danger that might threaten the companion he tended with such exquisite care. He barked orders at their attendants, plotting their trusty donkeys' course across the barren landscape in order to ensure that the brilliant sun was kept from irritating the creamy pallor of the young blossom of womanhood by his side.

She sighed and cupped her chin in the palm of her hand. Not only had the morning been wonderful but there was more to look forward to. In a short while Lord Ravenscroft and she would be dining at the palace of the khedive's own secretary, Abd al Jabbar.

Absently she wondered if Harry would be present. With any luck, she decided, he'd have left for Luxor by now and would be gone a few days. Time for her and Blake to become better acquainted without Harry's disruptive presence. Time for Blake to provide a much-needed tonic to Harry.

Harry. She'd thought she'd known him as well as she knew herself. Better. Blake had told her that Harry's hunger for position and acceptance, his yearning for the things Blake owned and Harry did not, his failure to achieve his desires in England had ultimately driven Harry to Egypt.

A week ago she would have discounted such a tale as nonsense. But these past few days she'd seen shadows in Harry's eyes she'd never dreamed existed, heard in his voice something unrecognizable, seen something potent and desirous in his expression. Or had she imagined them? It worried her that she was once more spinning fantasies around Harry Braxton.

She frowned and caught a glimpse of the timepiece swinging from a gold chain around her neck. Little more than half an hour before Blake arrived. Hastily she went in search of something vastly becoming in which to attend dinner. Something with yards and yards of lace.

She opened the giant, battered armoire and gazed inside with a sense of resignation. The few dresses that hung in lonely isolation within the vast expanse looked dowdy and outdated. Undoubtedly because they *were* dowdy and outdated. And there were no yards of lace. Clothes, nice as they were, were not high on her long list of priorities.

Closing her eyes, she thrust her hand into the wardrobe and grabbed the first dress her hand fell on. She peeked at it. It was the light champagne-colored muslin thingie, with a sweetly draped bodice and limp ruffles hanging from the demisleeves.

At least it would be cool, she thought, disrobing. Lord Ravenscroft seemed to have a passion for coolness. Several times during their excursion yesterday he'd remarked in awed tones on how fresh she looked. Poor Lord Ravenscroft hadn't fared so well.

It would be difficult staying "fresh" all bound up in jacket, vest, shirt, tie, and trousers. Dizzy resolutely admired, while she wondered at, such a strict adherence to a personal dress code.

Whenever he was outside the city, Harry immediately shed his jacket. He went about in a shirt, trousers, and a *khafiya*, the nomad's headdress, his sleeves rolled up over his tanned forearms and the loose edge of the headdress flipped over his shoulder. Harry always looked comfortable. And masculine. And casual.

Well, comfort wasn't everything.

A light rap announced Magi just as Desdemona finished buttoning her bodice.

"Oh, good, Magi. You're just in time to help me."

"There is a problem?"

"This dress doesn't want to fit. It looks all rumply. Not like a proper dress at all."

"Proper." The word came out flat.

"Yes. Ladylike. Smooth. Form-fitting."

"Tight."

"Yes."

"Turn around. I will tie you in." Obediently Desdemona presented her back. Magi took hold of the faded silk grosgrain sash and gave it a vicious tug.

"Ouch!"

Magi ignored her, pulling the sash tighter, grunting with her effort. "Why aren't you wearing a corset? All admired English ladies wear corsets. You will never be admired by an admirable English gentleman if you do not wear a corset. Oh, yes. I forget. You *hate* corsets. Perhaps you are not such an English lady after all . . . hating corsets as you do."

Desdemona would have answered this impertinence but she couldn't breathe. With a snap, Magi finished the huge bow. "That man is here," she said.

"Lord Ravenscroft?" Desdemona gasped, working her finger under the sash and loosening it.

"Yes."

"Well, show him to the sitting room," Desdemona said. "And get some lemonade for him. Tell him I'll be down directly. Ladies never hasten to meet their gentleman callers . . . do they? Is there any lilac water left? Do you remember where I put it? Is my

hair tidy? Are my teeth clean?" She lifted her lip for
Magi's approval. The woman just stood there. "And
stop glowering at me."

"Desdemona," Magi said, "you deserve a corset."

"Wake up, *Master* Harry."

He couldn't quite accommodate the oily, familiar
voice. He was hot, his head pounded, his side
throbbed, and his shoulders burned as if—

He cracked open an eye and peered upward. He
closed it again. Bloody hell. He'd been strung up by
the wrists like a side of beef in a pest-infested
slaughterhouse. The buzzing wasn't just inside his
head, it came from hundreds of flies.

Not only had he failed to "fight his way free" of
his assailants, he'd been clipped across the back of
his head like the greenest tourist.

He swallowed. His throat was parched. He had no
idea of how long he'd been out. The weak light
washing the dingy surfaces of the walls suggested it
was late afternoon. That meant he'd been unconscious at least a day. All he could do was hope that
when he'd failed to meet Blake at the house, his
aristocratic cousin had realized something was
wrong and gone for help. Fat chance.

"Come now, Master Harry. I am waiting."

He recognized the voice with a sinking sensation.
Maurice Franklin Shappeis, one-time overseer for the
Cairo Museum—until Harry had taken it into his
head to make sure no more children died as a result
of Maurice's directives. The flies suddenly made

sense. Maurice was not a proponent of personal hygiene.

"Aren't you supposed to be dead or something, Maurice?" he asked. "I thought your men had finally had enough of you and torn you—"

The rest of the sentence was cut off as Maurice's fist hammered into Harry's side, low, over his kidneys. Agony ripped through his body. He gasped, sagging forward. The sudden weight yanked his arms in their sockets, burning bright pain through his shoulders.

"What do you want, Maurice?" he gasped.

"To hurt you." The man's oddly feminine, casteless features broke into a sweet smile. Though he sported a French Christian name, it was impossible to guess his antecedents. Slavic, French, Italian, Turk . . . at one time or another he'd claimed them all.

"Well, you've achieved your goal. Can I go home now?"

Another blow, this one higher up, over ribs that felt as if they'd been mule-kicked. This time, however, Harry was ready. He rolled with the impact, absorbing as much as the blow as he could. It still hurt like hell. Maurice must have done some damage while he'd been unconscious. Harry wasn't sure if he approved or not.

"Come on, Maurice," he panted. "You may want to get some of your own back from me, but not unless you can make a profit from it. You're too savvy a businessman to allow personal feelings to make you take such a risk. Remember?"

"What risk?" Maurice asked.

"I'm still a citizen of Great Britain and you . . . ? Well, are you a citizen of any country?"

For a simple rhetorical question it had a nasty effect on Maurice's temper. He backhanded Harry across the face. Harry's head snapped sideways and his lip sliced open on his teeth. He groaned loudly, letting Maurice know his blows were working. No sense encouraging any extra effort on his behalf.

"Who hired you?" he croaked.

Maurice shrugged. "You are right. I work for another. Better pay than the chickenshit I got as Paget's foreman. I could almost thank you for that, Harry."

A tic started at the corner of Maurice's eye. He didn't look particularly grateful.

"Who?" Harry repeated, glancing around at the room. It was dirty and sparsely furnished with a stool, a chair, and a table covered with oiled paper. An earthen jug sat atop it and alongside that a fat satin pouch.

"My employer prefers to remain anonymous. And as for the money he pays me"—Maurice pointed at the purse—"I am to make your life . . . uncomfortable."

"Why?"

"You make many enemies, Harry. People do not like you to make fools out of them. Are you still making a fool out of the women?" he asked, studying him closely. "The fine Mrs. Douglass?"

"I don't know what you mean."

Maurice laughed. "Oh, I have learned much about you since our last encounter, Harry. I have made it my *business* to learn. There does not seem to be anything you care about. But I, most especially, know this isn't true. You mask your feelings well. Who, for instance, would have guessed you carried such strong emotions regarding the death of one little Arab brat?" Though his words were soft, virulence twisted Maurice's small features. "So what is it you care about? Not the English widow who chases after you, Mrs. Douglass."

Harry probed his lip with his tongue.

"Your artifacts?" Maurice suggested softly, his animalistic eyes intent on Harry's face.

"Yeah."

"Sir Robert or Miss Carli—" Maurice's eyes grew round, gleamed with fierce perception. "Ah! Miss Carlisle! I see it. There. In your eyes, in the muscles that leap with the mention of her name." He threw back his head and laughed. "Miss Carlisle! Most pitiful. She does not even know you exist."

Harry couldn't speak, he could only stare, sudden winter running in his veins. Fury choked him. He jerked savagely against the ropes holding him.

"Now, now, Harry . . ." Maurice clucked, backing up a pace.

"Don't touch her. Don't even look at her."

"Oh, I look. Very delicious little morsel. But I have been paid to hurt you, not the pretty little Miss Carlisle. So"—he shrugged—"I will comply. But after I am done with you . . . perhaps someday, for my own sake, I will visit Miss Carlisle."

Enraged, Harry surged forward, snapping to a halt at the end of the rope tethers. Straps cut into his wrists, his tendons tore with his effort. He ignored the pain, wrenching again and again against his restraints, the blood pounding in his temples.

Maurice laughed. And then there were a lot of blows.

Desdemona convinced Lord Ravenscroft to walk the short distance to Jabbar's palace. As they rounded the corner of the boulevard, they were greeted by the sight of the Nile, smooth tea-colored waters flowing beneath them as, in the background, the Great Pyramid sparked with sunlight, a tiny triangle shimmering above a veil of heat.

"I'm surprised you can see it all the way from here," Lord Ravenscroft said, leading her along the railed promenade beside the river.

"Yes. Magnificent, aren't they?" She pointed out at the pyramids. "Legend has it that the last Mameluke Bey, the one routed by Napoleon, signaled his wife Fatima from atop the Great Pyramid after he'd paid Napoleon's ransom for her."

"Such a pretty storehouse of knowledge." Lord Ravenscroft picked up her hand and raised it to his lips. "I did not get a chance to thank you, Miss Carlisle, for this morning's excursion."

He pressed a lingering kiss on her knuckles, his gaze intent. His hand was large and pale, unmarked by scars or calluses, the hand of a nobleman.

"You are most welcome, m'lord," Desdemona said, watching the way the setting sun caressed his black, glossy hair. "You seemed in something of a hurry when we parted company. I trust that there were no extenuating circumstances demanding your attention?"

"Oh, no. No, indeed. It was all just rather overwhelming. I . . . I felt I needed some solitude in which to assimilate the experience."

"I understand. The pyramids have that effect on me, also." She nodded, pleased to find herself in such accord with him. "I hope I did not overwhelm you with too many details?" she added worriedly. It had crossed her mind once or twice during their tour that perhaps Lord Ravenscroft did not find the subject of ancient Egyptian customs as fascinating as she did.

"No, indeed," he said, relinquishing her hand and leaning forward over the rail so that the breeze ruffled his long black locks. "You are an exemplary guide. So much information. So many facts. Your discourse on the embalming methods of the ancients was a revelation. And how conversant you are regarding eviscera!"

Desdemona laughed uneasily. "I'm afraid I sometimes get carried away. I've lived here for so many years that I forget what makes nice conversation. Forgive me."

"Not at all, not at all. It was all most absorbing. Even the Coptic jars . . ."

"Canopic," she corrected him. "Copt is a religion."

"Whatever." His gaze traveled over her face, her shoulders, her—

"Did you enjoy the sunrise?"

"Very much," he murmured. She moved back a

step. There was a lazy, sensual quality to his regard that she was unused to and therefore uncomfortable with. His gaze played over her entire person whenever she spoke, not stopping at her face and eyes, but slipping down her body, making her feel unclothed, aware, above all the things she knew herself to be, that she was *a* woman. *One of many.* She dismissed the traitorous thought.

"The first rays of light bathing the pyramids are quite the most arresting vision one might have in Egypt," she murmured.

"There was another vision, closer at hand, that arrested my attention," Blake said. His voice whispered in her ear. "You are surpassingly lovely."

"Oh, my." Her hand fluttered to her throat.

He made her forget patched dresses, ledgers that wouldn't balance, street orphans, and her grandfather's debts. He'd strode right out of the pages of the wondrous Ouida's romances and he found her, *her*, appealing. And yet she couldn't still the inconvenient thought that her value wasn't limited to her looks. She could translate—

"I see I am precipitous." His magnificent eyes abruptly clouded. "I am a bold man, Miss Carlisle," he said. "But I have never known a woman like you. You are unique. If I am too forward, forgive me. I would not offend you. Some would say that life had dealt cruelly with me. Perhaps that may account for my manner."

She stopped and turned, her unease evaporating in a rush of sympathy. "Miss DuChamp?" It slipped out before she could stop herself. Shocked by her audacity, she covered her mouth with her hand, staring at him in dismay. "I am sorry, Lord Ravenscroft."

"No matter." His expression grew shuttered, tense. With an effort he made himself smile. "And please, call me Blake. And I would like to call you Desdemona."

"Why, yes. I'm sure no one will think it untoward. We are a close little community here."

"So I gather. And how close are you"—his eyes glinted—"to my cousin?"

"Harry?" She blinked. "Harry is . . . Harry and I don't . . . he doesn't regard me as . . . we've never . . ." She stuttered to a halt, feeling her cheeks grow hot as memories of frantically kissing Harry crowded her mind. "We are friends," she finished lamely, realizing that she spoke the simple truth and yet the word didn't seem nearly intimate enough.

"Good," Blake said firmly. "Harry's years here have only made more pronounced the undesirable aspects of his nature. I wouldn't want to think you'd become overly familiar with him. He has, I believe, for all his shortcomings, considerable charm."

She cleared her throat uncomfortably. "I suppose you could say that. What do you mean 'undesirable aspects'?"

He looked down at her, his face solemn. "Yesterday afternoon he got into a street fight with some peasants. Undoubtedly he'd swindled them. He told me to run rather than face his adversaries. I did not like it, but I was even more unwilling to physically harm men I was unsure deserved it. And indeed, my worst suspicions were confirmed for afterward, rather than seeking me out and explaining the situation, Harry disappeared. I assume he was ashamed to face me. Harry would not have an easy time admitting culpability to me."

Desdemona's brow furrowed violently. "That doesn't sound like Harry." *But did it?* she could not help wonder.

"What would you know about Harry, Desdemona?" Blake asked not unkindly, and she could not help but think that she'd just been asking herself that same question. "I assure you, he is not that man you think. He's not anything like the man you imagine he is."

"But—"

"I won't say more." Capturing her elbow, he led her down toward the palace garden's gate. A small Arab boy dressed in rags scurried up toward them.

"*Sid! Sid!*" The child tugged at Blake's jacket. "You buy scarab. Nice *antika*. Very old. Belong pharaoh."

Desdemona stopped. It was Salik. Though thirteen years old, Salik looked like he was eight. Every bit of him was covered with filth.

She bent, examining the grubby palm holding up a cracked clay blob. It had been painted a startling blue, but the paint was chipping and the incision marks were sloppy.

"The lad wants *baksheesh*?" Blake asked, digging in his purse for a coin.

"No." Salik scowled at Blake. "I am no beggar. I sell *antika*, relics. Good relics. Very ancient."

"Well, this certainly doesn't fall under that heading, Salik," Desdemona said sternly, dropping the little beetle back into the boy's open hand. "Put your money away, I beg you, Lord Blake."

The boy grumbled.

"I have told you before, Salik. You should listen to me. Find Matin. He will teach you how to make a proper scarab."

The boy's grimy face turned thunderous. "I do not need Matin. I sell many, many scarabs."

"You would sell many, many more if you'd just swallow that oversized—and completely unwarranted—lump of pride stuck in your throat and learn from a master," she returned.

"Bah!" Salik grumbled, turning his back on Desdemona and jabbing a skinny, bony little digit at Blake. "You then, Good Master. You buy *antika*? Bring home to ladies, make a good impression," he said, sidling closer.

"My lord, Miss Desdemona," Blake said, "do you actually know this urchin?"

"Yes," Desdemona said, eyeing Salik darkly.

"Well," Blake said, holding out the coin he'd extracted, "we must encourage such an enterprising lad."

Salik snatched the coin from Blake's hand and scooted away.

Blake turned and beamed at her. "Resourceful little imp."

"Yes."

"You don't seem very pleased, Miss Desdemona. Should I have given him more?"

"No." She sighed. "I have been trying to convince Salik to join Matin for months. That boy could be learning a useful skill and making a real living rather than subsisting on pennies for those atrocities he's trying to foist off as scarabs."

"Matin?"

"A true genius at producing fake, er, *faux* scarabs. Most people can't tell them from the real ones."

"You've certainly come into contact with some interesting people here in Egypt," he said.

"Actually, I bought quite a few of Matin's facsimiles before I realized they were not authentic."

"You?" Blake asked in surprise. "But you're an expert."

"At languages," Desdemona answered. "Oh, I'm no Egyptologist. I know a few things, I have an adequate eye, but I am certainly not an expert in the leagues of my grandfather or Harry."

At the mention of Harry's name, the severe expression returned to Blake's face. Desdemona gave up trying to fathom the rivalry between the two men. And rivalry it undoubtedly was. What else could cause such taut animosity? She sighed. "Anyway, Matin now has his own workshop."

"Workshop?"

"It's actually a small turkey farm. The boys make the scarabs and then feed—" She stopped. She couldn't possibly explain to Blake that the turkeys' digestive juices added just the right patina of age to the carvings. And that then the aged scarabs had to be harvested from the droppings. And that she had helped Matin find a market for his wares—for a small percentage. It was not at all the sort of thing a young English lady did.

He was waiting, his grave handsome face puzzled.

"It's not all that interesting," she said. The words felt like a betrayal.

CHAPTER EIGHTEEN

"Mrs. Douglass, please try the fruit. Very sweet. Very nice," said Jabbar, the khedive's secretary, cutting Simon Chesterton off in midsentence. Marta inspected the heaping silver platter one of the legions of silent servants offered her.

The desperation on Jabbar's dark face had grown as the evening wound toward an end and Simon's harangue on the uneven distribution of relics between French and English archeological factions hadn't. "Or some cheese?"

Marta plucked a slice of melon from the platter and dangled it inches from Cal Schmidt's mouth. "Would you like some?"

Cal's eyes crinkled appreciatively at the corners. Instead of taking the ripe, moist-looking fruit from her fingers, he encircled her wrist, guiding her hand and its offering to his lips. "A pleasure, ma'am."

In many ways—certainly the most important ones—the tall American was as mature as she. Over

the past few days he'd pursued her with a singleness of purpose that had at first amused her and
finally charmed her. His directness and unapolo-
getic materialism were refreshing contrasts to English posturing. And if he lacked sophistication, he
possessed a native shrewdness that made up for it.

Cal released her hand and winked.

Of course, Marta thought, no matter what his attractions, he still wasn't Harry, whose intelligence
was flavored with such a piquant irony, whose sophistication was underscored with an element of
ruthlessness. Harry had *lived*. It was unclear how or
in what way life had marked him, but marked he
was. The scars were subtle . . . and provocative.

"*Please*, Colonel Chesterton. Eat!" Jabbar insisted,
interrupting Marta's thought.

Georges Paget, attending the party as France's
representative, paid no attention to Simon's diatribe.
He'd heard it all before. Besides, he was too busy
eating.

"If your sultan were to give England the director-
ship of the Cairo Museum instead of those
French—"

"Here, Colonel Chesterton, you must have a fig."
Jabbar popped the wrinkled brown fruit into Simon's open mouth. Though an act of fond familiarity in keeping with Turkish etiquette, Marta was
certain it served a dual purpose. It was a big fig.

With obvious satisfaction, Jabbar relaxed in his eb-
ony-and-malachite inlaid chair. He clapped his
hands and a troop of servants appeared. Smoothly,
snowy Irish linen was whisked from the table as

crystal bowls were slid in front of each guest. In each bowl of warm, scented water floated a single water hyacinth. Earlier they'd dined on solid gold plate.

Despotism had its rewards.

"I have heard extraordinary reports of your great linguistic abilities, Miss Carlisle," Jabbar said, dipping his fingertips in the water and waiting while an attendant dabbed them dry. "Are they true?"

The others politely turned their attention toward where Desdemona Carlisle sat beneath Blake's possessive gaze.

"You must be very proud," Jabbar prompted.

A frown turned Desdemona's lips. A woman had to have a care not to frown in front of men, Marta thought. Too bad the girl's mother hadn't lived long enough to impart such basic wisdom.

"As I have never striven for this accomplishment," Desdemona said slowly, "it isn't something I expect I have the right to take any pride in."

"You are too modest."

"No," she insisted. "I am not. Reading languages comes naturally to me."

"But how interesting," Jabbar said. He flicked a fingertip and another troop of servants swept in to replace the wine goblets with champagne flutes. For a despot's lackey, Jabbar had unusually European tastes.

Desdemona smoothed her muslin skirts. At one time—at least three seasons ago—the gown might have been termed champagne colored. Now, however, it was simply "not white." Marta gave a shiver of distaste. No matter what one's financial situation, a woman could *always* afford a new dress. And really, Desdemona should reveal more flesh if she was to keep Lord Ravenscroft's interest. A happenstance Marta had every intention of encouraging.

"That's real fascinating, Miss Desdemona," Cal said. "Is it true you can read a full dozen languages? Every word? Even the pronouns?"

She colored. Good. Men like Blake Ravenscroft loved pink girls.

"Yes," she said shyly.

"Even the ones like Latin?" Cal prodded.

"Yes. And Greek, Hebrew, Swedish . . ."

"How bizarre!" Marta exclaimed, and Blake shot her a glare. "Charmingly so, of course. I've never heard of the like."

"She can do it." Simon nodded, his beard bobbing up and down. "It's the Anglo-Saxon blood. Much better suited to scholarly undertakings than the fevered blood of"—he shot a look at Georges—"other cultures."

"Come now, sir," Cal protested with a laugh. "You don't really believe that."

"The blazes I don't! How many French chits do you suppose knew five languages by the time they were eight? How else do you account for her?"

"Intelligence?" Blake asked dryly.

Marta smiled. It was all going very well. She settled back preparing to give herself over to Cal's attention when she noted Georges's demeanor. Apparently his long-suffering silence had finally found an end. He drained the last of his wine and set the flute down with a bang.

"Intelligence is not the soul province of the English—"

Simon ignored him. "Intelligence coupled with British cool-headedness," he declared. "The khedive ought to see these attributes more properly recommend the Eng—"

Jabbar poked another fig in Simon's mouth.

"I'm all agog, Miss Carlisle," Cal said. "How can someone speak a language that hasn't been heard for thousands of years? Could you demonstrate?" He leaned forward, lacing his fingers together expectantly.

"Oh, no. I couldn't. You see, I can't actually speak the language, I can only translate them." She shifted uncomfortably.

Drat the girl. She should take advantage of every opportunity to pique Lord Ravenscroft's interest. Especially here, now, when Harry wasn't present, Marta thought. There was nothing for it, she would have to step in.

"My dear," Marta said, "a demonstration of your abilities would be a delightful interlude in . . . the conversation. I'm sure we'd all be thrilled to have an insight into the mind of the Egyptian."

"But I don't know any real Egyp—"

"Whatever you can offer will be appreciated," Marta said sternly, casting a speaking glance at Simon who'd nearly finished gulping down his fig.

"Oh!" Whatever her blind spot concerning Harry, Desdemona was no fool. She would oblige if she thought she could help her host out of an uncomfortable situation. "Of course. Let's see." She paused, obviously casting about for something suitably entertaining. "Ah, yes. I recently read this charming love poem. New Kingdom"—she grinned mischievously—"I think." She cleared her throat and began:

> Whenever we part, I go breathless
>   Only death is lonely like I am.
> I taste my favorite honeyed cakes,
>   they are as salt to me,
> Where is your tongue to sweeten my mouth?
>   The most luscious wine, once lovely,
> is bitter, bitter gall.
>
> Stroking you, love, taking your kiss
>   my heart speaks clearly:
> This is as breath to me, let me live!
>   Aton himself gifted me with you,
> Holy bequest, my love to outlast forever.

"Did you say *Aton?*" breathed Simon.

Georges froze, his fork half raised to his mouth. "Where did you read this extraordinary missive?" he whispered.

"A papyrus. It purports to be scribed at the behest of Nefertiti herself." Desdemona vested the word "purports" with added emphasis.

"Nefertiti?" Cal said.

"Where the devil"—Simon caught Jabbar's hand as it swooped in carrying another fig—"stop it, Jabbar—where the devil did you get hold of it, Miss Desdemona?"

"I acquired a scroll when I was, er, visiting a trader's encampment last week."

"What encampment?" Simon leaned across the table, resting heavily on his meaty forearms, the end of his beard dangling in the water bowl.

Marta's interest quickened. Could the girl actually have stumbled onto something important? Idly she swatted Cal's hand from her knee, attentively watching Simon and Georges's reaction.

"Oh, Colonel Chesterton!" Desdemona chuckled. "I'm sorry I've teased you. I can assure you the papyrus is forged."

"Oh, oh, yes, of course." Simon and Georges slumped back down in their respective chairs, their disappointment nearly palpable. "Ridiculous to think that it could be otherwise," Simon said. "Why would traders allow a young gir—" He broke off, his face suffusing with bright red color. "If they were real, your grandfather would be strutting about the table crowing, not poking about in El Minya."

"This Nefertiti is that Akhenaton fellow's wife, right?" Cal asked, stretching his long legs beneath the table where they rubbed intimately against Marta's. He grinned lazily.

Georges continued a melancholy study of his empty plate. "Yes. The great queen-wife of the heretic."

Simon nodded. "If someone did find something—" He glanced at Desdemona and grimaced. "You shouldn't give an old man heart palpitations like that."

"I'm sorry," Desdemona said contritely. "They are rather good fakes. The author has a definite feeling for New Kingdom verse: word usage, cadence, imagery. But the subject matter is too earthy to have been written by the consort of a pharaoh. Indeed, in some cases it is openly lascivious."

"Really?" Georges asked interestedly. In fact, Marta noted, all the men from Jabbar to Cal looked interested. Men hadn't changed in four or five millennia.

"Yes."

"You know, I still wouldn't mind taking a look-see at them," Simon offered. "Purely from an academic standpoint."

"Me, too," Georges said.

"Not necessary, sirs," Desdemona said. "I've offered them to a New York publisher. You give me hope that they may provoke some interest—purely academic, of course." She grinned.

The blasted girl didn't see the disapproving frost in Ravenscroft's eye, Marta thought. The chit had spent too many years with too many conversations open to her, privy to too much knowledge and too many . . . "experiences."

"Drat!" Cal said.

"Unfortunate," Simon murmured.

"I'm sure you wouldn't want to waste your time on them," she teased further.

"Of course they wouldn't," Blake said suddenly. "Who could have foreseen that salacious scribbling would be of any interest to such . . . *learned* men?"

The learned men sank back in their chairs, looking properly chastised if not particularly convinced.

"How chivalrous you are to champion Miss Carlisle, Lord Ravenscroft," Marta murmured. Even though the girl looked perplexingly unimpressed with Ravenscroft's gallant intercession, what romantically inclined girl could resist such chivalry? Marta smiled.

None.

Desdemona thanked her host and followed Cal Schmidt and Marta out of the palace and down the wide stone steps leading to the front gardens. Behind Georges bolted out the door, Simon hot on his trail. She stopped, awaiting Blake, and looked around in pleasure.

Above, a milky moon disappeared beneath indigo-colored clouds. The scent of night-blooming flowers flavored the cool air. An occasional black-winged kite screeched during its phantom flight overhead.

Cal paused at the bottom of the steps, twirling his watch fob. Red light flashed from its many inlaid jewels. Marta, too, had noticed the sparkling bauble. She was smiling in a distinctly predatory manner.

"You had those two going in there, Miss Carlisle," Cal said in impressed tones. "Little bit of a thing like you." He shook his head and chuckled. "Who'd a thought there was an imp under those gold locks?"

Desdemona laughed. She couldn't help herself, the American's easygoing humor was contagious.

Marta didn't seem to see the humor. She looked relaxed but aloof, her smile uninterested.

"Listen, Miss Carlisle, the more I think about that Apis bull, the more I want one. You say you were at a trader's camp the other day. Did you see one?"

"I'm sorry, Mr. Schmidt. I wish I had." He'd never know how much.

"Oh, that's okay. I know Mr. Paget is trying his best and Mr. Braxton. I 'spect between the two of those fine gentlemen I'll get what I want." He turned his attention to Blake. "Say, Lord Ravenscroft, maybe we should pool our resources and share a carriage."

"Oh, Mr. Schmidt," Marta said, leaning limpetlike against his arm. "I was rather hoping to walk. It is such a lovely evening and you're such a big, strong man. I feel quite safe in your care."

"But your house is a good two miles away, ma'am," the American said.

"Is it? Perhaps. But then, if I recall correctly, your hotel is not."

The American broke into warm laughter, and blood raced up into Desdemona's cheeks. The woman was shameless. How could Harry ever have—

"Let's go, Miss Carlisle," Blake clipped out, taking her elbow and guiding her onto the footpath intersecting the gardens. At the gate leading to the street Blake stopped and looked around for a carriage, once more, as he had all evening, acting on her behalf. He'd championed and protected her womanly sensibilities. All the things a hero did. He was becoming enamored of her.

It was wonderful.

Wasn't it?

"We may have to wait awhile, Desdemona." He was standing very near. She could smell the bay rum he used, see the shadowy cast of his incipient beard. He stepped closer, taking her hand and pressing it.

"We could walk, too," she suggested.

"Yes." His voice was low. His dark head bent nearer. Her breath caught in—anticipation that felt like anxiety.

A sudden low sound drew her attention. With a curious sense of relief, she backed away from Blake and peered around, looking for its source.

"Damn it," Blake said.

A figure detached itself from the night, and for a second the masculine form was silhouetted against the street torches before it staggered toward them.

Although darkness masked his features, Desdemona could see that the man's shirt hung open and torn from his lean torso. The ragged *khafiya* draped his throat like a charmer's snake. With each step, his gait grew more unsure. He called out in a hoarse, thick voice, but his words were so slurred and painful she could not tell what he said. She started forward but Blake caught her upper arm, stopping her.

"For Chrissakes," Blake bit out, "you'd think Jabbar would have the beggars kept off the palace grounds!"

The moon suddenly escaped the embrace of scuttling clouds, revealing the man's features, swollen and battered and somehow—

"Oh, my God!" she breathed. "Harry!"

He stumbled to a halt before her and sank to his knees in the dirt. "Diz," he muttered thickly, "you're not hurt."

"Dear God, Harry! What's happened to you?"

He grinned crookedly. The moonlight caught the dark gleam of blood on his lip. "Well, Diz . . ." He gasped. "You always said . . . you'd see me . . . on my knees." He pitched forward.

She caught him before he hit the ground.

CHAPTER NINETEEN

"Open up, Magi!" Desdemona called.

"Aha! It is time you are home!" Desdemona heard Magi's voice at the same time the inside bolt slid back. "You are most late. An English gentleman should know better than—"

The front door swung open. Light spilled out of the front door illuminating Blake at the bottom of the stairs, Harry slung over his broad shoulders.

"Allah have mercy." Magi gasped as Desdemona pushed past her.

"Bring him in," she said to Blake.

Blake shifted Harry's weight and struggled up the stairs. With each step, Harry's head bobbed. He was unconscious again, as he'd been most of the way here.

"To one of the bedrooms?" Magi asked.

"No," Desdemona said, "at least not tonight. I need light. We'll use Grandfather's library. Follow me," she ordered Blake. She strode down the narrow, cluttered hallway and flung open the door at the far end. "Duraid," she said, spying the boy peeking around the corner, "bring fresh linen, iodine, soap, and hot water."

Blake, burdened with Harry's long, limp form, lurched up the last few steps into the hallway.

"Sometime before Harry succumbs, Duraid," Desdemona suggested grimly, and the round-eyed boy fled toward the kitchen.

"But where can we put him?" Magi asked.

Desdemona quickly surveyed the room. The "library" was no more than an anteroom separating the main body of the small house from the little walled courtyard behind. It was already packed to overflowing with relics in various stages of readiness for shipping to London. Books, treatises, papers, and files littered every available surface. Crates, some empty, some packed, stood stacked along the walls. The desk and drafting table were lined with cartons and vessels and pottery.

She considered the floor and discarded the notion. Aside from being dusty and cold, it would be impossible to drape with the netting essential in keeping night-flying insects from feasting on Harry's open wounds. She bit her lip, searching for someplace to set Harry. Blake, hunched panting in the doorway, grunted.

"In there," she finally said, pointing. "It's high enough so I can see what I'm doing and narrow enough to keep him from rolling over."

"But surely, Miss Desdemona—" Blake protested.

"Just until we can scare up a cot."

Looking doubtful, Blake eased Harry onto the blankets Magi quickly laid beneath him. Desdemona raised the gas jets on the wall as high as they would go and turned. Her breath caught in her throat.

The hissing light exposed Harry's torn and battered form with awful clarity, revealing injuries far uglier than any she'd imagined.

So much damage. So much blood. Such filth—

"Miss Desdemona!" Blake caught her about the waist. He urged her toward the desk's chair but she shifted out of his embrace, impatient with her uncharacteristic squeamishness.

"I'm fine," she said firmly, bending over Harry and examining his face. "I am." His swollen left eye was discolored, a deep gash crossed the high angle of his right cheek, and a jagged tear scored his lower lip. Poor beautiful lip. She drew a shaking breath.

"I have the things, *Sitt*," Duraid said from beside her.

Without looking up, she accepted the small, steaming saucer of water and thick wad of square linen bandages that Duraid handed her. "Magi," she said, probing the torn edges of the cut on his cheek, "pour some iodine over this gash while I swab it clean. Allah only knows what is encrusted in there."

"Yes," Magi murmured. She dribbled liquid into the deep laceration and Harry jerked. His eyes flew open and he stared at her, his expression wild and fierce and intent.

"It's all right, Harry. I'm—"

"Magi!" The word burst from his lips.

"Magi's here, too." Did he think she wouldn't

care for him, as well, as determinedly as Magi? Did he think she felt so little for him? "I promise I'll do—"

"Where's Magi?" he demanded hoarsely.

"I am here, Harry." Magi put her hand on his brow. He grabbed her wrist. "You have . . . you . . . have . . . to—" He ground his teeth against whatever pain he felt and squeezed his eyes shut. Slowly the white-knuckled grip with which he held Magi's wrist eased. He'd fallen unconscious again.

"For God's sake," Blake burst out.

"It's better this way," Desdemona assured Blake. "Better that he's unconscious. I must work fast."

She eased the edges of the cut apart and swabbed little flecks of grit from the gash. Then she flooded the area with clean water and looked up. Her next request had already been anticipated. Magi placed the threaded needle in her trembling fingers.

"Hold his head, Duraid."

The boy slunk forward and bracketed Harry's pale face between his young hands. Clamping her lips together, Desdemona pinched the ragged edges together and forced the needle through the resilient flesh. Harry flinched and moaned.

"I said hold him still!" She blinked rapidly, her eyes watering with concentration.

"I think I'm going to be sick, *Sitt*."

She didn't have time for such delicacy.

"Maybe I can help, Miss Desdemona," Blake said quietly.

She looked around in surprise. For a minute,

she'd forgotten he was there. "Can you hold him still?"

"Yes." Blake's face was as white as his shirt, his expression concerned, but there was unmistakable determination, almost anger, burning in his eyes. Duraid backed off and Blake took the boy's place.

True to his word, though Harry's body jerked, his head did not move in Blake's hands until Desdemona had pulled the last thread taut and clipped the end. She straightened, wiping the sweat from her brow with the back of her hand.

"What else can I do?" Blake asked.

Else? Dear God, Blake was right. They'd only just begun, and it had already seemed they'd been working for eternity. Harry lay there seemingly lifeless; even his unconscious flinches had stopped. So still. So quiet. Once again, her vision swam.

"Ah." She cleared her voice to keep it from quavering. "There's some brandy in the bottom of that cabinet over there. If Harry wakes up too soon, he'll need it."

By the time Blake returned with the brandy, she'd finished cleaning Harry's face. She took the bottle and glass and set them aside. Harry wasn't going to wake up.

"Lord Ravenscroft, would you lift Harry? We can start getting his shirt off."

"Shirt? *Start?*"

She nodded. "Yes."

"You aren't suggesting that you'll be tending Harry's other bodily wounds yourself?"

"Yes," she said. "Why?"

"Miss Desdemona," Blake answered stiffly, "you are a young Englishwoman of genteel lineage. Young women of your type do not tend half-naked males. They do not *see* half-naked males."

She blinked in total incomprehension. She *saw* naked men all the time. Well, mostly naked. She needed only to walk through the *suq*, or visit a dig site, or stroll down the riverside to see them working, bathing, or playing. Young, middle age, old. Men. Naked. Mostly.

"Harry's shirt stays on until we can find a physician to care for him."

She relaxed in comprehension. Blake assumed a physician would be caring for Harry. Of course he would. He would not have any other experiences to guide him. She felt a touch of sympathy for him. Everything here must seem so foreign to him, so uncivilized.

"How best can I send for a medical chap?" Blake asked.

Magi caught her eye. A wealth of contempt was revealed in that one short glance. "We care for our own, Lord Ravenscroft," she said.

"Oh, I don't mean one of your native chaps. I mean an English physician."

"There are none," Desdemona said.

"I don't believe it," Blake said. "Cook's steamers must have some quack attending the aches and pains of his clientele."

They didn't have time for this. "It would take all night to make the trip to the dock, find the fellow—assuming he exists—and convince him to return here," Desdemona said. "In Cairo, a night of untreated, open wounds can be fatal, Lord Ravenscroft."

"I see." He did not like the situation. It offended him on every level.

Her sympathy toward him faltered. "Magi, will you help me?" she asked.

Blake forestalled Magi by stepping behind Harry's head. "It seems I have no choice but to do as you bid or look the churl."

Desdemona gave him a dazzling smile. Thank God, he was not so hidebound by convention as to risk Harry's life to preserve his English sense of modesty. Of course he wasn't!

"But," he said sternly, "not his pants."

She barely heard him, her attention having been caught by Harry's sudden, involuntary grimace. She'd never seen him like this.

Vulnerable.

To her, Harry epitomized the stamina, endurance, sheer tenacity of a desert scavenger. Oh, yes, he was a bit ragged around the edges, battered, but never fatally so. He was a survivor. But now Harry's tanned flesh glistened with sweat, his breath staggered in his chest, and the pulse fluttering at the base of his throat looked too mortal for the likes of a Jackal Prince.

"Please hurry," she said softly.

Blake lifted Harry and she peeled his shirt off, exposing his dirty, blood-smeared torso. Wringing cloth after cloth in the bowl of warm water Duraid raced to keep filled, she carefully sloughed the grime from his chest and arms. When she was done, she placed a hand at the small of her back, arching into the cramping muscles.

"Are you all right, Desdemona?" Magi asked.

"Yes. Just tired. I think he'll be fine." It was true; so far she'd found nothing wrong with Harry that time and some nice strong horse liniment wouldn't heal.

There was a nasty bruise over his ribs and a half-dozen angry red welts across his shoulders. He had raw abrasions encircling both wrists, as if he'd been tied, and some scrapes low on his stomach, as if he'd been dragged over rough ground. But her fingers could find no broken bones and—

She lowered her head and laid her ear on his chest. She held her breath, listening before closing her eyes in relief. His lungs sounded clear of fluid, his heartbeat was regular. Gently, thankfully, she fanned her fingertips over his heart's steady drumbeat. She'd found the only areas where disease might find a home. At least on his upper body.

She rose to find Blake watching her with a guarded expression. She had to get him out of there. He'd never understand, or condone, or possibly even allow her to examine a man's nether regions.

"There," she said, picking up a towel and wiping her hands dry. "I think he'll do."

"You are heroic, Miss Desdemona," Blake said. He cocked his head. "A regular Florence Nightingale. I wish Harry were more deserving of such endeavors."

"Sir?" Magi said.

"Obviously his nefarious activities have led him to such a pass. When one plays with fire . . ."

"Mr. Harry has played with fire many times," Magi avowed loyally. "He has never before been burned." And then, catching Desdemona's caustic expression, she amended. "Well, not so badly burned as this. Once or twice swollen knuckles. The odd cut. Oh, on occasion a black eye. A few stitches taken for vanity's sake. But nothing more."

"There doesn't have to be more!" Desdemona threw the towel on the floor, suddenly angry.

Blake was right. Whatever Harry had gotten himself into was undoubtedly a product of his own manufacture. *Whatever* it was he'd gone looking for, it wasn't worth the price of his blood!

She'd thought Harry had more wit than to imperil his life for profit. And imperil his life he had. Well, he wasn't going to die before giving her the opportunity to voice her views on such monumental stupidity. And in order to make absolutely certain he didn't die, she needed to get his pants off.

"Harry is a most circumsp—"

Desdemona cut off Magi's diatribe. "My. I suddenly feel light-headed." She fixed Magi with a stare.

Magi's eyes widened slightly and Desdemona knew her unspoken message had been understood.

"You *do* look most tired, Miss Desdemona." Magi caught her hand and patted it consolingly. "Allah keep your revered self from succumbing to ill health as a result of your saintly ministrations."

She was going to have to teach Magi not to mix her religious allusions.

"An angel, you most certainly are, but an angel in human form. You must care for the fragile vessel that shelters your sublime spirit."

"I am rather . . . fatigued," Desdemona allowed faintly, brushing her hand across her eyes.

"Oh, course you are, m'dear." Blake wrested her hand from Magi's and took over patting it. "May I suggest you get some much-needed rest?"

"I believe I'll take your advice, Lord Ravenscroft." She pulled her hand free and dragged her feet toward the library door. She paused at the portal. Blake wasn't following her. "Lord Ravenscroft . . . ?"

"Don't worry." He removed a carton from a chair. "I'll stay with Harry."

"No!" Magi chimed. "Really, Lord Ravenscroft, I am surprised you would suggest such a thing. Miss Desdemona is a maiden woman, little more than a girl, and her grandfather is not here."

"Don't worry," Blake said sardonically, "I promise I have no ulterior motives in mind and I will, of course, be the soul of discretion."

"I am sure you would, sir," Desdemona said. "But I would not like"—she scrambled around for something she wouldn't like—"I would not like us found in an untenable situation because of your determination to stay with your cousin."

"Really?" Blake gestured toward Harry. "And what about him?"

"Oh, Harry. No one will think anything of that.

They all know Harry. And me. Besides, he can't
. . . do anything."

Now she did blush. *Blast.*

"*I* will make sure all is proper," Magi said. "I wil
set Duraid to sleep before Miss Desdemona's door."

"What?" Duraid croaked. "I don't want to sleep
on the floor. I never slept on the floor before when
Harry—" Duraid's protest cut off abruptly. Magi
glowered at him. "I-I will, *Sitt*," he stammered. "Of
course, *Sitt*. Like always, *Sitt*."

"It is for the best, Lord Ravenscroft. Really," Desdemona said.

With a touch of petulance, Blake capitulated. "I
suppose you're right. We must be mindful of appearances. But if you should need me for any reason, send the lad."

"Oh, I will," Desdemona promised, escorting him
to the front door and waiting while he descended
the stairs. "Thank you." She heard a muffled groan
from deep inside the house, a sound of pain. Infection could set in in a matter of hours, and God alone
knew how long Harry had been staggering through
the streets of Cairo while she'd been eating curry
and dates.

"I am yours to command," Blake said solemnly,
leaning against the rail at the bottom of the stairs.
She didn't have time for declarations . . . as much
as she would liked to have heard them.

"That's very nice."

"I mean it."

"And I appreciate it." Another groan, louder this
time.

"I want you to know—"

"I do. Good night, Blake." Before he could respond, she backed into the house, closed the door firmly behind her, and hurried back to the library. "I heard him."

"He is fine, just waking up a bit," Magi declared. "But we'd best hurry and get these pants off of him before we have another male's delicate sensibilities to contend with."

Without further prompting, Desdemona bent over and began unbuckling Harry's belt.

"You look most disgruntled," Magi said.

"All this trouble just to get a man's pants off," Desdemona muttered, tugging the belt free of its loops.

"It is not usually so difficult," Magi assured her serenely.

CHAPTER TWENTY

"*I* see you're awake."

At the sound of the voice, Harry heeled over and banged his nose. He opened his eyes and stared at the rough, chiseled wood a few inches away from his face.

She'd put him in a packing crate.

He rolled on to his back and stared at the ceiling.

"I hope it was worth it."

Dizzy. He squinted into the painfully bright light. His chest heaved with relief. The searing impetus that had driven him to her, battered and barely conscious, had diminished when he'd found her last night. It was only a temporary refuge, however. There was still the matter of Maurice Shappeis. Harry wouldn't rest until the implicit danger represented by the mongrel had been removed.

"Well?" Dizzy demanded. "Was it worth it?"

"Was what worth what?" he mumbled, taking stock of his injuries. His left eye was swollen nearly shut. Carefully he felt along the ridge of his teeth, probing for any loose or missing member. He sighed with relief when he didn't discover any. He was rather proud of his teeth.

"I cannot believe you have been so careless. So incredibly stupid. So abysmally cavalier."

"What the devil are you talking about?" he asked.

Her face swam into hazy focus above the edges of the crate. She braced her hands on either side of him and leaned closer, peering intently. Behind her the sunlight turned her hair into a nimbus of spun gold. It streamed over her shoulders, lightly swinging against his bare chest. He could smell the lavender from her linen pillow cases still tangled therein.

For some inexplicable reason that fragrance aroused in him a welling of protectiveness. Nothing must ever happen to her. No part of anything he'd done must ever cause her harm. He'd do everything in his power to make it so.

"I hope you've learned your lesson, Harry," she was saying. "Akhenaton's tomb itself isn't worth a beating such as you've undergone."

"You can say that again."

"You might have died." Her face wore a thunderous expression.

"I know."

"What did you do? Play one of your desert rat friends false? Skim a little too much profit off the top?"

Her bitterness hurt him. What irony. She thought his wounds were the result of a deal gone sour. And well she might. It was what he'd taught her to expect.

He had no answer for her disillusionment, her disappointment. "You put me in a packing crate," he said instead.

"No, I didn't," she said. "I put you in a sarcophagus. The original owner wasn't using it."

He stared at her, nonplussed. "Couldn't you have at least found a cot?"

And now, finally, her lush, tender lips found their natural habit in a smile. Albeit a dry one. "Foresight and planning," she said. "Isn't that what you always advocate? I simply took your advice."

"How so?"

"This way, if you'd succumbed, we'd have been able to ship your remains back to England with the least amount of trouble."

He broke out in a surprised laugh. "So expedient, Diz. I'm proud of you." His chuckle became a cough. Immediately she hovered nearer.

"Desdemona," she corrected him distractedly, her fingers moving with breath-stealing gentleness over his lips and cheeks and swollen eye. "You should have ice on this."

"How'd I get here?"

"Your cousin carried you."

Damn Blake. Not content with exerting all that brooding charm, now he had to play at knight-errant, as well. "Nice to see all that brawn is good for something."

"I cannot believe you're so ungrateful. Blake—"

"Blake?" He jumped on her use of his cousin's Christian name.

She blushed and with that telling color ferocity stirred in his heart. He wanted to haul her into his arms and, with hand and mouth, erase that telling pink stain from her cheeks, replace it with a memory worth blushing over.

"Lord Ravenscroft, then." She did not meet his eyes. "He carried you all the way from Jabbar's mansion. Well, not all the way. We took a carriage most of the way. But he did carry you to and from the carriage. A good twenty yards."

"Remind me to tip him next time we meet," he said, trying to rise up on his elbows. Pain knifed through his side. "Chrissake," he muttered. "Did they have the damn mule work me over, too?"

"Oh!" Her hushed distress caught him off guard. She straightened abruptly, her color high, her eyes flashing not with answering humor but with real ire. He stared back, confused and despairing.

"I'm sorry, Dizzy," he said. "I am grateful to Blake. I'll make certain to express that gratitude at the first opportunity."

She turned her face from him, as if the sight of him were unbearable. He found, to his grim amusement, he could not bear that. "Please, Diz," he said softly.

He reached out and braceleted her wrist with his fingers, pulling her hand to his mouth and pressing a light kiss across her knuckles. Her fingers trembled in his clasp. "Please, Diz," he repeated. "Don't look like that. I'll write Blake a sonnet if it'll keep you from looking so. You've never looked at me with loathing before. Disappointment, frustration, suspicion . . . but not this." He smiled lopsidedly. "I find I hate it."

She snatched her hand away. "You idiot!" She dashed the back of her hand across her cheeks.

God, she was crying. He pushed himself upright, ignoring the lance of pain piercing his side, stretching out his arm for her. "Dizzy—"

"Idiot!" she repeated forcefully, backing away. "I don't give a bloody damn if you write Blake a hundred thank-you letters. Don't you *ever* risk your life for some useless piece of junk again! You might have become septic and died, you bloody, bloody fool!"

His mouth fell open.

"I've patched up your hands and plastered your cuts and, from time to time, I've even taken a few stitches in your miserable hide. But never anything like this. And I won't ever do it again. Do you understand?" Her voice was loud, strident. "Do—you—under—stand?"

"God help me, I think so. I hope so."

"You scared me!" she wailed. She backed into a chair and toppled down onto the seat. She promptly buried her face in her hands.

"Dizzy, I wasn't trafficking. I wasn't." He hitched a leg over the side of the crate, ready to go to her. It was a bare leg. Surprised, he hauled it back. He stared down at himself. Except for a sheet winding around his loins, he was naked. "Who took my pants off?"

She ignored the question. "Semantics. Trafficking, illegal dealing, theft . . . all the same thing."

"I hadn't stolen anything. I didn't betray anyone."

"Am I supposed to believe that? Am I supposed to believe *anything* you say? I don't feel like I *know* you anymore!" she said. "There's this odd animosity between you and Blake, and I find that your self-professed 'standard English boyhood' is shrouded in secrecy and hints of impropriety, and now this madness!" She sniffed noisily.

"Is that what he's hinted at. Impropriety?" He trailed off helplessly, unable to answer the one charge, unwilling to answer the others.

"I wasn't involved in any sort of deal gone bad, Diz." This at least he could explain. "Do you remember a brute named Maurice, worked as Georges Paget's foreman?"

"Big fellow, womanish features?" she asked in an odd, defeated tone.

"That's him. Well, he and I had a bit of a confrontation during the last excavating season."

"Yes," she said consideringly, "I recall. You were supposed to have administered a drubbing to him." She screwed up her mouth. "No one ever told me about what so I didn't put much stock in the story." She peered at him. "Should I have?"

"We fought," he answered. "He lost."

"So, he beat you up for revenge?" She raised her brows, openly skeptical. "Come now, Harry. I know revenge is a dish best served cold and all, but that incident happened last year. His revenge would be glacé by now."

Harry grinned. She charmed him, absolutely. Even suspicious and cold as she was now. "He wasn't motivated by revenge. It just helped his enthusiasm for his job. Someone paid him to work me over."

Her dark *houri's* eyes flashed. "Why?"

"I don't know. But I have my suspicions."

"What? And do not tell me you suspect Blake is responsible." Something immediate and hard chilled her tone. "It's clear you're in competition with him, that you mean to discredit him. How better than to accuse him of orchestrating your beating?"

"I don't think Blake is at fault," he answered, hating her acid tone, hating the distance that seemed to be opening up between them, desperate for some way to bridge it. "Maurice never said who it was, he was having far too much fun beating me up to answer any questions." He shrugged. "Luckily, I have a low pain tolerance and winked out pretty damn quick."

"Oh, Harry. I wish I knew what to think." For an instant pity was betrayed in stark look she gave him. He smiled and it vanished abruptly. "Oh, no. I won't fall for that little-boy-lost look. I've spent far too many hours fretting over you as it is. Not anymore. How did you get away?"

"Bribery."

Her brows rose questioningly.

"Honest."

"Aren't you afraid of lightning bolts, tossing out words like that?"

He grinned. "Really, Maurice's sort doesn't attract a fanatically loyal following. All I did was promise his henchman twenty pounds and I was hightailing it through the back streets of Cairo."

"Crawling" better described his progress, but she needn't know that, just as she needn't know how long Maurice had "merely followed orders to make him uncomfortable" before leaving for his dinner.

"Twenty pounds? And the man *believed* you?" she asked incredulously.

"Whatever you think of me, Dizzy, I have a reputation for being bound by my word."

She wandered to her grandfather's desk and picked up a broken piece of a funerary vessel, her expression absorbed.

He followed her movements, his lingering gaze tabulating each subtle, rich variation of the desert hues that comprised her beauty: the dark buff-colored gown, tawny streaked hair, burnt-toffee eyes, buttery glazed complexion. She might have been an exquisitely crafted amber goddess in some ancient's tomb. Might have, except she was not nearly as durable.

She was small. He often forgot just how small. But seeing her dwarfed behind her grandfather's desk, it distressed him to see how very fragile she'd been formed. Maurice could hurt her without even trying.

"I want you to take care, Dizzy."

She stopped toying with the shard. "Excuse me?"

"I want you to be very careful, Dizzy. Don't go anywhere alone. Stay with people." *Stay with me.*

His palm opened toward her, an involuntary movement. He shut it.

"What are you talking about, Harry?"

"Maurice knows that . . ." He didn't know how to explain. She wouldn't recognize or believe the truth if he told her, that she was in danger because he loved her. She'd be angry and offended and think he mocked her. "Maurice might come here, looking for me."

She returned to his side and patted his hand. "I'll be fine, Harry." She sounded as if she were reassuring her maiden aunt. "You yourself have always said no sane Egyptian would even consider harming an Englishwoman."

"No one has ever accused Maurice of sanity. And he's not Egyptian."

"Semantics again. Don't you worry on my account," Dizzy said in that balmlike voice. *Don't fret the invalid.* She had no intention of heeding his warning.

"Good." He nodded, not in the least relieved, and lay back in his sarcophagus, his mind racing as he formed a plan to keep Dizzy safe. He'd have to act fast, before Maurice disappeared into the backwash of the criminal underworld.

"Harry—" Whatever Dizzy had been about to say was interrupted by a discreet tap on the door. "Come in," she said.

Magi entered followed hard on her heels by Blake. His expression lightened upon spying Dizzy. Dizzy, Harry noted with a twisting in his chest, returned his welcoming smile.

"Lord Ravenscroft, how kind of you to call."

"Desdemona." Blake strode into the room and took her hands. "You look as lovely and fresh as if you'd just woken from a delightful dream rather than spent hours laboring over my reprobate cousin. I trust your patient hasn't—" He glanced at Harry. "Who took his pants off?"

"Ah, Blake." Harry lifted himself into a sitting position, allowing the cotton sheet to slip from his bare chest and settle over his hips. Yawning, he stretched one arm and then the other high over his head, keeping the smile plastered on his face even though his side screamed in protest. "Diz here tells me I owe you a debt of thanks. Thanks."

"Go get him a shirt," Blake snapped at Magi. She glared at his preemptory tone, but went. "You don't have much regard for Miss Desdemona's sensibilities, do you, Harry?"

Dizzy's gaze found his. Reproach clouded their wild honey clarity. Damn Blake, he'd won that point.

"It's all right," she said, lifting her chin. "It's just Harry, after all."

His face ached with his effort to keep his supercilious grin in place.

Blake shot him a savagely triumphant look. "Ah! 'Just Harry.' Oh, well, then . . ." His amused gaze passed insolently over Harry's sarcophagus and suddenly Harry saw himself as absurd, his nakedness as vulnerability.

"Amazingly, Harry old man, you don't look half

bad. I imagine you'll be able to scoot back to your little ghetto today."

"I suspect I—"

"No." Magi reentered, carrying one of Sir Robert's clean white shirts. "Infection," she said sententiously, "is still a distinct possibility."

"Magi is right," Dizzy agreed. "Harry should stay here. He has no one else to care for him."

"Surely he has a valet or a houseboy or someone?"

Dizzy shook her head. "No. No one. He relies strictly on himself. His secretaries live in their own homes; even the housekeeper is only employed thrice a week."

"Yes," Magi declared. "Master Harry should most definitely stay here. Look and see how red this cut is." She leaned over the sarcophagus and, her action concealed by its wooden sides, jabbed the cut on his cheek.

"Ow!"

Dizzy hastened forward. Harry moaned loudly as he slipped his arm through the shirt sleeve Magi held for him.

"It does look angry." Dizzy's fingers brushed his forehead. "And he feels warm to the touch, too. Magi, get him some water."

"I'm sure it's just his body's natural defenses," Blake said as Magi left. "And besides, remember your grandfather is gone. In Sir Robert's absence you cannot have him here for any extended period of time."

"Sir Robert is gone?" Harry asked. Given that

happenstance, there was no possibility that he would leave Dizzy alone in this house with only Magi and Duraid for protection.

"I appreciate the vote of confidence in my manly vigor, Blake, but I can promise you," he said weakly, struggling to look pitiful as he buttoned his shirt. It wasn't nearly as much play-acting as he'd have liked, "that playing fast and loose with Dizzy is the last thing on my mind."

His statement didn't appear to reassure Blake. He sneered, an exaggerated pull of his upper lip exposing one gleaming canine.

"That makes two of us," Dizzy said. "But much as I might like it otherwise, I have a duty to him. A Christian duty. I can't take chances with his health."

She turned to Blake but her fingers still glided lightly along Harry's cheek, over his swollen eye. If she kept this up, he might purr.

"That's right." Harry nodded. "You have your Christian duty. My back hurts, too."

"No wonder." She abandoned his face and ran her hands lightly over his now blamelessly covered shoulders. They may as well have been bare, he felt her touch so keenly. "You have welts. We have some liniment that I, er, Magi could rub in."

Blake, having lost his bid to have Harry removed from the house, dragged a chair over toward the head of the sarcophagus and sat down. "What did you do?" he asked.

This close, with the sun full in Blake's face, Harry realized that his cousin was angry. No, more than angry. Though his voice was light, his black eyes were filled with rage, his ridiculous aristocratic nostrils positively flared. He was furious, Harry realized, and for the life of him he could find no reason for such extravagant emotion or why Blake held it so rigidly in check. It was like watching oatmeal about to boil over. It looked as if Blake might erupt any minute.

"Well?" Blake demanded. "However did you manage to make someone so angry with you, Harry?"

"Just a knack."

"Reminds me of school," Blake said. "Always showing up with some new mark or other. The other lads made your life rather tiresome, didn't they? Spent more time being patched up than in classes, didn't you? Not that it mattered much."

Damn him.

"You went to school together?" Dizzy asked. "I thought you went to Christ's College and Harry was at Oxford."

"Harry and I were at prep school together. Eton," Blake said. "I'm afraid Harry was a prime target for the cruelties of the other lads."

"Wasn't I though?" Harry murmured softly.

"They hurt you?" Dizzy's voice registered her shock. Damn him again.

"Yes, they did," Blake said, and now the rage in his eyes was swamped by other emotions—remorse and pity and satisfaction—a black, fetid pool.

"Lucky Harry," he said tightly. "He's found a place for himself here. Desdemona is under the impression that you've made quite a name for yourself as an Egyptologist of sorts, if you can warrant that."

"Desdemona is given to impressions, I'm afraid." Harry contrived calm.

"Come now, Harry. I've seen how you live. I've spoken with some people. You're quite highly regarded here. I can't see you leaving to return to England. Here you're a success. There . . ." He shrugged apologetically. "I can't see you returning to England no matter what the incentive."

"Can't you?" Harry returned mildly. He kept his face bland, composed. He'd learned early never to give the satisfaction of exposing one's pain to public scrutiny.

He had the satisfaction of witnessing Blake's pity become frustration. Poor Blake, Harry thought, didn't stand a chance. Harry had been baited by experts. Compared to them, Blake was an amateur.

"Things would be difficult for you there," Blake said tightly. "All those reminders of what you can't possibly . . . have."

"What can't Harry have?" Dizzy asked, her brow furrowing.

"Darkmoor Manor?" Harry offered ironically. Blake swallowed his anger. No, he would never go back to England. But he wasn't going to tell Blake that. Blake glared at him and Dizzy's face was set with concentration.

"You," Blake suddenly said, snapping his head in Dizzy's direction, "you would love London. And London would love *you*, Desdemona. I can see you riding in Hyde Park or visiting the galleries, in a box at Ascot, or gracing one at the opera." She smiled, entranced by the picture he painted.

Blake leaned back, his gaze sliding back to Harry. Blake hadn't finished with him yet. "You had quite lofty aspirations at one time, as I recall. Wanted to be a scholar, didn't you, Harry?" Bleak and savage gladness filled Blake's voice, and now Harry thought he understood Blake's passionate response.

Blake, the consummate gentleman, was pithed on honor's point. Blake believed it was his duty to warn Dizzy about Harry. At the same time his aristocratic cousin recognized that such a warning was disloyal to family. Thus he both hated and delighted in the telling.

"You wanted to be an academician, Harry?" Dizzy was asking.

"Something of the sort."

"Why didn't you? You would have made a splendid scholar. You already know more than nine-tenths of those who come here. You have so much knowledge to impart—"

He cut her off. "I saw how ridiculous such a desire was. There's no money to be had. What good are academic lauds when one can't afford to fix a leaky faucet let alone purchase the champagne to toast one's own success?" He meant to taunt Blake, but Dizzy's little catch of breath alerted him to his error. He'd never meant to remind her of her material poverty. "Dizzy, I'm sorry."

"It's quite all right." Her cheeks wore brilliant ruddy flags.

"Please, I never meant—"

"*Sitt*," Duraid said, stepping inside the room.

"Yes, Duraid?"

"There is a Mr. Paget to see you. He says business."

"Oh? Show him to the sitting room, Duraid," Dizzy said. She rose. "If you'll excuse me, gentlemen?"

Blake stood up. "Of course. I'll just keep the invalid company for a while, shall I?"

"I'm sure that would be nice," Dizzy said.

Harry wasn't nearly so sanguine.

CHAPTER TWENTY-ONE

Thoughtfully, Desdemona made her way toward the sitting room. She'd always assumed Harry had been the Golden Boy, favored and cosseted by adoring parents and sisters. Certainly his self-confidence supported such an estimation.

But he could not have won such poise from the unhappy childhood Blake described, in a schoolroom where he'd apparently been singled out by his peers to be tyrannized. Why would they do that? Harry could charm vultures into fasting should he set his mind to it. It made no sense.

And Harry had wanted to be an academician? Again, she'd always assumed that Harry had always achieved exactly what he had wanted to achieve, that there was no brass ring beyond his reach.

Her brows knotted. Harry *was* an expert. He could date an artifact after a casual perusal, find the single genuine shard in a mountain of rubble, descry an eloquent history from a broken vase. Yet he'd been expelled from Oxford, fled England and his dreams. Even though he'd declared he'd done so for money, she didn't believe him. There was more here. There was frustration, aspirations, abandoned dreams . . . failure.

A fallible Harry seemed all too human. It would be hard to believe his devil-may-care, bon vivant attitude could be mere window-dressing masking . . . sensitivity? She smiled at her own folly. She was romanticizing Harry again. If he had been beaten up by the other lads at Eton, it had very probably been a well-deserved thrashing. Still, her own companionless childhood probably prevented her from ever really understanding him. Or anyone else.

She lifted her chin in a consciously defiant gesture. She refused to believe that. There was something else going on.

"—from the turkey farm."

Desdemona blinked. Duraid stood beside her, waving a scrap of paper under her nose, his face troubled. "What did you say, Duraid?"

"At the farm last night, a pack of dogs got into the pens. A quarter of the turkeys are dead and a full half have run off."

The thought of turkeys leaving scarab-studded offerings throughout the streets of Cairo brought an unwilling smile to her lips.

"My friend there says already many of the boys have gone back to the streets, certain that the factory is closed for good."

"Rubbish." A seed of anxiety flavored her tone.

"Matin says it will cost fifty pounds to replace the turkeys and make repairs."

"I don't have fifty pounds, Duraid." She didn't have ten pounds.

"Yes, *Sitt*." Duraid nodded, but his eyes pleaded with her for reassurance. "*Sitt* will think of something though, will she not?"

Always *Sitt* would think of something, come up with something, find something. She pinched the bridge of her nose between her fingers, struggling with this newest financial disaster. Those children *needed* the turkey farm.

"Won't *Sitt* think of something?" he prodded. Duraid had once begged in Cairo's streets. Several of his friends from those days depended on the scarab factory for their livelihoods.

She dropped her hand. "Of course I'll think of something." Somehow she invested confidence in her voice. "Soon. Now go to the kitchen and have Magi make some tea for Mr. Paget." She opened the door and entered the sitting room.

Georges scurried to his feet, abandoning the thrice covered settee he'd been perched on. "Ah, Miss Desdemona! I hear you have a houseguest."

"Yes. Harry met with some difficulty the other night and is recuperating here."

The little Frenchman shook his head. "Difficulty, you say. Ah, Harry. He is incorrigible. Nothing too bad, I trust?"

"He'll recover." She motioned for him to retake

his seat and took the one opposite him. "Duraid said you were here on a matter of business?"

"Yes. Last night you said you had acquired a papyrus."

"Papyrus? Oh, you mean the poetry. But, Monsieur Paget, I also told you it was a forgery. Nothing the Cairo Museum would bother with," she protested.

"I am not speaking of the museum, Miss Desdemona." His tone was playful.

"Oh?"

"Sometimes, outside of my duties to the museum, I have been known to engage in a bit of independent commerce. I can find a buyer for such works."

Though she had known this for years, Georges had never openly admitted his unofficial business practices before.

"I will take the fake papyrus off your hands for a nice profit to yourself. To a collector"—he lifted one slim brow—"it may prove valuable. May I see it?"

Business was business and she needed money. Though she'd hoped to sell the papyrus to a nice, distant New York publisher, if Georges Paget offered her enough money, it was his. She started to nod before remembering that it was in the library. Harry was in the library. She wasn't going to reveal her secret hiding hole to his all-too-interested gaze. Georges would have to wait.

"I'm afraid that at the moment that's not possible," she said. "Perhaps tomorrow? Or the next day?"

"Oh." His disappointment was nearly comic. His bland face collapsed into slack, aggrieved lines.

"I'm sorry, Mr. Paget," she said.

"So am I," Georges said unhappily, as Duraid arrived with the tea service. "So am I."

"How did they catch up with you?" Blake asked, watching Harry struggle out of that . . . that *coffin* . . . and limp across the room.

Harry stopped beside Sir Robert's desk and began poking the various objects littering its top.

"Catch up with me?" Harry murmured in a distracted voice, tying the sheet around his waist and wincing as he did so. Apparently he found whatever he sought on the cluttered desk. His hand closed about a small figurine. "Duraid!" he shouted.

"Tell me how the men who were chasing you caught up with you," Blake demanded. "You were always so bloody fast. How did they catch you?"

Harry spared him an annoyed glance. "Really, Blake, how would I know? They caught me. I wasn't clocking them." He used the tone an adult would when dealing with a tiresome child. Blake's resentment swelled.

How dare Harry treat him so condescendingly? How dare Harry play the hero, forcing him to play the craven? "You *didn't* run!"

Harry held up the statuette, scrutinizing it closely, ignoring him completely.

"Damn you. I said you didn't run!"

Startled by Blake's shout, Harry looked up. His gaze sharpened on him for a second before returning to the figure. "No," he murmured. "There was no place to run. The other corridor ended in a blind alley."

"You knew that when you sent me up that corridor, didn't you?"

"Yes. If you'll excuse me?" Painfully he made his way across the room, favoring his bruised side. At the door he poked his head into the hallway. "Magi!"

"I won't be beholden to you," Blake said. "You may think you've proven something by forcing me to desert you, after you knew . . . after I told you how wretched I'd felt about abandoning you back at Eton . . ." He stopped, seeking control before going on. "You haven't proven a thing, to me or to Desdemona. It was a pitiful act that in no way proves you're a better man than I."

"Magi!" Harry's voice reverberated once more down the cramped passage before he turned his head. His expression was flat with dislike. Blake returned it, easily surpassing his cousin's animosity.

"I don't have time to address whatever grievance you're nursing against me, Blake," Harry said. "And frankly, even if I did have the time, I don't have the inclination. I just don't give a damn."

Blake could hear the truth of Harry's words in the tiredness with which Harry regarded him. It infuriated Blake. Harry held hostage his very birthright, had cost him the woman he loved. Harry threatened everything Blake valued. He was a defective, utterly inadequate, a victim who improbably wore the mien of the victor.

Rage and frustration clouded Blake's thoughts, roiled darkly in his heart, and he fought the urge to lash out. His lack of self-control, these base impulses were intolerable.

Blake was the scion of the family. He had a heritage to uphold. A standard to maintain. By God, he would do what was right. He was a gentleman.

It was all that was left to him.

"Harry?" The housekeeper appeared in the doorway. "You called for me?"

Without wasting another glance at Blake, Harry stepped into the hall with the housekeeper. Blake stayed where he was, refusing to leave until he'd done what he'd come to Cairo to do. He would tell Harry about the new will. It was what honor demanded.

He waited and watched Harry bend over the slight, dark woman. He heard the gibbering lilt of Harry's Arabic words and the monosyllabic replies of the Egyptian. Harry placed the figure in her hand, closing her fingers around it and gesturing. Nodding gravely, she turned and disappeared down the hallway.

Harry reentered the room and, finding Blake still there, sighed heavily. "Blake, go away."

"I came to Cairo to see you, Harry."

"Really?" Harry said incuriously. "That's not the reason my mother gave out."

"And what was that?"

"She says you're recovering from a broken heart." Everything in Harry's manner betrayed how unlikely he found this explanation. Damn him.

"A broken engagement."

"Oh?"

Harry's careless tone infuriated Blake, shredding his determination to act as a gentleman, dimming his nobler resolutions. "Do you know why Lenore DuChamp dissolved our engagement?" He spoke quickly, violently, shocking himself.

"Do I want to know?" Harry mused, still unconcerned.

"Because of you, cousin."

Harry laughed and Blake's hand jerked shut into a clenched fist.

"Oh, come, Blake," Harry said with sharp amusement, "I've been blamed for a good many things, and in most cases I'm willing to plead guilty, but I've never even *met* Miss DuChamp."

"You didn't have to. She'd only needed to hear about you, your defect, to call off our engagement."

And now, finally, Blake had the savage satisfaction of seeing Harry's brown skin turn a sickly cast, his eyelids flicker shut as if he'd been struck.

"That's correct, Harry." Blake stretched his lips, trying to smile. "I told her about you myself. It was the only decent thing to do. She decamped after the courtesy of a final interview. She expressly told me that she could not face the possibility of bringing an abnormal child into the world. And what with your *inadequacy*, our bloodline was suspect, to say the least."

"Jesus."

As soon as he'd said the words, Blake experienced their loss. He'd kept the reason for Lenore's departure strictly to himself. He hadn't even told his grandfather, even when the old man had answered the news of her desertion by disinheriting him.

Harry absorbed the information as if he'd been struck. Even as he watched, Blake witnessed Harry master the pain, somehow become ennobled by it. Blake, for all his months of secret suffering, had not become nobler. He'd become bitter. And he knew it.

Once more he found himself wanting in comparison to Harry. Fury lashed his self-contempt into a white-hot resolve.

No more. Not again. Not ever again would he be found wanting in comparison to his imbecile cousin. He leaned a white-knuckled fist on the desk separating them, forced words through stiff lips. "It doesn't matter."

"Don't be a fool. Of course it matters."

"No. Not anymore."

"Does Miss DuChamp realize that we might not even share the same grandfather—"

"No! Besides, a better chatelaine than Lenore exists." He hadn't meant to say that, but once spoken, he was glad. His elation outpaced his self-disgust. It wasn't as if the words weren't true. He just hadn't realized before how well suited Desdemona was for the role of his viscountess. He hadn't said the words out of spite. He hadn't!

Harry looked as if he'd sustained a heart blow. He swayed ever so slightly . . . so gratifyingly. "No."

"Don't ever presume again," Blake spat out. "My future and that of *any* woman I contemplate forming a union with are no concern of yours. None. Don't dare to presume, don't dare!"

"You'll destroy her!" Harry's words tumbled out, low and throbbing with intensity. "She's artless and honest and decent. You'll never forgive her for being better than you are, Blake, for having nobility you can only approximate, and you'll chip away at her until you've destroyed her, until she's—"

"Shut up!" Blake squeezed his eyes shut.

He would not listen to Harry discuss Desdemona. The thought of their intimacy made his head swim with dark and violent impulses. He hated how casually she touched him, how he followed her with his gaze . . . "Shut up!" he shouted again to still the flow of images. "You've everything! Everything."

"Everything," Harry echoed hollowly.

"Everything! You've been named Grandfather's sole heir." Blake squared his shoulders and opened his eyes to find Harry regarding him in flat disbelief.

"It was because of Lenore," he went on, determined to finish this, to prove himself. "Grandfather doted on her and after she left, he was furious with me. He punished me by naming you his heir, knowing how I loved Darkmoor Manor, knowing how much it meant to me and how little it meant to you."

Harry frowned, skeptical and unconvinced. "And you came to Cairo? Why? To tell me in person, about my . . . fortune?"

"You bastard."

"I'm disappointed," Harry said, his flip tone at odds with his tense posture. "You've always been careful to make sure your epithet are accurate. Idiot, fool, moron. If nothing else, you know I'm legitimate."

"Don't you understand? You will own Darkmoor Manor!"

"I understand perfectly," Harry said, his bright eyes narrowing thoughtfully. "I've been named heir to Grandfather's estate in retaliation for your losing an approved fiancée. Miss DuChamp must have been a buxom girl. Grandfather was always partial to buxom women. No, I understand that part. What I haven't figured out is why you've come all this way to tell me.

"If I were you," Harry continued, "I'd be out scouring the English countryside for a suitably well-endowed replacement so I could wiggle into the old man's good graces before he died."

Jesus. Blake had never considered the possibility that Grandfather could die while he was gone— He looked up. Harry smiled knowingly.

"Damn you."

"You're being redundant."

"I will do everything in my power to regain what is rightfully mine," Blake said. "But my first responsibility is to Darkmoor, to seeing that it is properly cared for in the interim. That's why I'm here."

"Yes?" Sharper interest now.

"It's falling apart. If something is not done soon, the foundations will give way and the house will slide into the sea." He watched intently, trying to gauge Harry's reaction. "I need money to make the necessary repairs. Lots of money."

"You want me to give you—"

"No," Blake clipped out, insulted. "No. I asked the bank for a loan but they won't give me one. They will only lend that sort of money to someone with the collateral to back it—in other words, to Darkmoor's heir. *You.* That is why I've come here. I want you to sign the bank papers." He reached inside his coat and withdrew a thin packet: the bank's loan papers and a copy of the will naming Harry Darkmoor's heir.

Harry took the proffered papers, his smile ripe with grim humor. "You want me to sign papers that will make me responsible for repaying a loan that will be used to restore *my* inheritance after which you will then do your damnedest to do me out of that same inheritance?"

Blake nodded.

"It would seem I come by my brass honestly. Perhaps we're related after all." Harry tossed the papers onto the desk.

"If I had any other recourse, I would have taken it. Time is precious. I need the money now."

"How do I know these are what you say? I'm sure you remember I can't read. You might be asking me to sign a confession to some heinous crime you've committed back in England. You're not the Ripper, are you, Blake?"

Blake glared at him. "I give you my word as a gentleman they are what I say. If you have any doubts, hire someone to read them for you. I'm sure you must employ someone's services in that area fairly frequently."

"True, and of course, I shall do just that. But even

if these are what you say, I don't see how this would be a practical business move on my part, Blake. I mean, I take all the risks, incur all the debt, and you get all the fun of turning my supposed grandsire against me. A rather despicable role and one I humbly suggest I'm far better suited for."

Blake stiffened. "I will, of course, accept full responsibility for repaying the loan."

"Of course." Harry held all the cards and he knew it.

"Darkmoor means nothing to you."

"That's true. But I'm a businessman, Blake. You don't need to read to be a businessman. You only need to understand the simple concept of profit and loss. And I'm asking myself, what profit I?"

"What do you want?"

"Leave Cairo," Harry answered harshly.

"You bastard!"

Harry did not smile this time, but met and held Blake's furious gaze with one of his own, his eyes flat and hard and brilliant. "That's what I want."

"I can't believe you entertain *notions* about Desdemona Carlisle. You can't honestly want to force that lovely girl to live here, like some Arab tramp, with *you* for the rest of her life? She's extraordinary, gifted. You must have some natural affection for her. Want what is best for her."

"*That's* what I want," Harry repeated, breathing hard. "I'll sign the papers when you board the boat."

Blake snatched his hat up from the table. "I won't be blackmailed."

CHAPTER TWENTY-TWO

*H*arry paced restlessly around the cluttered library until he caught sight of the packet of papers Blake had left with him. He picked up the thin packet and unfolded them. Letters spilled in unrecognizable patterns across the sheet, meaningless and provocative. He tossed them back down.

It had been nearly two days since he'd offered to sign those damned mortgage papers in return for Blake's vacating Egypt. Two days since he'd offered Darkmoor Manor in exchange for Dizzy.

Since then Blake had avoided him. Blake hadn't, however, avoided Dizzy. He spent more time here than at his blasted hotel. She allowed it. She was "at home" whenever he called.

For the hundredth time, Harry cursed himself for acting so rashly. All he'd needed to do was sign the bloody papers and within a few days Blake would have been hightailing it back to Jolly Old, making lists of repairs to the family manse. Now bloody

Blake would stay until bloody doomsday proving how noble and sincere his aristocratic sentiments were.

Bully for bloody Blake.

Harry rammed his shoulder against the frame of the door leading out into the small walled garden behind the house. His lip curled at the blameless poppies nodding in the early-spring sunlight outside.

If Dizzy found out he'd tried to blackmail Blake into leaving Cairo, she'd have his head. But when Blake had presented him with a chance to be rid of him, he'd fallen on it. He should have realized how Blake would react to extortion. Blake's righteous outrage should have been pitifully easy to anticipate. The man was a walking cliché.

Luckily, Blake's intrepid discretion was just as easily assumed. He wouldn't tell Dizzy about Harry's attempted coercion. His gentleman's code would never allow it. Not that Harry gave a damn. He simply wanted Blake gone.

Leaving Dizzy to him.

His beloved.

Even now, he could hear the murmur of Dizzy's and Blake's voices from the sitting room. Though he strained his ears, all he could discern of their conversation was the tone: intimate and maddening.

He raked his hair back from his temples and returned to the library and the book he'd been perusing. Carefully he paged through the dog-eared book, treating it as if it were fragile vellum instead of the cheap foolscap novels of this type were generally printed on. He'd spent the morning skimming the illustrations of this and the other books he'd found tucked along the uppermost ledge of the bookcase.

They had striking similarities. They all featured an insipid-looking, open-mouthed girl and a rock-jawed man with a constipated expression. On the last page of each book was an inevitable picture of the pair, their arms entwined as they strolled toward some moss-mantled manor on a distant hill.

Harry closed the book.

Darkmoor was no pink-and-pastel fairy castle, but it was a manor.

And he could have had it; Darkmoor and, by transference, respect—or at least the qualified approval that came with the ownership of such ghastly rubble piles. He could return to England and, with his financial acumen, make the right investments, cannily parlay his money into wealth. He could force society to acknowledge his success if not his worthiness.

He would never make a name for himself as an Egyptologist. He would never find success in the fascinating field he'd devoted the last decade to studying. But he *could* have a measure of respect, and that was what he'd always wanted. Or imagined he'd wanted.

Because he'd heard Blake's disclosure and felt not one whit of triumph, of hope, of eagerness. Because it meant *nothing*, nothing at all, except that he would have been able to offer Dizzy at least part of the fairy tale.

Would have been.

Unfortunately, owning Darkmoor would not stop the sidelong pitying glances of some damned curate's wife, the condolences whispered to Dizzy behind his back, the assessing gleam in too-interested masculine eyes as they softly queried, "Why would a woman like that marry the likes of *him?*"

Abruptly Harry reached up and shoved the book back in its place.

"Harry?" Duraid's voice interrupted his black musings.

"Come in."

Duraid entered, spotted the serving platter heaped with half-attended food, and grimaced. "Magi will be upset with you for not eating," Duraid warned as he began stacking plates.

Harry forestalled him. "Has Lord Ravenscroft left yet?"

"I will look." Duraid abandoned the luncheon dishes and went out into the hall.

Harry had to find some way to remain in the Carlisle house until he was certain Maurice was no longer a threat. Unfortunately, his bruises were fading. While he could count on Dizzy's soft heart allowing him to stay, once Sir Robert returned he had little doubt he'd be expelled like yesterday's bathwater.

"He is going." Duraid closed the door behind him, immediately rousing Harry's suspicions. Obviously Duraid had been *told* to close the door. By whom? Dizzy? And why?

"Open that blasted door, Duraid," Harry snapped, and then, meeting the startled reproach in the boy's eye, "We need some air movement in here."

"They are in the hall," Duraid whispered.

"So what?"

"They were in the hall when I came to collect the lunch things fifteen minutes ago. Whenever he leaves, it takes a long time. Even though they spend all that time talking, they must say nothing because whenever he leaves he still stands, talking." Duraid's caramel-colored eyes widened with mystification.

"What do they talk about?" Any feelings of sheepishness he might feel at pumping the boy for information vanished with Duraid's answer.

"England."

"Damn it!"

The boy shrugged, looking doubtful. "*Sitt* desires."

Abruptly the irritation that had held Harry's desolation at bay drained away. *Dizzy desires.*

There had to be some way to make her see how much she meant to him. Some manner in which to combat the hypnotic lure of England and lantern-jawed aristocrats and fairy-tale castles . . .

"Duraid, I want you to go to my house and get something for me." Motioning him near, Harry gave the boy instructions. He'd finished when Magi entered. Duraid passed her on his way out.

"It's finished," she said without preamble.

"When?"

"Early today the *shabtis* was secreted in this Maurice's house. When he sees Maurice return, the man who did this will inform the Turkish authorities. Maurice will be arrested at once. With such unassailable evidence of his theft, thefts from Sir Robert's home itself, he will not be released for a very long time."

"Good." Harry nodded.

"This is a dangerous game you play, Harry."

"The alternative is untenable. I won't wait for Maurice to decide he'll strike at me through Dizzy. Someday he would." He heard Dizzy laugh, a rich sound of enjoyment. His lips answered with a smile even as his heart contracted painfully.

"You are a fool," Magi said quietly.

"Seems to be the popular consensus."

"I mean it, Harry Braxton. I never thought to say the like to you, who has always seemed a resourceful and level-headed young man, but I must. You are a fool."

"Third time's the charm."

"Fool."

"You know there's a popular myth in England concerning modest, silent Eastern women—"

"This is not the time for your glibness. Do you want Desdemona to marry Lord Ravenscroft?"

"No." The word rang out, harsh and clear, an answer from his heart, his very soul. "She won't marry Blake."

"She will," Magi stated grimly, "because *he* has no fear. Unlike you."

"I'm not afraid of—"

"—anything but that Desdemona will pity you, not love you."

He looked away, unable to form a reply. Magi touched his arm, compelling him to meet her serious gaze.

"For years I have watched you mask your desire. She is drawn to you and you know this and you want this and you will not allow yourself to have it. You will not let her fall in love with you without telling her the truth about yourself, yet you cannot let her go." Magi's voice dropped.

"So you keep her like this, month after month, year after year . . . making her love you, making her distrust you . . . each day falling more in love with her yourself. Telling her to go away while you make her stay. Afraid of what she will do, what she will say, when she discovers the real Harry Braxton. Not a silly child's hero, not this Prince of Jackals she likes to call you, but simply a man who cannot read."

He heard his own heart's beat, smelled the ancient dust of the surrounding artifacts, the must of antique leather, the perfume of decay. "How did you know?" he asked without surprise.

"All of Cairo knows, Harry," Magi said softly.

He nodded. What did it matter? Cairo knew his secret and he'd still achieved success, wealth, some respect. He'd achieved everything . . . except Dizzy's heart.

Magi opened her palms in exasperation, seeking an explanation. "I do not understand. Why don't you tell her?"

"She wants to leave," he said simply. "Every day she plots and plans and strategizes how she will leave Egypt. Why tell her what I am? What purpose would it serve other than provoke her pity?"

Magi shook her head. "She should stay here."

Should she? Harry rubbed his hand across his eyes. He didn't know how to untangle his desire for her to stay from his desire for her happiness. He didn't even know where to begin.

"She deserves more than a crumbling Mameluke palace with a chorus of starving dogs singing her to sleep each night. She wants England."

"England. Bah!" Magi said. "She has made herself homesick for a fantasy, because no one has offered her reality. I remember when Desdemona came to us. Though grieving for her parents, in this new country her dreams were fresh and sweet and newly possible. She even found a hero . . . who laughed at her."

"If he hadn't laughed, he'd have sobbed with wanting her." He did not flinch from the condemnation in Magi's eyes. In this, at least, he was certain. "She was too innocent. Too young. And he . . . was too afraid."

"Ah, yes. Fear again. Is it any wonder that Desdemona is enraptured of the dauntless, suffering viscount? Even his pain recommends him to her. How better to engage Desdemona's soft heart than to need her? You, Harry, have never needed anyone. Or anything."

God, what lies he'd enacted.

"Tomorrow is her birth date," Magi continued. "Lord Ravenscroft will give her pretty things, useless things, things for her enjoyment. He is unique among her acquaintance. Here, at last, is a man who does not care that she can read a dozen languages, decipher hieroglyphics, balance a ledger." Her finger flew out, pointing at him in a scornful gesture. "He doesn't care what she *does*. He does not want the scholar, he wants the pretty, adoring young girl used to making do with little. The perfect wife for an impoverished viscount. He wants—"

"*I* want her." Harry broke in tersely. "Never doubt it."

"Then tell her. Tell her the truth."

Magi didn't know what she was asking. He wasn't the boy who'd damped untold pages with his tears of frustration, or the young man who'd arrived in Egypt certain his life would always be dictated by his inability to make sense of written words. He didn't want to remember those incarnations. He wanted them dead.

"You call her a romantic and sneer at her fantasies but you only offer her more of the same." Magi's finger jabbed the air, punctuating each sentence. "You withhold and reveal as you see fit. It is not fair. It is cowardly. Anything less than the truth is just more make-believe. Desdemona needs a lover who is not a chimera, no matter whose creation, yours or her own."

CHAPTER TWENTY-THREE

$\mathcal{D}$esdemona paused outside the door to the library and adjusted her bodice.

She hadn't seen Harry all day. Yesterday after Blake had left, she'd gone to visit the invalid only to be met in the hall by Magi. Face like a thundercloud, Magi had grabbed her arm and spun her around, advising her to "leave that stupid man alone." Desdemona had heeded the advice.

But now she wanted to see Harry's expression when he saw her transformation from dowdy girl to exotic woman. Magi's deft needlework had achieved wonders on her old champagne-colored dress. The petticoat had been refitted with new tiers of tallow-colored taffeta. The delicate muslin had been separated in front and draped back, exposing the gleaming ruffles. Magi had used the excess material in back to create a cascading train made brilliant with amber beading.

Magi had refashioned the bodice, too, patterning

more tiny amber beads on the muslin that criss-crossed low over Desdemona's breasts. So much breast, thought Desdemona, staring down at seemingly endless expanse of flesh beneath her collar bone. *Courage*, she thought.

She took a deep breath and pushed the door open. "The Turkish police just left," she said.

"Did they?" Harry, sprawled indolently in the chair, did not look up from peeling an orange. A snifter of brandy stood on the windowsill. He must have sent Duraid to his house for it. The Carlisle budget didn't provide for brandy.

Desdemona stepped fully into the room, adjusting the sweeping skirts. "They say that they found one of Grandfather's own *shabtis* at this fellow Shappeis's house. Perhaps that is why he captured you, Harry, to give himself time to rob us. He must be an amazingly cunning thief. I'm sure Grandfather wasn't even aware anything was missing."

"Fancy." Harry popped a section of orange into his mouth, licking the juice from his lips. Lord, she thought irrelevantly, he had the most sensually fashioned mouth.

"The police were tipped off as to his criminal activities. Apparently he's suspected in a number of crimes but they've never caught him red-handed before." When *would* Harry look at her? Until he was giving her—and her appearance—his full attention, she refused to tell him the most interesting part of her story: that the fellow had escaped while being taken into custody.

"I can't say I'm surprised. Maurice is—" He

glanced up and whatever he'd been about to say died on his lips. His gaze slued over her. "You're going somewhere."

"Why, yes." She preened, fluffing out the layers of ruffle and lace like an exotic bird. "Blake is escorting me to a concert and then to dinner."

Carefully Harry set the orange on the ground beside his chair and stood. He'd washed his hair. The late-afternoon sunlight glistened on his damp head. He moved closer, his face a careful study of pleasantness. No appreciation. Simply friendly interest. *Damn*.

"I see," he said. "A birthday celebration, is it?"

This close she could smell the sharp, bay tang of his soap. "Lord Ravenscroft is very kind."

"How is it a kindness to win an evening with a beautiful woman?" he asked gently.

She grinned at his teasing. He *did* like the dress. "Magi did it."

"Magi did what?" he asked.

"Made the dress. Well, really remade the dress. Isn't it lovely?" She twirled around.

"Exquisite." He hadn't moved a foot nearer, but with that single, low utterance she felt as if he'd suddenly surrounded her. Her heartbeat answered the odd, unnerving sensation by accelerating, her lips parted. He leaned forward and checked, drawing his head back and clearing his throat.

"Well," he murmured, his eyes never leaving her face, "now would seem as good a time as any to offer my gift."

"Gift?"

"Your birthday gift." He crossed the room and picked up a parcel wrapped in plain brown paper tied with a string. He held it out, the gesture oddly uncertain. "Happy birthday, Desdemona."

Eagerly she accepted and unwrapped the package. Inside lay a mirror that was—unless she knew nothing about antiquities and her grandfather's tutelage had been wasted effort—three thousand years old. Square in shape, its rounded corners were studded with tiny, colored stones. The surface, though pitted and uneven, gleamed with a recent oiling.

A woman, a noble Egyptian lady, had once gazed into this mirror. Perhaps it had been a love token from her spouse or her lover.

Delighted, Desdemona looked into the shimmering depth. Her reflection wavered, dim and unrecognizable, over the ancient surface.

"Do you see yourself?" Harry asked.

"Not really." She looked up and smiled. "Harry, it's lovely."

"Here," he said. "You must see yourself." His hands cupped her shoulders. They were warm and strong and for just an instant his touch seemed to linger. Then he turned her so that the sun caught the mirror's surface. Her image appeared from the dark, oiled depths of the metal as if conjured with a spell, exotic and glowing. Behind her, she felt the heat Harry radiated, scented the unique, warm masculinity that was his own.

Instinctively she verged back against the protective shield of his body. Her reaction alarmed her and she dropped her head in confusion, pretending to study the mirror more closely. She turned it over in her hand. The back was patterned with a lotus motif, little scratches between the stylized flowers marring the otherwise pristine surface.

She squinted, tilting the mirror to catch the full benefit of the sun, and discovered that the faint lines were not scratches at all but hieratics, the shorthand of hieroglyphics. She peered closer, trying to make out the words.

I have loved you through each long season,
Through the span of each day, each meter of the night,
*   that I have wasted, alone.*
In darkness I have lain awake—

It was a love poem. Her face flushed. Harry met her gaze, a touch of self-mockery in his own expression.

"Har—" She stopped just in time to keep from making a fool of herself and faced forward again. The tiny etchings were so faint they would elude casual observation. It was a mirror. Just a mirror. "Thank you."

"I found this last year in a Luxor market and I thought of you. As soon as I saw it, I knew you had to have it. I had thought . . ." He broke off and shook his head slightly as if rejecting some notion. "You're welcome."

His fingers skated along her shoulder to the base of her neck. With his thumb he gently pushed her head forward. "Your hair is coming down," he murmured in her ear. "Allow me."

He didn't give her a chance to argue, not that she would have. His fingers combed up her neck collecting errant strands. Of its own volition, her head fell more fully into the delicious sensation. He plucked a tortoise-shell hair pin from the thick twist Magi had arranged and a loose tendril escaped, falling across her cheek. His hand appeared over her shoulder, his knuckles grazing the tops of her breast, causing her breath to stop. But it was a chance contact and his slender fingers reclaimed the tress.

"There." He sounded as if he, too, had been holding his breath.

"Thank you."

He stepped away. The sudden removal of his body replaced his screening warmth with cooling air and she shivered, running her hands up and down her bare arms.

"So, you're off to dine with old Blake," he said in that odd, stilted voice.

"Yes. He would have been here by now but some message from home delayed him. I hope it isn't bad news."

Harry smiled crookedly. "Maybe some gulls plugged up one of Darkmoor's chimneys," he offered sardonically.

He needn't be so critical of Blake's solicitude for his birthright. "Your cousin loves his home very much," she said.

"I should say so. All the males in his family see Darkmoor Manor as a sacred trust," he said without a trace of his usual amusement. "What would you give for a bona fide English manor, Diz?'' he asked suddenly.

"Oh, anything. What woman wouldn't love a manor to play grande dame in?'' she answered, distracted by his tension and wondering at its cause.

"And if Blake could give this to you . . . ?'' He was quite still, quite grave, ignoring her flippancy. "Or if he couldn't . . . ?''

"No manor; no Desdemona,'' she answered flippantly, trying to cajole him into laughter. He didn't laugh.

"Why don't you and Blake get along better?'' she asked. "You are cousins. What sparked this rivalry between you? Is it''—she hesitated, uncertain how to go on with this suddenly hard-eyed stranger—"because of what happened at Eton? Or . . . or the scandal at Oxford that resulted in your dismissal? Did Blake play some part in that?''

He paused, no more than the space of a heartbeat, and yet she had the impression that much was being considered in that brief hesitation. "No,'' he finally said. "Even if there hadn't been any schoolboy rifts, Blake and I still wouldn't like each other, Desdemona. He had nothing to do with the Oxford debacle. He wasn't even there. That was entirely of my own making.''

Desdemona? That was the second time Harry had called her by her given name. He never called her Desdemona of his own volition. She wasn't sure she liked it. "I haven't any right—''

"You have every right. I would insist you take

it"—he smiled crookedly—"but I'm just not sure I have the courage to bequeath it."

"I don't understand."

"Oxford was a . . . an extraordinarily difficult time for me, Desdemona." She stared at him in amazement. "I . . . I was sent down for cheating." He expelled the last word in a rush of air.

"Cheating?" She knew very well that cheating was one of the gravest sins a gentleman could commit. But this was Harry, and certainly he'd never pretended he was a gentleman.

No, it didn't surprise her in the least, she found, that cheating had been the reason for Harry's expulsion. What did surprise her was the lack of censure she herself attached to the transgression . . . and the transgressor.

Indeed, she was far more amazed by the fact that Harry had needed to cheat in the first place than she was that he'd cheated at all. Harry was so intelligent. Some would say brilliant.

But even more unsettling than her lack of censure regarding his cheating, she realized that beneath her surprise, she was touched with annoyance that Harry, who, after all, made a career of cheating or something as near like it as made no difference, was so obviously distraught by his long-ago crime.

It seemed to her that he should have come to terms with his past by now. It seemed self-pitying. And that did not fit the Harry she knew. More and more often in the last week, she was confronted with evidence that she did not know Harry Braxton. Not at all. She did not know what he wanted, what motivated him, his desires or goals. The idea unnerved her, hurt her with a sense of betrayal.

Yes, she thought studying him despairingly, this was not the Harry she knew. His breath was ragged and his complexion pale. His recitation had cost him much in the way of self-composure. She scowled.

"As I said," he went on, "Oxford was not easy for me—"

"You know, Harry," she cut in gruffly, unwilling to let him reveal more self-pity, unwilling to relinquish the idea of him she'd held for so long, that he was cavalier and unrepentant and self-reliant, "Blake has not had an easy time of it, either. Your difficulties, though dissimilar in nature, ought to create empathy between you two, draw you together, not distance you."

"Blake? What difficulties? Is Darkmoor's pasture being defaced by a flock of sheep?" he asked bitterly.

"Don't be horrid. You might attempt to see that others have grievances just as important to them as yours are to you." He looked as if she'd struck him. Instantly she was contrite. This was Harry. If nothing else he was her friend. For the longest time she'd assumed he had no pain, no private sorrows. Whether she considered them worthy or not was not at issue.

"Forgive me for my pettiness and my self-indulgence," he said stiffly. "Pray tell me what Blake suffers?"

It was all going wrong. He'd kept so much back from her over the long, intimate years of their association: Eton, Oxford, his family, this contest between him and Blake. She worried her lower lip, considering how to answer.

If she could effect a reconciliation between Harry and Blake, might not a slight betrayal of confidence be worth the price? "Blake's mother . . . she is not . . . she is not a very nice woman."

"Blake's mother is a tart," Harry said flatly. "What of it?"

She was stunned by his insensitivity. "Harry! How can you be so heartless? Imagine what that would do to a little boy . . . the confusion, the disappointment! And Harry"—she moved toward him, took his hand, and pressed it between hers imploringly—"the one woman he loved, Miss Lenore DuChamp, she, too . . . that is, I suspect she was not faithful."

"Not faithful?" His grip tightened around her hand and he tugged her close, searching her face as if Lenore DuChamp's perfidy was of great importance to him.

She went willingly, until she stood as near him without touching as possible. She angled her neck to meet his aqua gaze, placing her free hand against his chest. It was like laying her hand on sun-heated stone. "Yes."

"Are those Blake's words or yours?" he demanded urgently.

"Mine. He said that he'd found her in a highly suspicious situation . . . with another man."

A wide grin broke out across Harry's lean face. For the first time since she'd entered the room, he relaxed and looked amused. Once more he was the master of the situation and himself. The old Harry. The Harry she knew.

Or thought she knew.

"So there was more to the story than Blake told me," he murmured.

"It's not funny."

"Found her in bed with another man, did he?" Unholy glee sparkled in his amazing eyes. "Now that *would* put one off one's feed."

"No!" she refuted. "I mean, I am sure I don't know and I *certainly* didn't ask."

"Too bad."

"Harry." She smoothed the linen covering his chest beseechingly. He stared down at her fingers, tan against the pristine white. "Harry, be nice."

"I'm trying. God knows, I'm trying."

She was lost in the sudden starkness of his gaze, the paleness of his face, the bruised flesh that looked fragile, vulnerable. It was a mask. Harry was the least vulnerable man she knew. Idly he rubbed her wrist with the pad of his thumb, a gentle hypnotic motion that sent shivers up her arm. Too many shivers. She pulled away.

"Harry," she tried again. "Can't you see how trying it has been for him."

"What? For whom?" he asked in a distracted voice, his gaze traveling over her features.

"Blake. All the women he has ever been close to have disappointed him, let him down. His mother is running his estate into the ground, besmirching the family name."

He shook his head, as if clearing his thoughts, or denying something. "Oh, it's not as bad as all that. More a spot here and there than a regular besmirch."

"How *can* you be so unkind? Blake *cares* about Darkmoor Manor. He *loved* Lenore DuChamp. He wanted to love his mother. How can you mock his pain? How can you not pity him?" she demanded.

"His pain." His manner went flat, his voice lost all inflection.

"Yes!"

He swung away from her, a single liquid motion that denied the battered appearance of his face or the wounds she knew had yet to heal beneath his clean white shirt.

"Harry?"

He pivoted slowly. A sharp smile cleaved his face. The smile of a devil, or a man bedeviled. "*His* pain? Let me tell you three things about old Blake, Diz, my love. He didn't have perfect parents, he won't inherit a debt-free legacy, and most important, he's never forgotten either circumstance."

"A sensitive child—"

"*Any* child. A thousand children. A million children have had harder lives than Blake. He has health, position, money, respect. Others have had no parents, no food, no bloody home to obsess about. Look outside, Dizzy." He thrust his arm out, jabbing his finger toward the window. "Do you think there is any street brat out there who would not trade his life for Blake's 'pitiable' one?"

He lifted his hands toward her and then abruptly

changed his mind, the gesture becoming one of contempt and dismissal. Involuntarily she flinched. He swore.

"No," he went on, "his mother isn't going to win any maternal awards, and his beloved Lenore is human and his house has a draft. So what?" He spoke hotly, so hotly in fact that it left no doubt in her mind that whatever lay between Blake and Harry was passionate and primal and, more, had not begun with whatever had happened at Eton and Oxford but merely surfaced there.

"Ever since Blake was a boy," Harry went on, "he has acted as if the world owed him an explanation for why his life wasn't perfect. *Perfect.*" He spat the word and flattened his palm against the wall, staring outside into the fading afternoon light. "Well, if anyone deserves an explanation, it isn't Blake. And if he should get to spend his life standing in line waiting for an answer, I bloody well better get the place ahead of him." He turned his head, but not before she saw his hurt and bewilderment. "I want answers, too. There are things that I should—" He broke off, but just for a second as if his anger was too great to contain. "Why isn't Blake's mother more virtuous? *Why the hell can't I—*" He stopped.

She stared back at him, her eyes widening in recognition. She'd glimpsed the other side of Harry's facile, glib facade. Injury. Hurt. Deeper and more painful than anything she'd ever sensed before. She'd been wrong. There was no self-pity here, only an old burgeoning hopelessness.

"Harry, what is it?" She seized his arm. He trembled.

"Desdemona?" Blake called from the hall.

She barely heard him. "Harry, what were you about to say?"

He shook his head, the movement sharp with self-contempt, and stared at her from across too far a distance. In his countenance she read an anguish and pride she'd never descried before.

"Please," he said softly, "do me the kindness of leaving. Before Blake comes in."

Before she could act, he walked out into the dying light of the courtyard. He closed the doors behind him.

CHAPTER TWENTY-FOUR

Through the span of each day, each meter of the night,
  that I have wasted, alone
In darkness I have lain awake
Filling the hours with the sound of your voice,
  the image of your body, until desire lives within me.

Harry studied the mirror's fragile inscriptions, a too-true reflection of his heart if not his visage. He laid it on the desk and cocked his head attentively, listening for their return.

For three hours he'd paced the library, prowled the hallways, and stared out of the front windows onto empty streets. He'd growled when poor Duraid had brought dinner and barked so at Magi that she'd fled in a flurry of indignation.

For the hundredth time he asked himself how he could have been such a self-pitying ass. Clearly, she'd been repelled by his narcissism, disgusted by what little history he had related.

The truth, Magi had advised. Well, it hadn't taken much truth to repel Dizzy. He'd meant to explain and only succeeded in sounding like a mewling brat whining that his wounds were more pitiable than another's—in this case, Blake's.

Dammit, she couldn't possibly have fallen in love with his cousin. Regardless of how hard she tried not to, she had to see beyond the romantic aura she'd spun around Blake.

It was not that Blake was evil. Harry wasn't altogether sure evil wouldn't have been preferable. At least evil had the recommendation of being self-generated. No, instead, Blake was a *gentleman*. Dizzy would die if she wed him, her spirit bludgeoned to death by his stolid morality, his rote nobility, his quaking superiority.

He heard something outside. Moving quickly, he exited the library and strode down the hall to where Magi stood like a statue before the open front door. He looked out. At the bottom of the steps stood half a dozen men, their upper bodies consumed by the enormous bouquets of red roses they carried. They looked like ambulating shrubs with their spindly legs poking out from beneath the greenery. Harry's lips twitched.

Magi's mouth gaped.

"What the devil is this?" Harry asked, his amusement vanishing with dawning suspicion.

A ratty-looking turban struggled free of a floral embrace and an old, seamed face regarded him dolefully. "Is this the house of *Sitt* Carlisle?"

"Yes," Magi answered.

"Then these are for her. They are from Lord Ravenscroft."

Of course.

Somehow disengaging one arm from his burden, the old man waved the other five shrubs forward. "You tell us where to put these, you," he commanded, staring disapprovingly at Magi's unveiled face.

Magi glanced about the crowded hallway. *"Fut! Ilhak'ni min karib,"* she commanded them to follow her, leading the way down the narrow corridor.

The men stumbled up the stairs and down the hall, disappearing into the library. Harry trailed after, catching up in time to hear Magi say, "Put them out there. In the garden where they will not clutter up the place. There. Now be gone."

The turbaned men eyed her sourly, their disapproval of her European manner and dress not noticeably sweetened by the coins she tossed their leader.

Harry lifted a brow at her as soon as the last had left.

"Ignorant men. I thank God that I am an enlightened woman and that I live in enlightened times." She heaved an exasperated sigh and looked about, shaking her head. "There must be over two hundred roses out there. Such extravagance."

He didn't answer. He could only gaze helplessly at the bounty of fragrant crimson blooms now destined to share his vigil.

How ever could he hope to compete with such a spectacular cliché?

* * *

Marta stepped out of the rented carriage, one eye on the Carlisle house where Harry was recuperating. She rummaged distractedly through her reticule for the fare.

"Allow me, ma'am." She looked up, startled to discover Cal Schmidt pressing money into the driver's open palm.

Her brow knitted with consternation before smoothing self-consciously. A woman could get wrinkles frowning like that. "Mr. Schmidt. How kind."

She was not entirely pleased at Cal's appearance. She'd planned so well, and her plans did not include him. Desdemona, she'd ascertained, would be gone for the entire evening with Lord Ravenscroft. It had seemed the perfect opportunity to finish the . . . conversation she and Harry had begun several days ago. Before he'd lit off after Desdemona.

She couldn't contrive a seduction with Cal in attendance. She gave an inward sigh. She supposed she'd just have to get rid of her ardent admirer. If possible, without hurting his feelings. He was a very nice man.

She started down the street. Cal fell into pace beside her, allowing her silence.

Odd. *Nice* men had never particularly appealed to her before.

"You're visiting your friend Mr. Braxton?" he asked.

"Ah? Yes. I'm visiting Harry."

"Heard he had a nasty encounter a few days back. I hope he's all right?"

"Harry? Oh, Harry has more lives than a cat."

"Does he?" Cal secured her hand and tucked it into the crook of his arm. "Still, I bet the poor guy is asleep. Fellow needs rest to heal. It's a mite late for someone so recently busted up to be awake. Fellow on the mend needs an awful lot of sleep. I bet it hurts him just to sit upright."

"Perhaps." That thought hadn't occurred to her. There *was* a good chance Harry was sleeping. Even if he wasn't, how much seduction can one accomplish on a . . . a busted-up man? And, too, if Harry was asleep, she'd be left facing the blankly condemning stare of the Carlisles' housekeeper, Magi. Not an engaging prospect.

"I'd bet a hundred bucks."

"Oh," she said, turning to smile up at Cal's angular, ruddy face. "And are you a betting man, Mr. Schmidt."

"*Mister* Schmidt?" His fine gray eyes widened with amusement. Even though she was aware, too late, that such formality with this man whom she had allowed certain pleasurable liberties was disingenuous, there was nothing cynical in his expression, just honest humor.

"Why, yes, Mrs. Douglass, I am. And yourself?"

"Oh, I've been known to make the occasional wager."

He stopped, pulling her to a halt by his side. "I have an idea."

An idea. She kept the smile on her face even

though inwardly a shard of disappointment pierced what had been evolving into pleasure. It was time for Cal to suggest they retire to his hotel.

He took both her hands in his large paws and danced them up and down. "I have heard of a new establishment opening down by the river. Farley's. It's a gaming house. Very reputable," he hurriedly assured her as she stared at him in open wonder. He was actually concerned about her reputation.

"Yes?"

"Well, ma'am, I would be honored if you'd come with me. You speak French so well and I've found that there's more Frenchies in these gaming places than Brits and certainly more than Yanks. I feel quite outnumbered."

"Oh. I'm sure you could hold your own."

"Maybe." He grinned. "But then I wouldn't want to if I could be with you. Please, won't you come?"

She glanced at the Carlisle house. It did look dark.

"It'll be fun," he said.

"Only if we win."

"If you come with me, Marta," he said quietly, "I already have."

It wasn't the subtlest compliment she'd ever received, but it may have been the most delightful. She smiled and accepted his invitation.

"You're as lovely as you are sweet," Blake said at the front door to the house.

"What?" Desdemona forced herself to concentrate on Blake. All evening, her thoughts had returned to Harry: Harry's secrets, Harry's anger, Harry's rift with Blake. She needed to discover the source of the pain she'd seen reflected so clearly in his face, to discover where envy had led Harry—if envy it was. But how else could she construe his earlier anger and the words *"I deserve"*?

Blake angled closer. His hand dropped lightly on her shoulder and his breath tickled her ear, recalling another's warm breath—

Harry's lips near her shoulder, his breath in her ear—

"What are you dreaming about, my dear?" he murmured.

I have loved you through each long season—

"Nothing." Whatever Harry was or was not, right now she was with Blake.

He smiled and reached past her, tapping lightly on the door. "England? I, too, whenever I hear Haydn's music, am filled with longing for our home. Or were you dreaming about something, or someone, else—"

The door swung open and Magi squinted down at them. She pulled her dressing gown closer. "Oh. It is you. Quite late."

Blake smiled indulgently. "Ah, the inestimable Magi. Good evening to you. May I ask if my offering arrived?"

"Offering? Go to church if you would make an offering."

Drat Magi, anyway. Her accent was pronounced, her syntax a caricature, and her expression petulant. Magi did not appreciate being woken from a sound sleep.

Blake laughed good-naturedly. "Well, then, did my gift for Miss Desdemona arrive?"

"Yes."

Blake turned to her. "Would you mind, my dear, if I am here to see you receive my present? Call it a vanity on my part, but I would like to watch your expressive little face when you discover them."

"You cannot come in," Magi declared. "It is most unseemly. Much too late. Very bad *ton*."

Blake craned his neck, peering down the hall, ignoring Magi's edict. "Where have you put them?"

"Them?" Desdemona asked.

"In the garden. Another reason you cannot come in. Master Harry—poor, dear, suffering Master Harry—he needs his rest. You remember Master Harry?" She glared at Desdemona.

As if she *could* forget him. Thoughts of Harry crowded her mind with confusion. Last week she would have said she'd known Harry like the back of her hand, but it wasn't last week. During the past seven short days their relationship had changed. The realization frightened her. If what they'd once had was forever gone, what, if anything, would replace it?

She shivered. She did not want to be alone. She'd had enough alone to last two lifetimes. She looked at Blake.

"You cannot disturb him by going through the library," Magi was saying to him. "And that is the only way into the garden."

"We could go around the outside of the house," Desdemona suggested, unwilling to follow her previous thoughts, needing to flee the specter of abandonment.

"But of course." The smile Blake cast at Magi was a shade victorious. "If you'll excuse us, Magi?"

Magi's mouth twined. "Fine. But you do not hurt my Desdemona's reputation by coming in. You stay in the garden. Now, I go to bed." Without another word, she closed the door in their faces.

"Magi is very protective," Desdemona offered as Blake took her arm and led her down the stairs and around the back of the tiny house.

"And I applaud her vigilance. She has a precious treasure to guard." He waited patiently at the high stone wall as Desdemona unlocked the wooden door set in a low arch. Then he stepped aside, bidding her enter before him.

Immediately inside the gate, the aroma of roses assailed her nostrils, cloying and sweet and heavy. She squinted, her vision slowly adjusting to the glow cast by the single lantern that Duraid lit nightly. She glanced at the library door, a small unexamined hope dying when she saw that though open, the interior was black. Harry must be asleep.

She shouldn't be thinking of Harry anyway. She should be concentrating on Blake.

She looked about. Everywhere were roses, their deep color uncertain in the faint light. Red, she supposed. They covered the wrought-iron table and stood in vases on the paving stones, they crowded the seats of stone bench and twin chairs and marched along the bottom of the garden walls.

"Oh, my." She'd never seen such abundance, so many roses crowded into so small a place.

"I hope you like them."

"They're impressive. Extremely." And tragic, she thought. For having been cut, they were dying. Already the blooms dipped on their stalks and the first fallen petals sprinkled the pale pavers beneath like dark drops of floral blood.

"They do not begin to rival the beauty of the one near me. She is a single perfect rose blossom: sweet, pretty, pure."

—My hot, harrowing desert and my cool, verdant Nile, infinitely lovely and unfathomable and sustaining.

She chased his words from her mind. "Lord Ravenscroft—"

"Blake."

"Blake, I am not perfect."

"I think I, who have had some experience with women, am a better judge than you. But then, that's only part of your charm. You don't even realize your own worth. It's delightful." He moved closer, capturing her in his arms, his head bending near. "It is provocative."

She closed her eyes. *This* is what she had always dreamed of. All of the wonderful, romantic, exciting sensations depicted in her beloved books were about to come true. A dark and noble aristocrat, smitten with her beauty, was unable to keep himself from kissing her. Unlike Harry, who'd easily managed to resist her. She tilted her head invitingly.

"Oh, my dear," he breathed.

She was crushed in the viscount's strong embrace, and

then her tender lips were bruised by his passionate kiss. She couldn't breathe. His embrace tightened and she was suddenly hefted into his arms and moored against the bastion of his mighty torso. Her dangling feet collided with something hard and the sound of a crashing pottery vase filled her ears.

She frowned into his kiss. That wasn't right. She should only be able to hear her racing pulse. She wrapped her arms tighter around his neck.

His broad hands cupped her delicate skull, holding her head still for the forcefulness of his ravenous mouth. Suddenly he tore his lips free from hers and set her aside. She stumbled back, upsetting yet another pair of vases as she struggled to regain her footing in the closed quarters and knocked into—

Blast the stupid flowers anyway! They were ruining her story. She reached her hands out toward Blake, determined to give it another go, but he backed away.

His mighty limbs trembled violently, his eyes darkened with ardor. "You make me forget myself."

"I'm sorry."

He stood silently, attempting to regain mastery of his tumultuous emotions. Ladylike, even now, she folded her hands in front of her, twining her long, delicate fingers anxiously, uncertain what to do, what to say.

"God help me, I can stay no longer," he mumbled.

He *mumbled?*

"I understand."

"Do you?" he demanded. "I doubt it. I have to go. Now. Before I forget myself." He did not look again in her

direction. Instead, he strode past her, his noble head high, his fists clenched at his sides.

And collided with no less than three more vases on his way out.

She blinked at the horizontal roses and the broken crockery and the puddles of water winking in the guttering light. In her mind's eye she saw instead a hazy, darkened alley, smelled tobacco and bay rum, felt Harry's lips—

She shook her head. She had just lived out the most romantic aspect of her most romantic dream. She had just been kissed by raven-haired, ebon-eyed, stern-faced Blake, and all she could think about was plain brown Harry. Harry whom she didn't know anymore.

She pursed her lips together. If she just thought about it long enough, that kiss could become everything she'd envisioned. Maybe Blake's arms should have "enveloped" instead of "crushed" and if his lips had "conquered" rather than "bruised"— She felt along her lower lip with the tip of her tongue, uncertain whether she tasted blood.

"My," a soft, masculine voice said, "that certainly looked painful."

CHAPTER TWENTY-FIVE

"No wonder Lenore looked elsewhere for her lovemaking," Harry mused. "Apparently the poor girl wasn't up to the task of dealing with all that manly exuberance."

Desdemona pitched around, searching for him. There, a dark form leaning negligently against the door jamb leading into the library, his arms folded across his chest.

"You were spying on me!" she accused hotly, her cheeks burning with indignation.

"No," he corrected in the same thoughtful voice, "I was simply a captive audience to a scene enacted outside of my bedchamber. An unwilling captive, I assure you, but what with all that panting and groaning going on, it was hard to sleep."

"We were not panting and groaning!" she denied. At least *she* had not been panting and groaning, she amended silently. "And that's no excuse. A gentleman would have made his presence known immediately."

He detached himself from the shadows, coming more fully into the dim light. The soft glow of the lantern picked out a hardness in his eyes that was at variance with his casual tone. "Ah," he said in mock sorrow, "but that's been the problem all along, hasn't it? I'm not a gentleman."

"No. You're not."

"But then, old Blake has hardly conducted himself like one either, or even a gentle man, for that matter. What a heavy-handed ox." There was a flash of real anger in his voice as he drew nearer. He was still fully clad, only his open shirt attesting to the fact that he'd been preparing to sleep. She could see the white linen bandage she'd wrapped around his ribs, a stark demarcation against his lean brown flanks.

He came close and reached up, gently brushing his thumb across her swollen lower lip. "Did he hurt you?"

"No," she said sullenly. Bruised a bit, disappointed certainly, but not hurt. You had to love someone in order for him to hurt you. She simply did not love Blake. As much as she'd wanted to.

"You know, Desdemona, it isn't supposed to hurt." His thumb still tendered her lip, back and forth, a touch so gentle it might have been imagination, soothing and conversely tantalizing. She jerked her head away. He followed the movement, stepping closer still. The air between them thickened with something electric and elemental and irresistible. "It is supposed to be . . . wondrous."

"A kiss? Wondrous?" She scoffed, disillusioned by the night, fearful of the morrow.

"Yes." His fingers skated away from her mouth, found the angle of her jaw, and moved with breath stealing grace over her cheeks, her temples. He raised his other hand and held her face still with the smallest possible pressure between his large, strong palms. He found the spot at the base of her neck and kneaded it gently, deeply with the tips of his fingers. "Wondrous."

He captured her gaze with his. She couldn't look away, could not read anything but what looked like alarm in his night-darkened eyes. She could hear him swallow, feel one hand shiver over her temple. Slowly, incrementally he dipped his head toward hers. His mouth, his beautiful, ravishing mouth, relaxed. His lips opened and his breath fanned her face for a long heartbeat.

He kissed her.

It was unexpectedly sweet, debilitatingly tender. My lord, she thought dizzily, his lips are just as exquisitely sensitive as they looked. And then conscious thought disappeared and the pure pleasure of sensation took precedence.

He angled his mouth over hers, grazing and polishing her lips with the petal softness of his own, erasing the memory of Blake's harshness with a soothing touch that did nothing to calm or soothe. Because somehow, with those feathering touches, he distilled gentleness into white-hot desire, a desire that had waited five years for a voice.

Blake could never awaken her body this way simply because he didn't have her heart. And Harry did. He always had. She recognized the truth with poignant sadness and overwhelming urgency.

Her own kiss grew imperative with the fear that he would stop, and yet he answered her yearning with such deliberate, such exquisite control that she almost mistook it for insouciance, the expert's patience with a novice.

Almost.

But his long body quaked and his breath sang unevenly in her ear and there was nothing casual in the stark beauty of his gaze or the intensity of his expression.

He wanted her. And "want" was more than he'd ever offered before.

She twined her arms around his neck, drawing herself up against him. His arms flowed about her, she could feel his forearms harden as he leaned over her, his mouth awakening to exigency by her response. She pulled her breasts full against his naked chest, gasping with the shivering pleasure of that contact. Warm, smooth, clean. Such a fine texture against her own heated skin. He heard her.

Without hesitation, he scooped her up and carried her through the library door to his cot. He lowered her slowly, sliding her deliberately down the length of his body, his lips roving her face, his tongue gently stroking her wounded lower lip. And when he finally eased her onto the bed, still she could not release him, agitated by the thought he might leave her now, here, like this, with every sense abraded by

anticipation and every inch of her body charged
with expectancy.

He had no intention of leaving her.

He'd been urged to the truth. This was his truth.
He loved her.

He thought for a second to tell her that other
truth, but it was a dim, shadowy thing, of no import
now, here. Always before he had come to the act of
lovemaking with a sense of gratitude, a feeling that
he was the recipient of a largesse for which he was
more than willing to demonstrate his appreciation.

This was not a gift. It was a prize. He did not offer
his body for her pleasure, but thought in giving her
pleasure to find his own, and more, in the physical
act secure the talisman of her heart. Her love.

In a life rampant with unanswered petitions, he
had never desired anything more. Exigency made
him clumsy. His limbs, unlike the liquid grace with
which hers enveloped him, were rigid, suffused
with passion, his motion cramped and stilted.

Experienced in the act of passion, he'd thought to
tutor her. But this was unlike anything he'd known
before. It stunned him. The flagrant disparity of
what he had done with other women and this, here,
now, made mockery of his "experience."

He'd known. With that first kiss he'd known
where it must end, had told himself that he would
go to any lengths, do anything, to bind her to him.
Though jealousy and fear had led him here, he
hadn't anticipated the journey.

Her hands slipped beneath his shirt, peeled away
the linen bandage that kept his skin from her explo-

ration, followed the line of muscle over his shoulders. He closed his eyes, drinking in the sensation.

"I want to touch you."

"Touch me," he breathed, desire robbing him of sensate thought, mindlessly mouthing the words she gave him.

She clutched a handful of shirt and he shrugged out of it, jerking his arms free of the sleeve and pitching it away. Her eyes, made subtle by the incandescence of the single gas jet outside, dilated.

"*Houri,*" he murmured, taking her hand and pressing a kiss into her warm, soft palm. He flicked his tongue across her delicate wrist. She was so small, so perfect. "Pleasure's dark-eyed handmaiden, sandalwood and ambergris. Always love."

She shuddered and pulled free of his light clasp, stroking his throat, his chest with deep, languid touches that fulfilled whatever need drove her.

"You are so beautiful," she said.

"Sweet Allah," he breathed, holding himself still, transfixed by the need to touch and be touched.

"Lovely." She touched his lips, teased them open and ran her fingertip lightly along the seam. Her own lips parted and her breathing deepened. "Your mouth. I want—"

He groaned, sucking her fingertip into his mouth. Her eyes fluttered shut and she gasped. He knew full well what she wanted with his mouth. Her words were clarion, even in memory.

"Let me make love to you," he whispered.

"Make love with me," she offered in a husky, sherbety voice, arching up with the voluptuous exquisiteness of desire as her hands stroked down over his back to his buttocks, she pulled him tightly against her.

"More," she half pleaded, half demanded. He combed the satin curtain of golden hair away from her flushed and yearning face before untying the silk ribbon at her shoulder. He pushed the shimmering cloth down around her slim waist, exposing her breasts. Golden pale, crested with coral, he watched, fascinated by the nearly imperceptible jounce of their ripeness as she rose on her elbows.

"Touch me," she said, and he could feel her words whisper over his chest. He shuddered and reverently skimmed the outside arc of one sweet breast, cupping it in his palm. He lowered his lips to traverse the vale between, stroking the tip of his tongue to one puckering nipple before taking it into his mouth.

She gasped, flexing into the pull of his suckling, offering more, her hands raking his hair and holding his head to her body. So soft, so small, so strong . . .

"Oh, my." Her breath hitched with each pull of his mouth, and she arched in little counterjerks, stunned sounds of arousal purring from her throat. He'd pleasured her. And God, dear God, there was so much more.

He abandoned her breast and with awkward haste worked open the ties and buttons and myriad other fasteners keeping her entire body from him. She moved, unconscious, searching movements, battering his overtired body with stimulation, making him clumsy. Finally the gown fell apart, the skirt loosened. With one hand, he stripped her of the offending garment, the other stroking the elegant curves and flowing line of waist and hip and thigh and knee and calf . . .

No sooner had he bared her luscious little body than he felt her hands fumbling at his trousers, tugging at the fastening. Her thigh pressed between his legs, hard against his erection, driving him past what little reason was left.

He closed his eyes, clenching his jaw as she worked at her task, and then he felt himself spring free of the confining trousers and she was pushing them below his hips. He rolled over, yanked them off, and waited, his breath stopped, his heart hammering dully in his chest and thundering in his ears.

She was a virgin. If she hesitated, he'd not raise one hand to stop her, say not a word to convince her. He could entice only so much from her; the rest she had to give.

Desdemona opened her eyes when she felt the air move between their bodies, chill where there had been warmth. Her complaint died on her lips.

He was perfect.

Lying quiescent on his back, his jaw set with some inner struggle, his beautiful, sensual mouth a firm seal, each line of his body was tensile and graceful, lithe and supple. Each muscle, from the hard planes of his chest to the thick cords of his thighs, flowed one from the other, sinew and heat. And that part that Magi had gone to pains to describe, that seemed all of a part in keeping with the rest, potent and proud and male. She propped herself on one elbow, hovering above him, her long hair swinging against him. The muscles flinched in his hard, flat belly.

She rubbed her knuckles shyly across the silky brown hairs that grew thicker low on his stomach. Tentatively she curled her fingers around his rigid member. A sharp hiss brought her gaze flying. His eyes were open, banked between a thick hedge of short dark lashes, intent and watchful, guarded and yearning.

Instinct had led her here, instinct and desire and five years of wanting this one man, loving this one man. But now, with his long body trembling in an awful parody of repose, she was confounded by her stupidity. She felt the first flush of shame. What could she give Harry, who knew lovemaking as an art? She was abysmally inept. She did not know what it was he waited for, and wait he obviously did, for something from which her monumental naïveté exempted her.

"I don't know what to do."

Her confession caught him off guard. He stared at her, his chest heaving like a bellows, his gaze flashing with his own confusion.

"I don't know," she insisted in a hushed voice. "Tell me. Just . . . Only teach me. I want this to be . . . *wondrous.*"

His self-restraint vanished. He captured her face between his trembling hands and rolled her onto her back, bracing himself above her on his forearms, bracketing her body. The heat and hardness of his silky arousal lay between them.

"Want me."

"I do. But what can I—"

"For the love of Allah, just want me, Dizzy. As I want you."

"Yes."

Then he was kissing her again . . . sweet, wild, wet kisses. A flavor of urgency replaced the sense of discovery, of moving toward a culmination, an end to this torturous stimulation. She could not even tell whose crisis she anticipated, his or her own. All she knew was that an ache had begun in her breasts and thighs and down between her legs and each press of his hips made her ache more acutely until finally she sought that press of his body there, low, against her. It was the only thing that offered more pleasure than frustration. She instinctively moved in an ill-timed counter to his hips' rocking cadence.

He rose above her, his head thrown back, neck arched, magnificent lips parting in a grimace of endurance. His hair clung damply to his temples. His chest gleamed in the half-light, sheathed in glistening moisture. Powerful emotion coiled in the banked gaze he lowered to her, and then his hand was between them, deliberately stroking the curl-covered mound between her thighs, petting her, building the fire, slipping between slick folds, rubbing against—

She gasped and arched, her eyes flying wide, clenching his shoulders, looking for an anchor. He smiled—sweet violence, pure triumph—and he replaced his hand with another, harder presence. Then he was pushing *into* her, his gaze tangled in hers, his jaw tight, his nostrils flaring with each breath he dragged through them.

She lifted her hips and there—oh, there—a pressure, not quite pain, not sharp, but a stretching, a deep final ache and—and the promise of ecstasy. She seized upon the rhythm, pitched her hips to meet his thrust, winning a growl of rapture from him. He moved with her, pushing her, filling her.

He tried to slow down, to give her time to accustom herself to the feel of him inside of her. *Inside of her.* The thought banished good intentions. Her body communicated with terrible clarity her urgent striving. He could feel her closing tightly around him, hear her gasping for air, see the feverish focus of her body in the glazed blindness of her half-closed eyes.

She clung to him with her knees, riding his passion, and he was lost. His head fell into the lee of her throat where he felt the dampness of her breasts, tasted the salty musk of her arousal. He urged her along the spiraling dance of repletion, where sensation and need now drove him. And yet . . . and yet even now, a deep indefatigable part of his soul recognized the unique form, the grace and strength of the woman he held. Dizzy.

All of his desires pinnacled on this moment, everything he'd been or achieved or strove for culminated here, now. It was too much. Not enough. He incited her with tongue and touch, bequeathing a small part of his own passion. His control was slipping. He'd never lost control before. He ground his teeth together, struggling to give her what she sought before his own passion catapulted him to completion.

Somehow it was enough.

She cried out once, every lithe and gorgeous line shivering with rapture. With the sound of her climax, he gave himself over to his own.

CHAPTER TWENTY-SIX

"Dizzy," Harry whispered. "Are you awake?"

"Hmm."

"Go back to sleep." There was a smile in his voice and she nodded drowsily, nuzzling her cheek into the pillow. As if from a great distance, she heard him moving away.

Slowly her eyes drifted open and then widened. Harry, his back to her, naked as a Greek god, retrieved his trousers from the floor. He didn't know she was awake and she took the opportunity to watch him, unobserved. He pulled on his trousers. Such a simple act and yet one she could watch for hours, years. He was so very handsome, so very casual about his masculinity.

If questions had arisen in the last few days, some answers had come to light, too. In his past Harry hadn't been valued much. It had only enhanced his magnetism. For never having been taught his own beauty, he'd reached adulthood without self-consciousness or vanity, and so there was nothing measured or sentient in his grace. Only a lithe athleticism that riveted the eye.

Pale in the predawn light, his skin was clean and fine-grained. Her hands and limbs and lips still felt his smooth, warm texture. Exquisite. Shattering. Impossible to define what they'd shared. She closed her eyes, adrift in sensual memory and exquisite lethargy.

"I'm going to make us breakfast," Harry's voice drifted softly into her ear and then her lips were brushed by velvety warmth. It was a quick kiss but one that effectively demolished her languor. She rolled over, opened her eyes, and stretched her arms out just as he disappeared into the hall. The door closed with a quiet click.

Wide awake now, she blew a noisy sound of disappointment and swung her feet to the ground, twining the linen sheet around her body. For a second she debated whether to join him in the kitchen, but decided against it. She needed a few minutes without the distraction of his touch, his voice, his lips in which to think. There hadn't been any thinking going on for the last six hours.

Overnight their relationship, already ill-defined and unrecognizable, had metamorphosed yet again into something unutterably sweet and tender and violent and passionate, and nothing like the lofty spiritual merging her books had outlined.

Desdemona rose and wandered to the window. Faint saffron and rose lights seeped from the dark horizon, staining the morning sky. She turned from the vista, smiling as she saw Harry's few possessions littering the library desk. Inexplicably uneasy, needing something of his to touch, she straightened his ivory-backed bristle brush and tortoise-shell comb, deposited his gold collar stays in their enameled box. Her hand drifted tenderly over these few, so personal effects passing over each to an unfolded packet of papers on the corner of the desk. Harry's name caught her eye.

Curious, she opened the sheets and began reading the top paper. Her face grew still. It was a will naming Harry the heir to Darkmoor Manor.

A tremulous sensation began in her stomach and raced along her nerves, anxiety slowly replacing contentment, emptiness threatening her former feeling of repletion. Like a poisonous black flower, suspicion unfolded in her imagination, a dozen images and thoughts spurring on its ugly blooming.

The intense sense of contention she'd noticed immediately between Blake and Harry. The open rivalry with decades-long roots. The sincere concern in Blake's voice when he'd assured her Harry was not the man she thought. Harry's expulsion from Oxford. Blake swearing he would get his birthright back. Blake's telling Harry he couldn't go back to England because he would have to face the "reminders" of what Harry couldn't possibly have, and then Harry, his eyes brilliant with mockery, asking Blake if he meant Darkmoor.

She fell forward, her mouth opening to gulp the air that seemed to thicken in her throat. It couldn't be the way it looked. Harry could not have somehow orchestrated Blake's disinheritance. But, God help her, what else could it be? From the onset it had been clear Blake had not come to Egypt to recover from a broken heart, that his presence here had something to do with Harry.

Her hand crumpled the will. Another secret. Another lie. Some answers. Horrible answers.

She heard Harry a second before he backed into the room, carrying a wooden server stacked with cups and teapot and a basket of sweetbreads. He turned and spied her, grinning boyishly as he set the platter down on the floor. Her heart felt painful in her chest. Leaden and twisted.

"You're awake," he said, his voice filled with delight. He came to her, combing his hair back in a gesture appealingly boyish and self-conscious.

She thought of closing her eyes against the sight of his handsome face, his winsome smile, but couldn't. He looked so damn happy.

"Dizzy—"

"I have to go." She swallowed and gathered the linen sheet around her body, clutching the cotton over her breasts.

His brow furrowed in perplexity but still he smiled. "First—"

He leaned forward and kissed her. She could not help herself, she moved to meet his mouth. Passion, so lately satisfied, leapt to life with that brief contact. Shaken, she pulled away. He cupped her face between his palms.

"Dizzy. I love you."

He looked so sincere, with his wise, tender eyes

and crooked smile. She had never dreamed that pain could feast on pleasure. But it could. She'd waited five years to hear those words. She had never imagined they could hurt so much.

"Oh, Harry," she whispered, tears springing to her eyes, "I wish I could believe you."

"What do you mean?" He tried to keep his voice calm but he had told her the simple truth, words he'd never spoken to another woman, and all he heard in response was doubt. Doubt. The hallmark of his life.

"You can't hope to compete, Harry."

"You won't be able to make it through Oxford, son."

"Why waste your money on paying the curate to read you all these books?"

She was supposed to say "I love you, too, Harry." Fear burgeoned within him at her expression of resigned desolation.

"Harry," she said, "I have loved you for five years—"

He surged forward to take her in his arms. She put her hand up, stopping him with her palm flat against his chest.

"No. Listen. Please! I threw myself at you. You laughed—"

"That was three years ago."

She shook her head. "That doesn't matter now."

"I beg to differ," he said tightly. Only a supreme act of self-restraint kept him from shaking her. "I was not in the habit of stealing babies from cradles."

"I was seventeen."

"I don't give a bloody damn if you were thirty.

There's a difference between chronology and experience."

Once more she shook her head in that bewilderingly mature way. She would not be goaded, he realized, not be convinced. She would only come to her own conclusion. The thought appalled him, scared the hell out of him.

"You haven't ever, not by word or deed, demonstrated that your feelings for me are that of a . . . a lover."

That was what this was all about . . . *romance*? He raked his hand through his hair. "What did you want?" he asked fiercely. "Five hundred fucking roses?"

She paled and he cursed himself, his fists balling at his side.

"That's it, isn't it?" she whispered.

"What's it?" he demanded.

"The roses. Blake. Five years and you have never acted on your feelings for me before."

"No," he said hotly. "That's *not* it. I didn't say anything, I didn't tell you, because I didn't think there could be any future for us. My loving you didn't matter, it didn't change anything. I couldn't give you what you wanted. I couldn't take you back to England. I couldn't go back there."

"Why?"

"Because I can't read."

She froze, her eyes searching his face, her expression confused, wary. "I don't understand."

"That's why I left England. That's why I won't go back. I got kicked out of Oxford, Dizzy. I couldn't complete the written exam. Hell"—he didn't recognize the bitter laugh as his own, it was so acid bright—"I couldn't *start* the written exam."

"What happened to you?"

He closed his eyes. She still didn't comprehend. She thought some accident, some illness, had robbed him of a facility he'd once owned. "Nothing. Nothing happened," he murmured tiredly. "I've never been able to read or write."

"But I've seen you," she protested.

"Simple, familiar phrases. Some word."

A deep line scored the smooth place between her brows. "You went to Eton."

"For two years. They stopped trying after that and sent me home."

"I don't understand," she repeated.

How could she? No one did. Most of all himself. But he'd try. For her he'd try to find a way to explain the inexplicable.

"I see a word and it becomes in my mind *many* words and then *any* word. Sometimes I can recognize it and sometimes it seems as if it shifts through my memory, just beyond my ability to recall its meaning, taunting me with images I ought to recognize but can't. And then sometimes I'll be able to translate snippets from a page, a line, a word." He turned his palm up in a gesture of frustration.

"But the hieroglyphics," she said. "I know you translate them."

He nodded. "I can read some of them, many of them, because I can touch them. I trace the words and my hand reminds me of what it felt and my eye sees *and* in my memory, I *feel* the words. It all comes together," he said. He made a dismissive gesture, abandoning the effort to explain. "That's why I couldn't tell you I love you, Dizzy. Here, in Egypt, it doesn't matter that I can't read, that I can't write. I can still be involved in a field I love"—his voice grew low, fervent—"do things that have value. Discover things. Explore.

"In England, I'm just a man who can't read. I couldn't go back there to be the subject of pity. Or scorn. I *couldn't*." He could not keep the bitterness out of his voice.

He looked up to find her trembling, her expression chaotic with confusion, remorse, and resignation.

"Couldn't," she said. "But now you can."

He nodded, drew a deep breath. "Yes. I can. If you want. If you desire. I love you."

She shook her head then, a tense, negative motion. Tears spilled over her eyelids and rained down her cheeks. He started forward once again and once again she stopped him, pushing him away.

"Don't you see, Harry?"

"See what?" His voice contained a full measure of the fear and frustration coursing through him.

Truth. Well, there it was, bald and naked. He'd told her and now he saw that he'd been right for all those years when he'd withheld the truth from her. He'd related his defectiveness and he was going to lose her because of it.

"Blake arrives and it is all too clear that some long-standing rivalry exists between you."

"Blake?" His voice mirrored his shock. What had Blake to do with this?

"You bear him a grudge and he bears one for you." She lifted the papers and dangled them from her fingertips as if they were unclean. The damn papers Blake had brought. "You're inheriting Darkmoor Manor. You've somehow taken his birthright from him. That's why you can go back to England now. You've won the grand prize, Harry."

"Prize?" He should have burned the damn papers. "For God's sake, Dizzy, I couldn't care less about Darkmoor Manor."

She swallowed. "I know. That's what frightens me. You don't care about it but you're inheriting it anyway. What does that say about me? About . . . us?" Her voice broke.

Stunned and furious, he stared at her.

Her gaze fell to the ground, masking her dark, liquid eyes gleam. "It seems you've won me, too."

"I don't know what to say to convince you you're wrong," he said, the anger washed away in sudden comprehension, greater fear. "This wasn't a contest. You weren't the brass ring."

The words rang false. Last night, in his own thoughts, he'd called her a prize and he had been frantic to win her when he thought she was becoming enamored of Blake. But not for the reasons she thought. He'd stake his life on it. He'd already staked his heart.

"I've always loved you, Harry." She still stared at her feet, cold and pale beneath the pooling sheet she'd gathered around her. "No matter what you did, or what I thought you did. No matter what you can or cannot do. Scoundrel or not, I've always loved you."

"Dizzy—" He lifted his hand imploringly, helplessly.

"I simply love you too much. I could not bear to watch your interest in me fade at the same rate as Blake's passage home."

"Jesus." He shook his head and slumped down against the edge of the desk. His legs had gone numb, his heart, his thoughts were beggared of the ability to act. His hand fell between his knees and hung there limply as his world pitched into an endless black orbit. "I can't . . . how could you believe . . . that of me?"

"I don't think it purposeful, Harry," she answered faintly. "I don't know what to think. There's so much about you I never knew . . . don't know. So many secrets. So much you never told me. You're a stranger to me, Harry. But I do know you wouldn't intentionally hurt me."

"Well," he said bitterly, "thank you for that kindness." God. She thought he'd been scoring off Blake without even being aware of his own motives. "Jesus, Dizzy." He lifted his head, every ounce of his being concentrated in his bleak, blasted gaze. "I love you."

She drew a shuddering breath. "If I stay here long enough with you, I'll believe you only because I want to." Her voice was faint.

"Believe it!"

"I can't just take the easy course, Harry. It might not be as easy later on. It won't be fair. To me or you." She looked down at the papers in her hand and dropped them as if they burned. "I'm not plunder in this war you have against Blake or England or anyone else."

He clenched his fists, his mind racing, groping, fumbling to think of something, anything, to persuade her, to shatter her awful certainty. The thought of a future without her sent his thoughts spinning muddled and frantic, despair robbing him of reason.

When he looked up, she was gone.

Desdemona sat on the edge of her bed, staring out the window at the cool, winter sunlight. Her hands shook violently and she twisted the fingers until she felt some pain. Felt something, anything other than this overwhelming confusion and despair.

She'd hurt Harry when she'd only hoped to save them both from deeper pain. How could any pain be deeper than this?

Had she been right? Did the fact that he'd kept secrets from her, kept part of himself from her mean that he couldn't love her honestly, wholly? Honesty and Harry seemed such incompatible words. She closed her eyes. It didn't matter. She wanted to believe him. She'd never desired anything more. Maybe if she went back and he explained about Darkmoor . . .

"*Sitt?*" Duraid's voice called from beyond her bedroom door.

"Yes, Duraid?"

He slipped inside the door. "I know it is very early, *Sitt*. But this was waiting beneath the door when I came down this morning." He offered her a folded sheet of paper.

She accepted it, slowly focusing on Duraid's bleak expression. "Is something wrong, Duraid?"

The boy nodded miserably. "It is the turkey farm, *Sitt*. The owner of the property is demanding higher rent."

"Why wasn't I told of this?"

"Matin did not wish to worry you, *Sitt*. He knows you are trying to find the money to replace the turkeys. He was hoping to change the landlord's mind. But"—he lifted his shoulders and spread his palms wide—"the landlord will not wait."

Guilt added its piquant flavor to her misery. She'd completely forgotten about the turkeys. She'd failed the children. She got up and went to the sideboard and opened the empty silverware drawer. She withdrew the five-pound note she kept there for emergencies and pressed it into Duraid's palm. "Take this. Ask the landlord to wait. One week. Tell him I will pay interest on what is owed."

"Yes, *Sitt*. Thank you, *Sitt*. I will go right now. Immediately! Allah shines his face upon you, *Sitt*." The boy backed out of the room, dipping and bowing.

She dashed a tear from her cheek with the back of her hand and realized she still held the folded paper Duraid had given her. Incuriously, she opened it. It was written in a coarse hand in Arabic.

Sitt,

To me bring my papyrus and I will give you the bull you want. I am at Joseph Hassam's shop. I will not wait long.

Rabi Hakim

The bull she sought . . . an Apis bull?

She sighed at her foolishness. Rabi had probably manufactured some shabby facsimile. Still, however remote the chances were that he actually had an Apis bull in his possession, she needed to look into it. The letter offered her a chance to do something, for the turkey farm, for Matin, for her grandfather. She couldn't ignore her responsibilities.

She glanced at the gilt clock on her desk. It was already eight-fifteen. She pocketed the note and went to the armoire where she'd hidden the papyrus she'd taken from the library. From inside, she withdrew it and the small hard-sided cylinder her grandfather used to transport papyrus.

Quickly she draped a dark shawl over her head and slipped into the hall, looking for any sign of Magi. Magi would never allow her to go to the bazaar without a male escort, and with Duraid gone, there was only one male available. With one last despairing glance at the door to the library, she stole down the quiet hallway and out the front door.

Outside, the residential area was quiet. Only a closed carriage stood at the corner of the street, the horses sleeping in their traces. She'd nearly made the corner when she heard the click of European heels behind her. She looked around.

Marta Douglass, her thin elegant face set in determined lines, hastened toward her house.

"Mrs. Douglass?" she called, puzzled by Marta's appearance so early in the day. She started back toward the house.

Suddenly a thick arm looped around her, hauling her off her feet. She twisted frantically against her unseen assailant, opening her mouth to scream only to have a rag thrust into it. Her frantic gaze locked with Marta's shocked one. And then she was being dragged into the waiting carriage.

Marta wheeled around, looking somewhere, anywhere for help. There was no one around but a ragged-looking Arab boy who slunk quickly into the shadows when he realized he'd been spied.

From inside the carriage that man, Maurice, barked an order.

"El Aguza?" The driver called down the name of a district south of the city.

"*La!*" Maurice yelled the Arab word for 'no.' "El Bakwi. *Yalla!*"

Hurry. Marta's Arabic was rudimentary, but she knew enough to understand that the man had ordered the driver to an ancient desert road. She hastened up the steps of the Carlisle house. Harry would know what to do. He'd save—

She stopped, her hand raised to knock, her heart racing in her throat. Fear warred with self-interest. If Harry saved Desdemona, the girl was bound to finally realize his feelings for her. And Harry would never look at Marta again.

Last night . . . Last night had been wonderful. Cal and she— But there wasn't going to be any "Cal and she." She clenched her teeth in anger at her stupidity. She wasn't going to trade one alien culture for another, Egypt for Texas, even if Cal was to ask. Which he hadn't. She wasn't going to risk it all, ever again. She wouldn't fall in love with him. She couldn't. She wanted Harry.

But Harry was smitten with Desdemona and Desdemona was infatuated with the British viscount, the arrogant and powerful Lord Ravenscroft. Marta's hand dropped and she looked down the street. Dust still billowed from where the carriage turned the corner.

A thought, born of panic, formed bright and tempting. Let Lord Ravenscroft play knight-errant to Desdemona's damsel in distress.

She spun around. With a speed no one had ever witnessed in her before, she ran down the street.

Behind her, Rabi Hakim emerged from the shadows and trotted off in the opposite direction.

woburn contains that Desdemona was an English citizen. Between us, that narrowed I say she learned.

CHAPTER TWENTY-SEVEN

"*I* want all my trunks shipped back before week's end."

Marta heard Gunter Konrad's thick accent as she finished penning a note to Lord Ravenscroft at Shepheard's lobby desk. The huge Austrian strode by her, four bellhops trailing in his wake like pilot fish after a behemoth. He stopped and pointed at a huge pile of luggage at the foot of the staircase.

Apparently Gunter was leaving Cairo, Marta thought. Very odd as the archeological season was barely under way.

She handed a bellhop her note and instructions and then settled back in the chair, catching Gunter's eye as she did so. He blushed and fidgeted like a naughty little boy who'd been caught leaving the cookie jar with its lid askew.

"Mr. Konrad," she hailed him, glad for the distraction. Every minute Desdemona was held by Maurice she might be subjected to—no, she wouldn't consider that. Desdemona was an English citizen. Maurice wouldn't dare harm her. "I say, Mr. Konrad!"

At the sound of her voice, he heaved a sigh and pivoted with military precision. "Madame?"

"You're leaving us so soon?" she asked mildly. "You did not receive a concession?"

"Yes, I got a concession. Of course I got a concession. I am Gunter Konrad."

"I see. No trouble in your family, I hope?" She was being shockingly forward but she really didn't care. If only Ravenscroft would appear—

"No trouble."

"Then . . . ?" She let the phrase dangle invitingly.

His florid face grew even brighter. "You are most inquisitive, Mrs. Douglass. But for your own safety, I tell you this. There is a man in Cairo who hires his services out in any number of capacities. I employed him to do some work for me. He . . . he went above and beyond the intent of my directions."

"Yes?" Marta prompted, perplexed.

"He is become a nuisance and, more important, I am not at all sure he isn't dangerous. He comes to me, big Gunter Konrad, and he threatens me, telling me I owe him more money for this thing he has done. He is obviously not right"—Gunter rapped his forehead with his knuckles—"up here. I decide it is better to leave Cairo this season."

"I see."

Apparently he did not appreciate her tone. "Certainly I could hurt this little man. But that would make unpleasantness with the authorities. I am not sure if he holds citizenship here and I, Gunter, do not want trouble. It is best I leave. For this little man's sake."

"Of course."

He slammed his fist into his palm. "A rabid dog does not care what the size is of the man he bites, Mrs. Douglass."

"No," she said. "I don't suppose it does."

His lips compressed and he spun about, barking commands at the attendants hovering over his mountain of trunks. As she watched, Lord Ravenscroft made his way around the luggage, nodding perfunctorily at Gunter.

"Mrs. Douglass." Ravenscroft inclined his head as he approached.

"Lord Ravenscroft," she said, "I come to you on a matter of the gravest import—"

"Doubtless. But I am sure whatever your errand, it will not be served by a public scene," he answered, securing her elbow and leading her out onto the balcony.

"Now, what is this all about, Mrs. Douglass? Flattering though your appearance here is, I must inform you that my attentions have already been engaged—"

"You arrogant fool!" she spat. "I don't want *you*! I have come to tell you that Desdemona Carlisle has been kidnapped."

His features went slack. Any other time she might have laughed, certainly she'd have left him standing there gaping like a fish. But precious time had already been wasted.

Guilt and anxiety, unique emotions for her, impelled her on. "Early today I saw Miss Carlisle forcibly removed from the street outside her home and deposited into a waiting carriage. I heard the kidnapper give instructions to the driver. I know who he is and I think I know where he took her."

His eyes widened with shock. "We must contact the authorities—"

"What authorities?" she asked in a low, harsh whisper. "The Turks? The French? The English? They'll run around for days making plans with their usual ineptitude."

"I see," he said gravely. "Where has this person taken her?"

"A desolate area on the edge of the Bahariya Oasis. El Bawki."

"How do I get there?" he asked, his jaw congealing into a tense line of determination.

"You'll need a guide. And a horse. You can arrange for them in the lobby."

He looked at her with distaste. "I still say we should go to the authorities. They have the resources necessary. They will know who has the most to gain by—" He left off abruptly. The deep furrows on his forehead cleared. "Tell me, Mrs. Douglass, why would anyone kidnap Miss Carlisle?"

"I don't know," she said.

"Miss Carlisle, by her own admission, is far from wealthy. She is dependent on her grandfather for her livelihood. And it is common knowledge that he is in financial difficulties. If this was a kidnapping, there is simply no one who could pay the kind of ransom such a risky endeavor would demand."

"I don't know," she repeated forcefully. She'd gambled too much of Desdemona's welfare already. She would not be able to live with herself if her plan brought the girl irreparable harm. "I have to find Harry," she muttered.

"Let me be blunt," Lord Ravenscroft said, his tone officiously superior. "England owns Egypt. Regardless of what the penny dreadfuls claim, genteel, well-connected Englishwomen are not plucked from the streets to fill Eastern harems."

"Your point?"

"Miss Carlisle has a romantic nature. Could she, perhaps in order to induce a . . ." He trailed off. "Last night," he said uncomfortably, "I, er, took certain liberties without making clear my intentions. A romantic, sheltered young woman like Miss Carlisle might feel compelled to prompt assurances that she may have felt were lacking."

Desdemona arranging for her own kidnapping? Impossible. "No, Lord Ravenscroft. It doesn't make any sense. There were no witnesses. I was only there by chance. And, quite frankly, I doubt Desdemona is that fanciful."

"Well, whether she has had a hand in this or not, she needs rescuing," he said, smiling. Whatever she believed, Lord Ravenscroft obviously thought he'd found an answer to Desdemona's kidnapping. "I can imagine her supreme embarrassment if I were to approach the authorities only to have the situation revealed as a self-orchestrated . . . *tableau.*"

The monumental ego of the man! "I should wait about and see if a note arrives. But then again, why? Come, Mrs. Douglass, let us go see about that guide."

"Bihyatak—" Desdemona started to say. The carriage pitched sideways, throwing her into the door. She righted herself, fighting tears, cursing violently under her breath, only her anger keeping her panic at bay. Twice now in less than a fortnight she'd been kidnapped. She was getting bloody, bloody sick of it!

But this man was infinitely more threatening than Rabi. He terrified her. She gulped and tried again. *"Bihyatak—"*

"Speak English," the man, Maurice, said. "I cannot understand one word of your . . . Arabic, is that?" He gave her a mocking smile and his smooth, hairless skin crinkled like delicate tissue beneath his dark eyes and at the corners of his small mouth.

He looked very young and yet she knew he'd been working the dig sites for more years than she'd had life. With his androgynous features, dark hair, and European accent, it was impossible to tell his nationality. From what Harry had told her, it was his stock-in-trade.

"I was imploring you to return me to Cairo."

"Imploring. How nice. So few young persons these days have good manners. But"—he

shrugged—"I am afraid I must disappoint you.
You've not yet fulfilled your function."

"You're going to cause an international incident,
you know, kidnapping me like this," she said, trying
to sound unaffected. Harry would have handled this
with so much more élan than she was showing.

Harry. Dear God, let him find her.

"So?" Maurice laughed. "What do I care? I certainly have no love for Egypt. Or France. Or England. Or of any other nation. Let them read
political intrigue into my actions. Let each claim me
as the other's agent."

"And whose agent are you?"

He tipped his head slightly as if acknowledging
an accolade. "My own."

"But—"

He leaned across the carriage and set one knuckle
gently on her lips. She jerked her head back, rubbing
her mouth with her sleeve. His eyes went flat and
reptilian, and she prayed he wouldn't touch her
again.

If he forced her to do with him what she and
Harry had done— She could not stand that. She
knew too newly, too clearly, what making love was
to have it desecrated by him. *Love.*

Let Harry find her, she thought again, and even as
the thought was born she realized she'd not questioned whether he *would* come but only if he would
find her.

Harry *would* come for her. Harry, she remembered
Magi saying, would always come for her. And she
knew it was true. She knew it as surely she knew the

sun would rise, the desert would burn, and the sea was salt. It was as elemental and irrefutable as the planets' course across the heavens. Harry would come because he loved her.

She recognized that love now as the simple honesty upon which all of his actions had been anchored. It did not matter when he proclaimed his love. It had been there all along.

They careened along half-obscured roads, through the roan and ocher landscape. Outside, thousands of dragonflies encircled the carriage, their crisp, crystalline wings sparkling in the heat waves as they hovered and dipped disturbed in their flight by the carriage's passing. As the day wore on, the air within grew hot and weighted with dust, clogging her throat and burning her eyes until finally a shout from outside brought the carriage creaking to a halt.

Maurice kicked open the door and shoved her outside. She stumbled, just managing to keep upright, her legs weak from their cramped disuse. With a sense of déjà vu, Desdemona shielded her eyes from the sudden sunlight as half-dozen veiled men surrounded her. She squinted past them.

Behind the men sun-scorched ruined buildings gave mute testimony to an ancient, long-abandoned community. Maurice had brought her to an Egyptian ghost town. A narrow crossroad separated crumbling hovels. Only one or two looked capable of any longer providing shelter. At one time the little cluster of ruins a long-emptied cistern squatted in decay. A woman, a goat tethered at her feet, crouched in what little shade was afforded by the half-tumbled wall house. She caught Desdemona's eye and looked away.

The fear that the interminable, nerve-numbing trip had held at bay came racing back. She had no idea where she was. There was nothing familiar here, only the familiarity of the desert, its huge sand apron spreading out for countless miles in all directions. From behind her Maurice grabbed her upper arm, yanking her forward, causing mutters from the men.

"*Usskut!*" Maurice said.

It was one of the few words Desdemona knew. In no uncertain terms, he was telling them to be quiet. The men fell silent.

She lifted her chin; the worst one could do with such an animal is to show fear. "What is the meaning of this?" she asked. "I am Desdemona Carlisle. I am a citizen of Great Britain and a subject of Her Majesty the—"

The woman with the goat gasped, and Maurice shot her a glare filled with black promise as his fingertips dug painfully into Desdemona's arm. "Shut up," he said calmly. "Shut up or I will kill you. It makes no difference to me."

No one had ever threatened her life before. Her eyes fill with frightened tears. "Why have you kidnapped me?" Good, she could barely hear the quaver in her voice. "Why have you—I want . . . I want to go home!" The words broke free in spite of her determination to be proud, to be brave. Tears spilled from her eyes and dripped from her chin.

"So sorry." Maurice shrugged. "Apparently it

isn't Allah's will and all that. Well, at least it isn't *my* will that you go home. And here, my will is all that matters."

"What is it you want?"

"Ah." He nodded. "A woman who gets to the point. So English. What do I want? I want you, Miss Carlisle."

"Why?"

His eyes went dark and lifeless, the oily servility died from his expression. "As bait."

"Bait for whom?"

"Harry Braxton, may he rot in hell."

CHAPTER TWENTY-EIGHT

There was macabre humor in the fact that in every scene he imagined, after every confession he'd rehearsed, Dizzy had been repelled by the deficit in his mind, never one in his heart. He could not find a smile for it.

Harry looked around. Like an exotic bird strewing rare plumage in her wake, Dizzy had draped her silk shawl across the back of a chair, abandoned a silk stocking on the cot, left her cloisonné bracelet on the edge of the worn Oriental carpet.

He retrieved it and fingered the delicate enamel pattern. Had he removed it from her himself last night? In the midst of passionate, heart-searing love play, had it slipped from her wrist as her hand roved over him—

He leaned forward, bracing himself on the desk with stiff arms. He loved her. His lips bared his teeth with self-contempt. So much that he'd let her go.

He had heard her specious reasoning and he had

done nothing to correct it. He'd only stared at her, made mute with self-righteous anger, furious that she could doubt him, emphatically ignoring the fact that he'd taught her to mistrust him. Why should she believe his declaration? From her perspective, his seemingly sudden avowal of love *would* be suspect, his courtship *would* seem to have been prompted by Blake's arrival.

Enough vanity. He loved her and he would find a way to convince her of that love. Whatever it took.

He reached behind the bed and yanked the bell pull. A moment later Magi answered the summons, her head popping around the corner of the door, smug complacency evident in one playfully raised brow. "Yes, Harry. What might I do for you?"

"Where's Dizzy? I need to see her."

Magi moved into the room and looked about. "Isn't she with you?" She frowned. "When I saw that her bed wasn't slept in, I thought . . . I was hoping . . ." Magi's brow furrowed. "What did you do to her, Harry? I will have your heart if you have hurt her—"

"Too late," he answered. "Already gone. As is she. I need to find her, Magi." He started past, but she grabbed his arm.

"Why did she leave?"

"She thought she'd become contested ground in a rivalry between Blake and me." Though his tone was raw, he spoke distractedly, calculating where Dizzy might be. He pulled away from Magi.

"Why would she think that?" The steel quality in

Magi's voice stayed Harry where her hand failed. Concern riddled her face with lines of anxiety.

"Blake had brought me a copy of my grandfather's will. He cut Blake out, naming me his heir. And Darkmoor's future owner," he added humorlessly. "Dizzy saw the copy. She thinks I'm accumulating things as a means of stealing a march on Blake. And she is simply one of them."

"Oh, Dizzy," Magi murmured sadly.

He shoved his arms into the sleeves as he headed down the hallway. Magi hurried after him.

"Where are you going?" she asked.

"To the museum," he said. "Sometimes she goes there when she wants to think."

"The museum is not open yet," Magi said.

He pulled his timepiece from his jacket pocket, glanced at it, and shoved it back with a curse. He'd lost all concept of time. It had seemed days since Dizzy had left him. It had been barely two hours. "Where else would she have gone?"

Magi lifted her shoulders. "I don't know. She would not walk alone in the gardens, and the *suqs* are closed."

"She has to be somewhere."

Magi's unhappy gaze met his. "Shepheard's Hotel."

Yes. She could have felt it necessary to see him. Blake. "Send someone to the hotel with inquiries."

"I do not know what the note said." Tears shimmered in Duraid's eyes. "I cannot read."

"Can't one bloody person around here read?"

Harry thundered, his fist crashing down on the desktop.

"You do not help by terrorizing the boy," Magi chided.

Curse it, Harry thought, she was right. "I'm sorry, Duraid. Tell me again what happened."

"Early this morning I find a note under the door at the back of the house. It bears the *Sitt*'s name. I can read that much." A hint of reproachfulness. "I am taking it to her when I hear my friend calling for me from the street. I go to meet him and he tells me that the turkey farm's landlord wants more money. Today. I am very worried for my friends at the farm. I go to find *Sitt*. *Sitt* will help."

"Go on."

"She is in her room. I do not think she feels well. She is very white and here"—he gestured toward his eyes—"it looks as if she is hurting."

"Duraid, just tell us what happened, boy," Magi said.

"I hand her the note and tell her about the turkey farm. She gives me money to take to the landlord. I do as she says. I come back and she is gone." He lifted his hands, palm up. "I swear, Harry, I would tell you if I knew where."

"I know." He willed himself to be calm. She'd only been gone a few hours. She was, as Duraid had said, hurt and unhappy. As far as being in danger . . . Maurice was safely in jail and Dizzy knew this city better than any Englishwoman ought to.

The servant Magi had sent to the Shepheard's slipped into the sitting room and whispered in

Magi's ear. The housekeeper's face grew tense with concentration.

"What is it?"

Magi dismissed the servant before addressing him. "The clerk at the front lobby said that Lord Ravenscroft secured a guide and horses for an overnight excursion."

"Well, if Blake has gone touring he won't be of much help finding Dizzy," Harry said. Another avenue closed.

"Lord Ravenscroft asked for two horses. He was, the clerk said, with an Englishwoman."

He froze. "Who?"

"He did not hear her name."

He heard the pained assumption in Magi's voice. She needn't have worried. Whoever had been with Blake, it had not been Dizzy. Dizzy might feel she needed to tell Blake that she could no longer encourage his attentions, but nothing more. Four hours ago, Harry thought, Dizzy said she loved me. She would never betray her heart.

"I can't stay here waiting for her to return," he said. "I'm going to the turkey farm. If she comes back while I'm away, keep her here until I return."

"What if she doesn't want to see you?" Magi asked.

"We don't always get what we want," he answered grimly.

Desdemona rested her forehead on her knees, hugging her arms about her legs and shivering. The single high window let in the last of the fading sunlight. Soon it would be night. She had nothing to protect herself from its frigid embrace except her shawl.

Earlier, the Arab woman had approached her cell with a stack of blankets. Maurice had cuffed her across the face, sending her and the blankets sprawling in the sand. No one else had come near. No one had brought food; no one had brought water. She ran her dry tongue over her cracked lips, tasting the powdery dust covering them.

Keys rattled in the lock and Desdemona bolted to her feet, pressing herself tightly against the far wall. The door swung open and Maurice entered. Wordlessly he threw a goatskin at her. She caught it and raised the flask to her lips, gulping down the tepid, alkaline water. Her parched throat sated, she wiped her mouth with the back of her hand.

"Let me go," she rasped.

"Do not worry. I do not intend you shall stay here long. Just until Braxton arrives."

"What do you want with Harry?" She'd already asked him the question a dozen times. He'd yet to answer.

"You are a nag, Miss Carlisle." He had no accent, though his voice held a faint cadence. "Has anyone ever told you this?" he asked. "I hate nagging women. There are places in the world where a woman pays for wagging her tongue by losing it. Not a bad idea."

She lifted her chin, gratified her lips were so stiff they could not tremble. "What do you want with Harry?"

He grunted appreciably.

"Well?"

"I want Harry to die."

"No. You can't." She shook her head in vehement denial.

"Oh, yes." His smooth, ageless face nodded in mock agreeableness. "I do."

"Why?"

"Because he is my . . . *nemesis*?" His eyes, black and shiny as a beetle's carapace, rolled thoughtfully toward the ceiling. "Yes. Nemesis. Even though it seems a romantic word and I am by no one's definition a romantic. I am a businessman. I perform services for profit. Everything I have done is for the sake of business. Does that seem unreasonable to you?" He looked as if he were sincerely interested in her opinion.

"No," she said.

"No," he echoed encouragingly. "I have never made the mistake of allowing personal feelings to interfere with business. Yet many times Harry has seen fit to thwart my endeavors."

"I'm sure . . ." She fumbled around for something to say. "I'm sure it is just business for him, too."

"Oh, no," Maurice said. "No. He enjoyed cheating me, discrediting me . . . reviling me. Did you know that at one time I was the leading procurer of antiquities in Egypt? At one time Braxton and I were partners."

"Impossible."

"Yes!" A flash of ire. "I knew where to go, because

I was the Cairo Museum's chief foreman, overseeing dozens of archeological digs. You cannot imagine the treasures I once had access to." His gaze grew clouded, his attention turned inward.

Holding her breath, Desdemona moved along the wall.

"Harry reaped the rewards of *my* expertise, *my* entrée into the dig sites. But then he interfered." An expression of aggrieved bafflement crossed Maurice's unlined face. "Do you know why Harry Braxton did this?"

She halted, pinned in her progress by his sudden attention, yet he did not seem to notice she'd moved. "Did he get too avaricious? Surely you can understand how he may have been tempted—"

"No," he cut in. "Greed I could understand, forgive. Greed is a part of business."

"Business."

He pounded one clenched fist into his open palm and she started. "Business reasons might make it necessary to interfere with a man's livelihood, a man's career. But it wasn't business! He interfered because of the brats."

She was nearly to the corner of the room now. Her foot bumped against something and she glanced down at the cylinder she'd put the papyrus in. She looked up and found Maurice studying her. "Brats?"

"Yes, brats," he said slowly. "The peasant children who worked the digs. One of them died, a mewling brat died, and Braxton organizes a mutiny!"

"Mutiny? I thought he beat you up." She froze when she saw the effect of her words. Madness chased beneath Maurice's smooth face, like worms flooded from their hiding spot during a deluge.

"You're right," he said, openly struggling to control himself. "He beat me. And *then* there was the mutiny. It was the end of my being a foreman. A man who cannot instill fear in these peasants cannot supply the necessary manpower to the dig sites."

He took a deep, calming breath. "Still, I did not hold a grudge. That would be . . . unprofessional. There were other careers available," he went on, "other lucrative business opportunities around, ones where I did not need to cross Braxton's path."

"That was good of you." She was a few feet from the open doorway.

"Oh, do not fool yourself." His amused snarl made clear her attempt to placate him had failed. "That doesn't mean I forgave Braxton for introducing sentiment into simple business practices."

A child died and this man called it a simple business practice. He *was* mad.

"Being an astute businessman, I determined to be prepared should Harry and I have another encounter," he said. "I asked around. I ferreted out his secrets. His weaknesses. I found none. Then"—his gaze flowed over her like fly studded honey, sweet and repulsive—"a stroke of providence, or luck, or whatever you'd call it, occurred. I was hired to fulfill my own desires. Business served pleasure. I was paid—and handsomely—to beat the hell out of

Braxton. And he told me of his Achilles' heel himself. *You.*"

She bit the inside of her cheek, refusing to give him the pleasure of her pain.

"Oh, not in so many words," he said. "But his face, his eyes when I spoke your name, when I suggested you were important." He laughed and Desdemona's stomach clenched. "He fought like a chained dog when I taunted him with your name. I have never seen the like. Even beaten, he still sought to free himself to protect you."

Rage, cold and implacable, obliterated her fear. This man had beaten Harry, brutalized him. And someone had paid him to do it. "Who paid you?"

"The Austrian," Maurice answered with a shrug. "It seems your Harry is not a very popular fellow."

She would have Gunter Konrad's head on a platter when she got out of— Her momentary fury died with the resurgence of her fear as she remembered her plight.

"But if you already got to beat Harry up, can't you call it a draw?" she asked in a rush. "I mean, he beats you up, you beat him. It all seems pretty well evened up to me."

Ugliness flickered over Maurice's smooth features again, like the churning of silt beneath the Nile's thick, smooth water.

"Doesn't it?" he asked. "But it *didn't* end there. Braxton saw to that. He set me up. He framed me!" His voice rose in fury. "He stole a funerary piece from your grandfather's own collection and planted in my home! And then he sent the Turk military pigs to have me arrested, thrown into prison. Do you know—" He moved close to her, angling to her side, leaving the doorway unguarded. His breath, fetid and hot, fanned her face. "Can you possibly conceive of what an Arab prison is like?"

She shook her head, mesmerized by the virulence in Maurice's unblinking eyes.

"Braxton and I aren't just enemies. Harry Braxton is my nemesis. He seeks my destruction. It is only reasonable that I strive to achieve his first. And I will," he said, "because I have something Braxton won't be able to resist coming for: you."

She leapt for the open doorway.

He was way ahead of her. He caught her hair, savagely jerking her back and spinning her around. His backhanded blow caught her across the mouth, slicing her lip open against her teeth. She gasped, dropping to her knees with the force of his blow.

"Any more questions . . . *Honored Sitt?*"

CHAPTER TWENTY-NINE

$\mathcal{H}$arry stared in the mirror, barely recognizing the image it gave back. He looked awful. Dark bruises encircled his eyes. His skin looked thin and cleaved too tightly to the underlying bone.

Dizzy hadn't come home.

"Someone has to have seen her." How many times had he said this, aloud and to himself?

"I have men scouring the area and I've sent word to Sir Robert in Luxor. Undoubtedly she has gone to join him there," Simon Chesterton said. He pulled the unlit cheroot he'd been gnawing on out of his mouth and rolled the soggy ends between his thumb and forefinger. He looked older, too, his ruddy face lined like thousand-years-old crumpled papyrus. Even his beard appeared thinner.

"Without clothes, money, or telling Magi?" Harry asked.

"We'll find her." Simon's words did not reassure him.

Harry had sent for the colonel late last evening, after everything he'd done, every avenue he'd searched had proved fruitless.

"Coffee?"

"Thank you, Magi," Simon said, allowing his untouched cup to be emptied and refilled with steaming liquid.

"The boy from the turkey farm," Harry asked again. "You're sure he hasn't seen any English-woman? Any at all?"

"No."

"What about a light-skinned native woman? Sometimes Dizzy dresses in—"

Simon shook his head gravely.

Nothing had been found. Not a single clue to where she'd been taken . . . and taken she'd undoubtedly been.

A young woman alone. Taken from the streets. Harry pushed his fingers hard against his temples and breathed deeply through his nostrils, seeking calm. Little more than a week ago when Rabi had snatched Dizzy from the *suq*, he'd spent a similar night, demon-haunted and terrified. He'd hunted then as frantically as he had last night, roaming the bazaars and footpaths and streets until dawn and word from Abdul had finally come.

This might be the same thing. Initially alarming but ultimately benign. It had to be.

He swept his hand over his eyes, vaguely aware his fingers grew damp on their passage.

* * *

"Marta, what's wrong, dear?" Cal asked. He waved the hovering waiter away and planted his forearms on either side of his plate. "I was delighted when your note arrived suggesting we breakfast on Shepheard's terrace together, but now I'm thinking that this isn't a purely social visit, is it?"

Even though she'd arranged this meeting, she was ashamed to face Cal. Her bottom lip must be raw from her chewing it. Her hair—She raised her hand, touched her coiffure. Her hair was coming undone. In a dozen years she'd never appeared in public with untidy hair. She stared stricken at the street scene beneath the balcony.

Cal reached across the table, capturing her chin with lean, strong fingers, and forced her to look his direction. "You best tell me, Marta. So I can fix it."

"Have you seen Lord Ravenscroft?"

"No. Why?" His mouth drooped with sad irony. "Are you plotting some new way to make Harry Braxton jealous, this time using Blake Ravenscroft?"

She blinked.

He sighed, sat back in his chair, and pulled his watch fob from his vest pocket. Casually he unlinked the jewel from its gold chain and bounced the ruby-crusted ball up and down in his palm. The seemingly idle motion belied the hard set of his features.

"Listen, Marta," he finally said. "I can't stay in this hand much longer. I always reckoned myself a good man with a bluff, but the stakes have never been this high before."

"I don't know what you mean."

"Fine. Then here it is, all bald and unpretty. I think it's high time you woke up. Harry Braxton doesn't love you. He loves Miss Carlisle. And you know it."

She reacted automatically, tossing her hair disdainfully. "Pshaw. Why would a man like Harry love a mere girl like Desdemona Carlisle?"

"You're a smart woman, Marta. How is it you can't manage to see those things that are right in front of your nose?" He tossed the bauble higher. The rubies winked red fire at the top of its arc. He snatched it overhand from the air and tossed it back up again. His movements grew quicker, more abrupt.

"I don't know what you're talking about," Marta snapped.

"Miss Carlisle's eyes look a mite wiser than a girl's ought, don't you think? And she tries so hard to emulate you." He leaned back farther in his chair, balancing on the back legs, still playing his solitary game of catch with his watch fob.

Marta's eyes widened in surprise. "Me?"

"Something in that girl's life has made her want to be something other than what she is. More the pity. There isn't anything wrong with Desdemona Carlisle just as she is, and I suspect Harry's the only one who makes her feel that way."

"It's amazing that you, on the merit of a few meetings, have managed to discern things about people that I, who have known them for years, have not."

He came down on the front legs of his chair with a crash, surging forward over the table as his watch fob fell unheeded to the tabletop. Ignored, it rolled off the edge, dropping to the tiled floor.

She could feel the intensity of his regard, his frustration struggling for voice. Her heartbeat quickened.

"You don't know Harry Braxton any better than I do," he said through tight lips. "You've just used him as an excuse, is all."

"An excuse." She twisted her suddenly cold hands in her lap. She felt as if she were standing on the crumbling edge of a dark, heated abyss, and, though she was frightened by its unknown depths, she was tempted by its promised warmth.

"Yup," he said, reaching across the table and capturing her wrist. He dragged her hand over the linen surface toward him. "Marta, you're chasing after a man who's already given his heart elsewhere and you know it. And I know the reason."

"I can hardly wait to hear." Her attempted sarcasm failed. Her voice sounded weak, breathless.

"Good, cause you're gonna hear it," he answered. "You chase Harry Braxton 'cause you don't have to worry about catching him. And if you don't catch a man, you can't be hurt by him."

Her eyes widened.

"Your husband died young. I know you and I have no doubts that you loved him passionately and wholly. And I'm real sorry you had so much pain. But a brave woman doesn't spend the rest of her life afraid of getting hurt again."

She closed her eyes. His words sounded with the clarion ring of truth.

"You're a brave woman, Marta."

"No," she said faintly. "I'm not."

"I love you, Marta."

Once more she heard the truth and recognized it. Her heart, clenched tightly against being hurt, slowly relinquished its fear. With that inner sigh of release, she experienced the unmistakable stirring of love. It didn't matter that Cal was younger than she or that he came from a wild, raw country or that he was unpolished and elemental. He knew her and he loved her.

Her fragile joy evaporated abruptly. Cal wouldn't love her when he discovered what her jealousy and alarm had caused her to do to Desdemona Carlisle.

"I've loved you from the moment we met, Marta." Slowly he lifted her hand to his lips and pressed an ardent kiss against her knuckles. "And you love me."

She did, but she couldn't find the words to tell him.

He mistook her silence for doubt.

"Marta, five thousand dollars' worth of pretty colored rocks just fell on the floor and you didn't even blink an eye. If that ain't love, honey, I don't know what is."

She could almost find a smile for him if she didn't fear she'd recognized love too late, that she'd already recklessly endangered a prize she hadn't even known she owned.

"Now, enough about Harry Braxton and Blake Ravenscroft," Cal said. "Be my wife, Marta. I'll take care of you."

"I saw Desdemona Carlisle being kidnapped." The words came out in a rush. "And I . . . I think I've put her life in danger."

He regarded her pensively, without condemnation. "What happened?"

"Yesterday morning I saw a man force Miss Carlisle into a carriage. I heard the directions he gave the driver. I know I should have told Harry but instead I told Lord Ravenscroft. He's had plenty of time to find her. They should have been back by now." Her voice broke. "I didn't mean anything bad to happen."

"Why didn't you tell Braxton? He knows these people, the lay of the land . . ."

"I thought if Lord Ravenscroft could effect a rescue, Desdemona would . . ." She trailed off miserably.

"She would think of Ravenscroft as her knight-errant?"

She nodded mutely.

"Oh, Marta." He sighed and rose from his seat, holding out his hand for her. She took it and he pulled her to her feet. "Come on. You have some talking to do."

"I can't tell Harry what I've done. I can't," she protested, trying to pull away. He wouldn't let her. He put his arm around her waist, drawing her gently but inescapably to his side.

"Yes, darlin'," he said firmly. "You can. I'll be with you. Forever, if you'll let me."

Grateful, she met his gaze. She couldn't think of anything, or anyone, she wanted more.

She took a deep breath and nodded. "Yes," she said. "I'd like that."

Marta watched Harry blanch as if he'd sustained a heavy and unexpected blow.

". . . and then I heard Maurice tell the driver to go take the El Bakwi road," she hurried on.

"Maurice? You're certain?" Harry asked.

She nodded.

"Maurice Franklin Shappeis. Jesus." Simon yanked furiously at his beard. "He's wanted by at least two other governments for various crimes. An export officer was killed . . ."

"Maurice is a *murderer*?" Marta asked faintly, reading her answer in Simon's miserable silence. "Oh, God, I never knew."

"He said El Bawki?" Harry broke in. He'd already absorbed the blow and recovered, far more rapidly than she'd have believed possible. "Are you sure?"

"I'm so sor—"

"Are you sure?" Harry repeated tightly.

"Yes," Marta whispered. She had a hard time reconciling her genial ex-lover and this stark-faced stranger. He turned from her, motioning the Carlisles' housekeeper near.

"Send Duraid to the livery where I stable my mare," he told her, "and have him meet me at my house with her, saddled and ready to ride."

She was forgotten, Marta realized. Her usefulness in Harry's time of crisis having ended, she'd been dismissed from his thoughts. She doubted he even realized she was still in the room.

"Fine, Harry," Simon Chesterton said. "I'll have my men marshaled in less than an hour—"

Harry dug out some crumpled notes and pressed the currency into Magi's hands. "I won't wait. Come when you can," he said, and strode from the room. Simon hurried after him.

Marta sat quite still as Magi, too, left to find the boy Harry had named. Only she and Cal remained. She felt him shift behind her. He'd positioned himself there early in the interview and had not moved.

As welcome as it was, his championship had been absolutely unnecessary. She needn't have worried about Harry's reaction to her duplicity. He'd had none.

Except for the information she'd provided, Harry had taken no notice of her actions at all. All of his being, his every mental faculty, centered on Desdemona. There was simply no room in that concentration for something so inconsequential as outrage over her actions. What would it be like to be the focus of such devotion?

Cal's hand cupped the curve of her shoulder and she covered his big, rough hand with her own. Pray God, she'd know.

CHAPTER THIRTY

"Thank God," Desdemona whispered as she stared out the tiny aperture at the horse and rider cresting a dune far in the distance. She'd known Harry would come. Love flooded her, relief making her shake. Now they only needed to wait a few hours before making their escape under the cover of night or until reinforcements arrived. She smiled, the sun and relief making her eyes dazzle.

The great ebony steed reared once and the fine manly figure . . .

Desdemona frowned. It didn't look like Harry planned on sneaking in later and freeing her. It didn't appear he was going to wait for the reinforcements. In fact, he was heading straight for the encampment. In broad daylight.

She blinked, finding it impossible to believe her canny Harry would be so reckless. It did no good. She still saw the same thing, a rider approaching pell-mell on a black stallion.

Black? Desdemona's foot slipped on the bucket. She righted herself. *Harry's horse wasn't black, and it wasn't a stallion. It was a milk-white mare.*

She grabbed the sill and scrambled up as far up into the narrow window as she could. It wasn't Harry's horse because it wasn't Harry. It was Blake Ravenscroft.

His dark head uncovered under the burning desert sun, his black waistcoat flapping behind him, he cantered toward the abandoned town.

Good God, she thought, *he is going to get himself killed.*

She raced to the door, grinding her cheek against the rough wood in order to see between the ill-fitting planks. Outside she saw one of Maurice's men crouch beneath a crumbling wall. Another scooted up over the edge of a half-ruined roof, like a lizard scuttling onto a warm rock shelf. Then she saw Blake ride by.

"Get out of here!" she hollered. "It's a trap!"

He leapt from his horse, his head swinging to and fro as he searched for the source of her voice.

"Get away!"

"Oh, but it's too late for that, my dear." Invisible to her eyes, Maurice spoke from the other side of the door just before he appeared, walking toward Blake. She saw Blake's head tilt with British superiority, his shoulders hitch in disdain.

"Honored *Sid,*" Maurice said, "to what do we owe the pleasure of this call?"

"You're holding an Englishwoman," Blake said. "Release her to me at once."

"I'm so sorry, but I'm afraid I won't do that."

"I, sir, am a subject of Her Royal Majesty Queen Victoria, and as such I demand—"

Maurice struck him, open-handed, across the face. Blake stumbled backward. "Shut up and listen, and you just may live through this." A tincture of excitement colored Maurice's voice. He'd liked hitting Blake. "You'll deliver this message to one Harry Braxton. Tell him that I hold his woman and that unless he comes for her, the things she shall endure by tomorrow's first light—"

"You dog!" Blake launched himself forward. Maurice sidestepped the attack easily, clipping Blake on the back of the head and sending him sprawling. Helpless, Desdemona watched Blake lurch to his feet, fists raised as if he were about to go a round of gentleman's fisticuffs.

Maurice took immediate advantage. He hammered both his knotted fists into Blake's stomach, folding Blake in half with the force of his blows.

"Don't be more of a fool than you can help," Maurice advised. "Just take the message to Braxton. You'll find him at—"

"I know where to find him," Blake panted hotly. "He's my cousin."

Desdemona, seeing Maurice's reaction, sobbed. Blake had just signed his own fate.

"Well, this puts a rather different light on things," Maurice mused. "I now have two baits rather than one."

Blake braced his hand on his knee and straightened. The effort cost him much for he was deathly pale now, his face sheathed in sweat.

"My," Maurice said, "I am impressed. You're quite a robust man, aren't you? Unfortunately, a robust fellow like you will bear more watching than I can afford right now." His gaze flickered behind Blake.

The man on the roof dropped like a spider from his lair and darted in swinging a short, stout pole. Before Blake could turn, the man slammed it into the backs of Blake's thighs. Blake screamed as he crumbled like an ox being felled by an ax.

"You won't be causing any trouble now, though, will you?" Maurice asked mildly, gazing down at where Blake lay, clench jawed in the dirt. *"Yalla!"*

Two men slunk forward and lifted Blake, dragging him toward her cell. Desdemona watched, tears streaming down her face. Tears of anger as well as sorrow. Blake's heroics endangered not only his life but Harry's, too, and all for what? A gesture. He could have easily sneaked in late tonight when Maurice was unsuspecting, freed her, and they'd have gone on their way. She banged her fist against the wall.

The door swung open and two men pitched Blake unceremoniously at her feet. He moaned. Immediately her fury disappeared. She knelt beside him.

"Are you all right?"

"I think my right leg is broken." He gasped.

She looked at Maurice standing in the doorway, coolly considering them. "He needs a doctor."

"Maybe Harry will bring one when he comes," Maurice suggested.

Desdemona shifted closer to Blake, avoiding his injured limb. Night had fallen. The smothering heat of the day had fled, replaced by night's piercing cold. Only the slivered moon's milky radiance, as frigid as the air, illuminated the small room.

She'd tried examining Blake's leg, but he'd have none of it. The only thing she could give him besides sips of water was the comfort of her presence. Small as that undoubtedly was.

He was in pain. His face looked strained and waxen. A sheen of moisture covered his forehead.

"I shouldn't have ridden in here like that." He'd muttered the same phrase over and over again and, truth to tell, his self-condemnation was beginning to annoy Desdemona.

"You thought it for the best."

"It was a fool thing to do. But when I heard you yelling so frantically I—"

"I was yelling for you to go away," she answered tightly, her compassion challenged by her irritation.

"Well, when one comes after a kidnapped woman and one hears this woman shrieking, one would naturally assume that she is being set upon by—"

"One would only assume that if one didn't have the presence of mind to listen to what was being shrieked," she bit out.

"I said it was a fool thing to do," he snapped. "You might try graciously acknowledging my concession."

"And you might try not harping *your* errors, *your* sins, and *your* shortcomings so much of the time. I didn't realize people could get as much enjoyment out of their hair shirts as you do."

He fixed her with an unreadable look and shoved himself into a straighter sitting position. Immediately he gasped with pain.

Her remorse was spontaneous. "I am so sorry," she said earnestly. "Please, forgive my outburst," she begged. "I—"

"You may be right."

Her mouth clomped shut.

Gingerly Blake rearranged his hurt leg before fixing her with a stern look. "Harry said something similar a few days back. I have always found that if two people make note of something under separate circumstances, it may bear considering." She smiled at him. He didn't return it. He looked intense and horrendously romantic with his white skin and black eyes and tumbled glossy locks. Exactly like Bertie Cecil would look under similar circumstances. And as grim.

She'd never wondered whether Bertie Cecil smiled much. Now that she did, she realized that of course he wouldn't. Berties weren't terribly good at joy.

Harry was good at joy. Harry was good at everything. Harry, unheroic, unromantic Harry. *Unromantic. Unheroic.* What a fool she'd been.

Harry said he loved her and she'd not believed him. She'd been too blinded by the idea that there were things about Harry she didn't know, that she'd questioned what she *did* know, had known for years; that he was honorable and loyal, that he never feigned an emotion or sentiment, that though undoubtedly unethical, he was highly moral, that he made her laugh and challenged her ideas and respected her wisdom. That she loved him.

She wasn't a normal English girl, or woman. She never could be. Just as she couldn't see herself living amid the eternal green gloom of England. She'd simply have to find her grandfather a companion when he went on tour with the museum's collection of artifacts. Her future was in her Egypt. With Harry. God willing she *had* a future. She forced the thought away.

Without remorse she gave good-bye to her fantasies. They'd served their purpose, they'd awoken her heart to its potential. But as far as using them as a template for her life . . . She was probably allergic to heather, and if Bertie Cecils did exist they did so in the person of Blake here, an unhappy man unable to look beyond himself: his code, his conduct, his grievances.

She leaned in closer to Blake. "Tell me about Harry and reading and Oxford and Darkmoor," she said.

With a sigh—it was impossible to tell whether of relief or annoyance—he leaned against the wall.

"Harry isn't very"—he searched for a word—"bright. He can't read. He can't write. But that's not why he was sent down from Oxford in disgrace. He was sent down for cheating. He paid another student to write his year-end paper for him. The lad

Connie Brockway

swore Harry dictated every word, but that doesn't change anything. Cheating is cheating. So he came here.

"Luckily," Blake went on, "Harry has a simple parrotlike ability to mimic that has served him well."

Desdemona stared at Blake, utterly at a loss for words. *A simple parrotlike ability? The ability to master the nuances and subtle intonations of half a dozen dialects?*

"I'm sorry," Blake said, misinterpreting her bemused expression. "Learning about Harry's lack of mental acuity is obviously a blow to you."

Mental acuity, Desdemona thought sourly. Saying Harry wasn't "mentally acute" was like saying a falcon didn't run very fast. The mouse cowering beneath the shadow of a diving falcon must think it quite fast enough without worrying about its ground speed.

"It is apparent you and he have some sort of relationship. I know this will undoubtedly change your feelings for Harry, and I am sorry you have labored so long under a false impression of him, but you will simply have to chalk it up to experience. Believe me," Blake said, ignoring her tightening lips and lowering brows, "Harry's retardation has affected all of us."

"How could Harry's inability to read affect you?" Her voice was low.

"I see no reason not to tell you." His face filled with tight dignity and old pain and she felt her anger bank. "Lenore DuChamp, in discovering my first cousin was abnormal, asked that our engagement be terminated. She couldn't bear the thought that any children of ours would be . . . less than whole. When my grandfather discovered that my fiancée had left me, he assumed it was because of something I'd done. In turn, he cut me from the will. He was very fond of Lenore."

"Harry didn't seek to become your grandfather's heir?" she asked faintly. Oh, God, she'd all but accused him of orchestrating Blake's disinheritance.

"No. How could he?" Blake asked irritably.

"Didn't you tell your grandfather why Lenore had decamped?"

"No. It would be dishonorable to blame Harry, who, after all, cannot help his unfortunate condition. A gentleman never seeks to lay culpability."

"You misunderstand me," she said coldly. "I meant why didn't you tell your grandfather what a small-minded, bigoted little twit Lenore was and good riddance to her?"

Even in the untrustworthy light, she could see Blake's face turn a dull red color. "Lenore did what any right-thinking, decent young woman who anticipates a family would do: She chose not to risk bringing another defective into the world."

"*Defective?* By God," Desdemona whispered, leaning over him, eyes dark and burning, "if Harry is a defective, the world should be fortunate enough to be so afflicted!" Her voice was low, throbbing and passionate. "If you are representative of what Harry had to endure at school, how he has managed to retain not only his charity and his laughter, but his self-esteem and heart, I will never know. His is the measure of a greater man than you can ever hope to be, Blake Ravenscroft. You deserve Lenore."

"And you are bizarre and unwomanly and deserve Harry Braxton," he returned hotly, his colossal self-containment finally crumbling, revealing the jealous and insecure little boy beneath.

She lifted her chin. For the first time those words were a source of pride and pleasure.

"Do you think someone with Harry's problem is even capable of love?" Blake asked stonily. "Has he ever even said he loved you?"

"He's been telling me for years," she said softly, "I just wasn't listening."

"Sitt!"

Desdemona blinked awake at the sound of the feminine voice whispering from outside the door.

"Sitt!" The soft, heavily accented word came again. *"Usskut!"*

Be quiet! Desdemona had heard that word enough times to be familiar with its meaning. She complied, looking over at Blake who was struggling upright, his shirt wet with his efforts.

The door swung open and cold air rushed in. The Egyptian woman stood outlined in the cramped doorway. It was the same woman who'd earlier tried to bring blankets. She motioned Desdemona forward with a hand, her head turned as she peered over her shoulder.

"You are really *Sitt* Carlisle?"

Desdemona nodded cautiously.

"*Yalla!*" the woman whispered, pressing a bundle into Desdemona's arms. "Horse packed behind. Guard sleep. Go now."

"Why are you helping us?" Desdemona asked, suspecting this was somehow a trap, but uncertain how it could possibly benefit Maurice.

From beneath her voluminous wrap, the woman withdrew an evil-looking dagger and a small greasy package. She thrust both at Desdemona and once more indicated the door.

"Here light. Food. Go!"

"Why?" Desdemona insisted.

"Turkeys farm." The woman struggled with the language. "My young brothers, no mother. No help. *Sitt* make turkeys farm. Food, bed. *Sitt* help. I help *Sitt*." She tugged at Desdemona's hand. "Come now."

Desdemona allowed herself to be pulled forward only to stop as if jerked short by an unseen tether. With his broken leg, Blake could never ride a horse.

"Go," Blake said, giving up the struggle to stand. He closed his eyes, fighting the pain. "Find Harry and warn him."

"But you—" God. If she didn't warn Harry, he would fall into Maurice's hands and Maurice would kill him. At least Maurice had no reason to kill Blake.

As if he'd read her mind, Blake said, "Maurice isn't going to hurt me simply to please himself. Bad business." He smiled bravely. He would have made Bertie Cecil proud.

"Please," the Egyptian woman implored. "*Yalla. Khamsin* comes. You go now. I find my man. Make him come. You go before *khamsin*."

Khamsin. The name of the horrifying, bone-scouring sandstorms that swept through the desert in the spring.

"When is it coming?" Desdemona asked. If she did not escape the desert before it hit, she might never make it out. Harry might never know how very much she loved him.

"Soon," the woman said.

Blake had found her papyrus container and was upending the scroll from it. He finished and tossed it to her. "Use this to carry the food and water."

She stared at him. She could never permit him to act as messenger for her heart. She knew what she had to do.

She pushed the parcel and water skin into the container and then knelt by the abandoned papyrus. She ripped a corner from it and smoothed the golden parchment with her hand. Then she reached behind her head and dragged a pin from the thick coil of hair. Without hesitation, she stabbed her finger with it. A bright bead of blood appeared and she dipped the end of the pin into it, ignoring Blake's horrified gasp.

Carefully she traced a few glyphs on the clean side of the papyrus. She waved it in the air a few seconds and handed it to Blake.

"If . . . if I don't reach Harry in time to stop him from coming, please, give him this." Wordlessly he accepted the scrap.

"Please, *Sitt!*" the Arab woman whispered urgently.

"I'll find help," she promised, sliding the dagger across the dirt floor to him. Before he could protest, she was gone.

CHAPTER THIRTY-ONE

"*Yalla!*"

Blake came fully alert just as the man's yell was abruptly cut off. He peered around. Above him the window was murky with predawn gloom.

The muffled sounds of a commotion continued outside.

They've captured Desdemona. Panicked, he dragged himself toward the door, gritting his teeth as agony ripped through his injured leg. Panting, he pushed against the door. Still unlocked, it swung open a few inches. He peered outside.

Fifteen feet away, Harry stood in the ancient street. Facing him, his lips folded back over his teeth, Maurice crouched.

Blake scanned the area for Maurice's other men. One lay near the corner of the building, his body crumpled in an awkward angle. Another slouched next to the door. If the woman had taken off with her lover, that left two others unaccounted for. And Maurice.

"I'll ask you one more time, where is she?" Blake had never heard so deadly a tone.

Maurice sidled forward a few steps, his head bobbing above his body, the motion sinuous and predatory, like a cobra before a snake charmer. "You bring this on yourself, Harry!" Maurice shouted. "It did not have to be so. We could have both profited. Now I have no choice but to kill you!"

Harry did not answer. If Maurice swayed like a cobra, Harry quivered with the suppressed anticipation of a coursing hound. He gauged Maurice's movements, his lean body tightening and relaxing, articulating a response to Maurice's position with each small adjustment.

Blake's skin prickled. For the first time he realized just how deadly an opponent Harry would prove.

Maurice needed no such instruction. Fear stamped his features. "You are the one who made this personal. Why? Why did you frame me?" Maurice demanded indignation somehow surfacing above his fear. "Because I beat you?"

"No," Harry said, his eyes marking Maurice's semicircular progress. "Because as long as you're free, your very existence implies a threat to Desdemona. You said so yourself."

"*Implies?* You would have me rot in jail because of what I *might* do?" Maurice stopped, grinning with feverish humor. "Don't you think that's a little extreme?"

"No. Any threat," Harry said softly, "implied,

perceived, real, or imaginary, is too much where Desdemona is concerned."

Then Blake understood.

He'd never stood a chance to win Desdemona's heart because Harry would fight with weapons Blake could never match. Harry would never be afraid for his own sake. He would do anything to protect her from whatever threatened her happiness, her well-being, or her future.

A surge of dark hurt slipped into his thoughts, invidious and familiar, twisting them with envy. He fought the impulse. Desdemona's reaction to his words regarding Harry's disability had hit its mark. She'd made him feel like a little boy who'd found in Harry an excuse to indulge his own jealous nature.

He slipped the dagger from his waistband, determined to aid his cousin as Maurice shuffled laterally, circling, forcing Harry beneath the ruined rooftop where—

"Harry! Watch out!" Blake yelled. Too late. With a horrifying sense of déjà vu Blake saw the man land, swinging his short, heavy club. Harry, alerted to danger, twisted and ducked, raising his arms just in time to deflect most of the club's impact. He grabbed the man's robes at the neck and jerked the Arab's head down as he drove his knee up into the attacker's face. The Arab grunted, pitching forward into Harry, catching him off guard. Harry staggered back from the man's impetus. His feet tangled in the man's robes and he toppled over, the unconscious Arab falling heavily atop him.

Maurice gave a short, eager laugh of triumph and

ran forward, scooping up the stout cudgel. In a white-knuckled grip, he raised it over his head even as Blake raised the dagger by its point. Fifteen feet and it might as well be fifty. He couldn't possibly hope to—

"We could have been such a team, Harry! We are two of a kind!" Maurice screeched, raising the cudgel higher. Harry stopped trying to fight free and gazed silently up at Maurice. Even from a distance, Blake could see the disdain in Harry's light eyes. He'd no fear. None at all.

"But you betrayed me! And now—"

With a sickening sense of impotence, Blake hurled the dagger. Maurice gasped as the blade struck his exposed flank. An expression of astonishment filled his face. Harry heaved the unconscious Arab from him and surged upward, his fist battering twice into Maurice's shocked face. And that was all. Maurice crumpled to his knees and then pitched facefirst into the sand.

Blake slumped in the open doorway. His gaze met Harry's. "I didn't run away."

"No," Harry allowed gravely. "Thank you." He bent down and ripped a thick strip of material from the hem of Maurice's robe. Efficiently, he tied Maurice's hands and feet. "There's another man tied and gagged out back," he muttered. He straightened. "Now, where is she? I looked in all the ruins and she's not there."

"She left last night," Blake explained, startled at the singleness of purpose that drove his cousin. "An Arab woman helped her escape."

Harry moved quickly to tie up the other Arab in the same manner. His face was horribly haggard, his eyes appeared preternaturally pale and intense. It was as if all the joy had been taken from him, which, Blake allowed with this new, painful perceptiveness, it had.

That was the difference he noted upon his arrival in Egypt and been at a loss to explain. The difference between the young Harry who'd fled England and this man. The boy who'd been sent down from Oxford had had humor and wit but little joy. Harry had found joy here in Egypt. Only its yawning absence fully relayed how much had been taken from him. Blake knew what had called into existence that joy. Or rather who.

Blake felt in his shirt pocket for the scrap of paper Desdemona had scribbled on. "She told me to give you this if I should see you before she did."

Harry raked his hair back from his face. "Read it. You know I can't."

Blake bent over the papyrus and unfolded it. He lifted his head. "I'm afraid I can't read it, either."

"What?" Harry's brows snapped together in a fierce scowl as if he suspected Blake mocked him.

"It's Egyptian." He offered it to Harry.

With something akin to uncertainty Harry took the scrap. He lowered his gaze, astonishment crossed over his lean features before he turned the scrap over.

Blake would have wagered all of Darkmoor Manor that whatever his cousin saw on that paper caused his breath, perhaps even his heart, to pause.

An expression of wonderment and joy—no, something far fiercer and more wild than mere joy—appeared on his face. His eyes glowed with inner triumph and his features set with savage determination.

"When did she go and which direction?" he asked.

"A few hours." Blake pointed east. "She went that way."

"Damn it to hell! There's a *khamsin* brewing out there."

"*Khamsin*. That's the word the Egyptian woman used. What is it?"

"Sandstorm. It can peel the hide off a rhinoceros if it gets whipped up enough," Harry muttered. He glanced down at Blake, apparently for the first time noting the angle of his leg. "You're hurt."

"What an astute observation." Blake might fight the jealousy that had marked him, but he would never like Harry. They were far too different to ever understand each other.

Harry ignored the sarcasm, turning and disappearing into one of the better preserved outbuildings.

"What are you doing?" Blake called.

Harry emerged carrying a sack. Unceremoniously he heaved it into Blake's shelter. "I have to find Dizzy before this storm arrives," he said. "Chesterton was behind me. If he doesn't make it before the storm hits, keep inside the hut. There's food and water in here. Keep your eyes closed and your mouth and nostrils covered with a wet cloth for as long as the storm lasts."

"And how long might that be?" Blake asked.

For the first time Harry smiled. It held no humor. "*Khasmin* is the Arabic word for fifty. And I don't think they were referring to hours."

Desdemona unhaltered the horse and swatted its rump, sending it out over the dunes. She'd little choice. It couldn't seek shelter with her in the gorge, and hobbling it would be its death sentence. She watched it until it had disappeared then picked up the leather cylinder and the horse's blanket and turned into the narrow, rocky defile.

It was the entrance to a gorge, the faint beginnings of what would become at some later point a *wadi*, or canyon, opening on to the Nile's wide flood plain. She glanced at the sulfur-violent sky to her west.

The *khamsin* was out there, gathering strength, sucking mountains of sand thousands of feet into the air. Eventually it would mask the sun itself. She had no idea how long it would be before it arrived, or, once it had come, how long it would last. Just as she had no idea where she was.

She'd ridden in the direction the Egyptian woman had pointed, but within a few miles of the camp the road had vanished beneath the billowing sand. With little knowledge of astronomy and no sun to mark the east or west, she'd ridden through the night searching for a familiar landmark. She'd not found any but with morning she'd spied a light mist. Only the flat surface of rocks held enough moisture to create a morning mist. Rocks could mean an oasis, or in this case the defile.

She picked her way down the incline, moving cautiously, scanning for a cave to take shelter in. The sides of the ravine grew steeper and the footing more difficult the farther in she went. She came to a rocky shelf above a narrow gash in the earth. She could try picking her way around it, but a glance to the west showed her that the storm was moving fast now. She took a deep breath. She would have to jump.

She hitched her skirts high and, grinding her teeth in concentration, leapt. She stumbled on the far side and fell, scrambling and clawing the broken shale as she slipped into the cut. She came to rest twisted on her side. Pain stabbed her knees. Sobbing, she rolled upright and lifted her skirts. She stared at her torn and bloody knees. She linked her arms around her leg and rocked forward, tears stinging sharp and bright as they flooded her wound.

The pain was tonic. Harry would be appalled at such monumental self-indulgence. She blinked her eyes clear and found herself staring into a low black aperture hidden beneath the overhanging rock she'd jumped from. She hobbled to her feet and cautiously ducked her head to look inside. It was a small, rubble-strewn corridor, dry and—luckily—free of snakes.

She thrust the blanket inside, her movements causing a small cloud of fine, choking dust to erupt from underfoot. She flapped her hand, coughing.

There was no sense in going in farther. She huddled near the entrance. She was safe there.

For the time being.

The wind beat fiercely. For hours now it seemed to have been picking up strength, lashing the stone outside, pouring through the window and between the door planks, drifting into mounds in the corner of the room.

Lord Blake Ravenscroft grimaced. He'd probably die in this infernal country, smothered in sand. And Darkmoor would become Harry's—if Harry survived. He probably wouldn't. Harry would die searching this trackless hell for his "Dizzy."

"Anyone here?" a voice hollered above the roar of wind. "*Sitt*, are you there?"

Blake raised himself up on his arms. It wasn't Chesterton. Another of Maurice's cohorts? What matter who it was? If he didn't get out of here he'd die anyway.

"In here!" he shouted. A moment later the door swung open, revealing a group of heavily veiled men.

"Where is the *Sitt*?" the one near the front demanded. "I am Abdul Hakim. I am a friend of the *Sitt* Carlisle. Where is she?"

"*You* are a friend of Miss Carlisle's?" It shouldn't surprise him. Desdemona seemed to have little sense of class distinction. "You have to help look for her."

Abdul nodded, unlinking the veil that covered his face. His turban was slipping from his head. With an impatient gesture he righted it. "I *am* looking for her. My worthless offspring here"—he shot a venomous look toward the rear of the group—"said she'd been taken to this place."

"She was. But she escaped. She's in the desert."

Abdul gave a gusty sigh of vexation.

"You don't understand. It is imperative you go now. A *khamsin* is coming—"

"No, no." The man shook his head. "Maybe farther north. Not here. Here it is just a little windy. No *khamsin.* Do you think we would be out here in a *khamsin?*"

The men behind him snickered.

"Don't worry. We'll look for the *Sitt.* Might take a little time but she has taken water with her, right?"

Blake nodded. "Yes, she filled her satchel with what provisions she could."

"Then she will be all ri—" Abdul's gaze found the papyrus scroll Desdemona had abandoned. His eyes widened. "This was left by *Sitt?*"

"Yes."

The man lifted the scroll and carefully unwrapped the papyrus. "It has been torn."

"Des—*Sitt* wrote a message to Harry, Harry Braxton, on it."

The men went quite still. The only sound heard was the relentless howl of the sand storm outside.

"Harry has this missing piece?"

"Yes. He read it and took out after her."

Abdul swung around toward the still-silent group crowding the doorway and spoke several hurried sentences. He then turned back to Blake, his expression baffled. "Make clear to me that I have the right of this," he said, squatting down in front of Blake and meeting his gaze with a level one of his own. "Harry was here. He saw this worthless scroll. He held in his own hand. He read from it."

"Yes." The fellow must be daft.

"And he left the scroll here, with you, taking with him only this scrap you say the *Sitt* wrote upon?"

"Yes."

"And he went after the *Sitt*?" His consternation had slowly given way to what appeared to be glee. Indeed, the native seemed inordinately amused.

"Yes, but—"

"Ah. Love." He gave a melodramatic sigh and turned to the group. "*Mashallah!* Braxton *murram Sitt!*" The men broke out in loud guffaws of laughter.

"You have to—"

"Listen now," the man said. "Listen well. I have come here to make a trade with Sitt. This—" He beckoned a man forward. He deposited a melon-size, silk-wrapped object at Blake's feet. "—for this. The papyrus was given to the *Sitt* without my consent by my worthless offspring. So you see, I do more than I need to in offering something in exchange for it."

A man rushed into the room, gesticulating and chattering. The others murmured in agitation.

"What did he say?" Blake asked.

"He says he sees twenty riders," Abdul explained. "English army. Five kilometers. Coming fast."

Abdul grabbed Blake's hands and shoved the large, silk-wrapped parcel into them. It was heavy. Very heavy. The form it concealed was hard.

"Here. We have traded." Abdul snatched the papyrus up and gingerly wrapped it in a clean tube of heavy silk. He barked an order at the men and they disappeared, leaving Abdul.

"Harry and Miss Carlisle need your help," Blake implored.

"How far can they get on foot?" Abdul said, his smile disappearing under his veil.

"They're both on horseback."

Abdul stopped, uttering what Blake supposed was an Arabic curse. "Then they *are* in trouble. The landscape changes in a wind. Still, we are Tuarek and Harry is one of our own. We will find Harry. And his Desdemona." And with that he disappeared.

Blake's head fell back against the wall, his relief nearly palpable. Chesterton would be here any moment. He glanced at the object in his hand and carelessly flicked open the silk wrapping.

A golden bull gazed placidly up at him.

"Dizzy!"

She came awake slowly, the sound of his voice calling her back from the drugging lethargy. Tragedy and anguish laced his tone. She rubbed the heels of her hands into her eyes and licked her dry cracked lips. It had been—days? hours?—since she'd drunk the last drops of water and laid her head on her knees to rest—

"Dizzy!"

She bent forward, her cramped shoulders and neck protesting dully, and peered woozily from her hiding place.

She could not see him clearly, his lean form was obscured and revealed by thick veils of blowing sand. The violent wind plucked his voice from his lips and carried it down the defile as he disappeared from sight.

She sank back against the rocky wall. Her head ached and her eyes felt heavy. So very tired. She smiled weakly. Her hero, her knight in shining armor had finally come.

Or so mirages would have her believe.

There was no chance even the most stalwart knight could find her in the vast magnitude that was the Egyptian desert. Still, it was a kind enough mirage and she'd little else left.

Her head drooped and her eyelids had nearly slipped shut when she saw him again. He emerged nearer her this time and here, in profile, she could see him in greater detail.

He was dressed in a soiled white shirt, a khafiya _covering his head, one end flapping loose in the violent wind, flaying his throat and shoulders. Bold and athletic he moved with grace and assurance among the rocky boulders. His noble features were obscured by the capricious wind, but she could descry behind the pall of sand a countenance at once tragic and stern, sorrowful and resolute._

Poor grieving knight.

"God, Dizzy, answer me!"

She must comfort him.

She rocked forward on to hands and knees and crept from the cave.

"Sir?" she called out in a hoarse whisper. He was beyond her now. All she could see of him was his shirt plastered to his broad back in the heightening wind.

"Sir!"

He spun. His light eyes blazed with an inner—

"Desdemona!"

She swallowed, reaching out for the man racing toward her, tears streaking his lean cheeks.

It wasn't a knight. And it wasn't Bertie Cecil.

It was Harry.

And that, after all, was all she'd ever desired.

*E*PILOGUE

*L*ord Blake Ravenscroft hobbled down the promenade deck of the Thomas Cooke's newest luxury excursion steamer. He found an unoccupied deck chair and lowered himself into it, staring broodingly out over the Egyptian landscape. He motioned for an attendant to bring him a scotch and water. The week-old wound to his leg throbbed and the blasted splint was a nuisance.

Only a few hours had passed since the wedding. He'd come directly from the church without bothering to change clothes. Though there had been no reason whatsoever to prolong his stay, he was pricked by the notion that he'd run away.

The bride had been lovely, Blake conceded, even though her gown had been an odd conglomeration of Eastern and English elements. The veil she'd worn had been some sheer piece of Oriental nonsense. Above the low décolletage she'd worn had been a collar, or a pectoral as Marta Douglass had informed him in awed tones, fashioned in the form of what looked, for God's sake, to be a jeweled vulture. The effect was disturbing.

But then, the bride was disturbing. Lovely and heart-stoppingly desirable, but decidedly disturbing. Bizarre, one might say. As was this entire Egypt, belonging as it did to no one though so many countries claimed it.

Blake's gaze slipped wearily over the Nile's tea-colored waters. In the far distance he could see the desert's shoulders, muscular and dun-colored, hunched above the river plains.

No one would ever own that.

Perhaps ultimately Egypt belonged to the desert. Who could tell? He only knew this country held nothing for him, no appeal, no charm, no romance. It would always be the battleground upon which he'd been forced to confront his own nature. He'd done so bravely, facing the truth about himself like a gentleman. Why did he feel as if somehow this godforsaken land had revealed some unworthiness in his nature that honor did not address?

No, Egypt wasn't for him. Just as Desdemona had not been for him. Both had proven to be enigmas he did not want to understand.

Well, he thought, accepting the iced glass of scotch the silent waiter offered him, at least he'd come away from this cursed place with some compensation. He slipped a hand into his inner jacket pocket, reassuring himself that the thick packet of American bills was still folded there. Ten thousand dollars for one bona fide Apis bull. The money would be enough to get him reinstated as his grandfather's heir. The old man was nothing if not practical.

Yes, Harry had Dizzy but he'd have Darkmoor Manor.

Blake's smile faltered as he stared into his glass. The damnable thing was that he suspected Harry had gotten the better deal.

Abdul watched his youngest son pack the cooking equipment. For the next six months Rabi would be doing woman's work, and he would be doing it uncomplainingly. It was Rabi's punishment.

Abdul shook his head. Not only had his youngest apparently lost his mind and kidnapped Harry's woman but then, as if to compound his crime, Rabi had given the woman the scroll!

Well, thought Abdul, pointing at a pan that had escaped Rabi's eye, by the end of his penance the boy would have a keener appreciation of his family's duty. A duty untold generations old. Though to be fair, Abdul thought, pointing impatiently at some bedding Rabi had yet to pack, it had not been completely the boy's fault.

Abdul should never have removed the scroll from the tomb. Occasionally, throughout the years and decades, it had been necessary, in order to ensure his family's well-being, to sell off some small bit from the enormous trove. Always they were small things, indistinguishable as coming from any specific cache. It was only after he'd translated a bit of the scroll that he'd realized it would lead a canny scholar immediately to its source. They were, after all, poems the beautiful queen had written her husband, Akhenaton.

And now Harry, one of the few men Abdul knew would be able to identify the papyrus for what it was, was in possession of a scrap of it.

Abdul had broached the subject of the papyrus on the journey back to Cairo as Harry cradled the *Sitt* tenderly in his arms and she had drifted in and out of slumber. The Tuareks had helped him find his woman, Abdul had explained, now Harry must return the piece of papyrus.

For a long minute their gazes had met and held. Abdul knew, perhaps more than any other man, what such a discovery could mean to Harry. Harry would obtain much honor among the scholarly community. He would finally achieve the recognition his inability to read had hitherto excluded him from. Abdul had held his breath. Though Harry was an honorable man, and he owed the Hassams much, even Abdul could not tell how he would answer.

Finally Harry's gaze had broken from Abdul's and he had looked down at the woman nestled close to his heart. Pure contentment spread over his features.

"I have in my possession only one piece of paper. It is"—he'd lifted his eyes to Abdul and passion and sincerity shined in their pale depths—"a private missive. To me it is priceless. I will never part with it, let it be seen by another, or sell it. To you or anyone else."

That had been an end to it. Harry never lied.

Abdul sighed and picked up the bedroll at his

feet. He threw it at his frightened-looking offspring before relenting and giving the boy a small smile. To give him his due, Rabi had found the woman and the scroll before any serious damage had been done.

Perhaps Rabi would soon be ready for the real family business: guarding Nefertiti's tomb until such a day as Egypt belonged to Egyptians.

Harry withdrew the vial suspended from a gold chain around his neck. It was warm from resting near his heart. Tightly rolled within the delicate yet strong crystal carrier was a piece of papyrus and on that scrap was a set of simple hieroglyphics.

"You are my own, my always love."

Even now, the simple message had the power to make his hand shake. He looked up, eagerly awaiting his wife. He could hear her moving about in the adjoining room. He could damn near feel her presence.

His wife.

Five days ago they'd struggled out of the desert under Abdul's escort. Harry had returned her to her frantic grandfather vowing—or, as Sir Robert later claimed, threatening—he'd be back to marry her.

He'd spent the next few days preparing for their wedding. First Harry had confounded Sir Robert's gruff reservations by offering the old man the first pick of whatever treasures Harry came into possession of—at in-law rates, of course. It had been painful to watch Sir Robert's paternal impulses war with his archeological ones. Dizzy, Magi later told him, had tipped the balance by declaring in irrefutable

terms that she did not want to go to England, had
never wanted to go to England, and that she'd only
said she had so that Sir Robert would feel free to
return to London and achieve the recognition he deserved.

Apparently Sir Robert's face had grown comical
with extravagant relief. He'd actually teared up; the
only words he'd been able to push past the constric-
tion in his throat were, "I hate tweeds."

That obstacle overcome, Harry had next bribed
the necessary Egyptian and English officials—with
Simon Chesterton's blessing—into hastening the li-
censing procedure. All the while he'd rehearsed
ways to convince Dizzy of the sincerity of his love.

If she wanted to live in England, in England
they'd live. He'd live anywhere on the bloody planet
as long as she was with him.

She hadn't wanted England; she'd wanted him.
When he'd appeared in her bedroom the night before last and told her he loved her and she'd be a
damn fool not to realize it and just let them live
happily ever after, in whatever the hell country she
desired, she'd told him she'd found what she most
desired—or rather whom.

The memory of her words pierced him with happiness, and he looked around impatiently. He heard
her a few seconds before she came into the room, a
vision of silken skin and silken gown, gold and
tawny and altogether lovely. She stopped before the
open window, shoving the shutters apart so that
midafternoon sun flooded the room. The sudden
light glowed on her skin, turned her hair into a

shimmering veil that spilled over her shoulders and down her back.

"You'd think at the rates they charge Shepheard's would endeavor to keep their rooms aired," she grumbled.

He laughed. "I love you, Desdemona. Lord knows, I love you."

She turned, a smile lighting her face.

He couldn't seem to say the words often enough, at first because it had been the simple truth that had gone for so long unvoiced but then because of the wondrous change each repetition wrought in her. From wonder to contentment to self-confidence, she flourished.

Just a few days ago, she would have blushed, her gaze would have dropped shyly from meeting his. Now her whole face lit with pleasure.

"You just love me because I can read and in marrying me you think you've gotten a free scribe for life."

His breath caught in his throat. A further illumination. All of his life his inability to read had been something to hide, a source of pain. But she . . . she *teased* him about it, gently, tenderly, casually. The effect of her teasing was astonishing. He'd never felt so empowered. So capable of doing anything. He might well author that treatise Sir Robert had for years been badgering him to do. Perhaps the method he'd used to learn hieroglyphics could be used to learn English. Anything was possible now.

Dizzy loved him.

"Don't try to deny it," she said, one brow lifted.

"How did you know?" he asked gruffly.

"You're a terrible opportunist, Harry Braxton. Everyone knows it. Just because I lo—" She paused, eyeing him wickedly. "Suffice to say, I mustn't allow my personal aberration to cloud my judgment."

"You said 'I lo—' You 'lo—' what?" If he adored telling her he loved her, his passion for hearing it from her was nearly as great. He moved closer. She laughed. Beautiful, wide curving lips.

"I love . . . your mouth."

He captured her, hauling her into his arms, spinning her around, the feel of her pressed to him heady, pulsing, delicious. The memory of their lovemaking returned with urgent clarity.

"Dear Allah, I am so damn *glad* you like my mouth." He could barely hear himself. His words came out in a hoarse whisper. He was too intent on the feel of her intimately rubbing against him. The warm satiny skin was his to touch, to stroke and caress and nibble and . . . He swallowed. Hard.

At this rate the honeymoon was going to be over before it began.

Her lips touched the base of his throat and roamed in shiver-inducing increments up his throat to the angle of his jaw and over his chin. Her arms crept around his neck and she suddenly swayed into him. She was, he realized, pushing him toward the bed.

"No," she reproved him in a throaty whisper, drawing her head back and causing him to groan in frustration, "I don't *like* your mouth. I *love* your mouth. I love the look of it." She swept her fingertip back and forth along his lower lip, her dark eyes nearly black with sexual intent. "I love the shape of it." She stood on tiptoe, her tongue following the path her finger had just forsaken, nearly bringing him to his knees with longing. "And the taste of it."

He lifted her into his arms, backing up until he felt the bed bang into the backs of his thighs.

"But most of all I love the *feel* of your mouth," she said, and opened her own mouth over his, kissing him deeply, passionately, succulently.

He toppled backward, dragging her down on top of him. They landed with a soft *whoosh* and sank deep into the down mattress, a tangle of arms and limbs, her hair spilling over his chest.

He closed his eyes, nuzzling his cheek against the cool, silky texture of it. She sprawled over him, all soft womanly skin against his heated male flesh. Abruptly he rolled to the side, carrying her with him, pinning her beneath him. His gaze riveted on hers, stealing her breath with the open hunger of his expression.

Color mounted her throat and cheeks and his lids slipped low as he watched. He opened his mouth and bent near, scenting her fragrance, her taste, the moist salty aura that shimmered a fraction of a degree above her flesh. Her breathing grew rapid beneath his lazy perusal, excited, nervous. She could not stand the strain of his silent intensity.

"What are you doing?" she asked, her voice pitched a full octave above her normal one. "You shouldn't look at me like that. It makes me—"

Her voice gave out abruptly.

He met her eye and smiled with roguish laziness. He knew full well what she was about. Slowly, one by one, he began unbuttoning the tiny seed pearls that marched primly up her bodice.

Her pulse raced madly as she vacillated, alternately shy and bold, light-headed with the longing his undressing her engendered.

"Lovely." He peeled back the first few inches of her bodice and brushed his fingertip over the exposed curve of her breast. She trembled. "Have I ever told you how I learned to read hieroglyphics?"

"How?"

"With my fingertips," he said softly. "Like this." He ran his hand beneath the lacy chemise, slipping beneath her breasts, stroking their roundness. "I can read your body just as easily."

He found her nipples and positioned the hard nubbins in the center of his palms and kneaded her breasts lightly. "I can read the arousal you're feeling. Not yet desire, but more than simple longing."

Without warning he left off his attentions to her breasts and swept her skirts above her slender thighs, finding the lacy garters that secured her silk stockings. With infinite delicacy and agonizing slowness, he rolled first one sheer stocking from her leg and then the other. His pale gaze never left her face.

"I can feel your thighs relax," he whispered. "They're still closed, furled. They need encouragement to ease open, like a hyacinth blossom." His hand brushed lightly on the most sensitive skin of her inner thighs. "Open for me, Dizzy."

She shivered. His touch was both familiar and foreign. Before when they'd made love, it had been a tidal wave of instinct and long-suppressed emotion. This was an inexorable step, the crescendo of an ever-building dance of which he was the maestro. She was being pulled along, uncontrollably and without volition, and he . . . He seemed so in control, so familiar with passion's heated music.

It disturbed her that he had mastery over this thing between them where she had none. She did not know what they were sharing and what she was simply receiving. She only knew she had no choice but to ride the rising tide of stimulation and desire that he so effortlessly awoke in her body and heart. She wanted so much to be a part of this, to give as well as take from him. To have it be unique and extraordinary and . . . and wondrous.

He seemed to understand her agitation, the inexpressible misgivings, for suddenly his hand moved away from that place between her legs. He captured her face between his palms.

"It has never been like this for me, Dizzy. Never. I only dreamed that making love could be this . . . important," he said in a hushed, reverent voice. "Diz, I have waited for you for all my life."

"Me?" She could not hide the tincture of disbelief in her tone.

"Always." He stared into her eyes. "Do you remember the mirror, Diz?"

She nodded.

"I'd waited years to give that to you, though the sentiment was true from the first time we kissed.

And one I carried with me for three years." His voice was low and hypnotic and flowed over her like ambergris and honeyed wine.

"I have loved you through each long season,
Through the span of each day, each meter of the
night, that I have wasted, alone.
In darkness I have lain awake
Filling the hours with the sound of your voice, the
image of your body, until desire lives within me.
Mere memory of you awakes my flesh, brings
singing to limbs that are numb without you.
I am impoverished without you.
Thus into the darkness I call: Where have you
gone, houri of my heart?
Why have you gone from him who could teach the
sun of burning?
Who is more constant than is dawn to day?
I hear no beloved voice answer and I, too well,
know how much I am alone."

A tear slipped from the corner of her eye. He caught it.

"Am I much alone, Dizzy?" he asked softly. For just an instant the old self-doubts, echoes of the past, clouded his brilliant gaze. She did not ever want to see their like again.

She shook her head roughly, her eyes liquid with reflected pain. "No. Nor am I."

He touched his lips to hers. He did not want tears from her, not now, not when his blood sang with desire and his heart beat a staccato of such exultation he felt he could not contain it. Now was for surging, joyous passion.

"And"—he took a deep breath and suddenly smiled, the old Harry and the new fully merged, whole and complete—"was that romantic enough for you?"

She did not hesitate a second before answering him, they were that alike, that closely allied in soul as well as heart. Because she discerned his intent and realized it was her own.

Joy.

"It's a beginning," she answered archly.

And, indeed, it was.

NOTE FROM THE AUTHOR

I admit it, I fell in love with Victorian Egypt and became fascinated by the history of archaeology. Howard Carter's predecessors were ancient grave robbers, Roman invaders, and modern plunderers the likes of Napoleon Bonaparte, Belzoni, and the forerunner of modern archaeology, Jean-Jacque Rifaud. By the time my Harry Braxton comes on the scene, serious scholars are usurping simple treasure hunters and Flinders Petrie has forced methodology upon the nascent science.

Harry, of course, walks the line between scientist and profiteer. But that's how he's managed to keep a hand in the game he loves in spite of his dyslexia.

Dyslexia is not a disease. It has no cure. Dyslexia is difficulty processing language. Dyslexics have problems translating language to thought, as in listening or reading, or translating thought to language, as in writing or speaking. Dyslexia varies from person to person, in both severity and how it presents itself.

Dyslexia was first identified in the late 1800s and was originally called "word-blindness." People with dyslexia were thought to be mentally retarded and regarded as substandard.

Harry Braxton suffers from visual dyslexia. He has no problem processing verbal language. In fact, he's excellent at it. His teaching himself to read hieroglyphics through what is now known as multisensory learning is perhaps stretching the bounds of probability and making a huge leap of faith, but then, I write romances and "leaps of faith" are my daily bread.

Thank you for "leaping" with me.

Connie Brockway